Walt Disney's

Donald Duck

in...

Executive Editor: Gary Groth

Senior Editor: J. Michael Catron

Colorist: Rich Tommaso

Cover Colorist: Keeli McCarthy

Designer: Keeli McCarthy

Production: Paul Baresh

Associate Publisher: Eric Reynolds

Publisher: Gary Groth

Fantagraphics Books, Inc.
7563 Lake City Way NE
Seattle, WA 98115

For a free catalog of more books like this, classic comic book and newspaper strip collections, and other fine works of artistry, call (800) 657-1100 or visit fantagraphics.com. Follow us on Twitter at @fantagraphics and on Facebook at facebook.com/fantagraphics.

ISBN 978-1-60699-852-6
Library of Congress Control Number: 2015932754

Printed in Malaysia

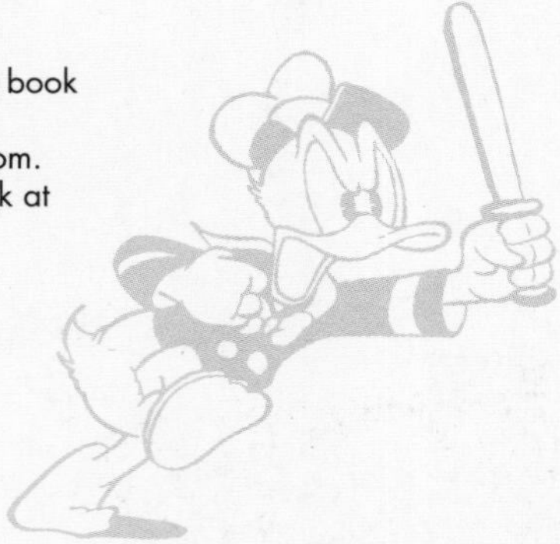

Also available:
Ghost of the Grotto • *Sheriff of Bullet Valley*

The Golden Helmet

FANTAGRAPHICS BOOKS

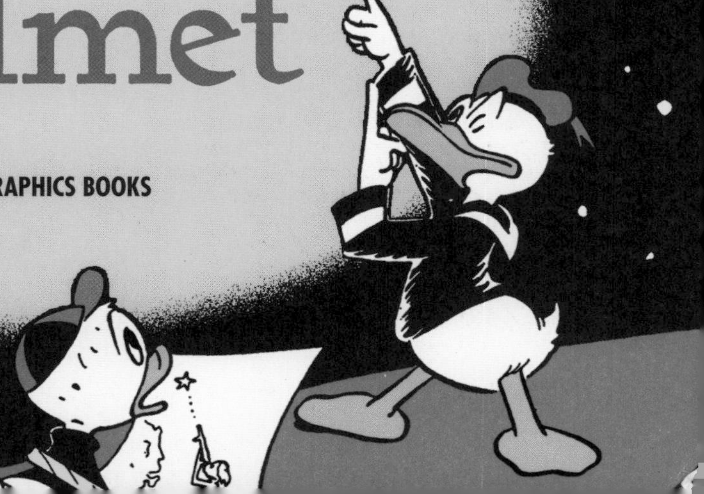

CONTENTS

ALL STORIES WRITTEN AND DRAWN BY CARL BARKS

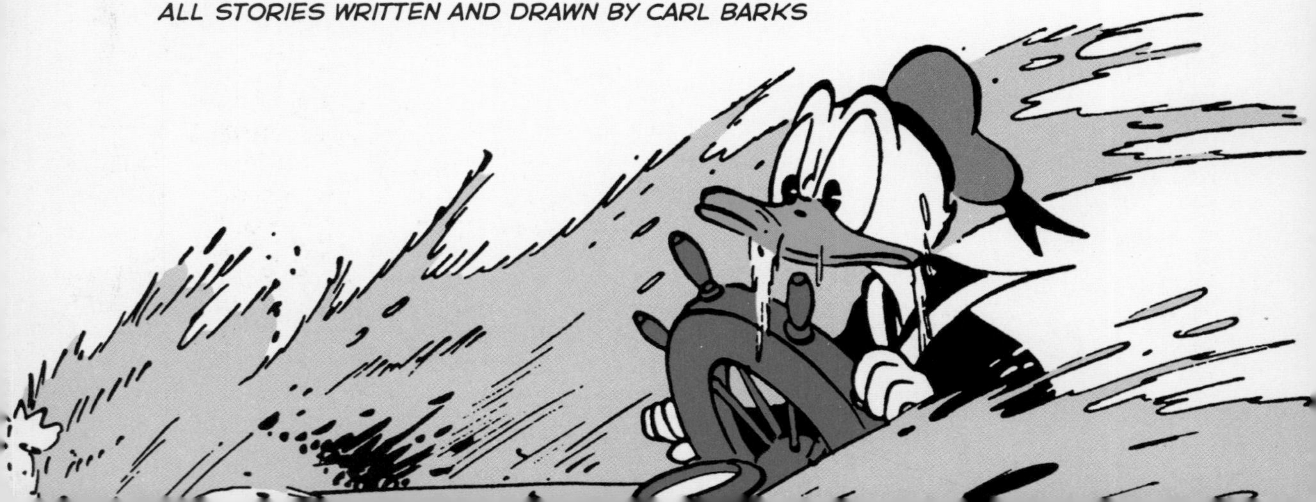

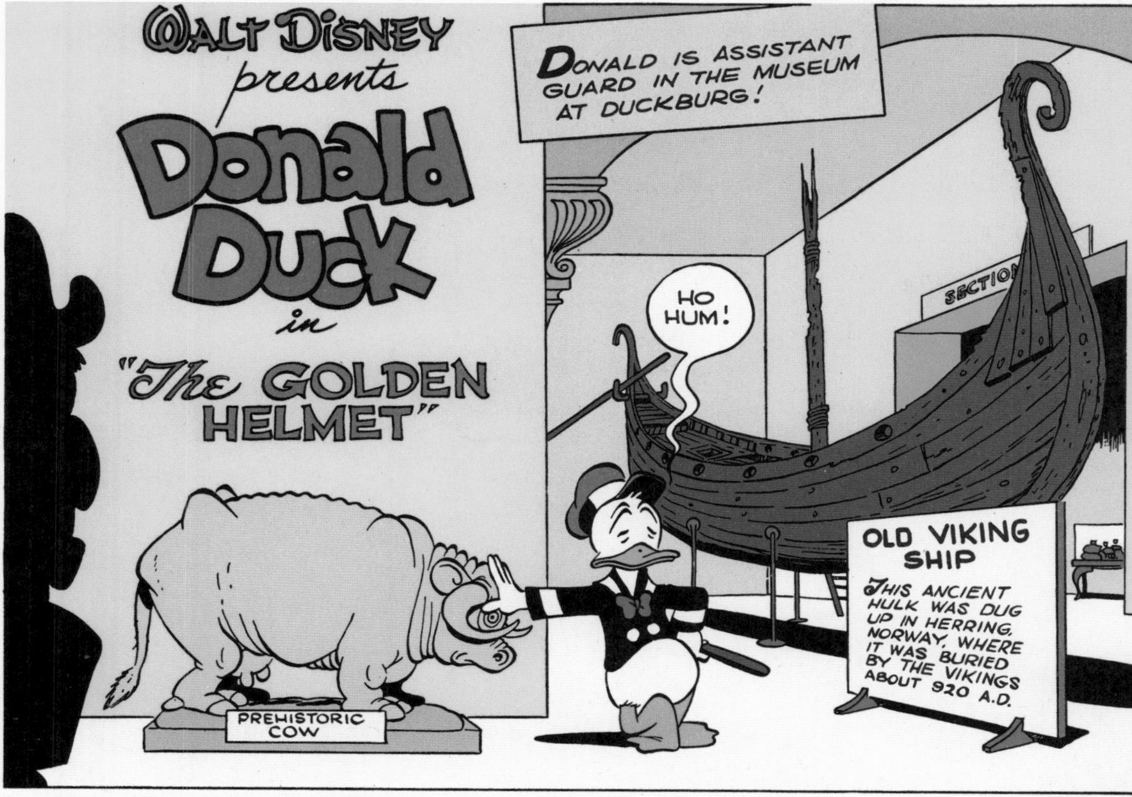
WALT DISNEY
presents
Donald Duck
in
"The GOLDEN HELMET"
DONALD IS ASSISTANT GUARD IN THE MUSEUM AT DUCKBURG!
HO HUM!
SECTION
OLD VIKING SHIP
THIS ANCIENT HULK WAS DUG UP IN HERRING, NORWAY, WHERE IT WAS BURIED BY THE VIKINGS ABOUT 920 A.D.
PREHISTORIC COW

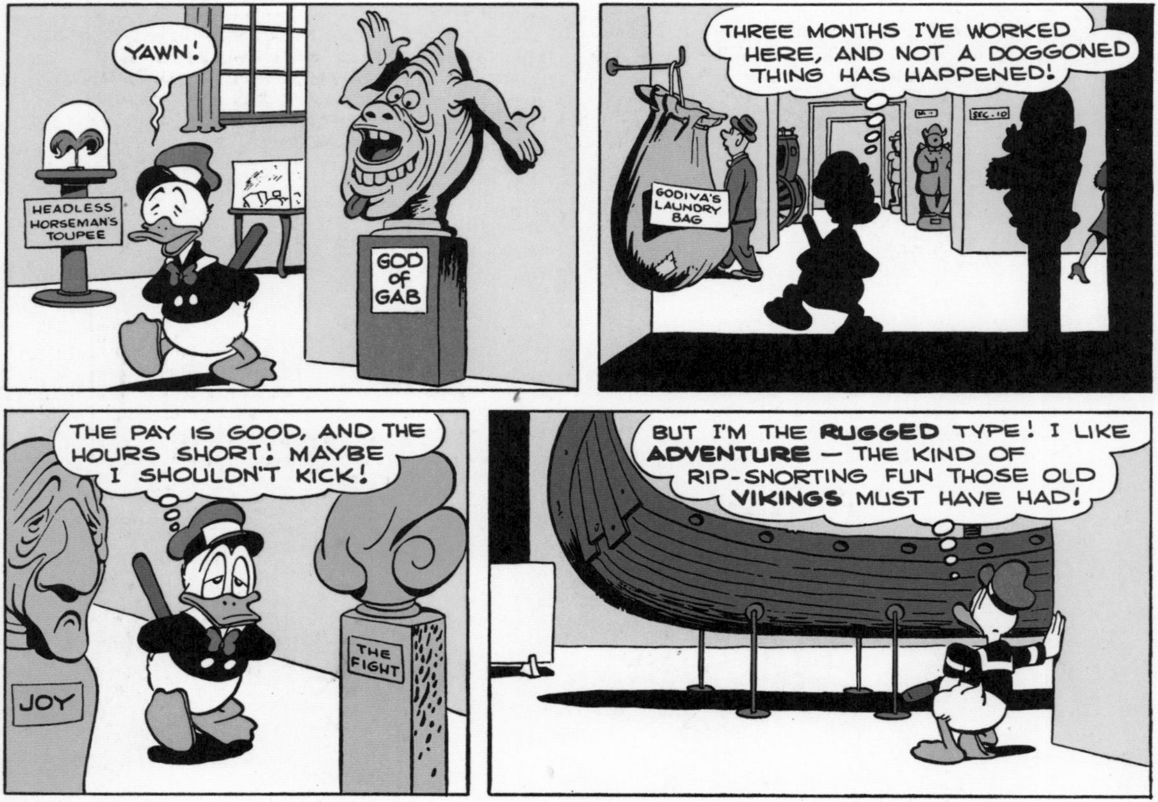
YAWN!
HEADLESS HORSEMAN'S TOUPEE
GOD of GAB
THREE MONTHS I'VE WORKED HERE, AND NOT A DOGGONED THING HAS HAPPENED!
GODIVA'S LAUNDRY BAG
SEC. 10
THE PAY IS GOOD, AND THE HOURS SHORT! MAYBE I SHOULDN'T KICK!
JOY
THE FIGHT
BUT I'M THE **RUGGED** TYPE! I LIKE **ADVENTURE** — THE KIND OF RIP-SNORTING FUN THOSE OLD **VIKINGS** MUST HAVE HAD!

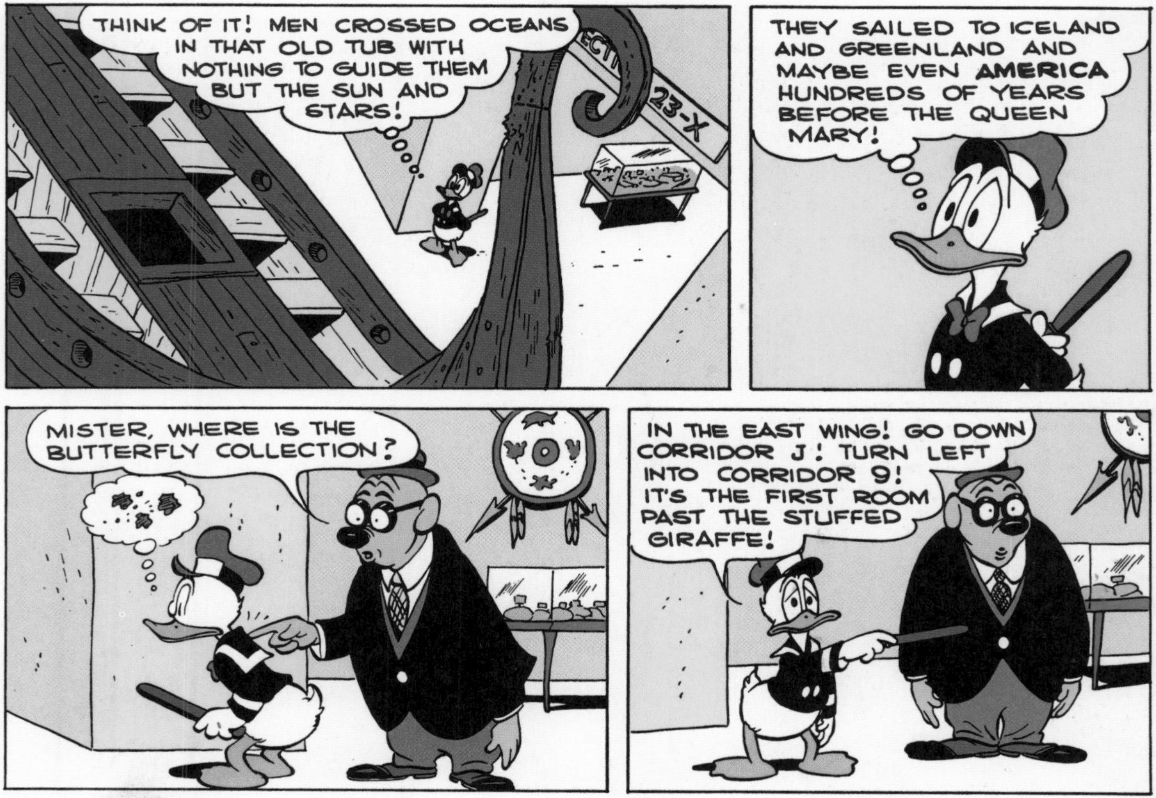
THINK OF IT! MEN CROSSED OCEANS IN THAT OLD TUB WITH NOTHING TO GUIDE THEM BUT THE SUN AND STARS!
23-X
THEY SAILED TO ICELAND AND GREENLAND AND MAYBE EVEN **AMERICA** HUNDREDS OF YEARS BEFORE THE QUEEN MARY!
MISTER, WHERE IS THE BUTTERFLY COLLECTION?
IN THE EAST WING! GO DOWN CORRIDOR J! TURN LEFT INTO CORRIDOR 9! IT'S THE FIRST ROOM PAST THE STUFFED GIRAFFE!

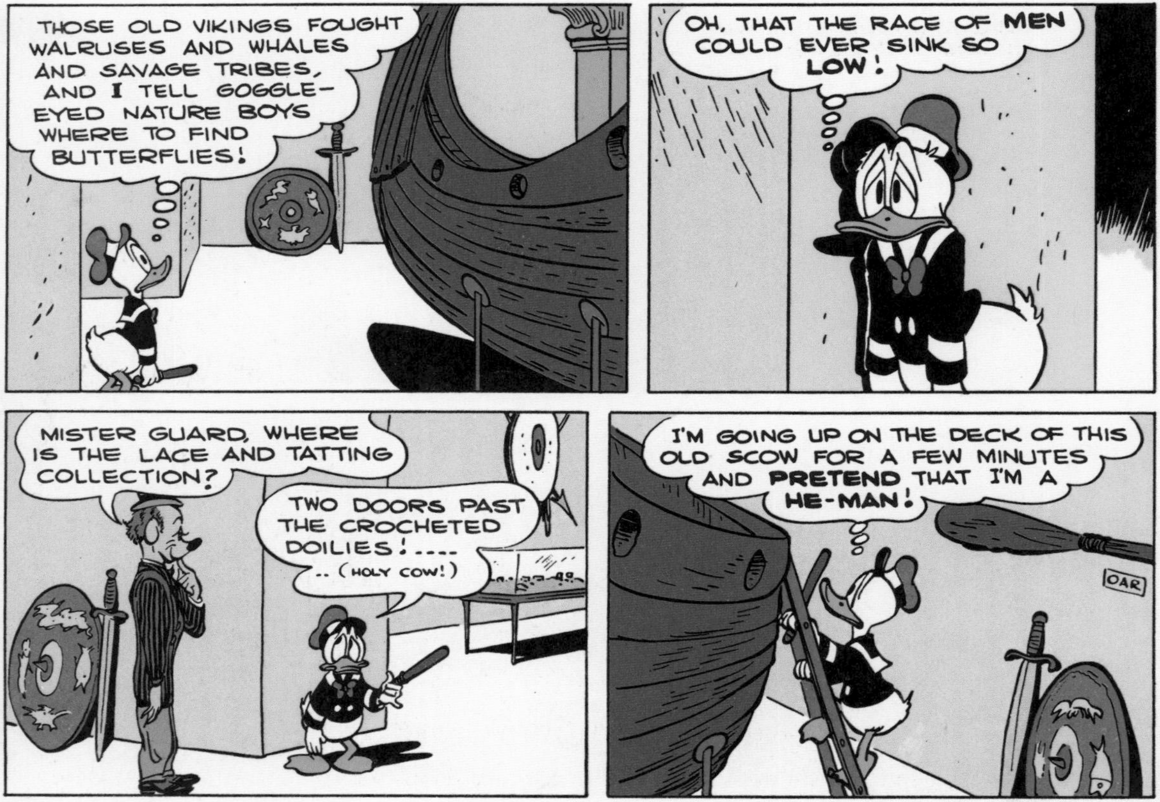
THOSE OLD VIKINGS FOUGHT WALRUSES AND WHALES AND SAVAGE TRIBES, AND I TELL GOGGLE-EYED NATURE BOYS WHERE TO FIND BUTTERFLIES!
OH, THAT THE RACE OF MEN COULD EVER SINK SO LOW!
MISTER GUARD, WHERE IS THE LACE AND TATTING COLLECTION?
TWO DOORS PAST THE CROCHETED DOILIES! ....
.. (HOLY COW!)
I'M GOING UP ON THE DECK OF THIS OLD SCOW FOR A FEW MINUTES AND PRETEND THAT I'M A HE-MAN!
OAR

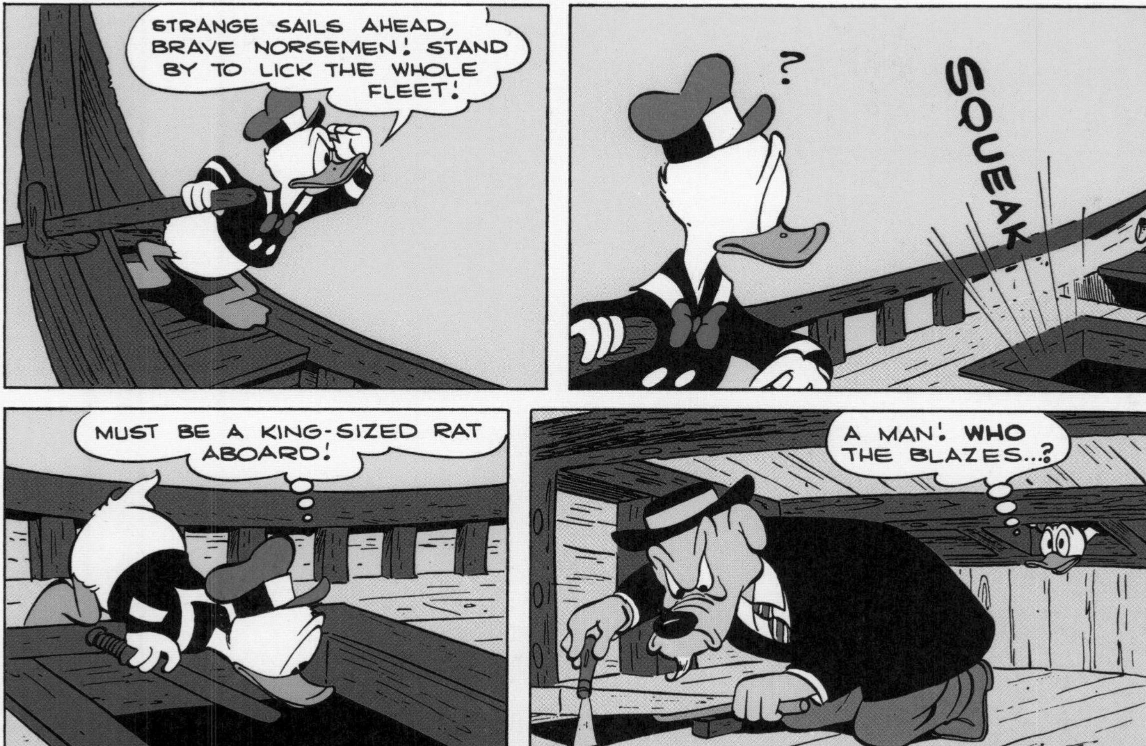
STRANGE SAILS AHEAD, BRAVE NORSEMEN! STAND BY TO LICK THE WHOLE FLEET!
?
SQUEAK
MUST BE A KING-SIZED RAT ABOARD!
A MAN! WHO THE BLAZES...?

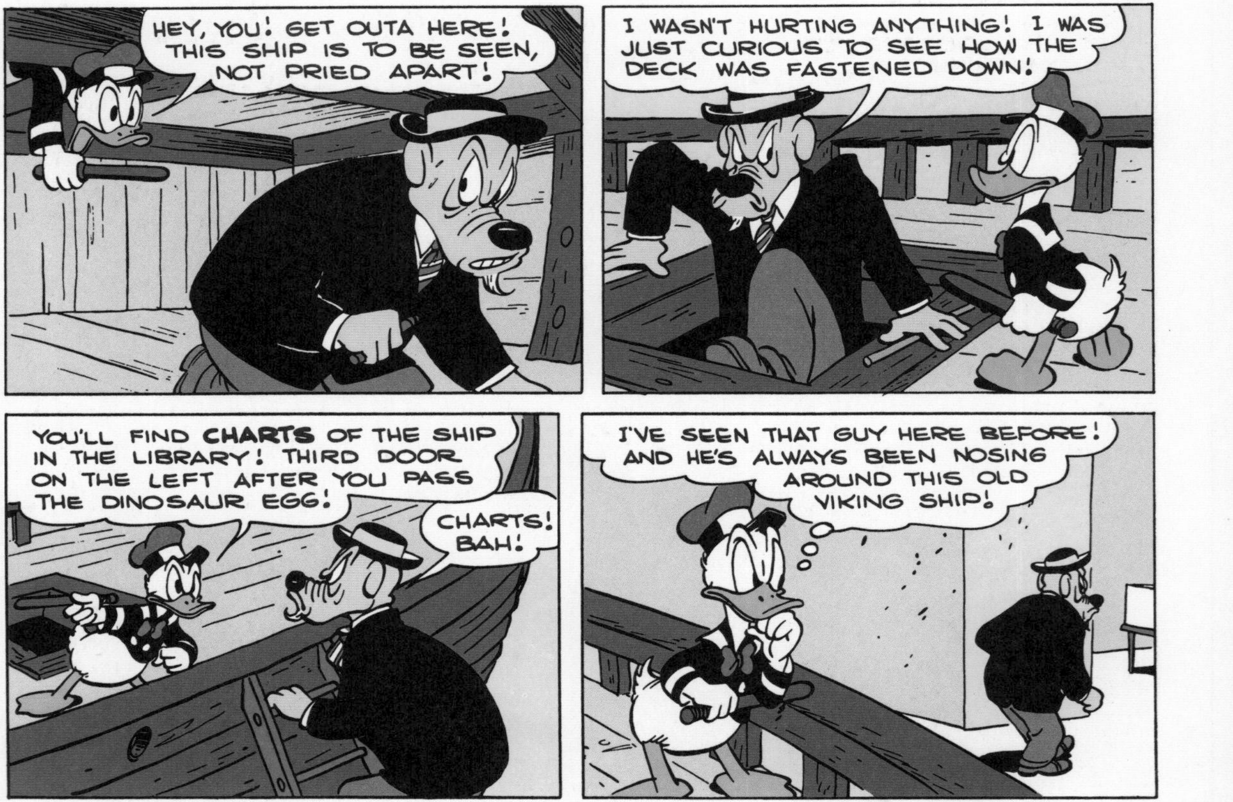
HEY, YOU! GET OUTA HERE! THIS SHIP IS TO BE SEEN, NOT PRIED APART!
I WASN'T HURTING ANYTHING! I WAS JUST CURIOUS TO SEE HOW THE DECK WAS FASTENED DOWN!
YOU'LL FIND **CHARTS** OF THE SHIP IN THE LIBRARY! THIRD DOOR ON THE LEFT AFTER YOU PASS THE DINOSAUR EGG!
CHARTS! BAH!
I'VE SEEN THAT GUY HERE BEFORE! AND HE'S ALWAYS BEEN NOSING AROUND THIS OLD VIKING SHIP!

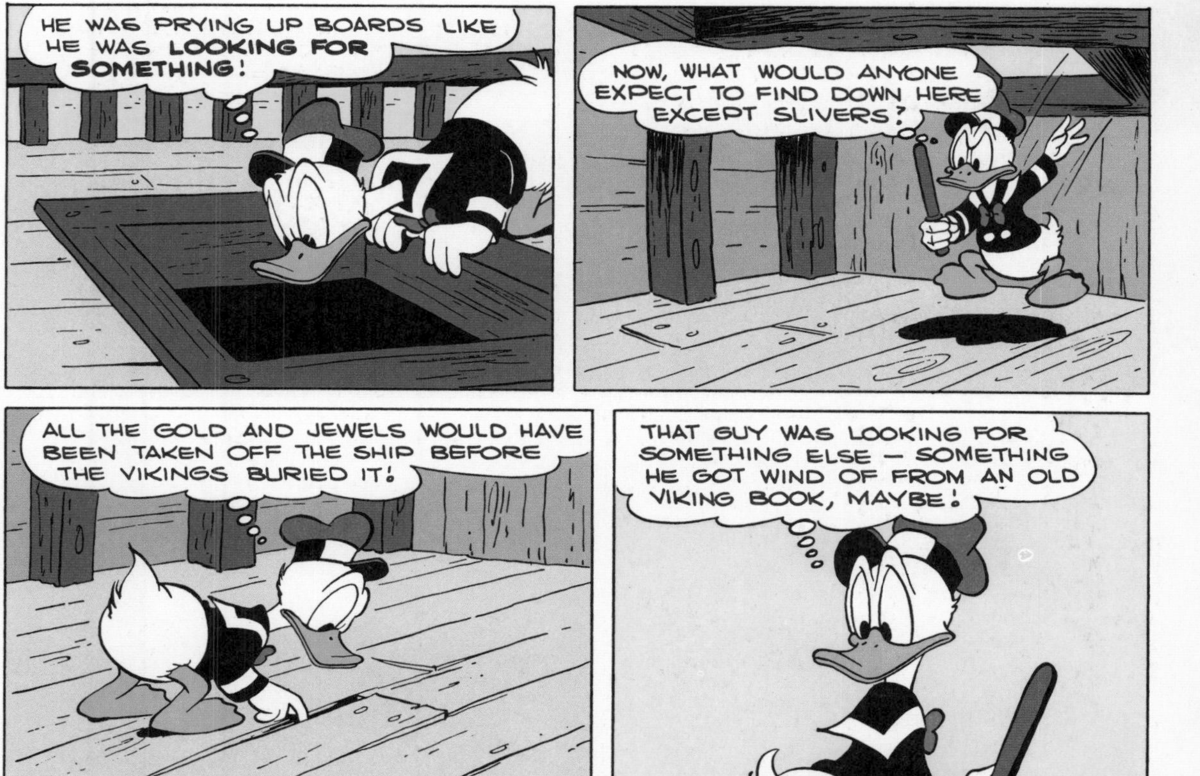
HE WAS PRYING UP BOARDS LIKE HE WAS **LOOKING FOR SOMETHING**!
NOW, WHAT WOULD ANYONE EXPECT TO FIND DOWN HERE EXCEPT SLIVERS?
ALL THE GOLD AND JEWELS WOULD HAVE BEEN TAKEN OFF THE SHIP BEFORE THE VIKINGS BURIED IT!
THAT GUY WAS LOOKING FOR SOMETHING ELSE — SOMETHING HE GOT WIND OF FROM AN OLD VIKING BOOK, MAYBE!

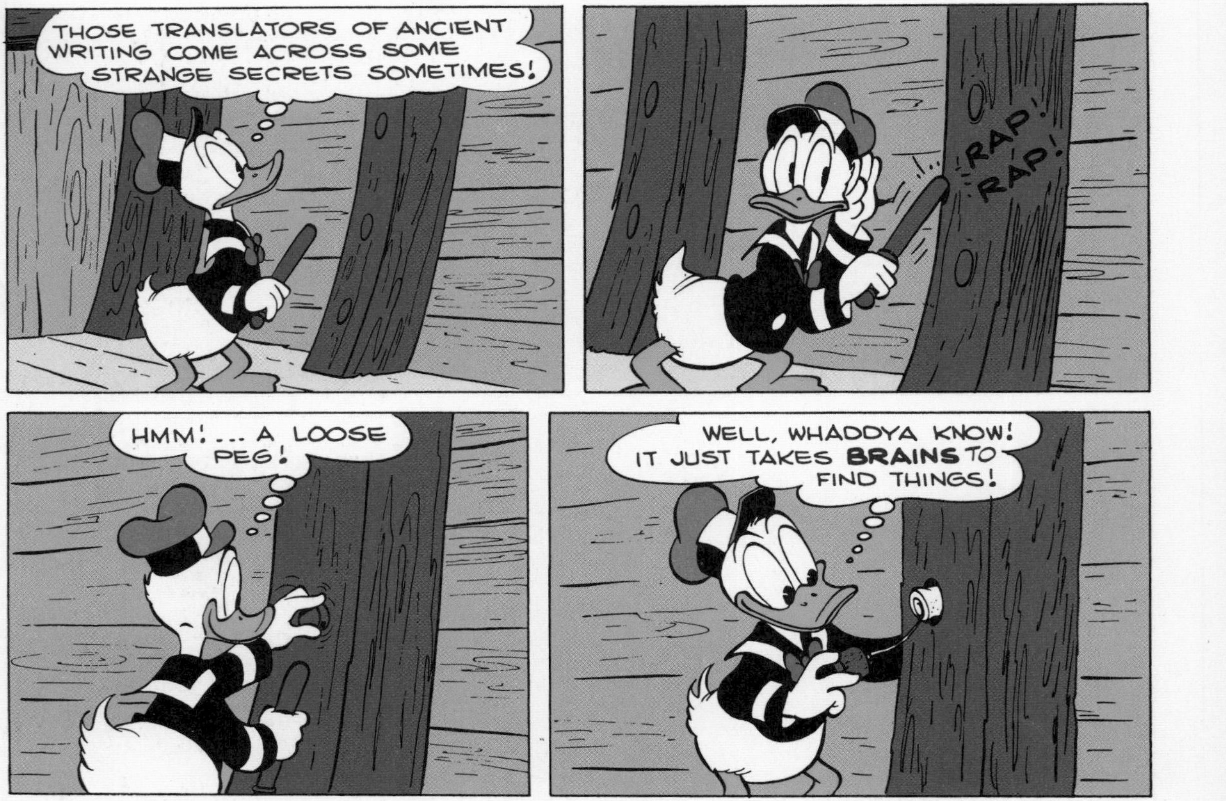
THOSE TRANSLATORS OF ANCIENT WRITING COME ACROSS SOME STRANGE SECRETS SOMETIMES!
RAP! RAP!
HMM! ... A LOOSE PEG!
WELL, WHADDYA KNOW! IT JUST TAKES **BRAINS** TO FIND THINGS!

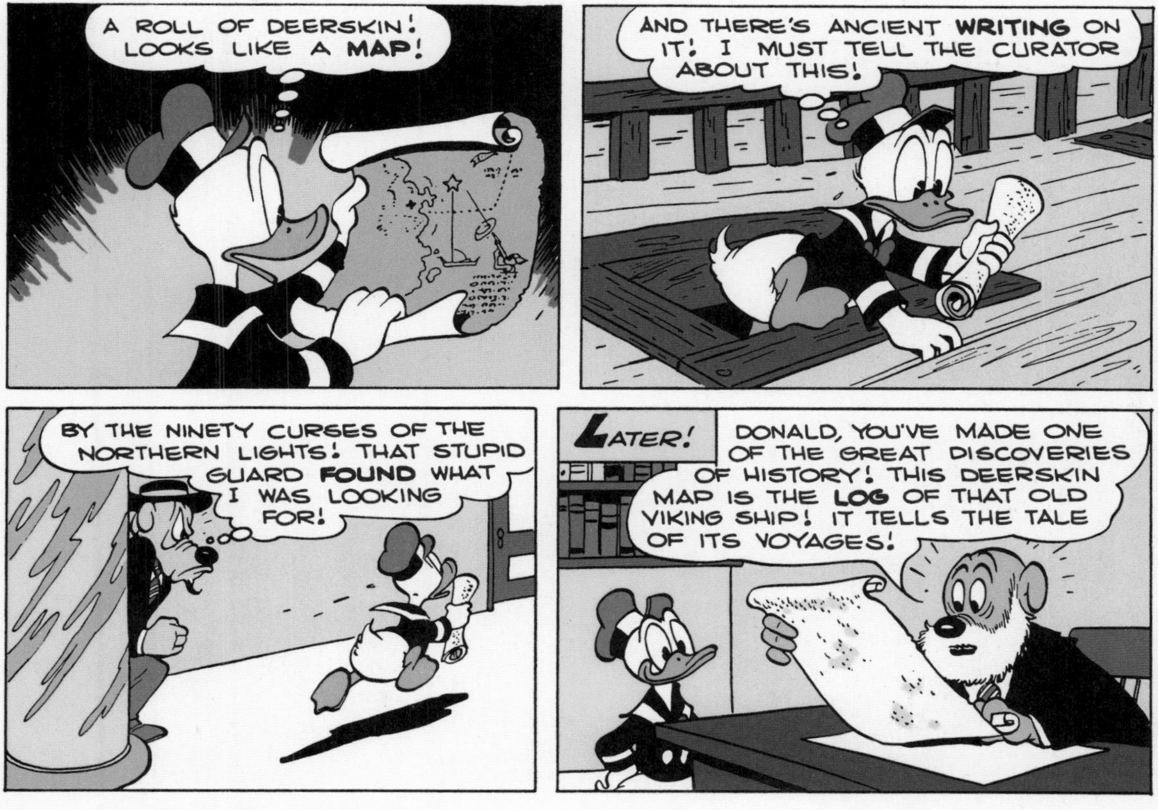
A ROLL OF DEERSKIN! LOOKS LIKE A **MAP**!
AND THERE'S ANCIENT **WRITING** ON IT! I MUST TELL THE CURATOR ABOUT THIS!
BY THE NINETY CURSES OF THE NORTHERN LIGHTS! THAT STUPID GUARD **FOUND** WHAT I WAS LOOKING FOR!
LATER!
DONALD, YOU'VE MADE ONE OF THE GREAT DISCOVERIES OF HISTORY! THIS DEERSKIN MAP IS THE **LOG** OF THAT OLD VIKING SHIP! IT TELLS THE TALE OF ITS VOYAGES!

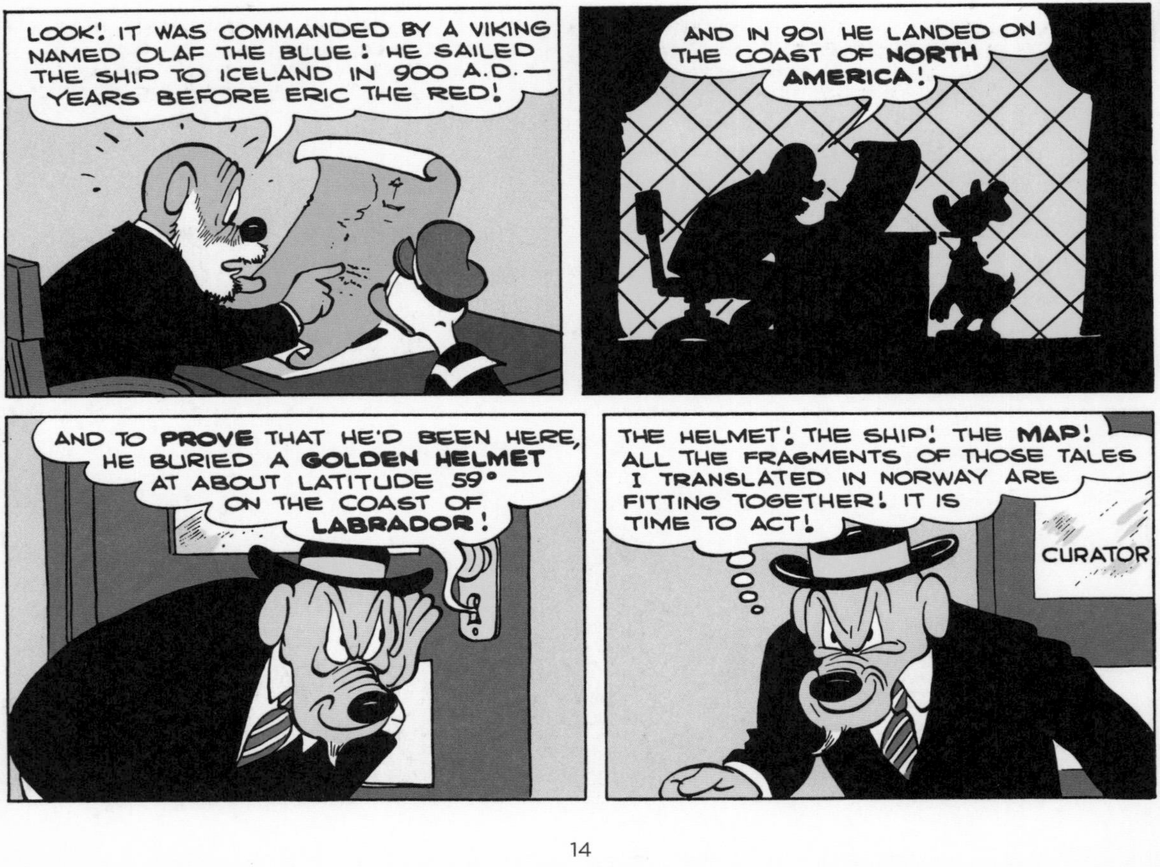
LOOK! IT WAS COMMANDED BY A VIKING NAMED OLAF THE BLUE! HE SAILED THE SHIP TO ICELAND IN 900 A.D.— YEARS BEFORE ERIC THE RED!
AND IN 901 HE LANDED ON THE COAST OF NORTH AMERICA!
AND TO PROVE THAT HE'D BEEN HERE, HE BURIED A GOLDEN HELMET AT ABOUT LATITUDE 59° — ON THE COAST OF LABRADOR!
THE HELMET! THE SHIP! THE MAP! ALL THE FRAGMENTS OF THOSE TALES I TRANSLATED IN NORWAY ARE FITTING TOGETHER! IT IS TIME TO ACT!
CURATOR

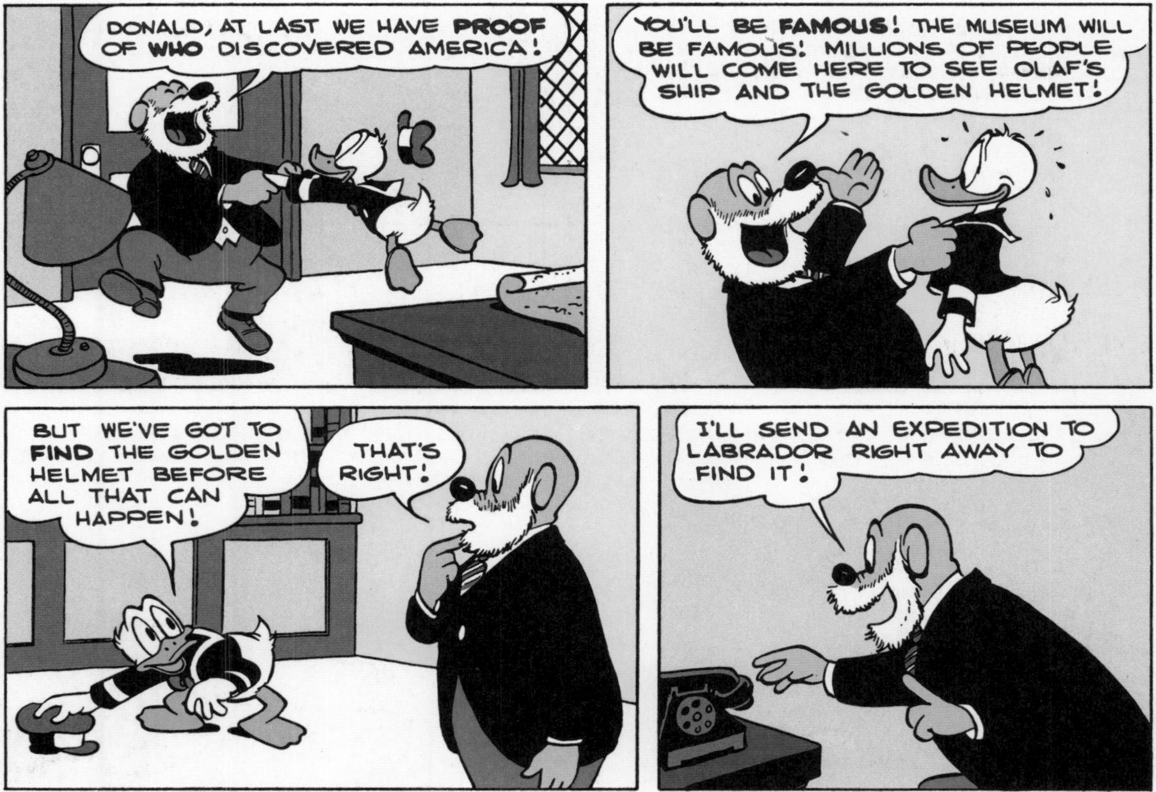
DONALD, AT LAST WE HAVE **PROOF** OF **WHO** DISCOVERED AMERICA!
YOU'LL BE **FAMOUS**! THE MUSEUM WILL BE FAMOUS! MILLIONS OF PEOPLE WILL COME HERE TO SEE OLAF'S SHIP AND THE GOLDEN HELMET!
BUT WE'VE GOT TO **FIND** THE GOLDEN HELMET BEFORE ALL THAT CAN HAPPEN!
THAT'S RIGHT!
I'LL SEND AN EXPEDITION TO LABRADOR RIGHT AWAY TO FIND IT!

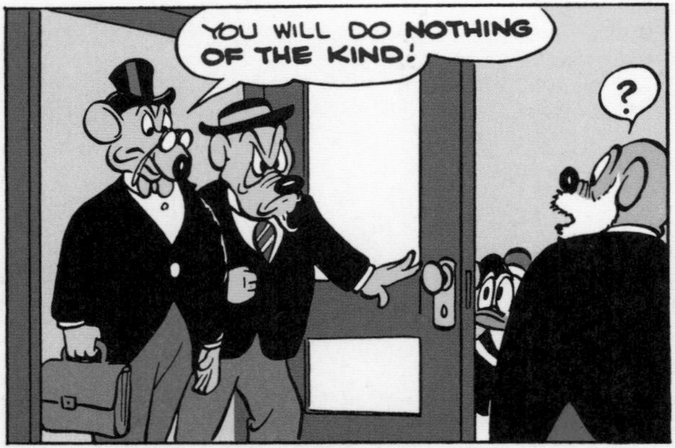
YOU WILL DO **NOTHING OF THE KIND**!
?
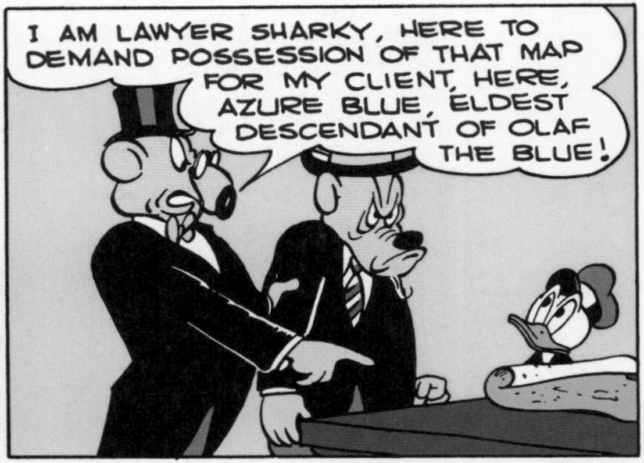
I AM LAWYER SHARKY, HERE TO DEMAND POSSESSION OF THAT MAP FOR MY CLIENT, HERE, AZURE BLUE, ELDEST DESCENDANT OF OLAF THE BLUE!
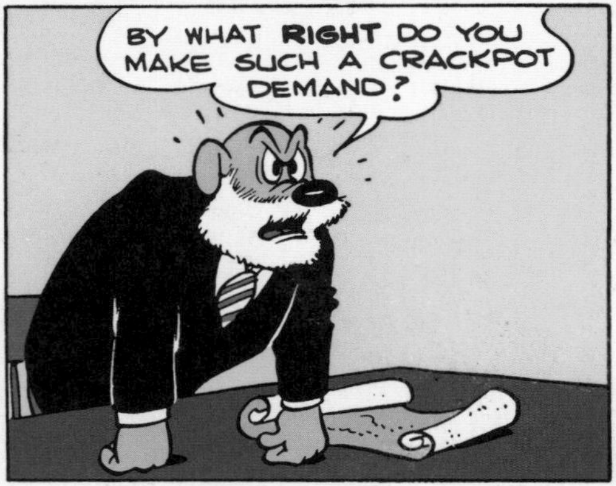
BY WHAT **RIGHT** DO YOU MAKE SUCH A CRACKPOT DEMAND?
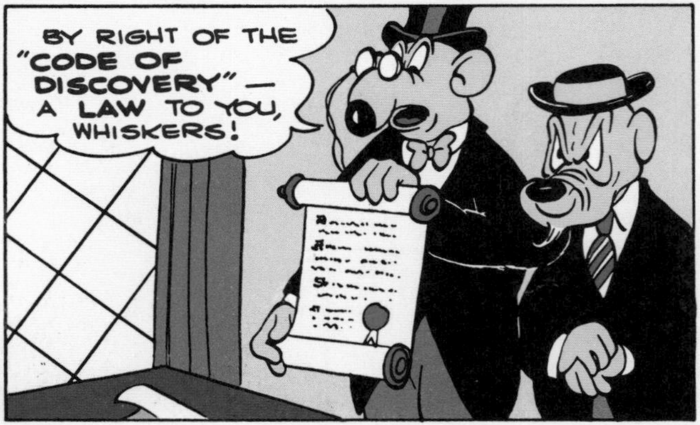
BY RIGHT OF THE **"CODE OF DISCOVERY"** — A **LAW** TO YOU, WHISKERS!

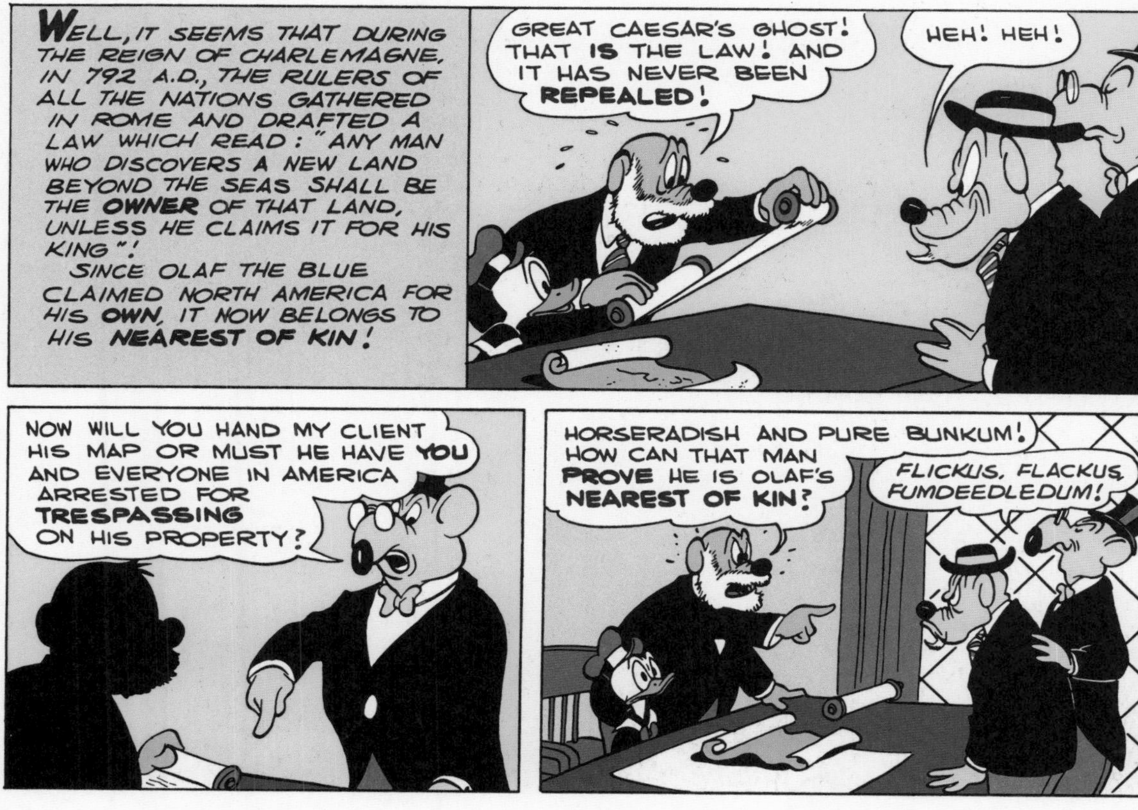
WELL, IT SEEMS THAT DURING THE REIGN OF CHARLEMAGNE, IN 792 A.D., THE RULERS OF ALL THE NATIONS GATHERED IN ROME AND DRAFTED A LAW WHICH READ: "ANY MAN WHO DISCOVERS A NEW LAND BEYOND THE SEAS SHALL BE THE **OWNER** OF THAT LAND, UNLESS HE CLAIMS IT FOR HIS KING"!
SINCE OLAF THE BLUE CLAIMED NORTH AMERICA FOR HIS **OWN**, IT NOW BELONGS TO HIS **NEAREST OF KIN**!
GREAT CAESAR'S GHOST! THAT **IS** THE LAW! AND IT HAS NEVER BEEN **REPEALED**!
HEH! HEH!
NOW WILL YOU HAND MY CLIENT HIS MAP OR MUST HE HAVE **YOU** AND EVERYONE IN AMERICA ARRESTED FOR **TRESPASSING** ON HIS PROPERTY?
HORSERADISH AND PURE BUNKUM! HOW CAN THAT MAN **PROVE** HE IS OLAF'S **NEAREST OF KIN**?
FLICKUS, FLACKUS, FUMDEEDLEDUM!

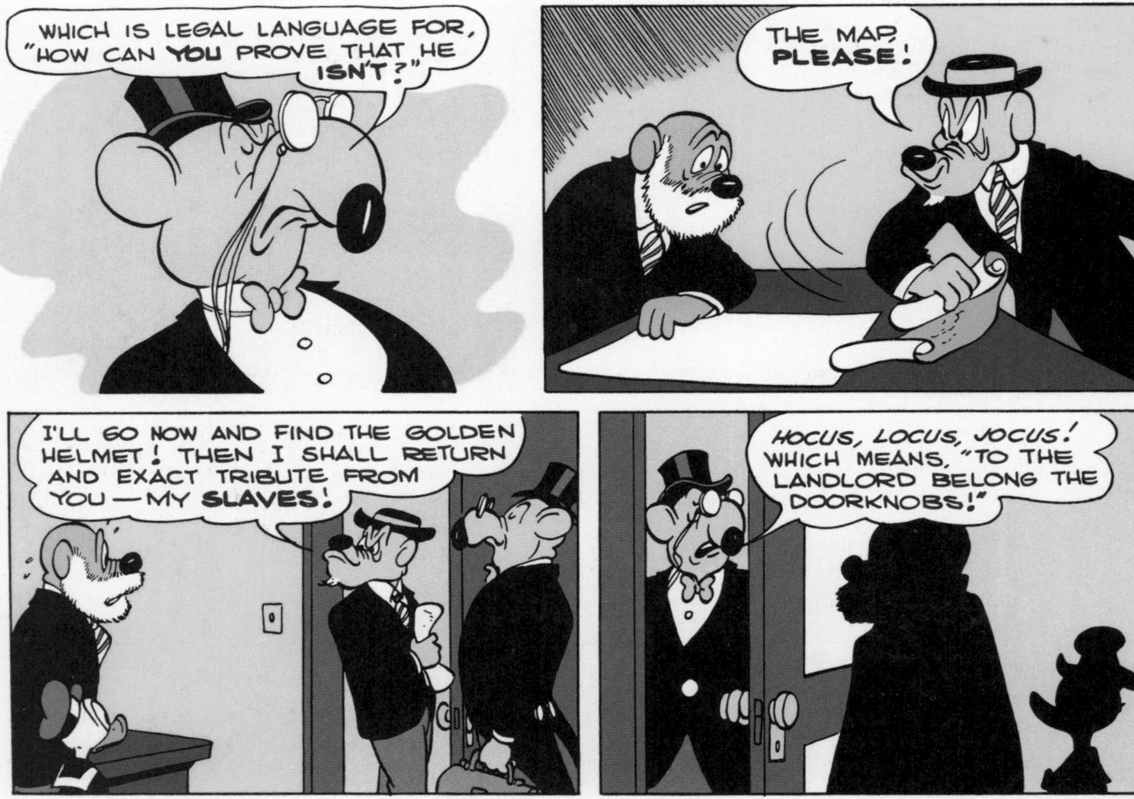
WHICH IS LEGAL LANGUAGE FOR, "HOW CAN **YOU** PROVE THAT HE **ISN'T?**"
THE MAP, **PLEASE!**
I'LL GO NOW AND FIND THE GOLDEN HELMET! THEN I SHALL RETURN AND EXACT TRIBUTE FROM YOU—MY **SLAVES!**
HOCUS, LOCUS, JOCUS! WHICH MEANS, "TO THE LANDLORD BELONG THE DOORKNOBS!"

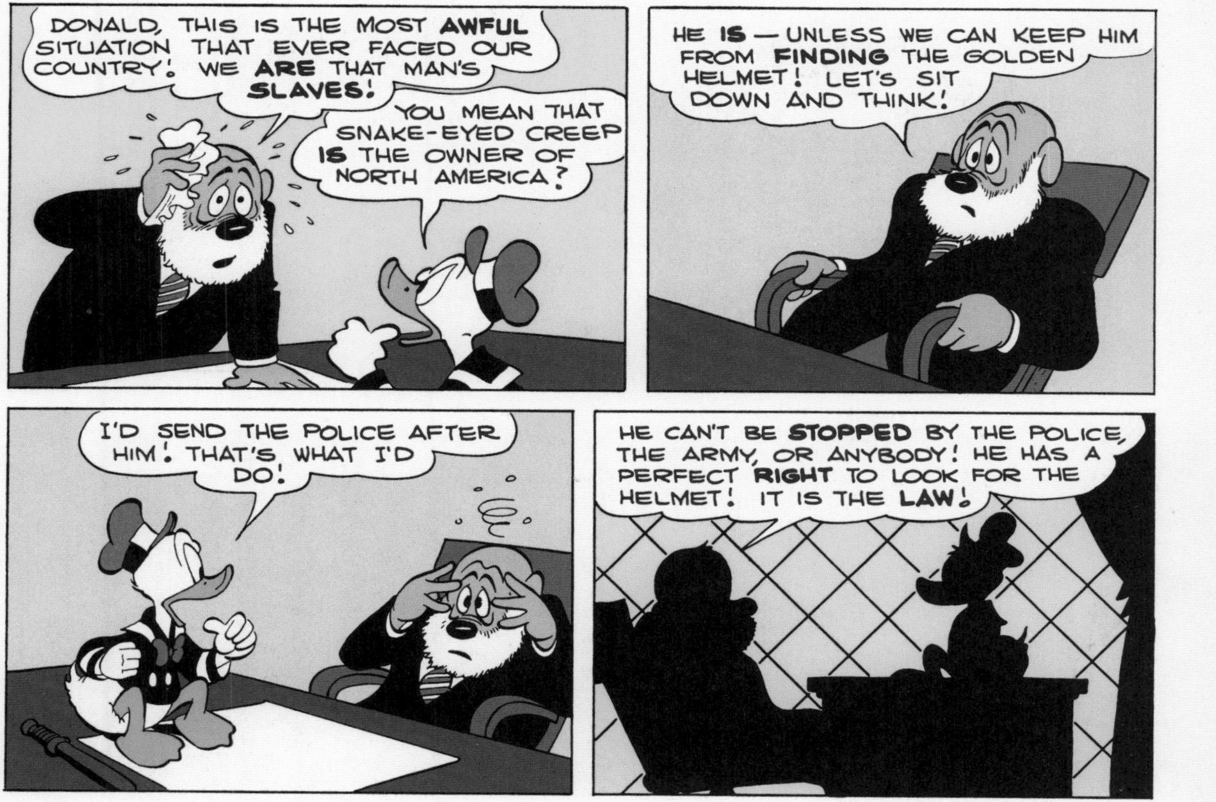
DONALD, THIS IS THE MOST **AWFUL** SITUATION THAT EVER FACED OUR COUNTRY! WE **ARE** THAT MAN'S **SLAVES!**
YOU MEAN THAT SNAKE-EYED CREEP **IS** THE OWNER OF NORTH AMERICA?
HE **IS** — UNLESS WE CAN KEEP HIM FROM **FINDING** THE GOLDEN HELMET! LET'S SIT DOWN AND THINK!
I'D SEND THE POLICE AFTER HIM! THAT'S WHAT I'D DO!
HE CAN'T BE **STOPPED** BY THE POLICE, THE ARMY, OR ANYBODY! HE HAS A PERFECT **RIGHT** TO LOOK FOR THE HELMET! IT IS THE **LAW!**

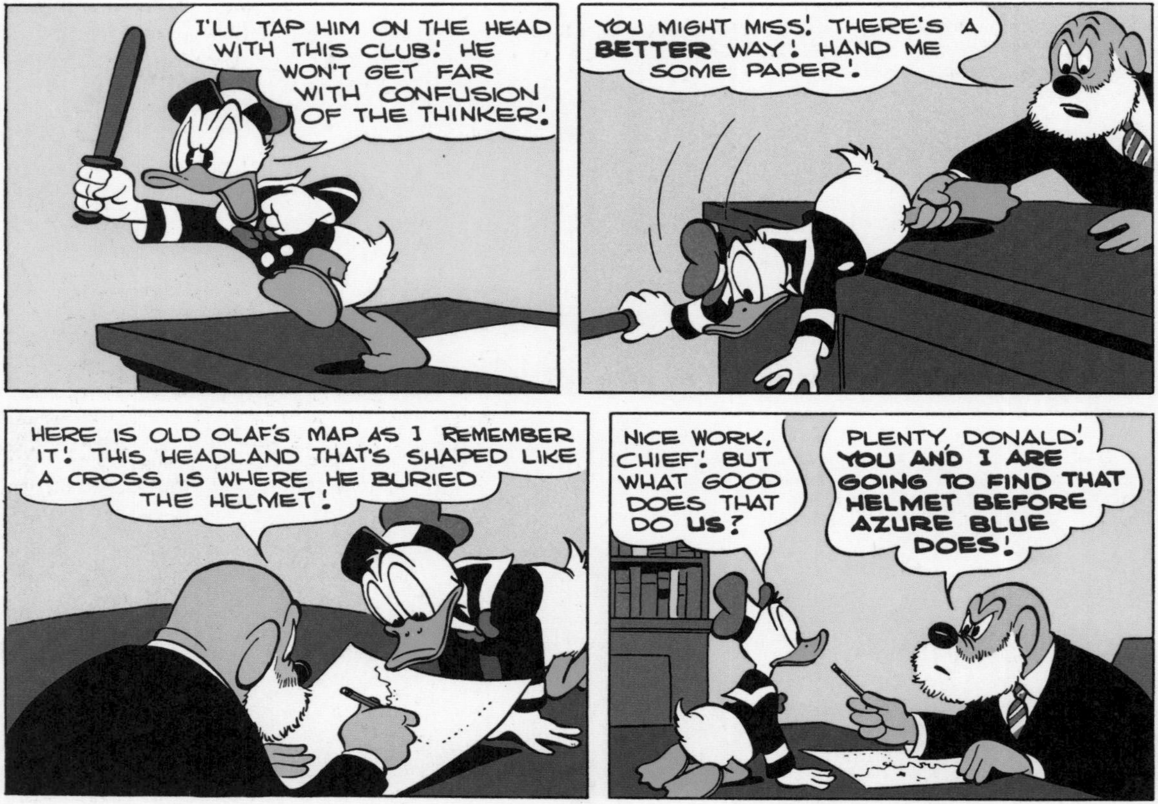
I'LL TAP HIM ON THE HEAD WITH THIS CLUB! HE WON'T GET FAR WITH CONFUSION OF THE THINKER!
YOU MIGHT MISS! THERE'S A BETTER WAY! HAND ME SOME PAPER!
HERE IS OLD OLAF'S MAP AS I REMEMBER IT! THIS HEADLAND THAT'S SHAPED LIKE A CROSS IS WHERE HE BURIED THE HELMET!
NICE WORK, CHIEF! BUT WHAT GOOD DOES THAT DO US?
PLENTY, DONALD! YOU AND I ARE GOING TO FIND THAT HELMET BEFORE AZURE BLUE DOES!

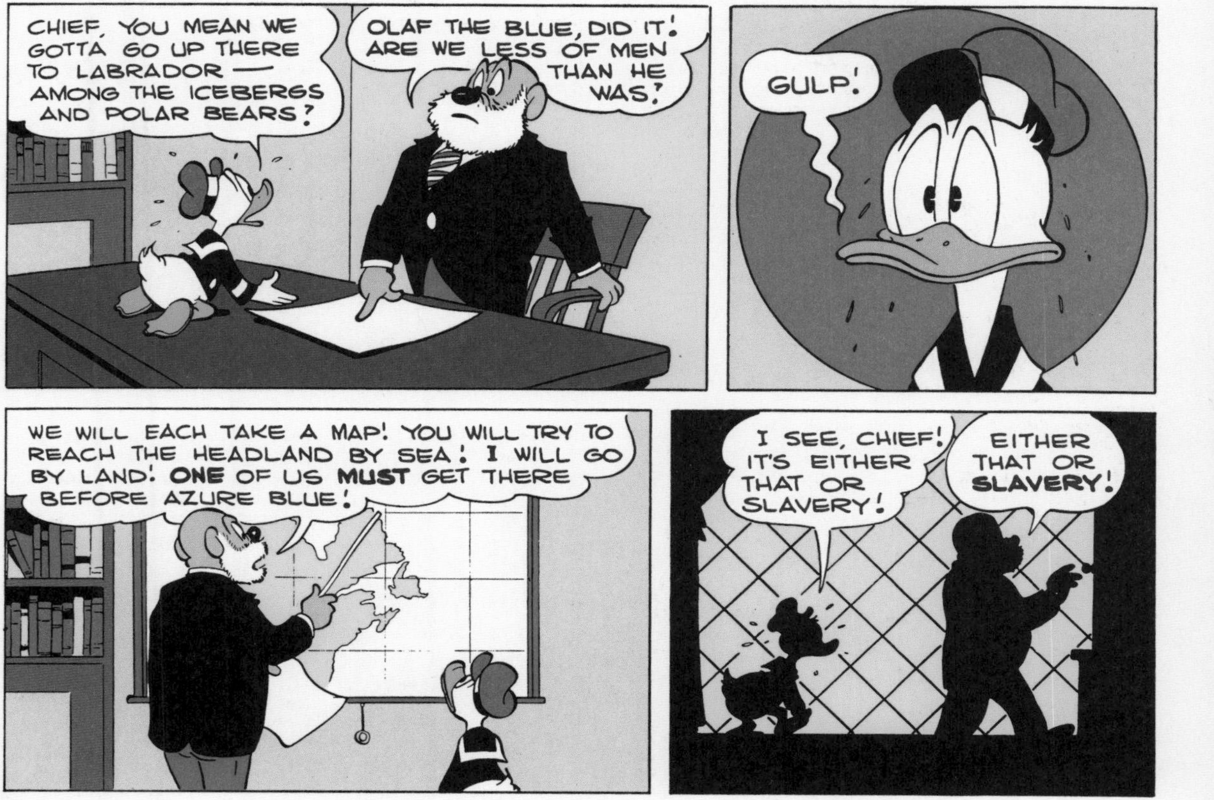

CHIEF, YOU MEAN WE GOTTA GO UP THERE TO LABRADOR — AMONG THE ICEBERGS AND POLAR BEARS?
OLAF THE BLUE, DID IT! ARE WE LESS OF MEN THAN HE WAS?
GULP!
WE WILL EACH TAKE A MAP! YOU WILL TRY TO REACH THE HEADLAND BY SEA! I WILL GO BY LAND! ONE OF US MUST GET THERE BEFORE AZURE BLUE!
I SEE, CHIEF! IT'S EITHER THAT OR SLAVERY!
EITHER THAT OR SLAVERY!

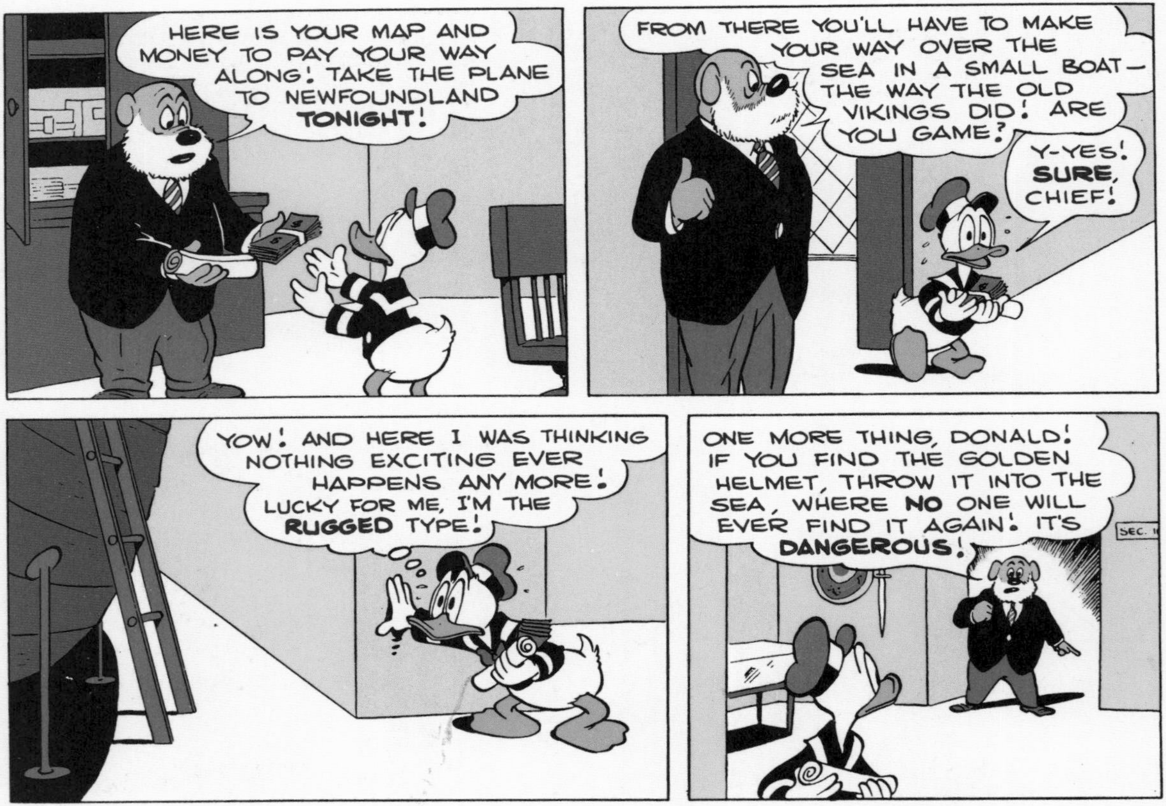
HERE IS YOUR MAP AND MONEY TO PAY YOUR WAY ALONG! TAKE THE PLANE TO NEWFOUNDLAND **TONIGHT**!
FROM THERE YOU'LL HAVE TO MAKE YOUR WAY OVER THE SEA IN A SMALL BOAT— THE WAY THE OLD VIKINGS DID! ARE YOU GAME?
Y-YES! **SURE**, CHIEF!
YOW! AND HERE I WAS THINKING NOTHING EXCITING EVER HAPPENS ANY MORE! LUCKY FOR ME, I'M THE **RUGGED** TYPE!
ONE MORE THING, DONALD! IF YOU FIND THE GOLDEN HELMET, THROW IT INTO THE SEA, WHERE **NO** ONE WILL EVER FIND IT AGAIN! IT'S **DANGEROUS**!
SEC. 1

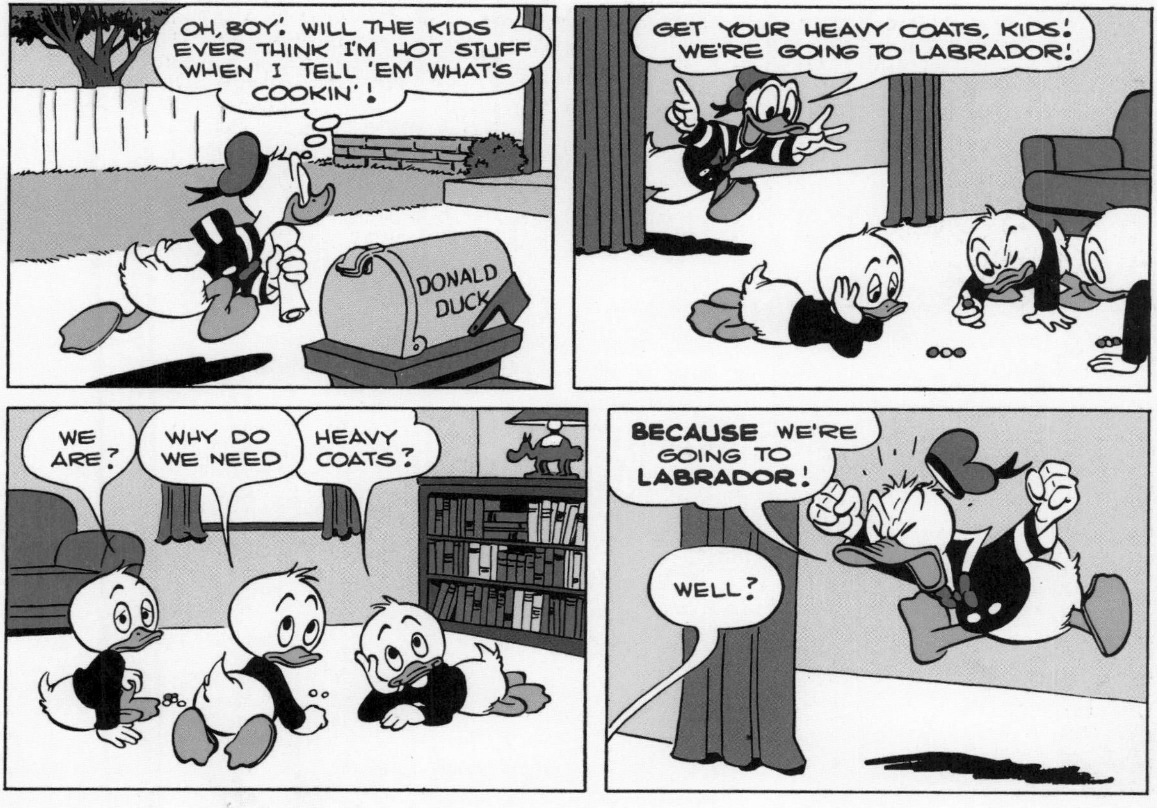
OH, BOY! WILL THE KIDS EVER THINK I'M HOT STUFF WHEN I TELL 'EM WHAT'S COOKIN'!
DONALD DUCK
GET YOUR HEAVY COATS, KIDS! WE'RE GOING TO LABRADOR!
WE ARE?
WHY DO WE NEED
HEAVY COATS?
BECAUSE WE'RE GOING TO LABRADOR!
WELL?

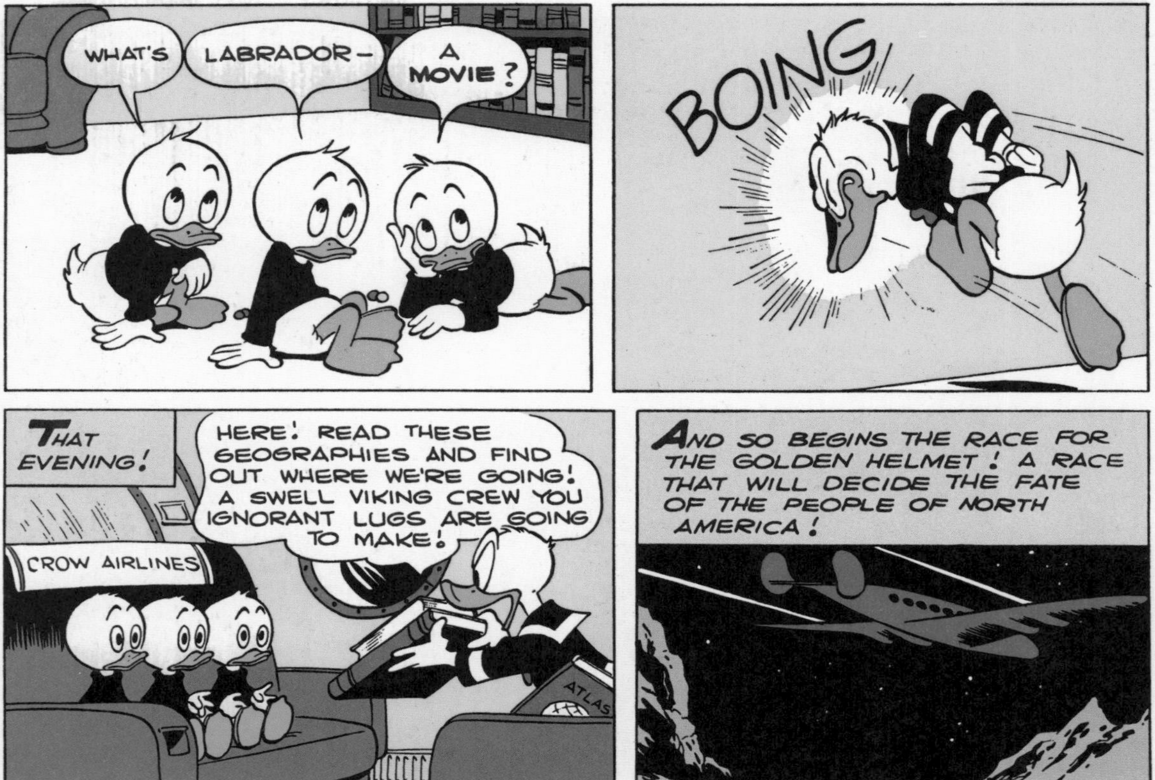
WHAT'S
LABRADOR—
A MOVIE?
BOING
THAT EVENING!
HERE! READ THESE GEOGRAPHIES AND FIND OUT WHERE WE'RE GOING! A SWELL VIKING CREW YOU IGNORANT LUGS ARE GOING TO MAKE!
CROW AIRLINES
ATLAS
AND SO BEGINS THE RACE FOR THE GOLDEN HELMET! A RACE THAT WILL DECIDE THE FATE OF THE PEOPLE OF NORTH AMERICA!

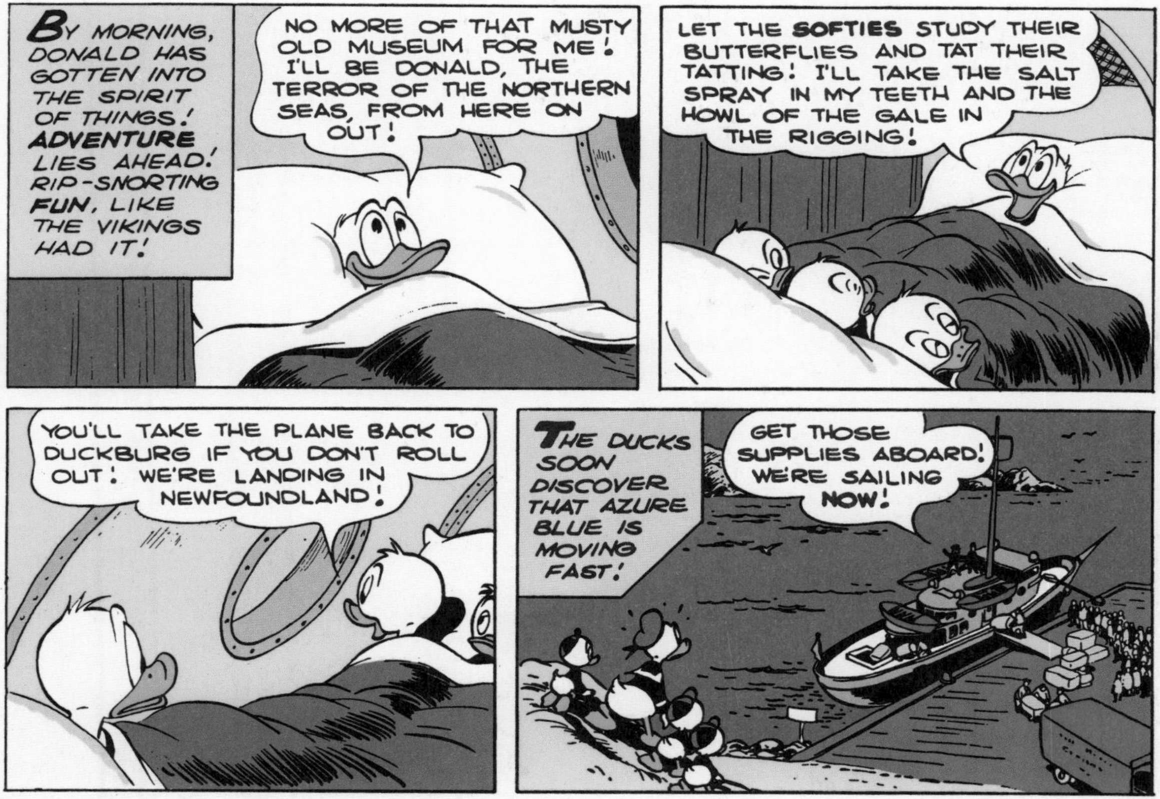
BY MORNING, DONALD HAS GOTTEN INTO THE SPIRIT OF THINGS! ADVENTURE LIES AHEAD! RIP-SNORTING FUN, LIKE THE VIKINGS HAD IT!
NO MORE OF THAT MUSTY OLD MUSEUM FOR ME! I'LL BE DONALD, THE TERROR OF THE NORTHERN SEAS, FROM HERE ON OUT!
LET THE SOFTIES STUDY THEIR BUTTERFLIES AND TAT THEIR TATTING! I'LL TAKE THE SALT SPRAY IN MY TEETH AND THE HOWL OF THE GALE IN THE RIGGING!
YOU'LL TAKE THE PLANE BACK TO DUCKBURG IF YOU DON'T ROLL OUT! WE'RE LANDING IN NEWFOUNDLAND!
THE DUCKS SOON DISCOVER THAT AZURE BLUE IS MOVING FAST!
GET THOSE SUPPLIES ABOARD! WE'RE SAILING NOW!

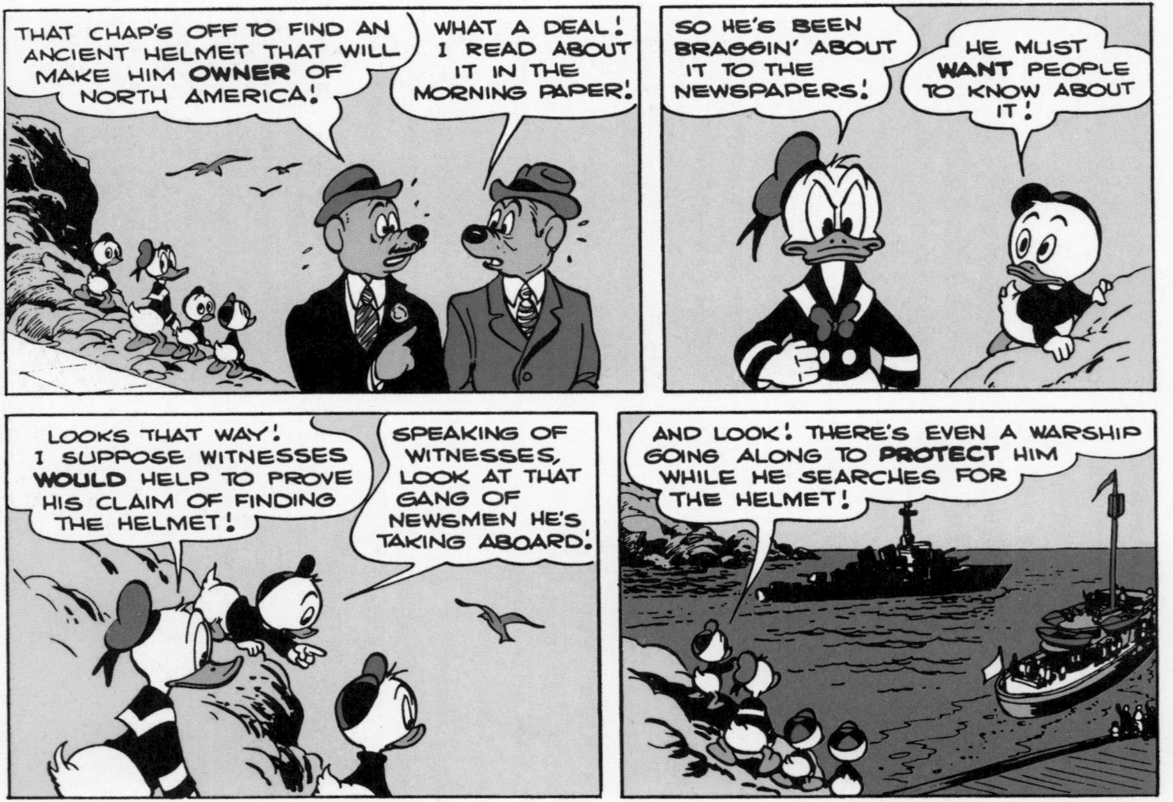
THAT CHAP'S OFF TO FIND AN ANCIENT HELMET THAT WILL MAKE HIM **OWNER** OF NORTH AMERICA!
WHAT A DEAL! I READ ABOUT IT IN THE MORNING PAPER!
SO HE'S BEEN BRAGGIN' ABOUT IT TO THE NEWSPAPERS!
HE MUST **WANT** PEOPLE TO KNOW ABOUT IT!
LOOKS THAT WAY! I SUPPOSE WITNESSES **WOULD** HELP TO PROVE HIS CLAIM OF FINDING THE HELMET!
SPEAKING OF WITNESSES, LOOK AT THAT GANG OF NEWSMEN HE'S TAKING ABOARD!
AND LOOK! THERE'S EVEN A WARSHIP GOING ALONG TO **PROTECT** HIM WHILE HE SEARCHES FOR THE HELMET!

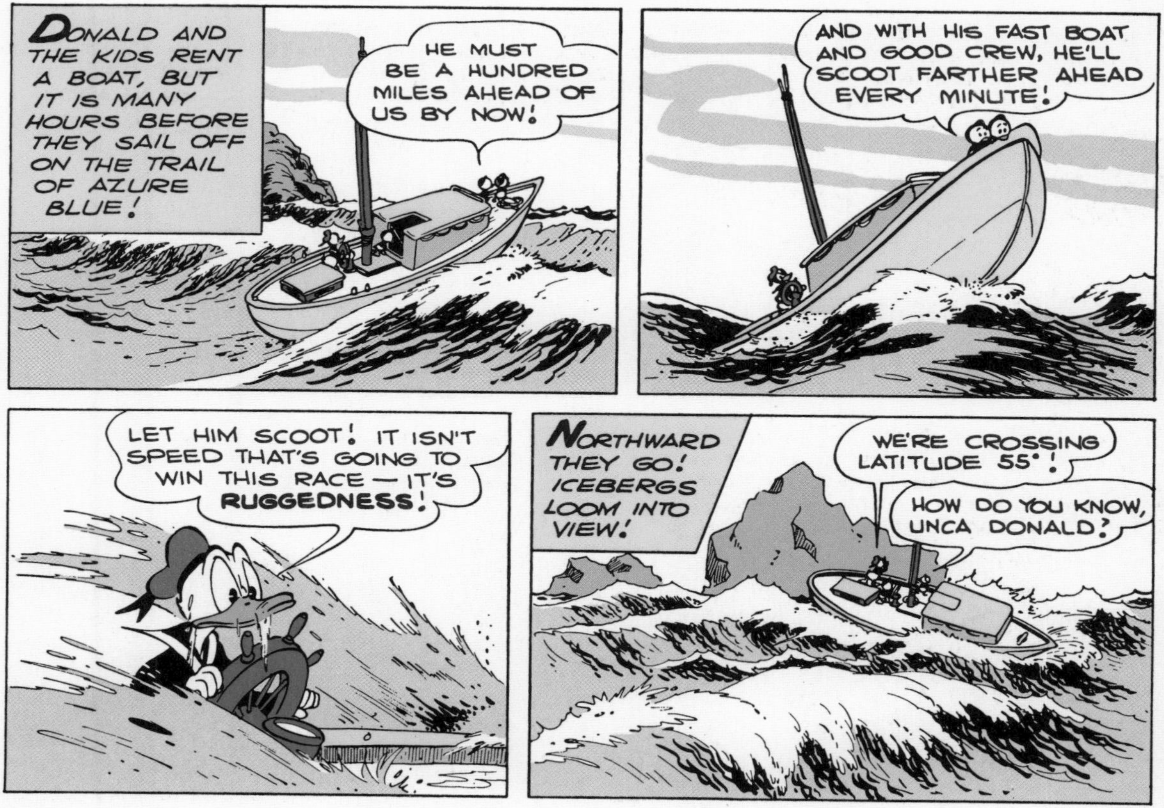
DONALD AND THE KIDS RENT A BOAT, BUT IT IS MANY HOURS BEFORE THEY SAIL OFF ON THE TRAIL OF AZURE BLUE!
HE MUST BE A HUNDRED MILES AHEAD OF US BY NOW!
AND WITH HIS FAST BOAT AND GOOD CREW, HE'LL SCOOT FARTHER AHEAD EVERY MINUTE!
LET HIM SCOOT! IT ISN'T SPEED THAT'S GOING TO WIN THIS RACE — IT'S **RUGGEDNESS**!
NORTHWARD THEY GO! ICEBERGS LOOM INTO VIEW!
WE'RE CROSSING LATITUDE 55°!
HOW DO YOU KNOW, UNCA DONALD?

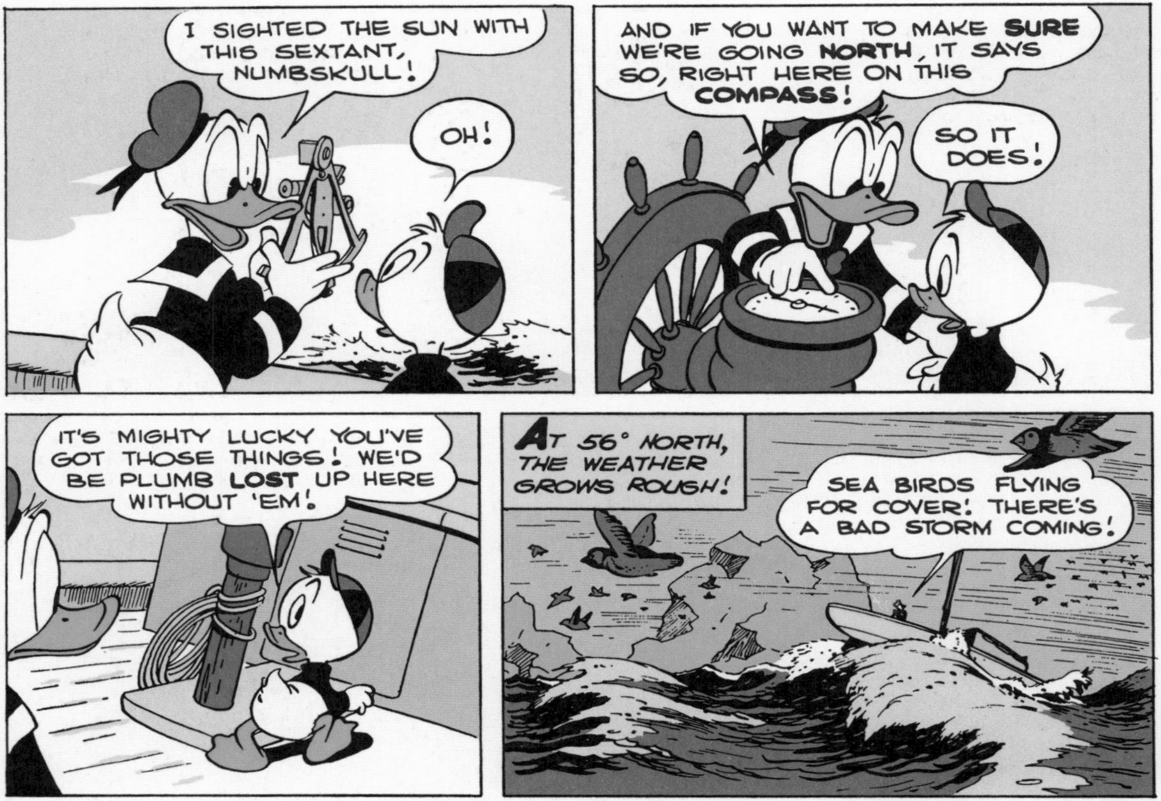
I SIGHTED THE SUN WITH THIS SEXTANT, NUMBSKULL!
OH!
AND IF YOU WANT TO MAKE **SURE** WE'RE GOING **NORTH**, IT SAYS SO, RIGHT HERE ON THIS **COMPASS**!
SO IT DOES!
IT'S MIGHTY LUCKY YOU'VE GOT THOSE THINGS! WE'D BE PLUMB **LOST** UP HERE WITHOUT 'EM!
AT 56° NORTH, THE WEATHER GROWS ROUGH!
SEA BIRDS FLYING FOR COVER! THERE'S A BAD STORM COMING!

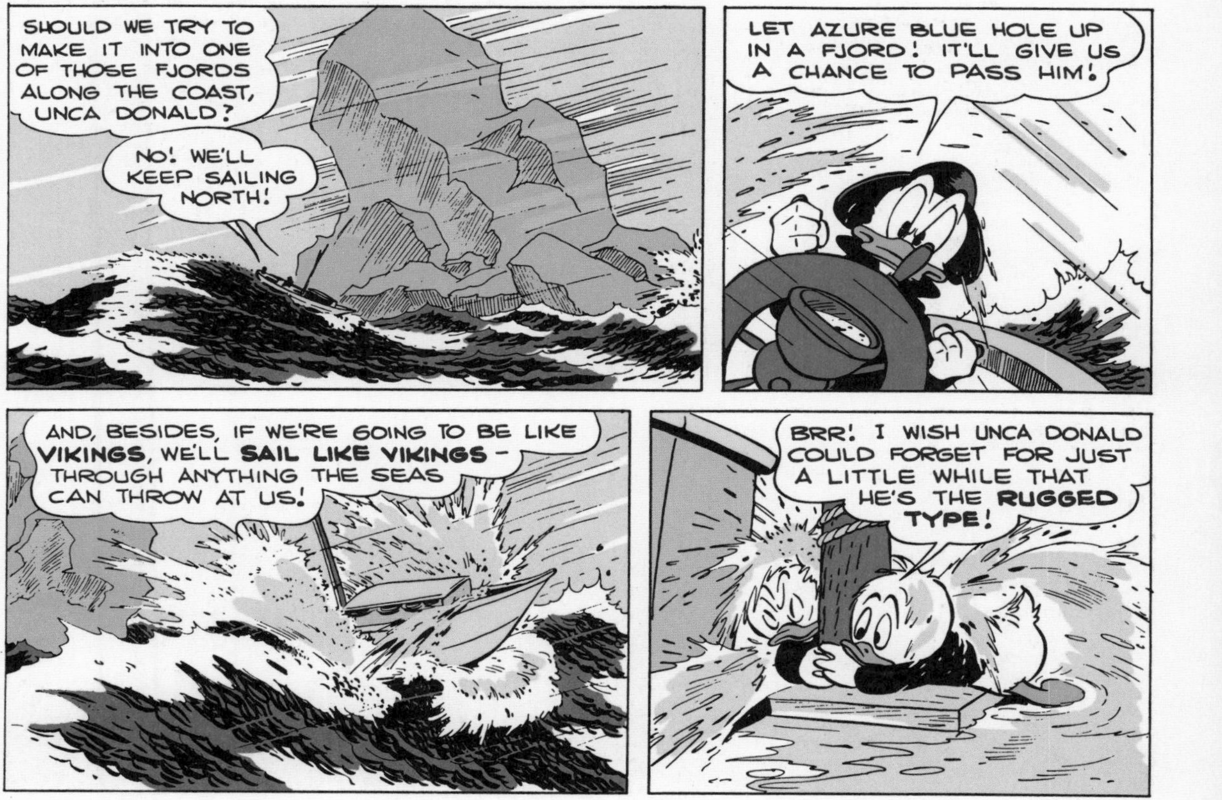
SHOULD WE TRY TO MAKE IT INTO ONE OF THOSE FJORDS ALONG THE COAST, UNCA DONALD?
NO! WE'LL KEEP SAILING NORTH!
LET AZURE BLUE HOLE UP IN A FJORD! IT'LL GIVE US A CHANCE TO PASS HIM!
AND, BESIDES, IF WE'RE GOING TO BE LIKE VIKINGS, WE'LL SAIL LIKE VIKINGS — THROUGH ANYTHING THE SEAS CAN THROW AT US!
BRR! I WISH UNCA DONALD COULD FORGET FOR JUST A LITTLE WHILE THAT HE'S THE RUGGED TYPE!

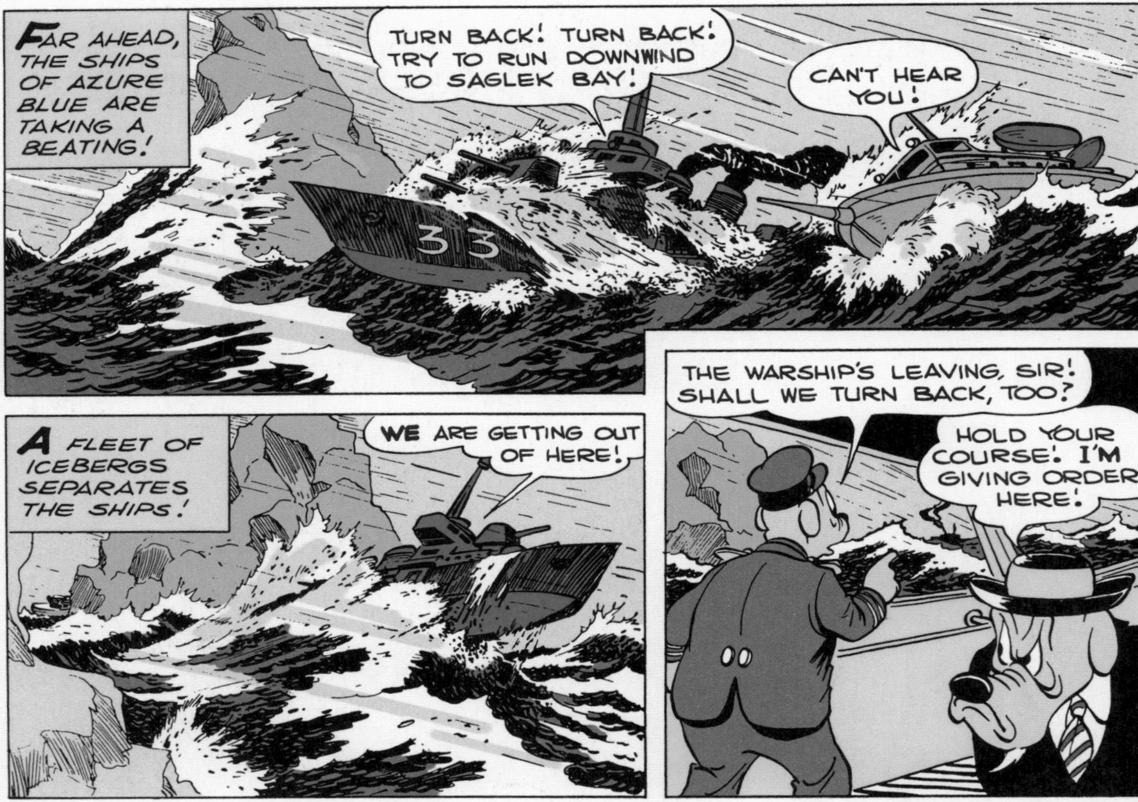
FAR AHEAD, THE SHIPS OF AZURE BLUE ARE TAKING A BEATING!
TURN BACK! TURN BACK! TRY TO RUN DOWNWIND TO SAGLEK BAY!
CAN'T HEAR YOU!
33
A FLEET OF ICEBERGS SEPARATES THE SHIPS!
WE ARE GETTING OUT OF HERE!
THE WARSHIP'S LEAVING, SIR! SHALL WE TURN BACK, TOO?
HOLD YOUR COURSE! **I'M** GIVING ORDERS HERE!

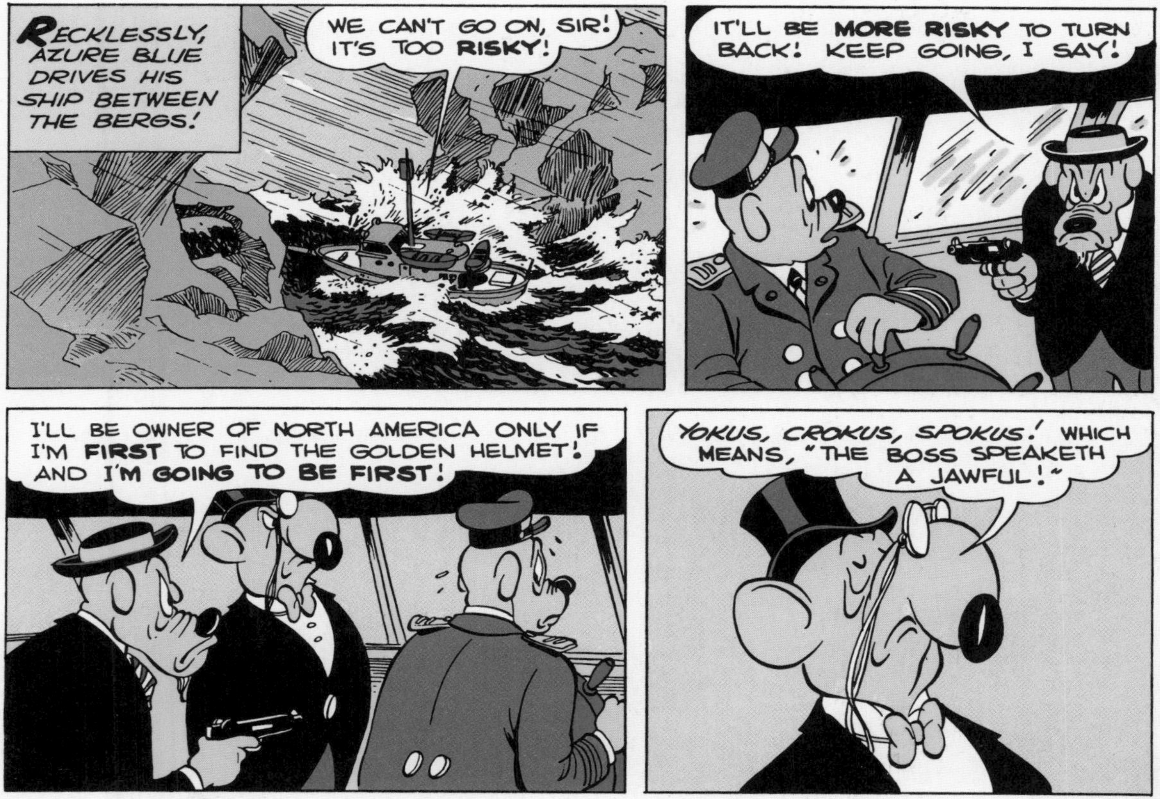
RECKLESSLY, AZURE BLUE DRIVES HIS SHIP BETWEEN THE BERGS!
WE CAN'T GO ON, SIR! IT'S TOO **RISKY**!
IT'LL BE **MORE RISKY** TO TURN BACK! KEEP GOING, I SAY!
I'LL BE OWNER OF NORTH AMERICA ONLY IF I'M **FIRST** TO FIND THE GOLDEN HELMET! AND **I'M GOING TO BE FIRST**!
YOKUS, CROKUS, SPOKUS! WHICH MEANS, "THE BOSS SPEAKETH A JAWFUL!"

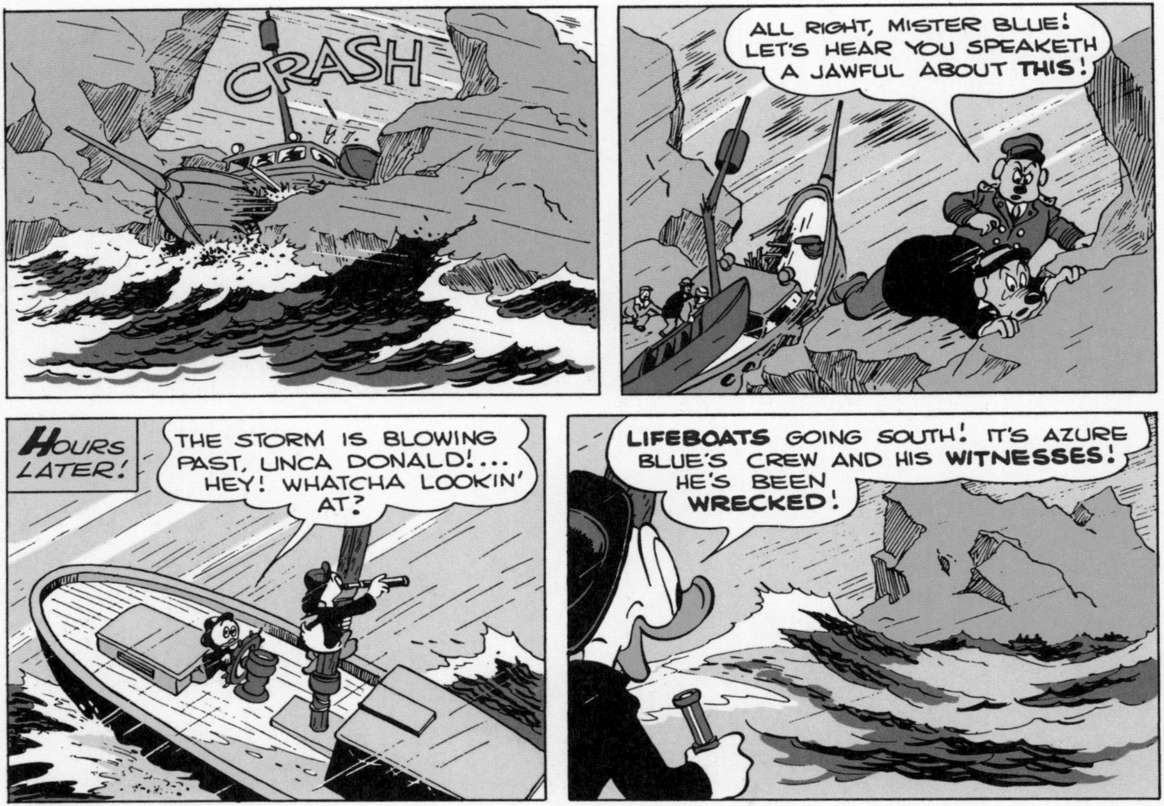
CRASH
ALL RIGHT, MISTER BLUE! LET'S HEAR YOU SPEAKETH A JAWFUL ABOUT THIS!
HOURS LATER!
THE STORM IS BLOWING PAST, UNCA DONALD!... HEY! WHATCHA LOOKIN' AT?
LIFEBOATS GOING SOUTH! IT'S AZURE BLUE'S CREW AND HIS WITNESSES! HE'S BEEN WRECKED!

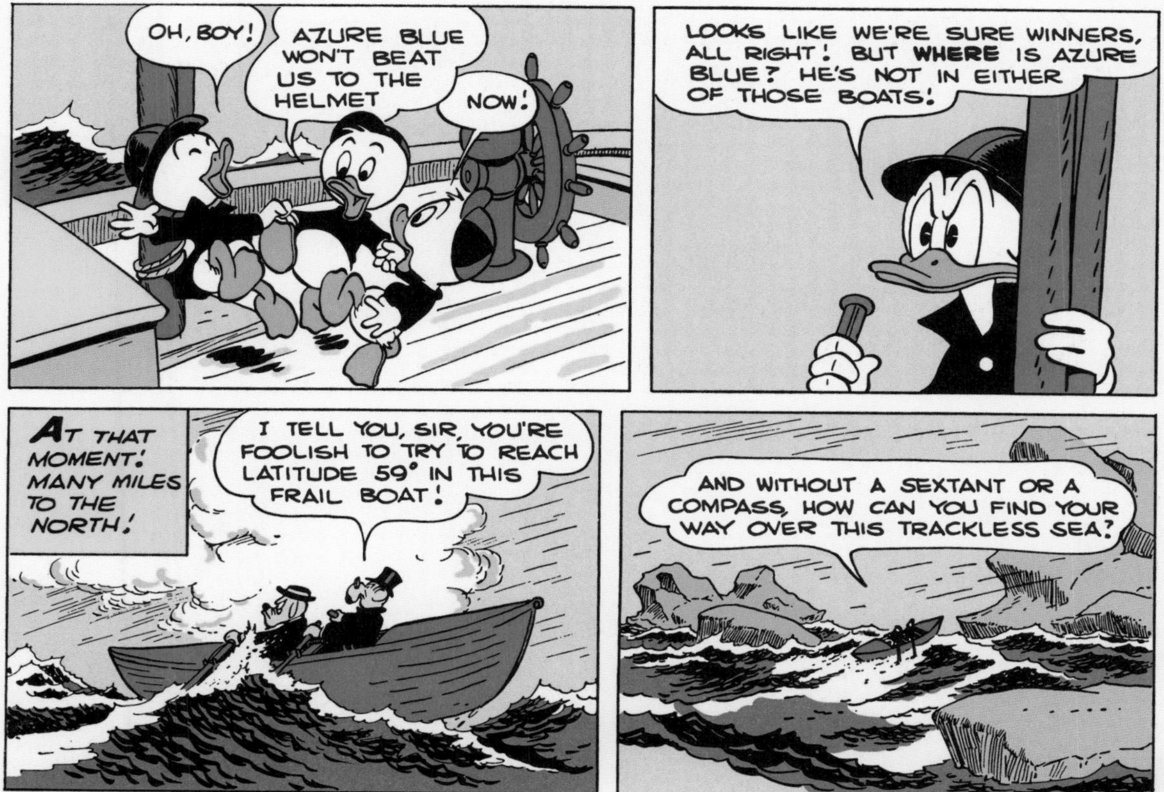
OH, BOY!
AZURE BLUE WON'T BEAT US TO THE HELMET
NOW!
LOOKS LIKE WE'RE SURE WINNERS, ALL RIGHT! BUT WHERE IS AZURE BLUE? HE'S NOT IN EITHER OF THOSE BOATS!
AT THAT MOMENT! MANY MILES TO THE NORTH!
I TELL YOU, SIR, YOU'RE FOOLISH TO TRY TO REACH LATITUDE 59° IN THIS FRAIL BOAT!
AND WITHOUT A SEXTANT OR A COMPASS, HOW CAN YOU FIND YOUR WAY OVER THIS TRACKLESS SEA?

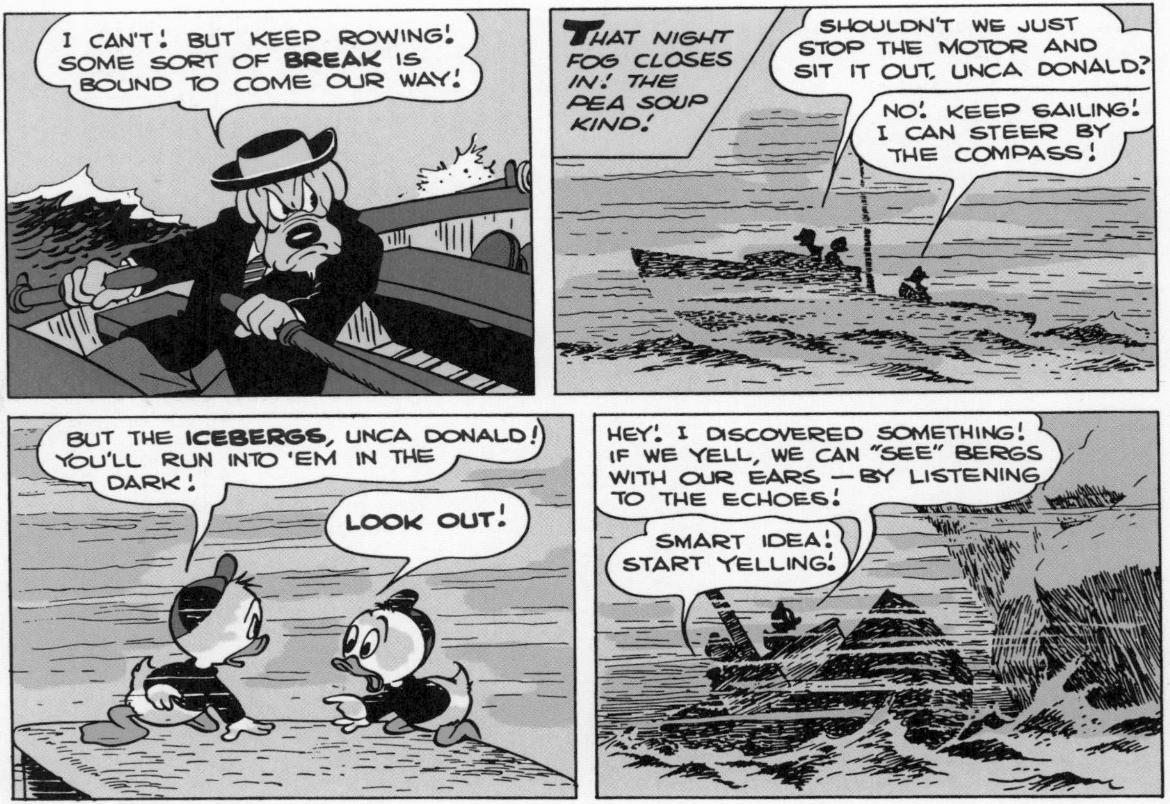
I CAN'T! BUT KEEP ROWING! SOME SORT OF **BREAK** IS BOUND TO COME OUR WAY!
THAT NIGHT FOG CLOSES IN! THE PEA SOUP KIND!
SHOULDN'T WE JUST STOP THE MOTOR AND SIT IT OUT, UNCA DONALD?
NO! KEEP SAILING! I CAN STEER BY THE COMPASS!
BUT THE **ICEBERGS**, UNCA DONALD! YOU'LL RUN INTO 'EM IN THE DARK!
LOOK OUT!
HEY! I DISCOVERED SOMETHING! IF WE YELL, WE CAN "SEE" BERGS WITH OUR EARS — BY LISTENING TO THE ECHOES!
SMART IDEA! START YELLING!

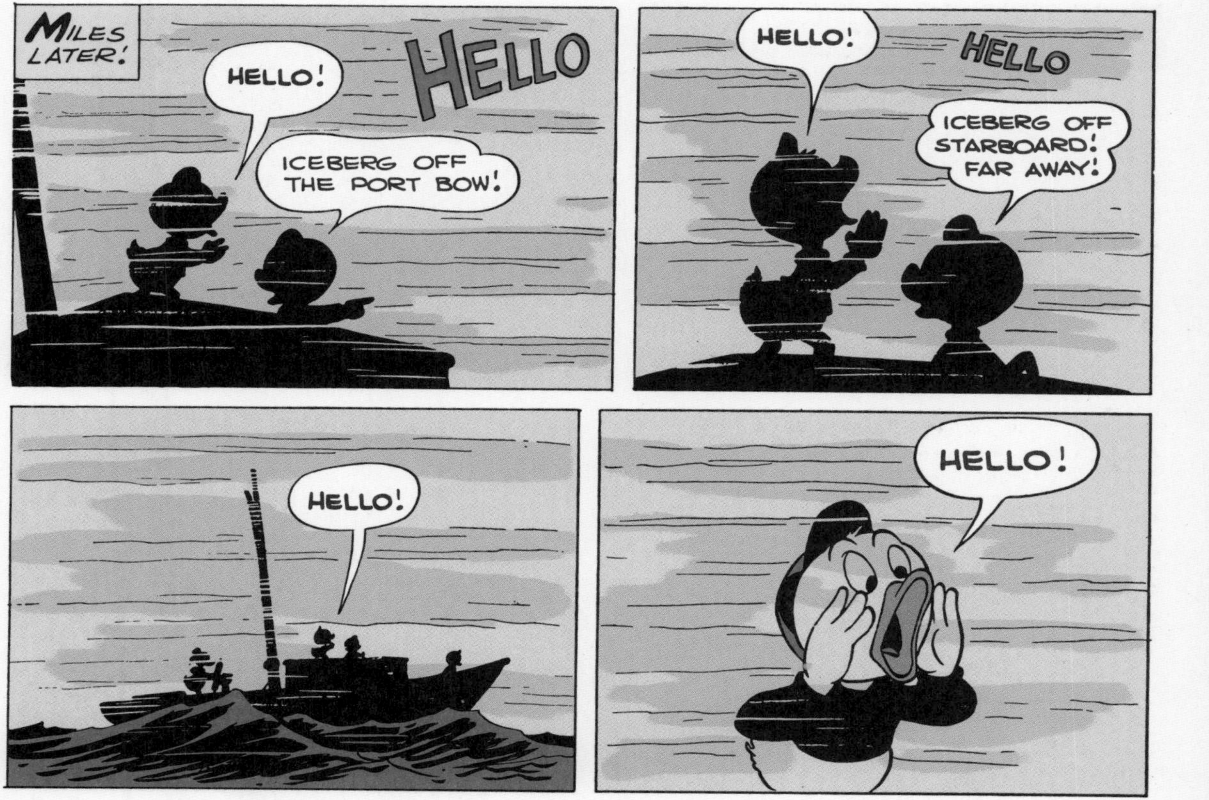
MILES LATER!
HELLO!
HELLO
ICEBERG OFF THE PORT BOW!
HELLO!
HELLO
ICEBERG OFF STARBOARD! FAR AWAY!
HELLO!
HELLO!

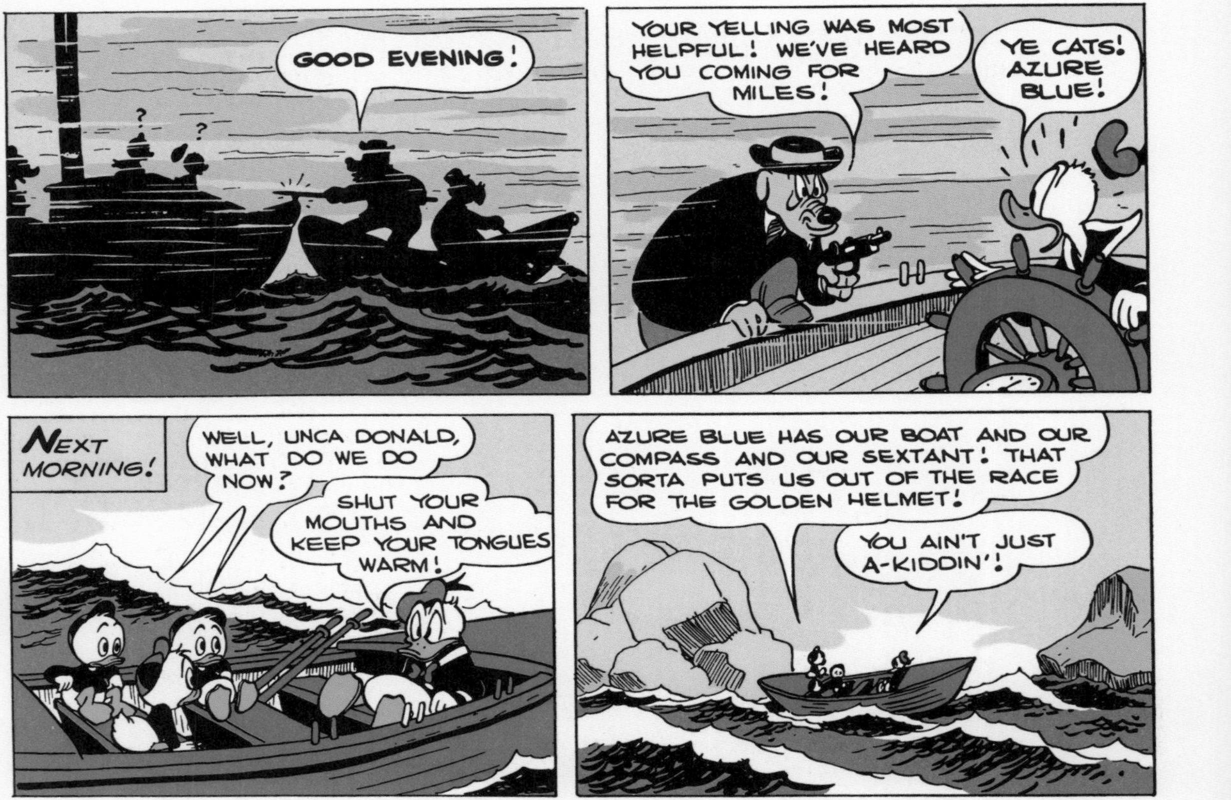
GOOD EVENING!
YOUR YELLING WAS MOST HELPFUL! WE'VE HEARD YOU COMING FOR MILES!
YE CATS! AZURE BLUE!
NEXT MORNING!
WELL, UNCA DONALD, WHAT DO WE DO NOW?
SHUT YOUR MOUTHS AND KEEP YOUR TONGUES WARM!
AZURE BLUE HAS OUR BOAT AND OUR COMPASS AND OUR SEXTANT! THAT SORTA PUTS US OUT OF THE RACE FOR THE GOLDEN HELMET!
YOU AIN'T JUST A-KIDDIN'!

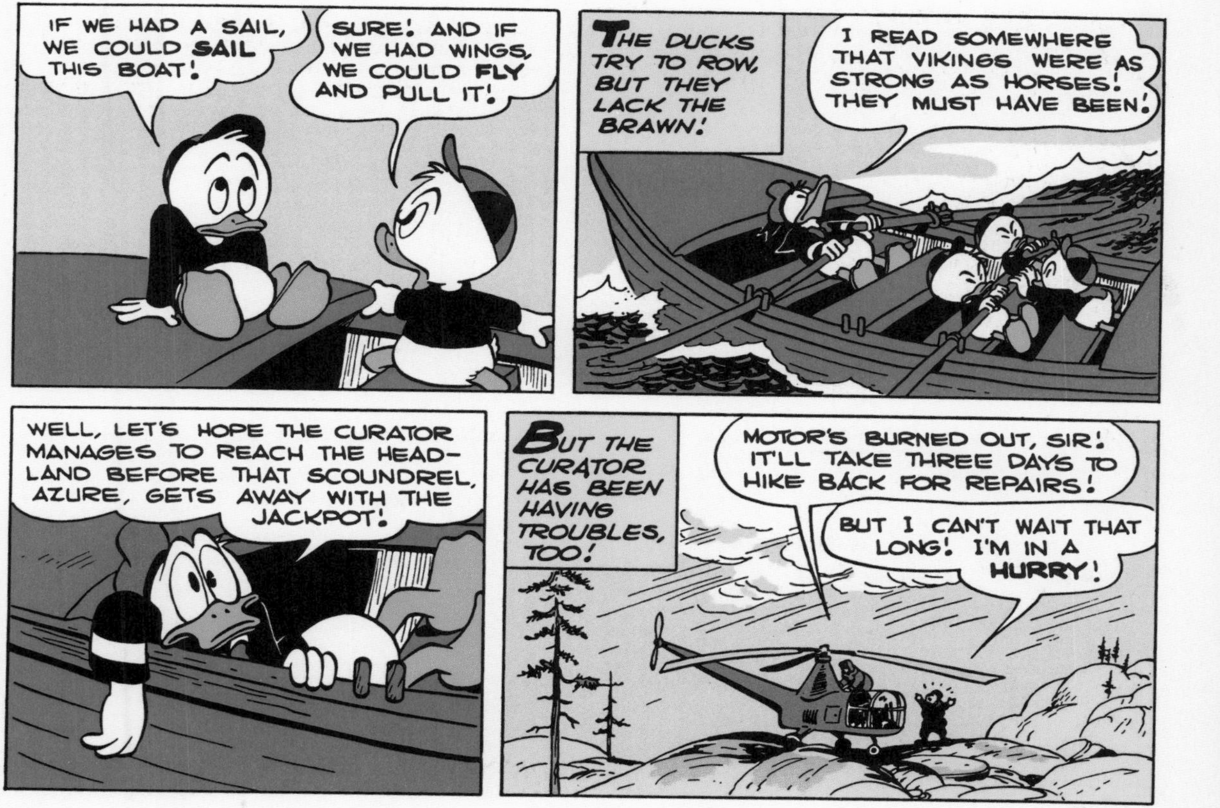
IF WE HAD A SAIL, WE COULD SAIL THIS BOAT!
SURE! AND IF WE HAD WINGS, WE COULD FLY AND PULL IT!
THE DUCKS TRY TO ROW, BUT THEY LACK THE BRAWN!
I READ SOMEWHERE THAT VIKINGS WERE AS STRONG AS HORSES! THEY MUST HAVE BEEN!
WELL, LET'S HOPE THE CURATOR MANAGES TO REACH THE HEAD-LAND BEFORE THAT SCOUNDREL, AZURE, GETS AWAY WITH THE JACKPOT!
BUT THE CURATOR HAS BEEN HAVING TROUBLES, TOO!
MOTOR'S BURNED OUT, SIR! IT'LL TAKE THREE DAYS TO HIKE BACK FOR REPAIRS!
BUT I CAN'T WAIT THAT LONG! I'M IN A HURRY!

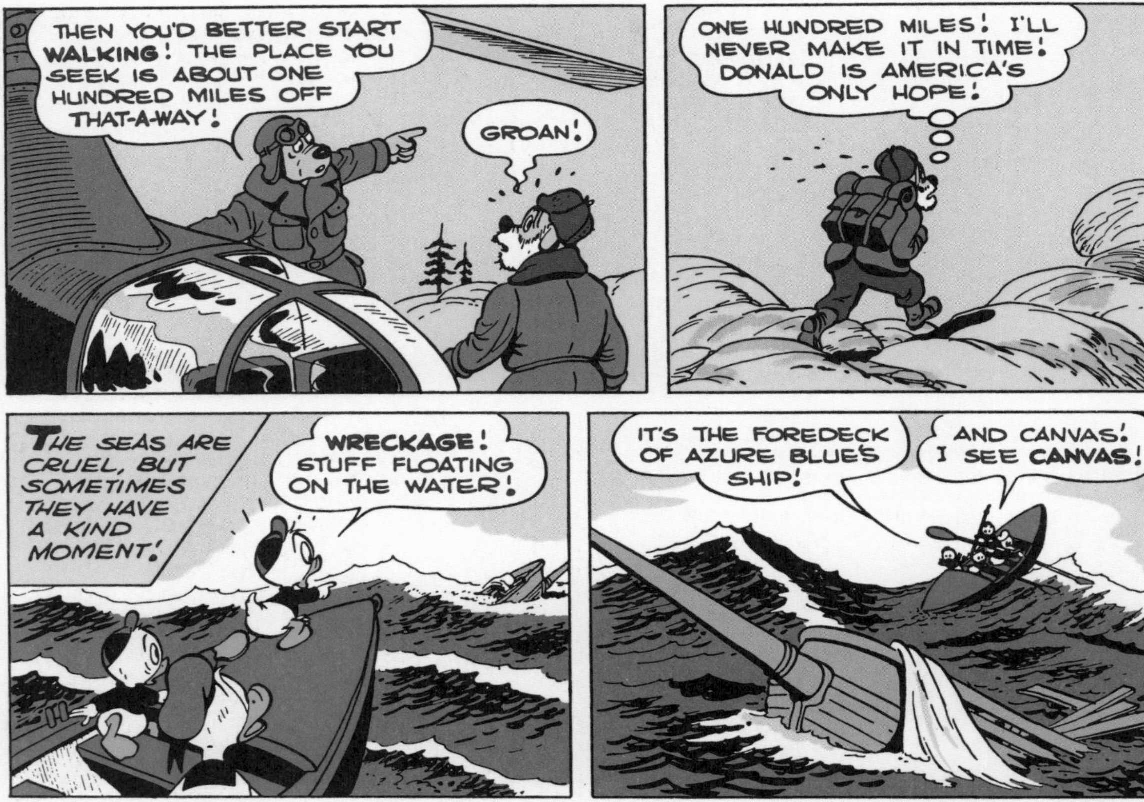
THEN YOU'D BETTER START WALKING! THE PLACE YOU SEEK IS ABOUT ONE HUNDRED MILES OFF THAT-A-WAY!
GROAN!
ONE HUNDRED MILES! I'LL NEVER MAKE IT IN TIME! DONALD IS AMERICA'S ONLY HOPE!
THE SEAS ARE CRUEL, BUT SOMETIMES THEY HAVE A KIND MOMENT!
WRECKAGE! STUFF FLOATING ON THE WATER!
IT'S THE FOREDECK OF AZURE BLUE'S SHIP!
AND CANVAS! I SEE CANVAS!

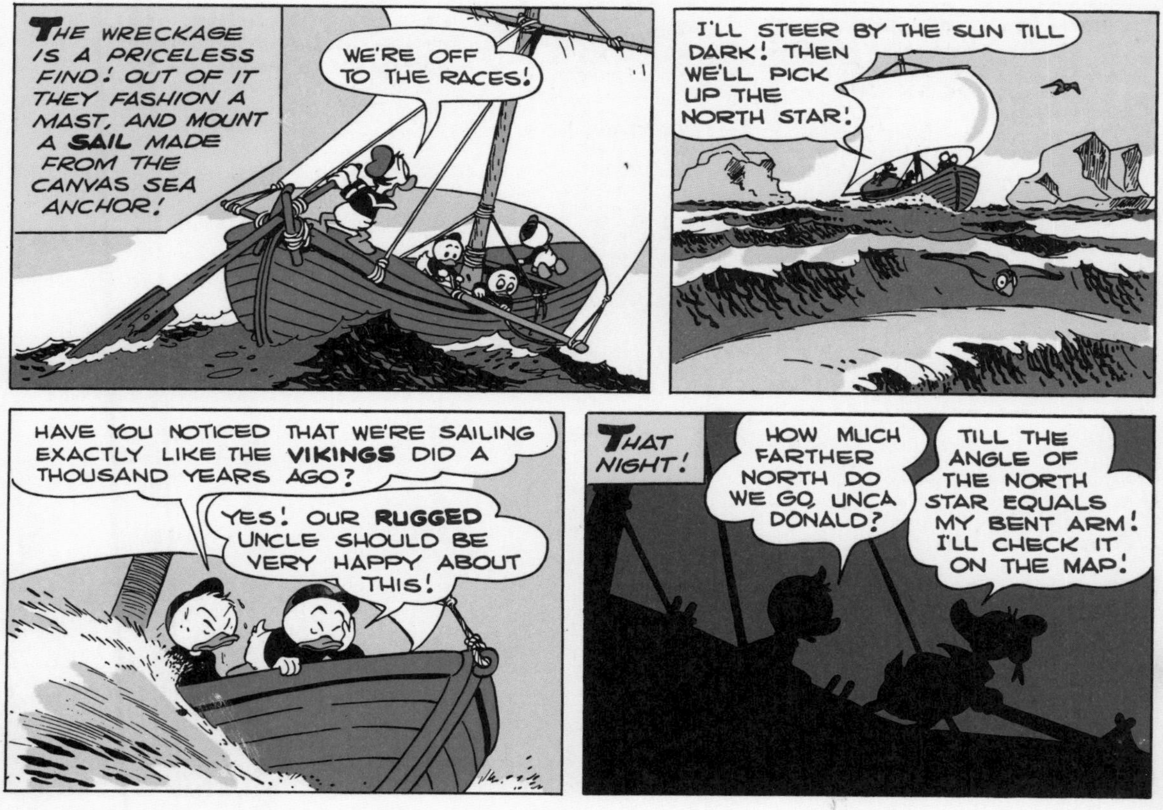
THE WRECKAGE IS A PRICELESS FIND! OUT OF IT THEY FASHION A MAST, AND MOUNT A SAIL MADE FROM THE CANVAS SEA ANCHOR!
WE'RE OFF TO THE RACES!
I'LL STEER BY THE SUN TILL DARK! THEN WE'LL PICK UP THE NORTH STAR!
HAVE YOU NOTICED THAT WE'RE SAILING EXACTLY LIKE THE VIKINGS DID A THOUSAND YEARS AGO?
YES! OUR RUGGED UNCLE SHOULD BE VERY HAPPY ABOUT THIS!
THAT NIGHT!
HOW MUCH FARTHER NORTH DO WE GO, UNCA DONALD?
TILL THE ANGLE OF THE NORTH STAR EQUALS MY BENT ARM! I'LL CHECK IT ON THE MAP!

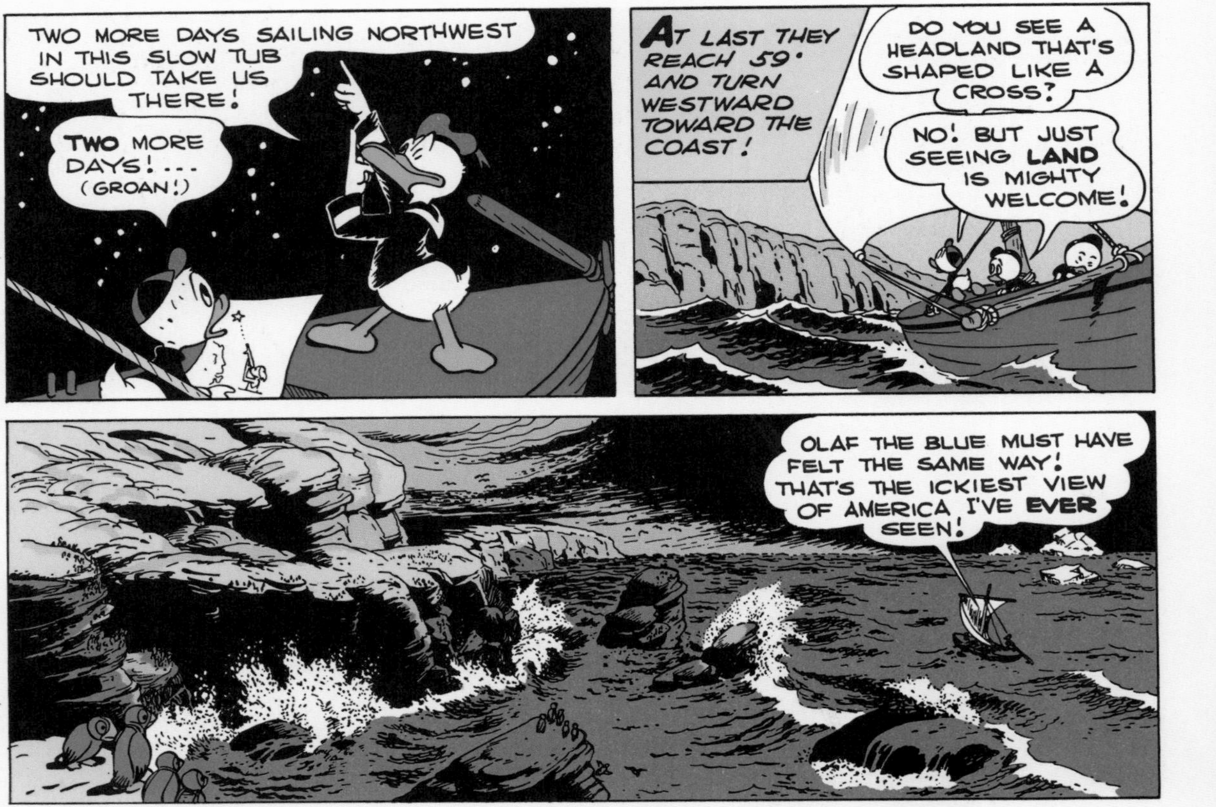
TWO MORE DAYS SAILING NORTHWEST IN THIS SLOW TUB SHOULD TAKE US THERE!
TWO MORE DAYS!... (GROAN!)
AT LAST THEY REACH 59° AND TURN WESTWARD TOWARD THE COAST!
DO YOU SEE A HEADLAND THAT'S SHAPED LIKE A CROSS?
NO! BUT JUST SEEING LAND IS MIGHTY WELCOME!
OLAF THE BLUE MUST HAVE FELT THE SAME WAY! THAT'S THE ICKIEST VIEW OF AMERICA I'VE EVER SEEN!

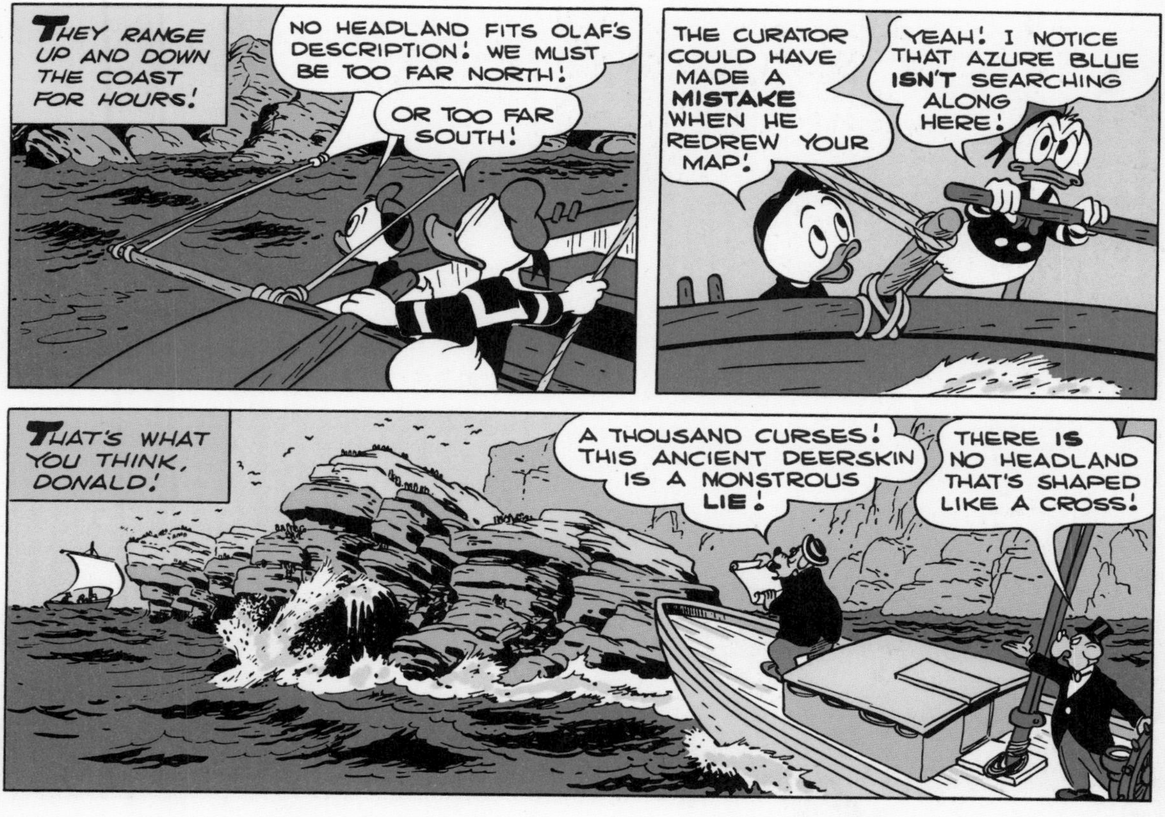
THEY RANGE UP AND DOWN THE COAST FOR HOURS!
NO HEADLAND FITS OLAF'S DESCRIPTION! WE MUST BE TOO FAR NORTH!
OR TOO FAR SOUTH!
THE CURATOR COULD HAVE MADE A MISTAKE WHEN HE REDREW YOUR MAP!
YEAH! I NOTICE THAT AZURE BLUE ISN'T SEARCHING ALONG HERE!
THAT'S WHAT YOU THINK, DONALD!
A THOUSAND CURSES! THIS ANCIENT DEERSKIN IS A MONSTROUS LIE!
THERE IS NO HEADLAND THAT'S SHAPED LIKE A CROSS!

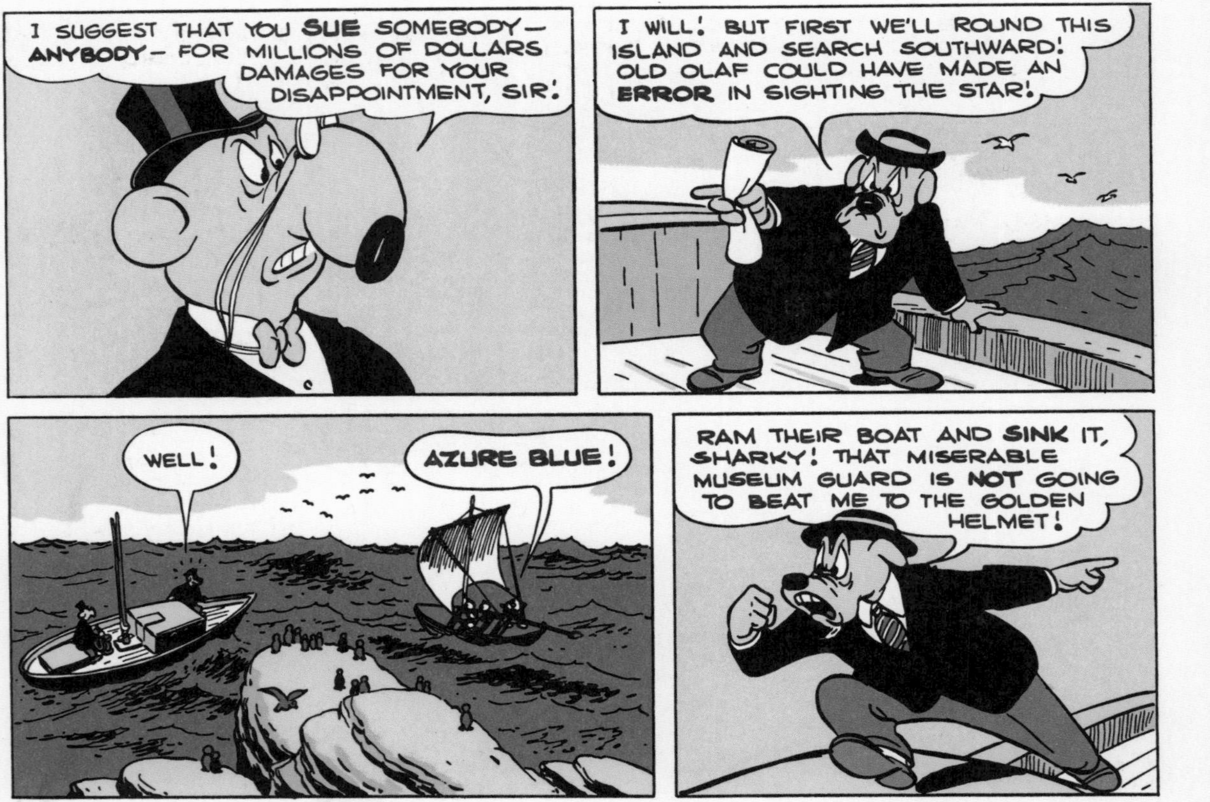
I SUGGEST THAT YOU SUE SOMEBODY— ANYBODY— FOR MILLIONS OF DOLLARS DAMAGES FOR YOUR DISAPPOINTMENT, SIR!
I WILL! BUT FIRST WE'LL ROUND THIS ISLAND AND SEARCH SOUTHWARD! OLD OLAF COULD HAVE MADE AN ERROR IN SIGHTING THE STAR!
WELL!
AZURE BLUE!
RAM THEIR BOAT AND SINK IT, SHARKY! THAT MISERABLE MUSEUM GUARD IS NOT GOING TO BEAT ME TO THE GOLDEN HELMET!

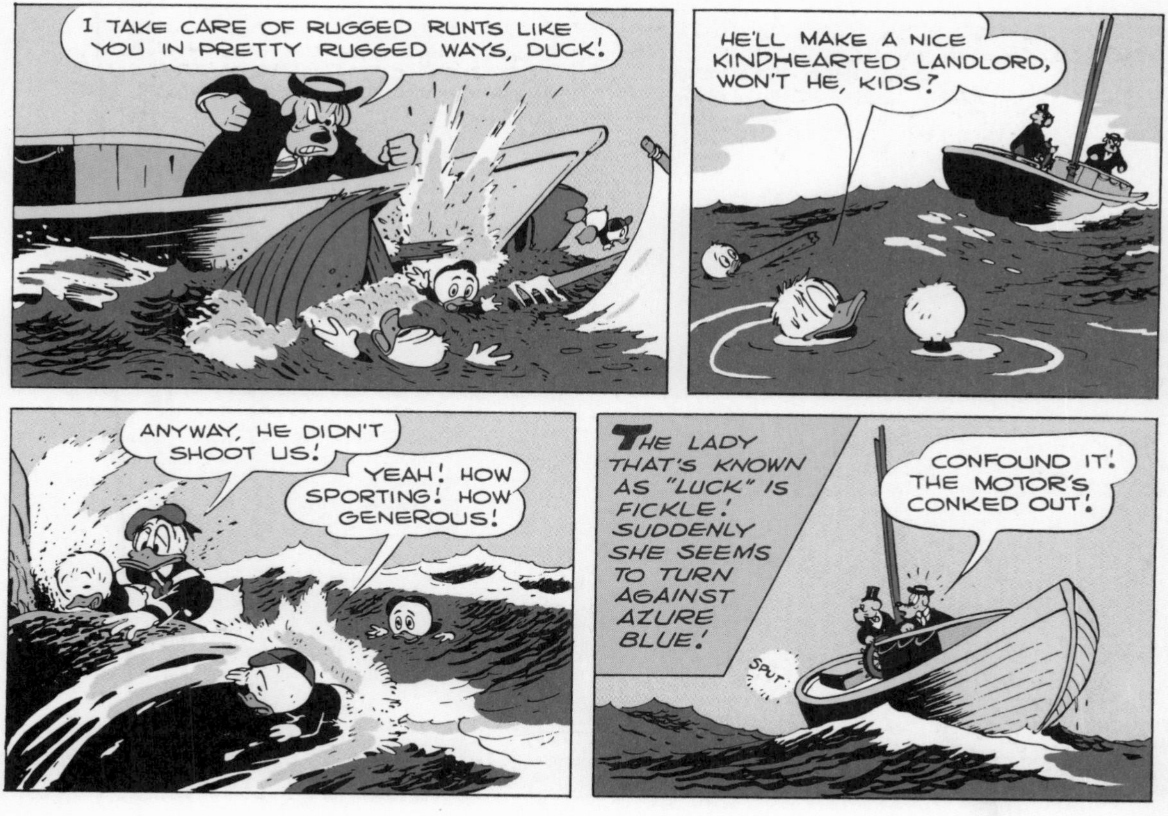
I TAKE CARE OF RUGGED RUNTS LIKE YOU IN PRETTY RUGGED WAYS, DUCK!
HE'LL MAKE A NICE KINDHEARTED LANDLORD, WON'T HE, KIDS?
ANYWAY, HE DIDN'T SHOOT US!
YEAH! HOW SPORTING! HOW GENEROUS!
THE LADY THAT'S KNOWN AS "LUCK" IS FICKLE! SUDDENLY SHE SEEMS TO TURN AGAINST AZURE BLUE!
CONFOUND IT! THE MOTOR'S CONKED OUT!
SPUT

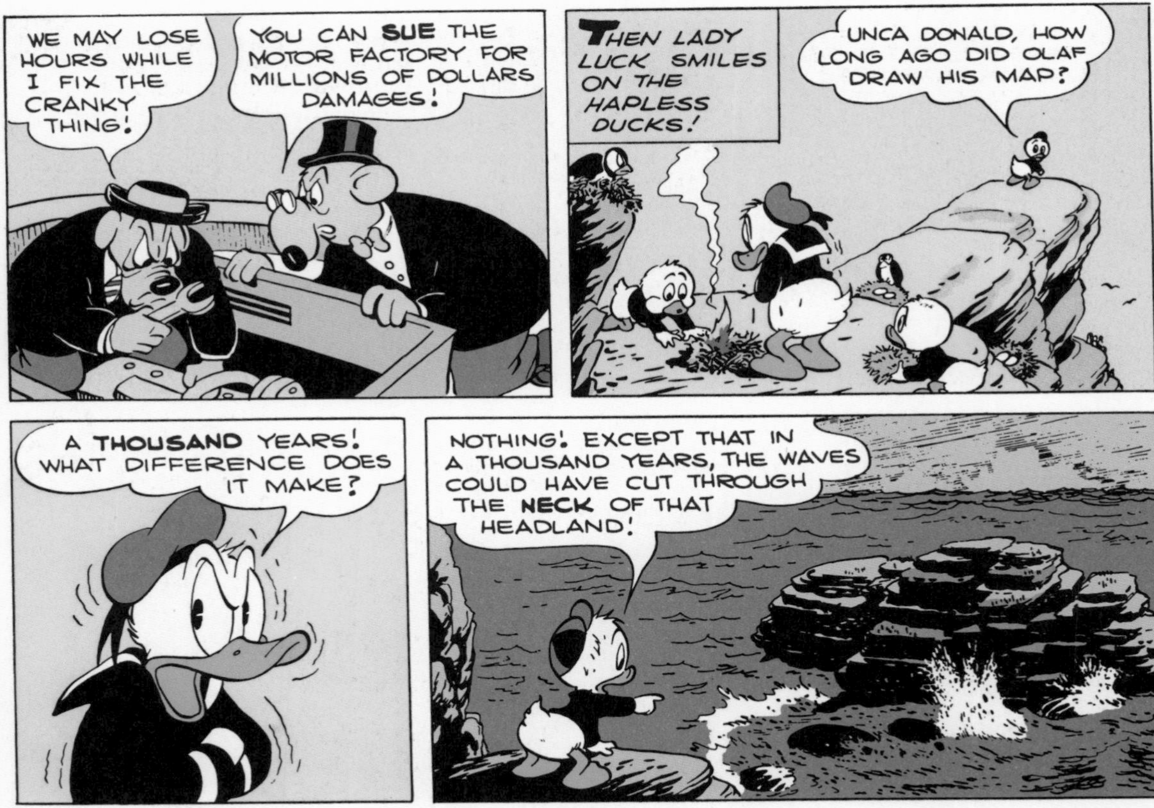

WE MAY LOSE HOURS WHILE I FIX THE CRANKY THING!
YOU CAN **SUE** THE MOTOR FACTORY FOR MILLIONS OF DOLLARS DAMAGES!
THEN LADY LUCK SMILES ON THE HAPLESS DUCKS!
UNCA DONALD, HOW LONG AGO DID OLAF DRAW HIS MAP?
A **THOUSAND** YEARS! WHAT DIFFERENCE DOES IT MAKE?
NOTHING! EXCEPT THAT IN A THOUSAND YEARS, THE WAVES COULD HAVE CUT THROUGH THE **NECK** OF THAT HEADLAND!

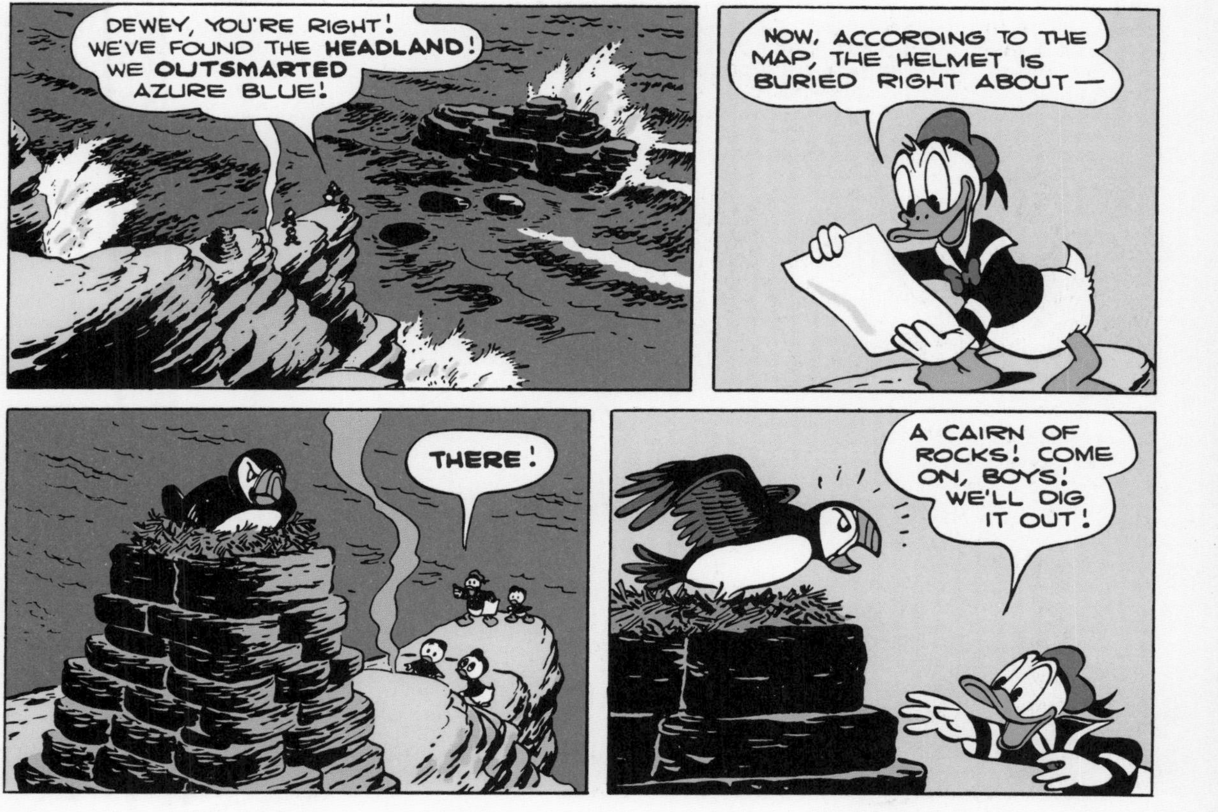
DEWEY, YOU'RE RIGHT! WE'VE FOUND THE **HEADLAND**! WE **OUTSMARTED** AZURE BLUE!
NOW, ACCORDING TO THE MAP, THE HELMET IS BURIED RIGHT ABOUT—
THERE!
A CAIRN OF ROCKS! COME ON, BOYS! WE'LL DIG IT OUT!

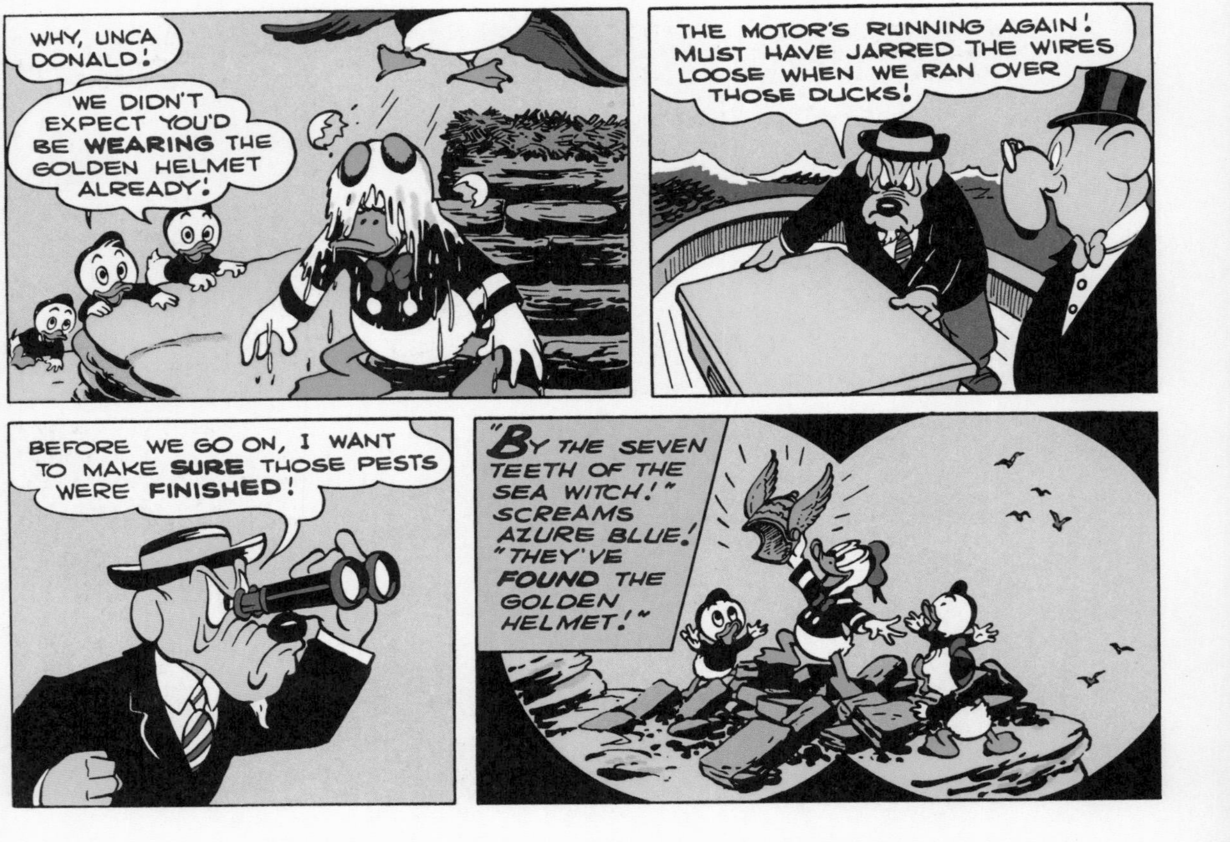
WHY, UNCA DONALD!
WE DIDN'T EXPECT YOU'D BE **WEARING** THE GOLDEN HELMET ALREADY!
THE MOTOR'S RUNNING AGAIN! MUST HAVE JARRED THE WIRES LOOSE WHEN WE RAN OVER THOSE DUCKS!
BEFORE WE GO ON, I WANT TO MAKE **SURE** THOSE PESTS WERE **FINISHED**!
"BY THE SEVEN TEETH OF THE SEA WITCH!" SCREAMS AZURE BLUE! "THEY'VE **FOUND** THE GOLDEN HELMET!"

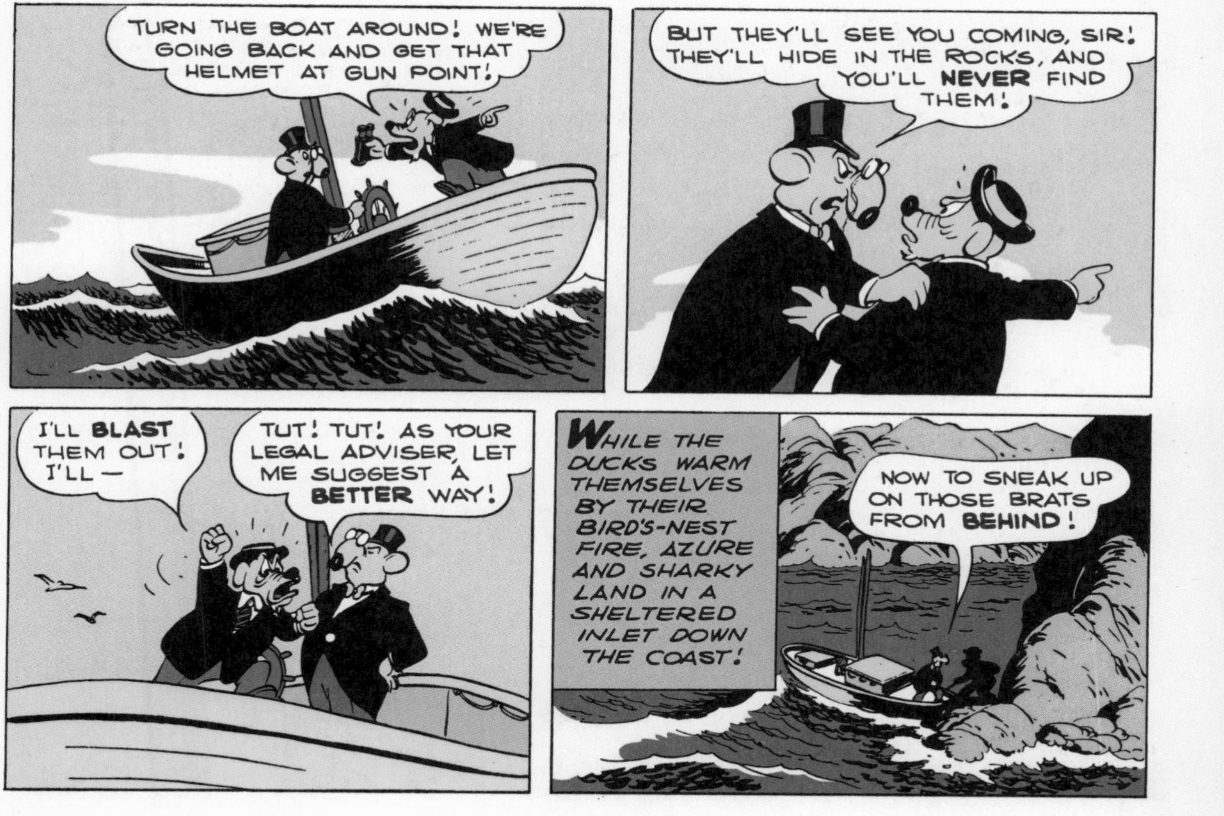

TURN THE BOAT AROUND! WE'RE GOING BACK AND GET THAT HELMET AT GUN POINT!
BUT THEY'LL SEE YOU COMING, SIR! THEY'LL HIDE IN THE ROCKS, AND YOU'LL **NEVER** FIND THEM!
I'LL **BLAST** THEM OUT! I'LL —
TUT! TUT! AS YOUR LEGAL ADVISER, LET ME SUGGEST A **BETTER** WAY!
WHILE THE DUCKS WARM THEMSELVES BY THEIR BIRD'S-NEST FIRE, AZURE AND SHARKY LAND IN A SHELTERED INLET DOWN THE COAST!
NOW TO SNEAK UP ON THOSE BRATS FROM **BEHIND**!

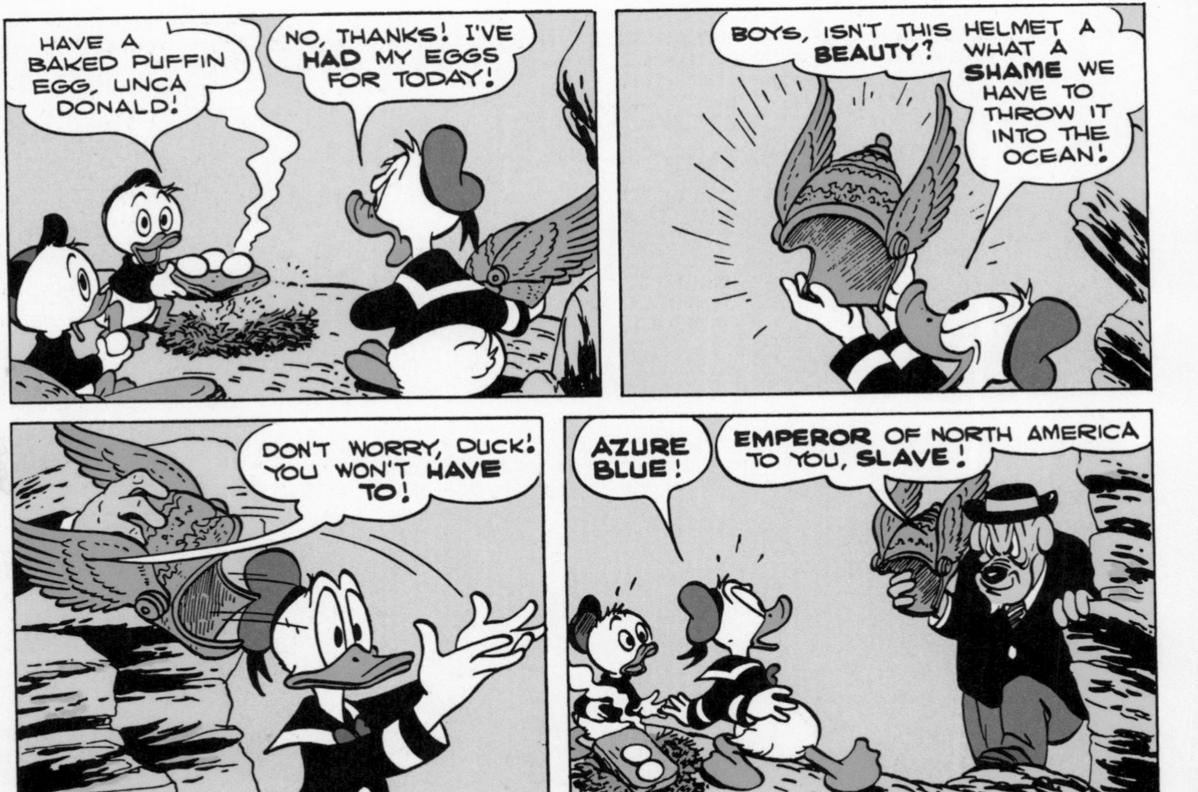
HAVE A BAKED PUFFIN EGG, UNCA DONALD!
NO, THANKS! I'VE **HAD** MY EGGS FOR TODAY!
BOYS, ISN'T THIS HELMET A **BEAUTY**? WHAT A **SHAME** WE HAVE TO THROW IT INTO THE OCEAN!
DON'T WORRY, DUCK! YOU WON'T **HAVE TO**!
AZURE BLUE!
EMPEROR OF NORTH AMERICA TO YOU, **SLAVE**!

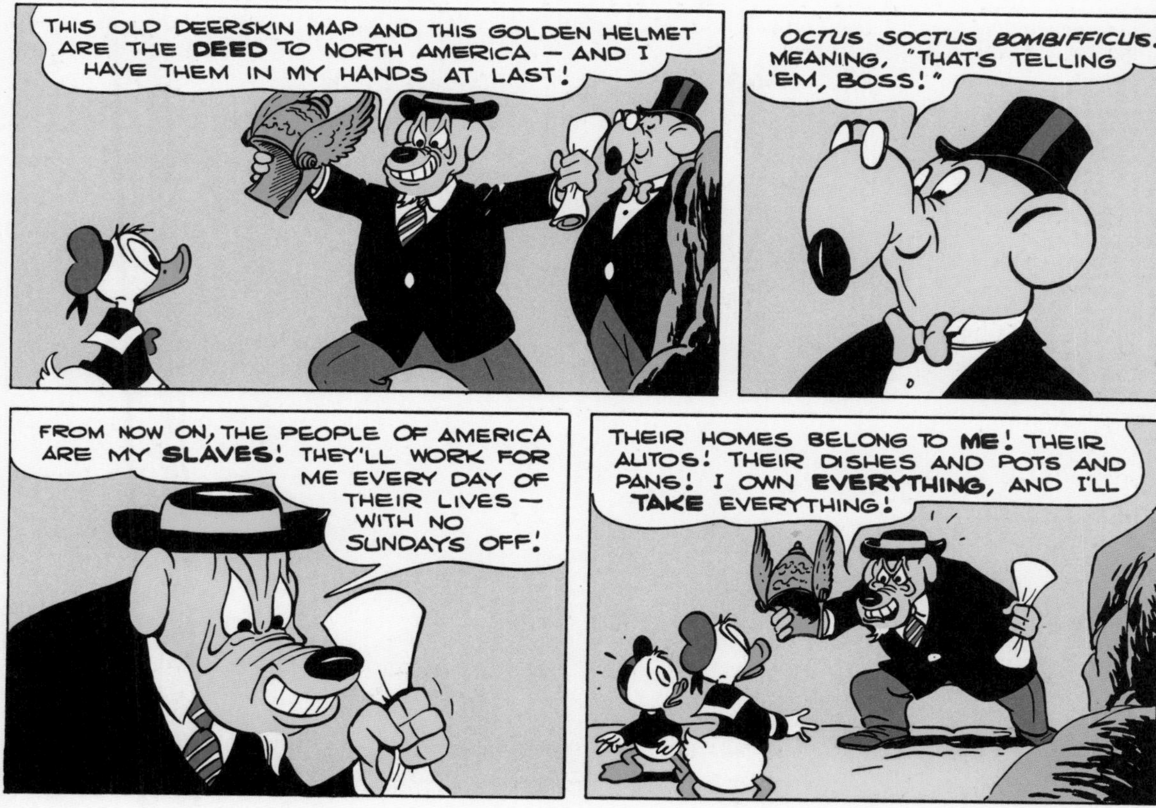

THIS OLD DEERSKIN MAP AND THIS GOLDEN HELMET ARE THE **DEED** TO NORTH AMERICA — AND I HAVE THEM IN MY HANDS AT LAST!
OCTUS SOCTUS BOMBIFFICUS! MEANING, "THAT'S TELLING 'EM, BOSS!"
FROM NOW ON, THE PEOPLE OF AMERICA ARE MY **SLAVES!** THEY'LL WORK FOR ME EVERY DAY OF THEIR LIVES — WITH NO SUNDAYS OFF!
THEIR HOMES BELONG TO **ME!** THEIR AUTOS! THEIR DISHES AND POTS AND PANS! I OWN **EVERYTHING**, AND I'LL **TAKE** EVERYTHING!

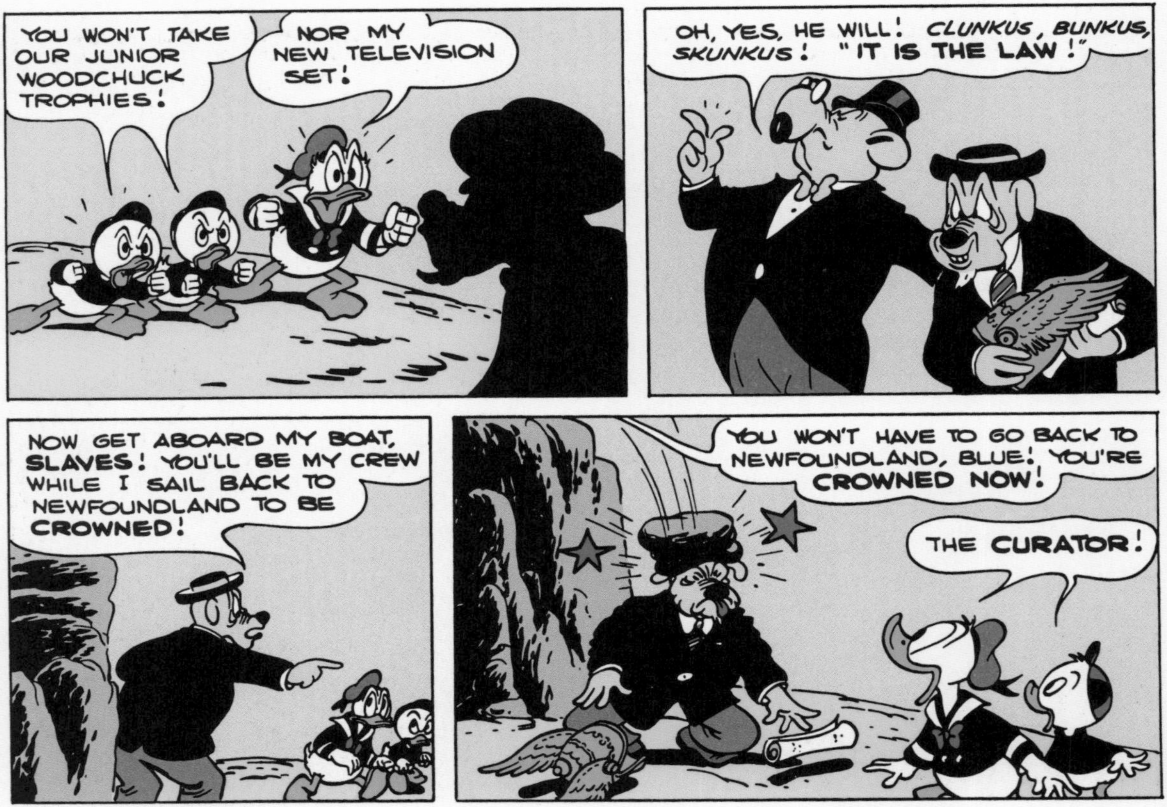
YOU WON'T TAKE OUR JUNIOR WOODCHUCK TROPHIES!
NOR MY NEW TELEVISION SET!
OH, YES, HE WILL! CLUNKUS, BUNKUS, SKUNKUS! "IT IS THE LAW!"
NOW GET ABOARD MY BOAT, SLAVES! YOU'LL BE MY CREW WHILE I SAIL BACK TO NEWFOUNDLAND TO BE CROWNED!
YOU WON'T HAVE TO GO BACK TO NEWFOUNDLAND, BLUE! YOU'RE CROWNED NOW!
THE CURATOR!

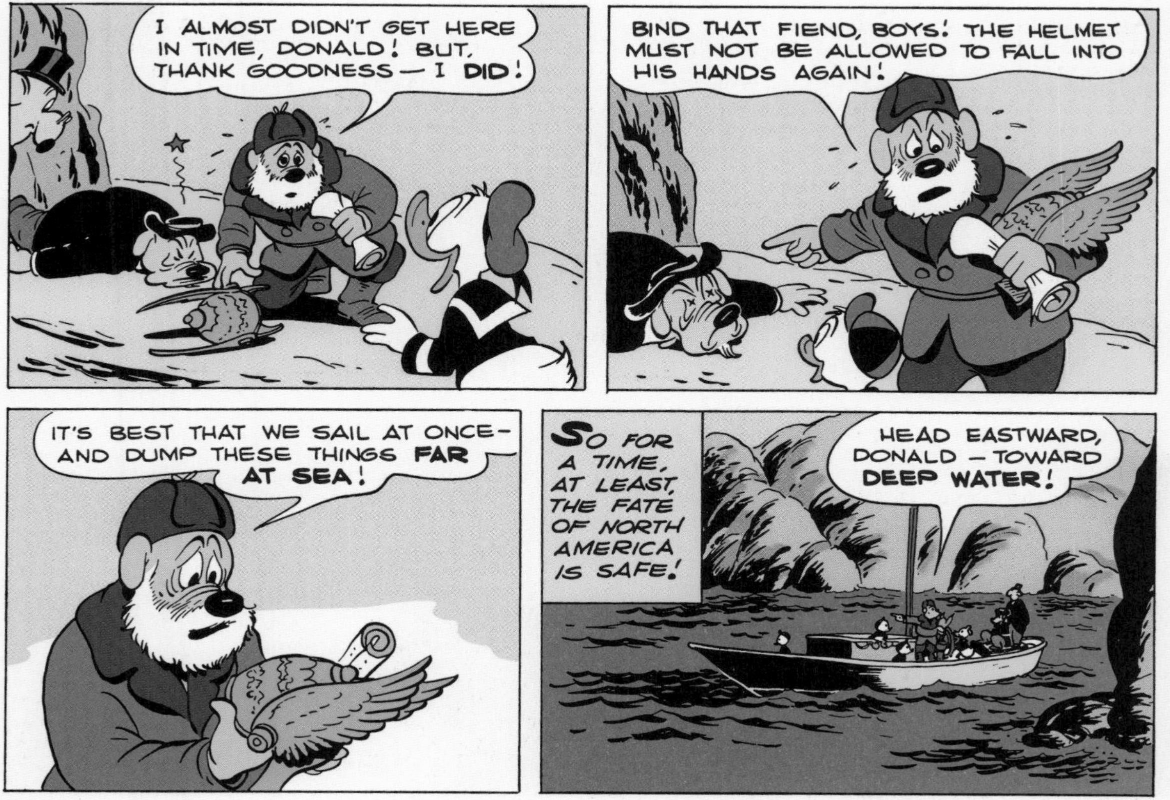
I ALMOST DIDN'T GET HERE IN TIME, DONALD! BUT, THANK GOODNESS — I **DID**!
BIND THAT FIEND, BOYS! THE HELMET MUST NOT BE ALLOWED TO FALL INTO HIS HANDS AGAIN!
IT'S BEST THAT WE SAIL AT ONCE— AND DUMP THESE THINGS **FAR AT SEA**!
SO FOR A TIME, AT LEAST, THE FATE OF NORTH AMERICA IS SAFE!
HEAD EASTWARD, DONALD — TOWARD **DEEP WATER**!

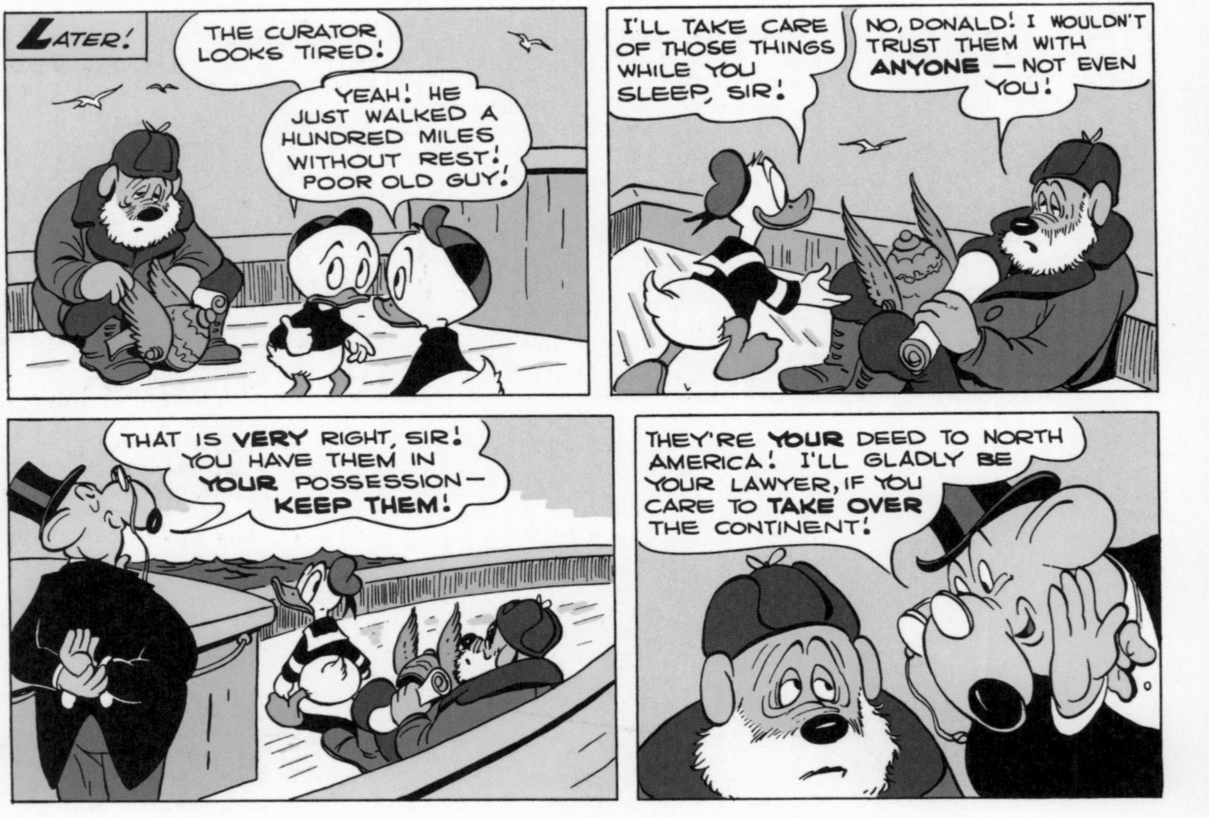
LATER!
THE CURATOR LOOKS TIRED!
YEAH! HE JUST WALKED A HUNDRED MILES WITHOUT REST! POOR OLD GUY!
I'LL TAKE CARE OF THOSE THINGS WHILE YOU SLEEP, SIR!
NO, DONALD! I WOULDN'T TRUST THEM WITH ANYONE — NOT EVEN YOU!
THAT IS VERY RIGHT, SIR! YOU HAVE THEM IN YOUR POSSESSION— KEEP THEM!
THEY'RE YOUR DEED TO NORTH AMERICA! I'LL GLADLY BE YOUR LAWYER, IF YOU CARE TO TAKE OVER THE CONTINENT!

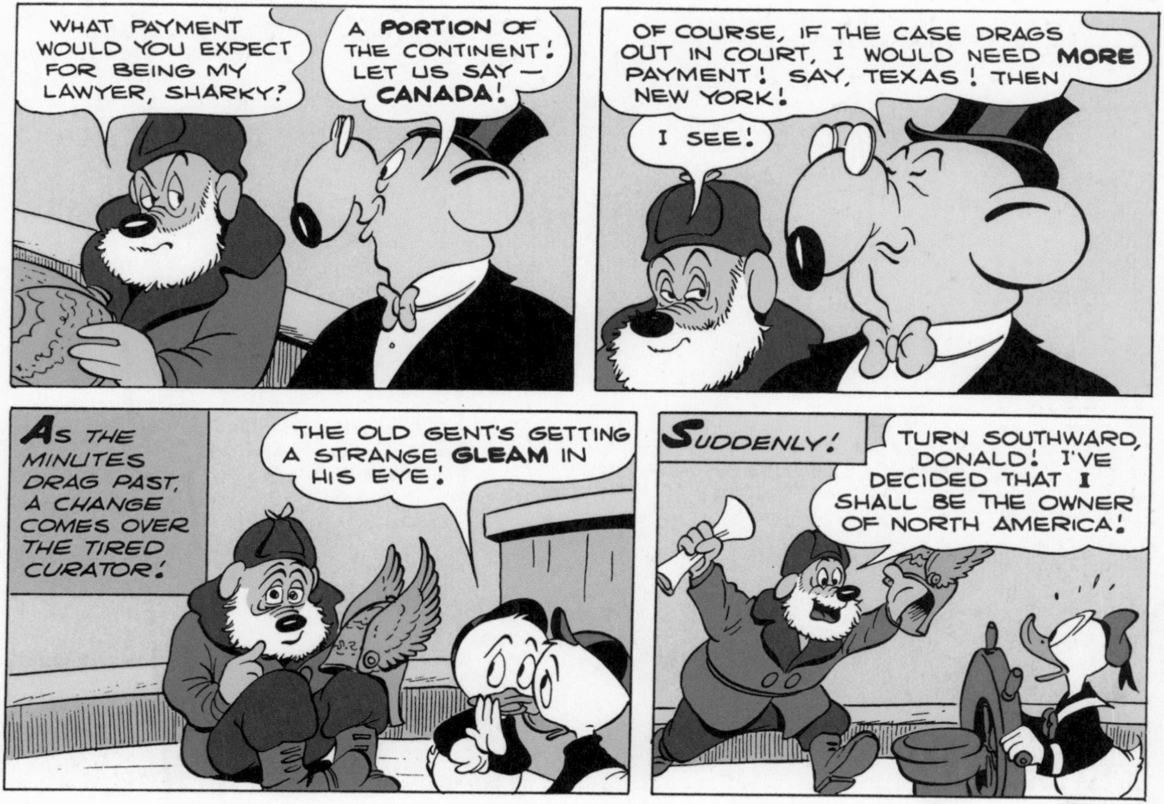
WHAT PAYMENT WOULD YOU EXPECT FOR BEING MY LAWYER, SHARKY?
A PORTION OF THE CONTINENT! LET US SAY— CANADA!
OF COURSE, IF THE CASE DRAGS OUT IN COURT, I WOULD NEED MORE PAYMENT! SAY, TEXAS! THEN NEW YORK!
I SEE!
AS THE MINUTES DRAG PAST, A CHANGE COMES OVER THE TIRED CURATOR!
THE OLD GENT'S GETTING A STRANGE GLEAM IN HIS EYE!
SUDDENLY!
TURN SOUTHWARD, DONALD! I'VE DECIDED THAT I SHALL BE THE OWNER OF NORTH AMERICA!

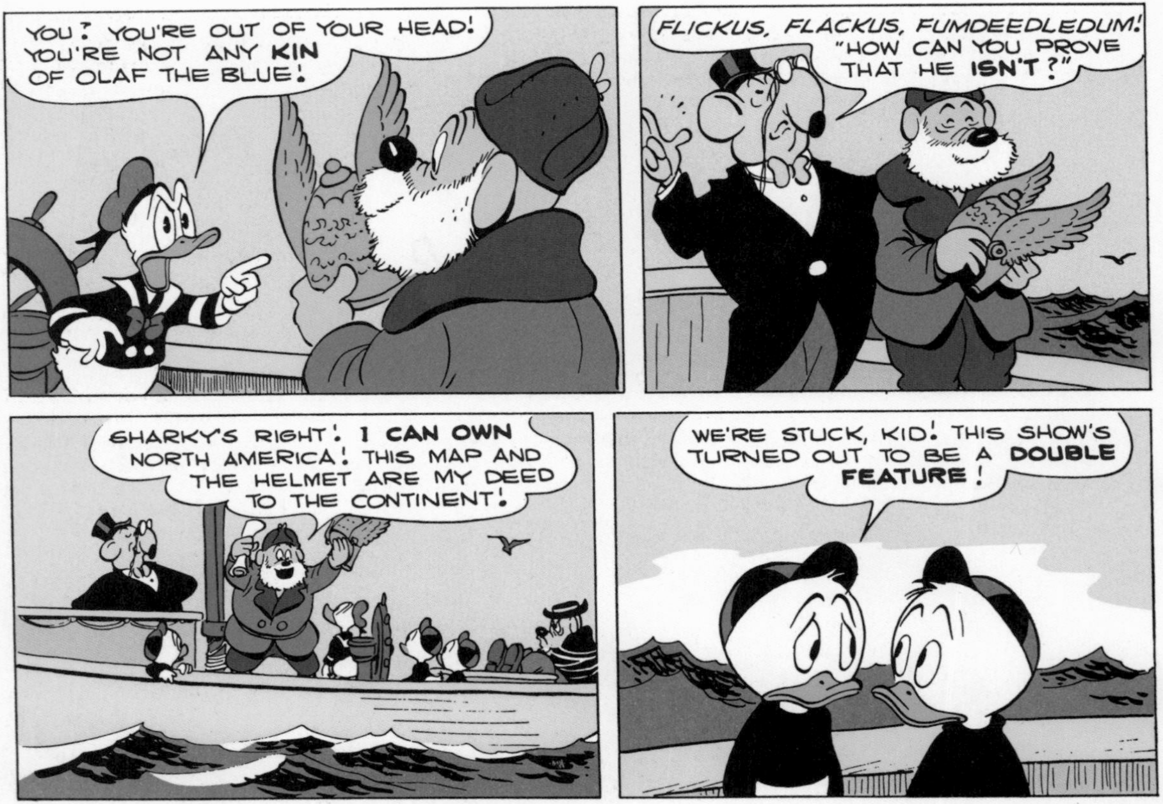
YOU? YOU'RE OUT OF YOUR HEAD! YOU'RE NOT ANY **KIN** OF OLAF THE BLUE!
FLICKUS, FLACKUS, FUMDEEDLEDUM! "HOW CAN YOU PROVE THAT HE **ISN'T**?"
SHARKY'S RIGHT! **I CAN OWN** NORTH AMERICA! THIS MAP AND THE HELMET ARE MY DEED TO THE CONTINENT!
WE'RE STUCK, KID! THIS SHOW'S TURNED OUT TO BE A **DOUBLE FEATURE**!

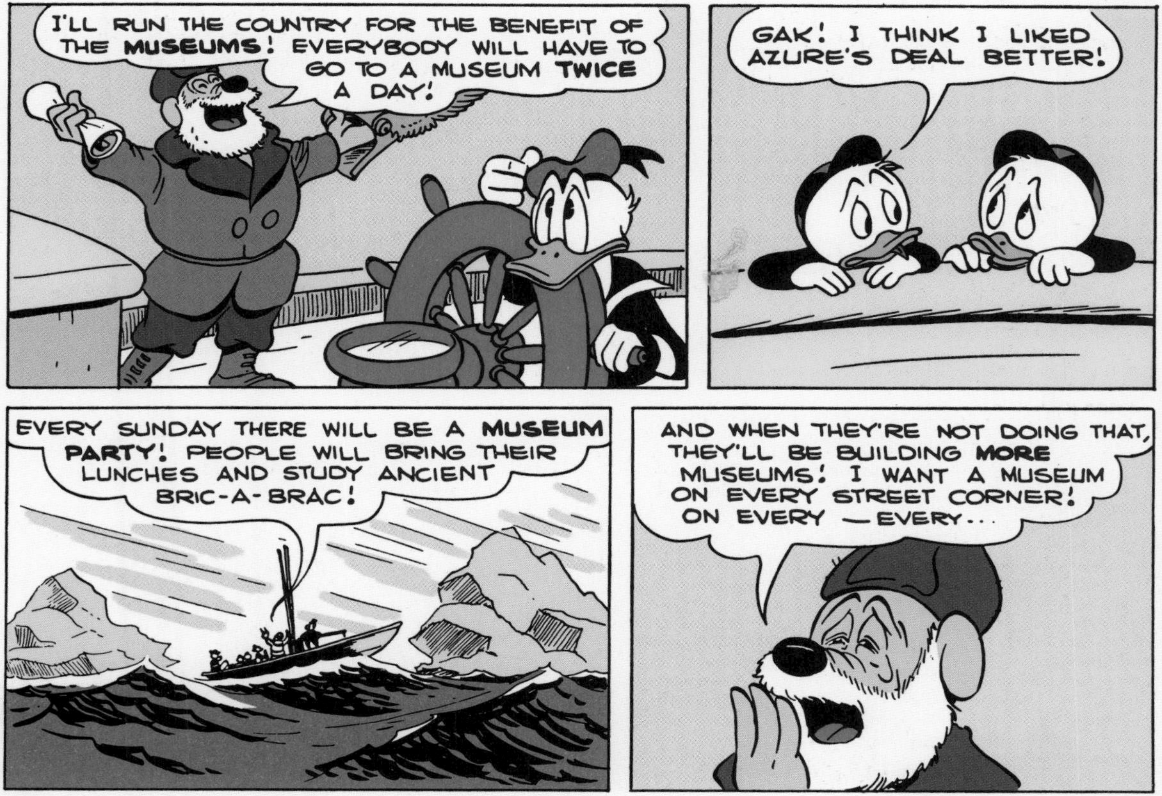
I'LL RUN THE COUNTRY FOR THE BENEFIT OF THE **MUSEUMS**! EVERYBODY WILL HAVE TO GO TO A MUSEUM **TWICE** A DAY!
GAK! I THINK I LIKED AZURE'S DEAL BETTER!
EVERY SUNDAY THERE WILL BE A **MUSEUM PARTY**! PEOPLE WILL BRING THEIR LUNCHES AND STUDY ANCIENT BRIC-A-BRAC!
AND WHEN THEY'RE NOT DOING THAT, THEY'LL BE BUILDING **MORE** MUSEUMS! I WANT A MUSEUM ON EVERY STREET CORNER! ON EVERY —EVERY...

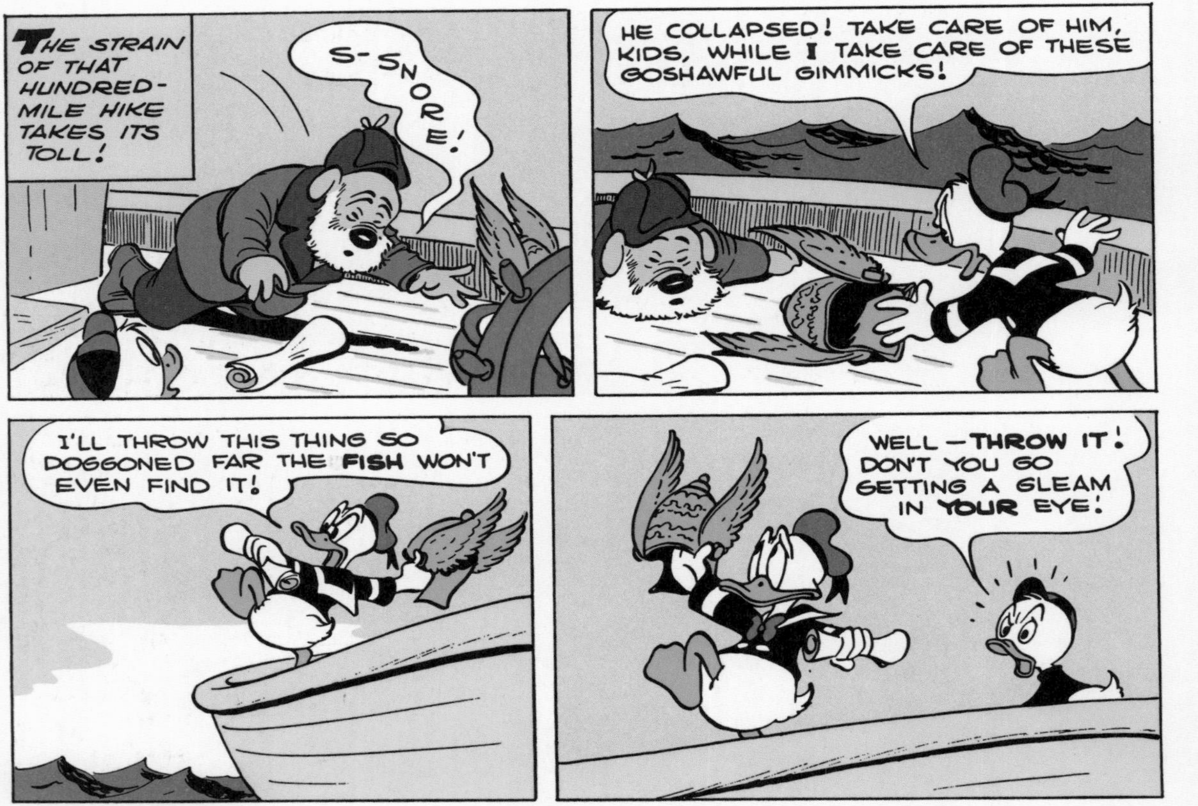
THE STRAIN OF THAT HUNDRED-MILE HIKE TAKES ITS TOLL!
S-SNORE!
HE COLLAPSED! TAKE CARE OF HIM, KIDS, WHILE I TAKE CARE OF THESE GOSHAWFUL GIMMICKS!
I'LL THROW THIS THING SO DOGGONED FAR THE FISH WON'T EVEN FIND IT!
WELL—THROW IT! DON'T YOU GO GETTING A GLEAM IN YOUR EYE!

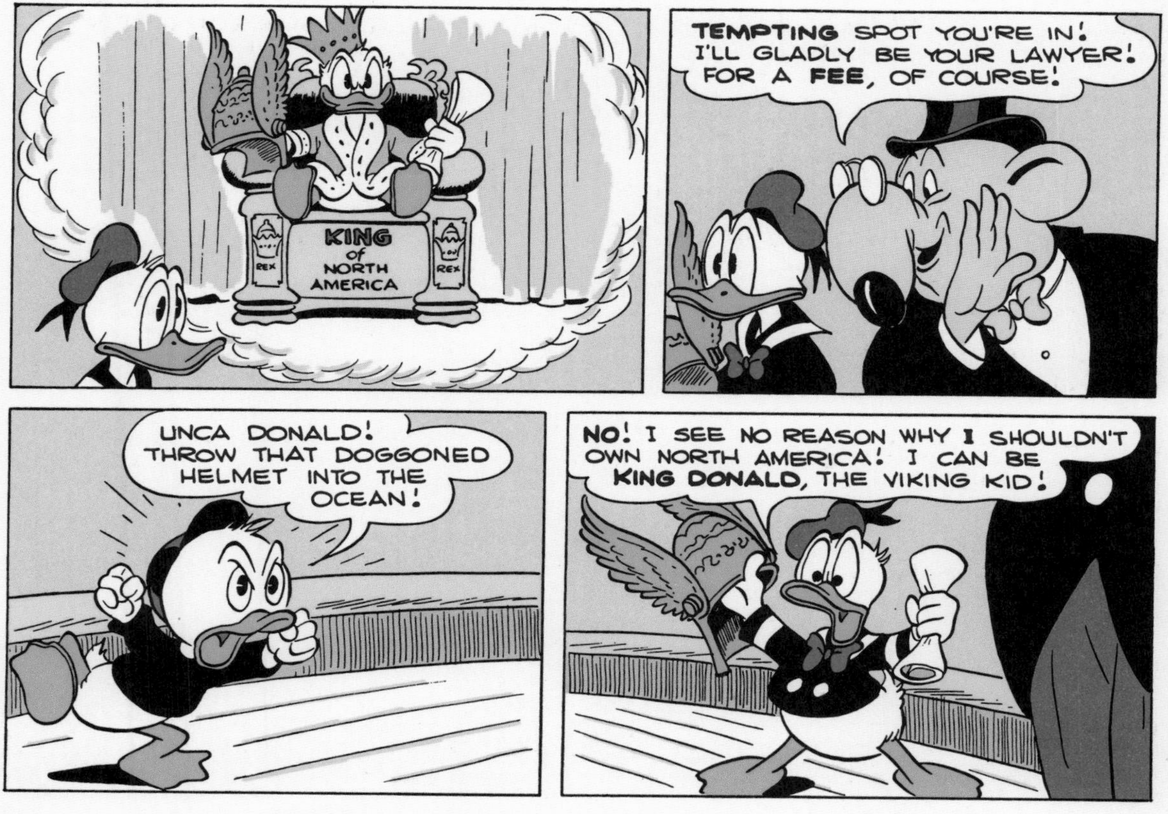
KING of NORTH AMERICA
REX
REX
TEMPTING SPOT YOU'RE IN! I'LL GLADLY BE YOUR LAWYER! FOR A FEE, OF COURSE!
UNCA DONALD! THROW THAT DOGGONED HELMET INTO THE OCEAN!
NO! I SEE NO REASON WHY I SHOULDN'T OWN NORTH AMERICA! I CAN BE KING DONALD, THE VIKING KID!

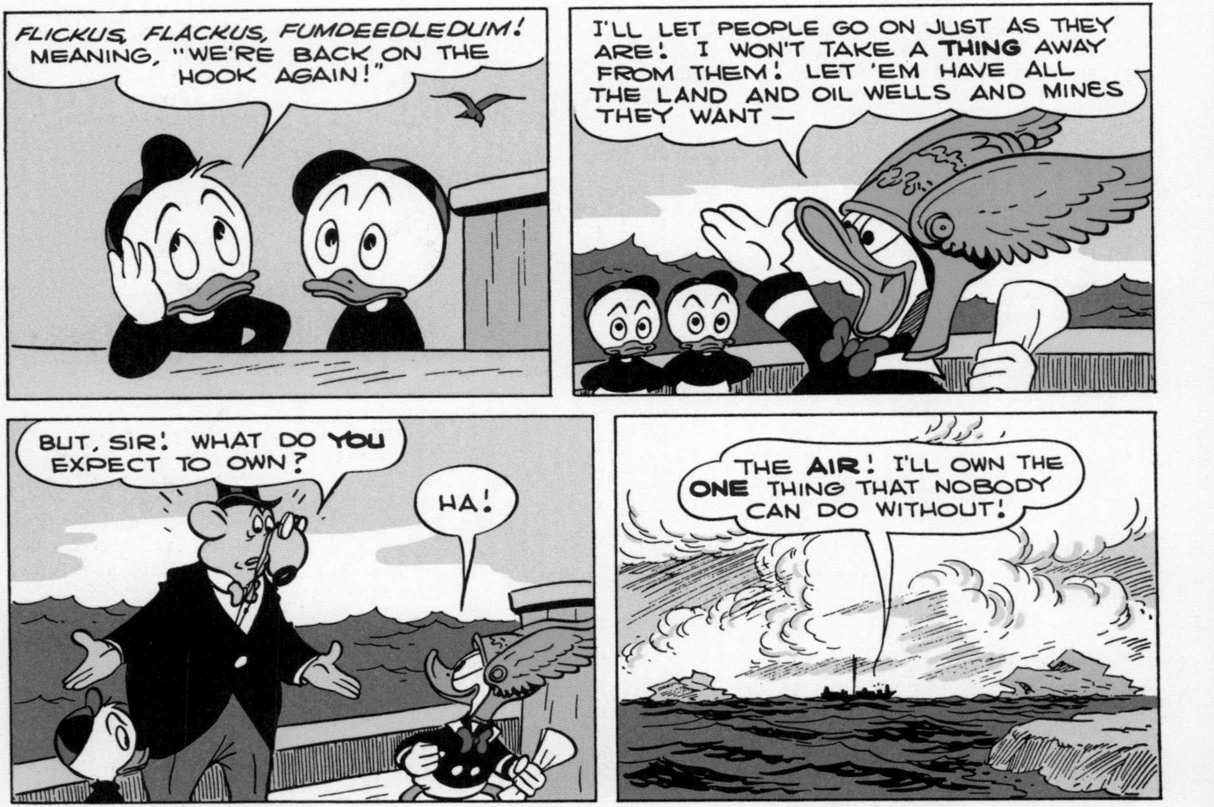
FLICKUS, FLACKUS, FUMDEEDLEDUM! MEANING, "WE'RE BACK ON THE HOOK AGAIN!"
I'LL LET PEOPLE GO ON JUST AS THEY ARE! I WON'T TAKE A **THING** AWAY FROM THEM! LET 'EM HAVE ALL THE LAND AND OIL WELLS AND MINES THEY WANT—
BUT, SIR! WHAT DO **YOU** EXPECT TO OWN?
HA!
THE **AIR**! I'LL OWN THE **ONE** THING THAT NOBODY CAN DO WITHOUT!

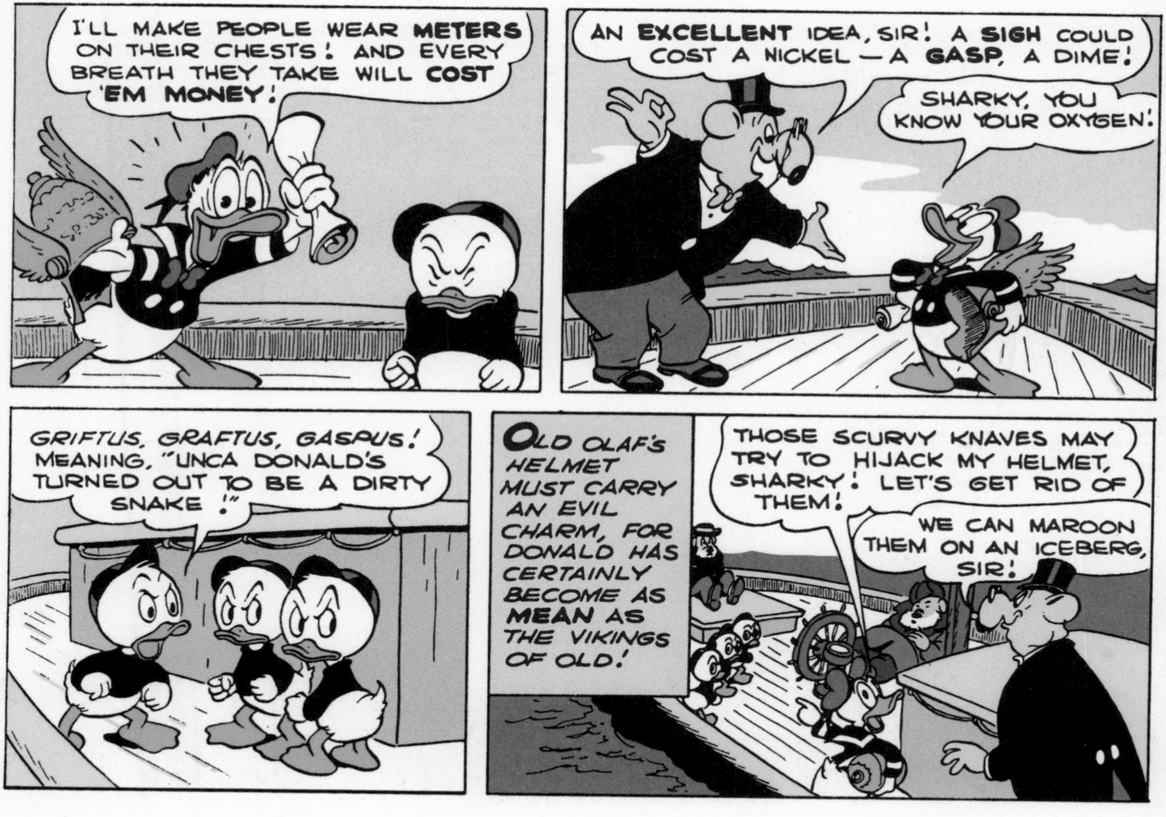
I'LL MAKE PEOPLE WEAR **METERS** ON THEIR CHESTS! AND EVERY BREATH THEY TAKE WILL **COST** 'EM MONEY!
AN **EXCELLENT** IDEA, SIR! A **SIGH** COULD COST A NICKEL — A **GASP**, A DIME!
SHARKY, YOU KNOW YOUR OXYGEN!
GRIFTUS, GRAFTUS, GASPUS! MEANING, "UNCA DONALD'S TURNED OUT TO BE A DIRTY SNAKE!"
OLD OLAF'S HELMET MUST CARRY AN EVIL CHARM, FOR DONALD HAS CERTAINLY BECOME AS **MEAN** AS THE VIKINGS OF OLD!
THOSE SCURVY KNAVES MAY TRY TO HIJACK MY HELMET, SHARKY! LET'S GET RID OF THEM!
WE CAN MAROON THEM ON AN ICEBERG, SIR!

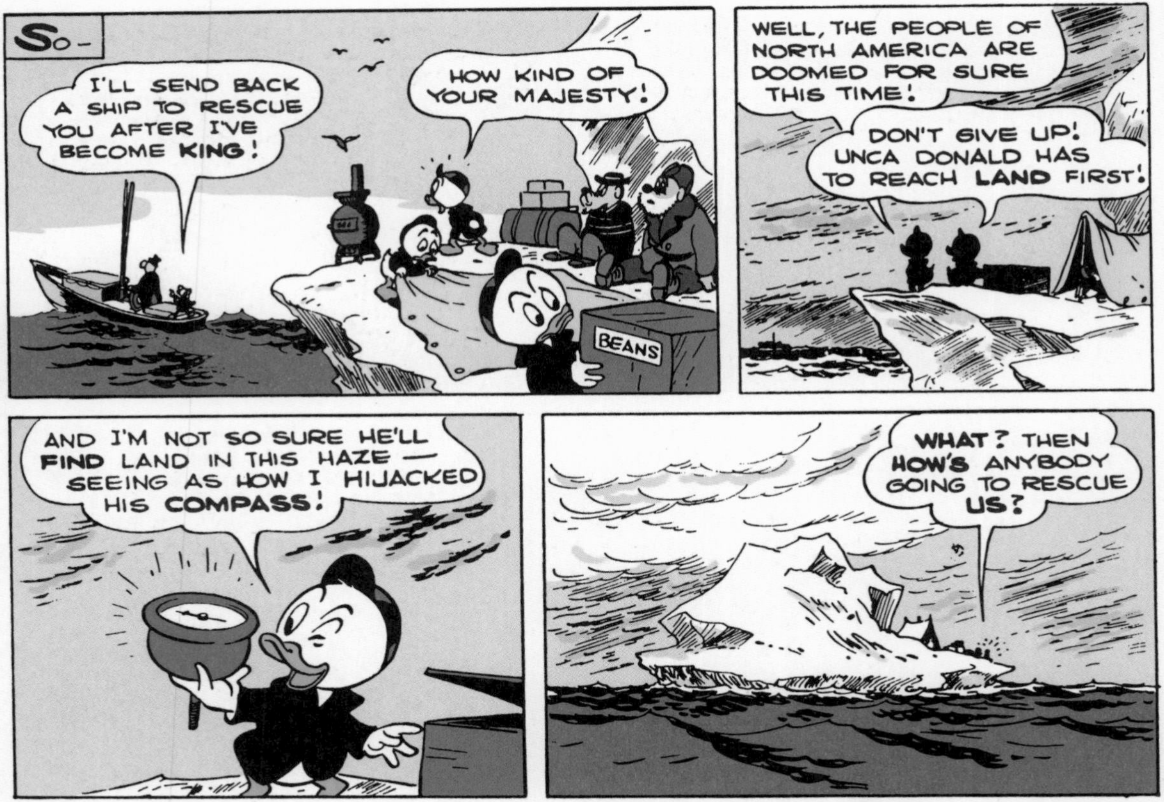
SO –
I'LL SEND BACK A SHIP TO RESCUE YOU AFTER I'VE BECOME **KING**!
HOW KIND OF YOUR MAJESTY!
BEANS
WELL, THE PEOPLE OF NORTH AMERICA ARE DOOMED FOR SURE THIS TIME!
DON'T GIVE UP! UNCA DONALD HAS TO REACH **LAND** FIRST!
AND I'M NOT SO SURE HE'LL **FIND** LAND IN THIS HAZE — SEEING AS HOW I HIJACKED HIS **COMPASS**!
WHAT? THEN **HOW'S** ANYBODY GOING TO RESCUE **US**?

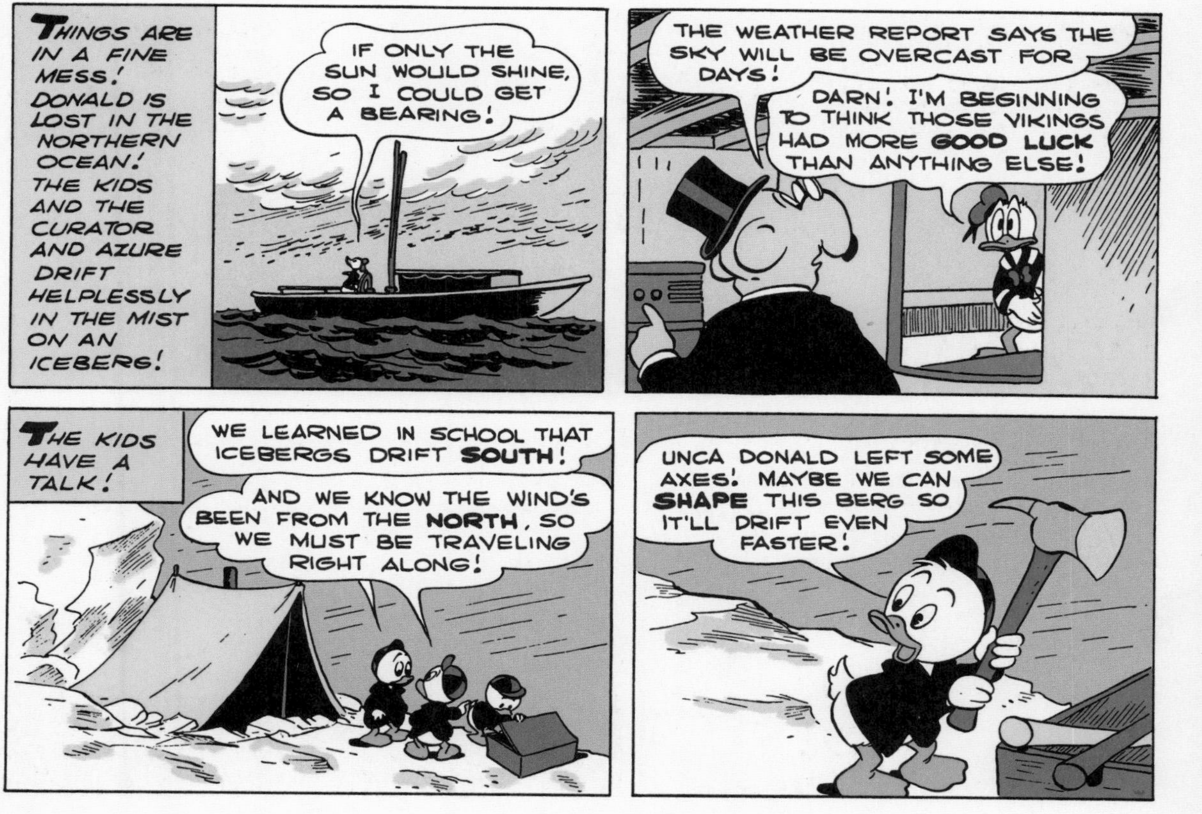
THINGS ARE IN A FINE MESS! DONALD IS LOST IN THE NORTHERN OCEAN! THE KIDS AND THE CURATOR AND AZURE DRIFT HELPLESSLY IN THE MIST ON AN ICEBERG!
IF ONLY THE SUN WOULD SHINE, SO I COULD GET A BEARING!
THE WEATHER REPORT SAYS THE SKY WILL BE OVERCAST FOR DAYS!
DARN! I'M BEGINNING TO THINK THOSE VIKINGS HAD MORE GOOD LUCK THAN ANYTHING ELSE!
THE KIDS HAVE A TALK!
WE LEARNED IN SCHOOL THAT ICEBERGS DRIFT SOUTH!
AND WE KNOW THE WIND'S BEEN FROM THE NORTH, SO WE MUST BE TRAVELING RIGHT ALONG!
UNCA DONALD LEFT SOME AXES! MAYBE WE CAN SHAPE THIS BERG SO IT'LL DRIFT EVEN FASTER!

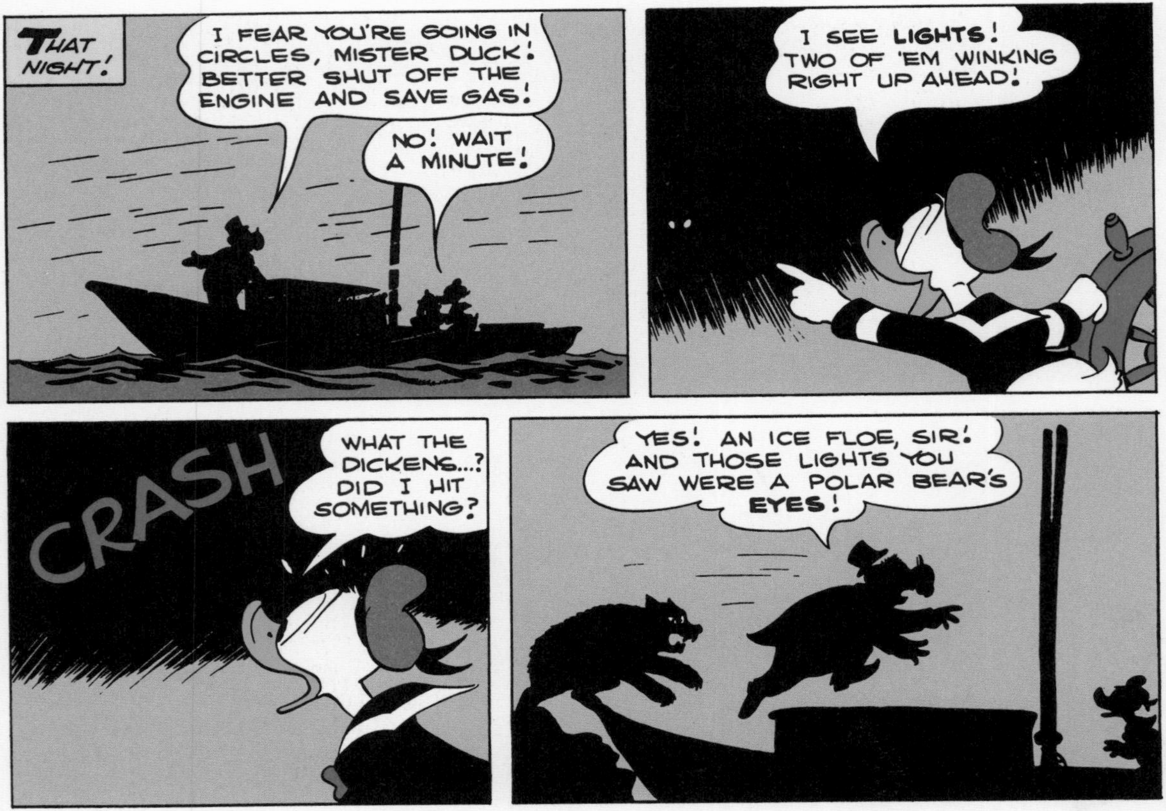
THAT NIGHT!
I FEAR YOU'RE GOING IN CIRCLES, MISTER DUCK! BETTER SHUT OFF THE ENGINE AND SAVE GAS!
NO! WAIT A MINUTE!
I SEE LIGHTS! TWO OF 'EM WINKING RIGHT UP AHEAD!
CRASH
WHAT THE DICKENS...? DID I HIT SOMETHING?
YES! AN ICE FLOE, SIR! AND THOSE LIGHTS YOU SAW WERE A POLAR BEAR'S EYES!

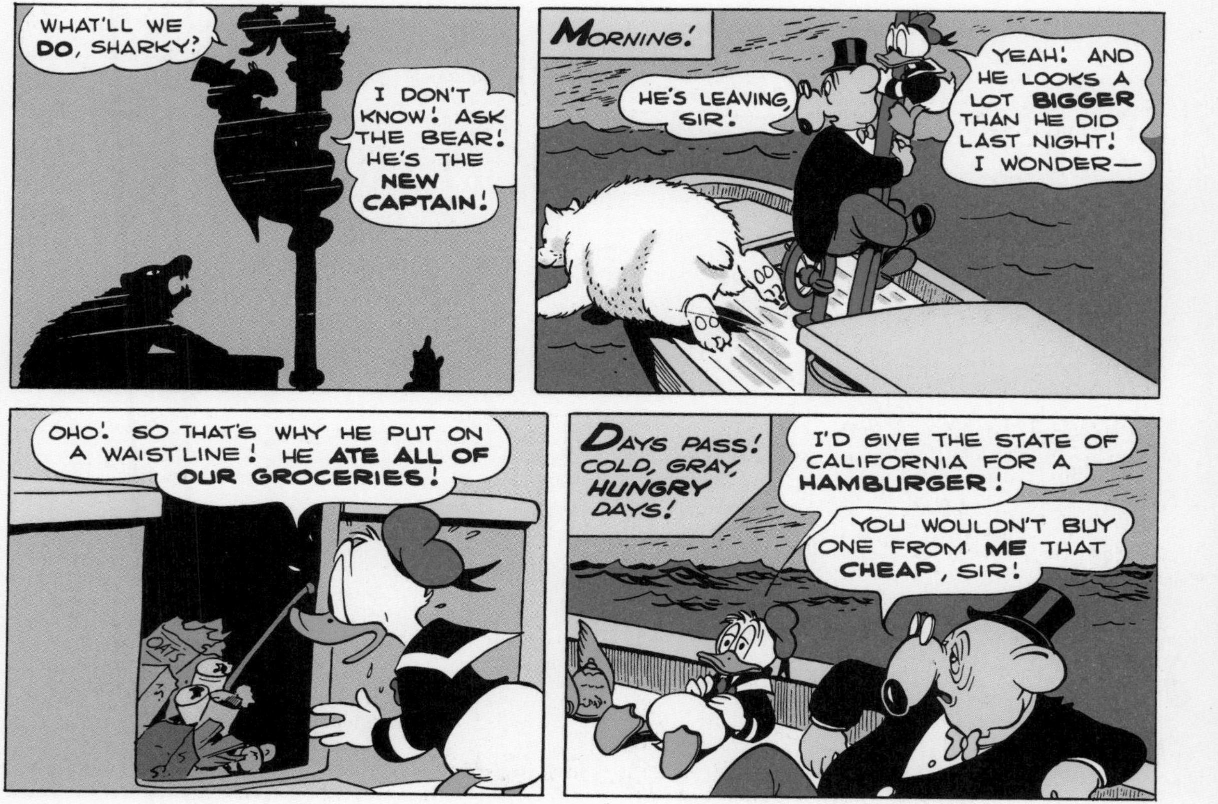
WHAT'LL WE DO, SHARKY?
I DON'T KNOW! ASK THE BEAR! HE'S THE NEW CAPTAIN!
MORNING!
HE'S LEAVING, SIR!
YEAH! AND HE LOOKS A LOT BIGGER THAN HE DID LAST NIGHT! I WONDER—
OHO! SO THAT'S WHY HE PUT ON A WAISTLINE! HE ATE ALL OF OUR GROCERIES!
OATS
DAYS PASS! COLD, GRAY, HUNGRY DAYS!
I'D GIVE THE STATE OF CALIFORNIA FOR A HAMBURGER!
YOU WOULDN'T BUY ONE FROM ME THAT CHEAP, SIR!

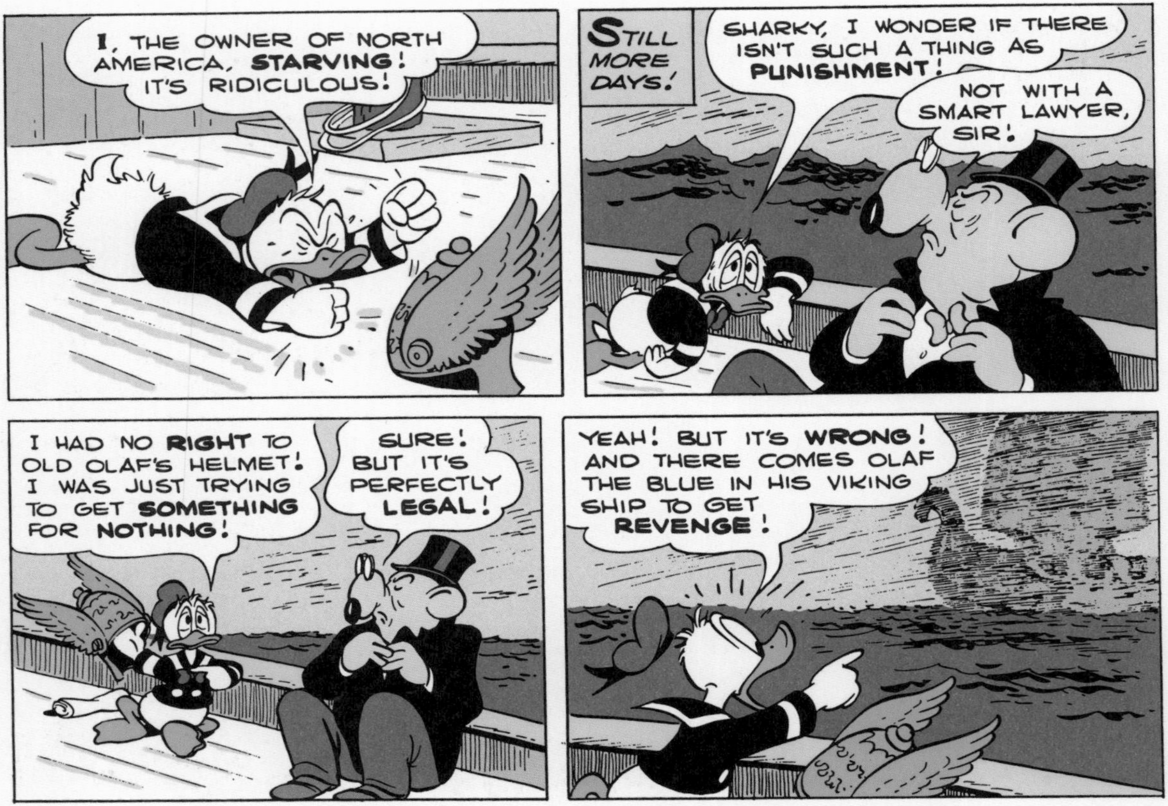
I, THE OWNER OF NORTH AMERICA, STARVING! IT'S RIDICULOUS!
STILL MORE DAYS!
SHARKY, I WONDER IF THERE ISN'T SUCH A THING AS PUNISHMENT!
NOT WITH A SMART LAWYER, SIR!
I HAD NO RIGHT TO OLD OLAF'S HELMET! I WAS JUST TRYING TO GET SOMETHING FOR NOTHING!
SURE! BUT IT'S PERFECTLY LEGAL!
YEAH! BUT IT'S WRONG! AND THERE COMES OLAF THE BLUE IN HIS VIKING SHIP TO GET REVENGE!

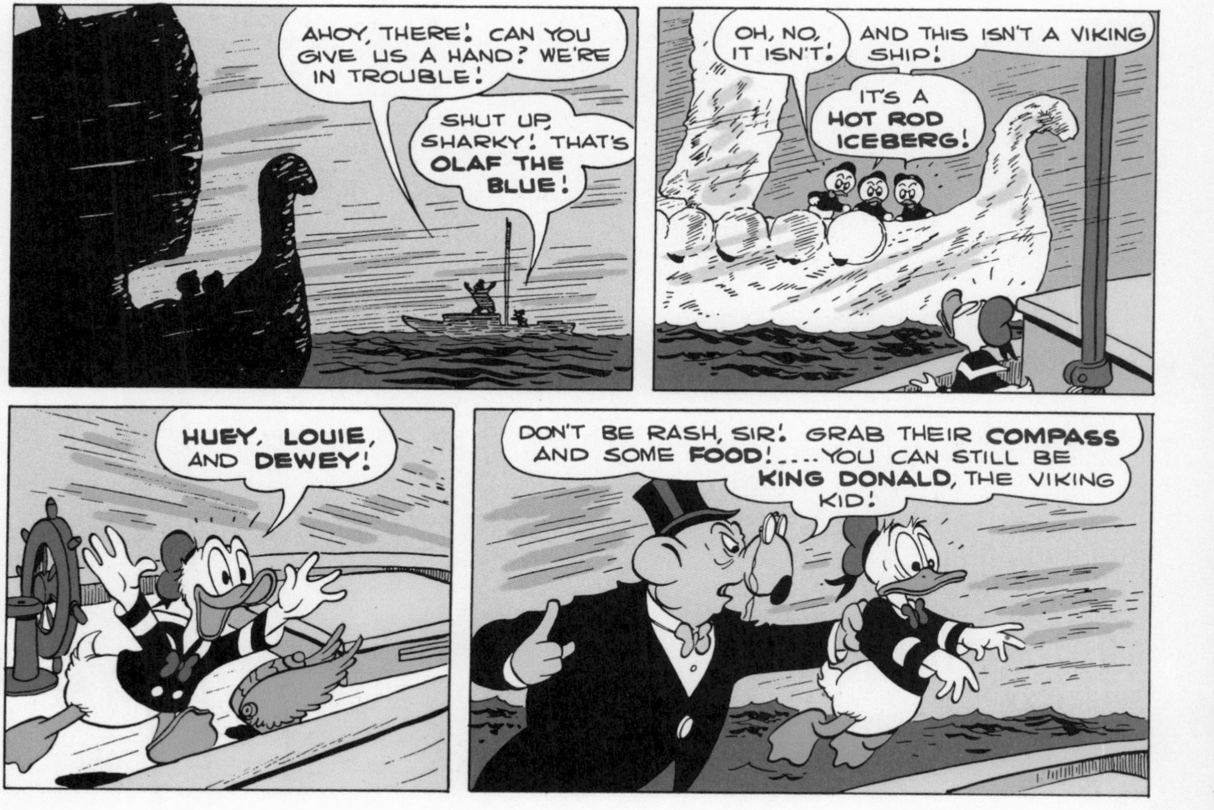
AHOY, THERE! CAN YOU GIVE US A HAND? WE'RE IN TROUBLE!
SHUT UP, SHARKY! THAT'S **OLAF THE BLUE!**
OH, NO, IT ISN'T!
AND THIS ISN'T A VIKING SHIP!
IT'S A **HOT ROD ICEBERG!**
HUEY, LOUIE, AND **DEWEY!**
DON'T BE RASH, SIR! GRAB THEIR **COMPASS** AND SOME **FOOD!**.... YOU CAN STILL BE **KING DONALD,** THE VIKING KID!

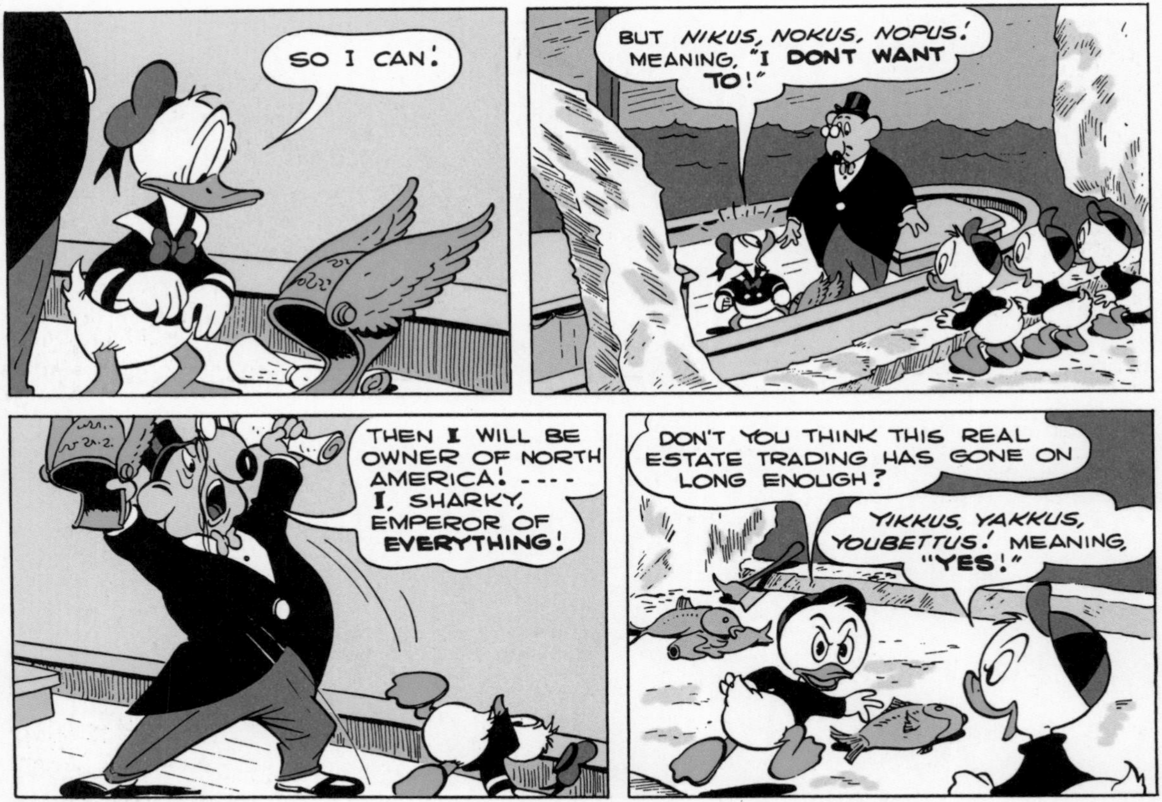
SO I CAN!
BUT NIKUS, NOKUS, NOPUS! MEANING, "I DONT WANT TO!"
THEN I WILL BE OWNER OF NORTH AMERICA! ---- I, SHARKY, EMPEROR OF EVERYTHING!
DON'T YOU THINK THIS REAL ESTATE TRADING HAS GONE ON LONG ENOUGH?
YIKKUS, YAKKUS, YOUBETTUS! MEANING, "YES!"

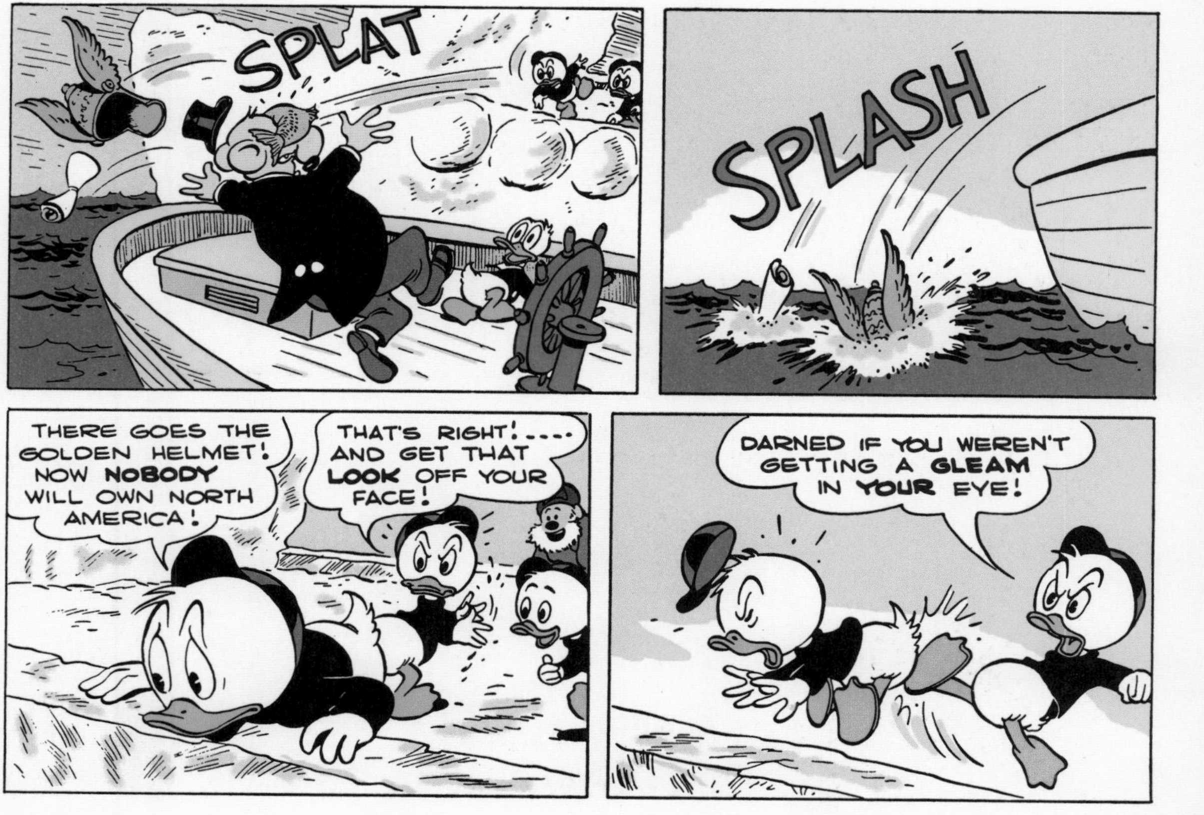
SPLAT
SPLASH
THERE GOES THE GOLDEN HELMET! NOW NOBODY WILL OWN NORTH AMERICA!
THAT'S RIGHT! .... AND GET THAT LOOK OFF YOUR FACE!
DARNED IF YOU WEREN'T GETTING A GLEAM IN YOUR EYE!

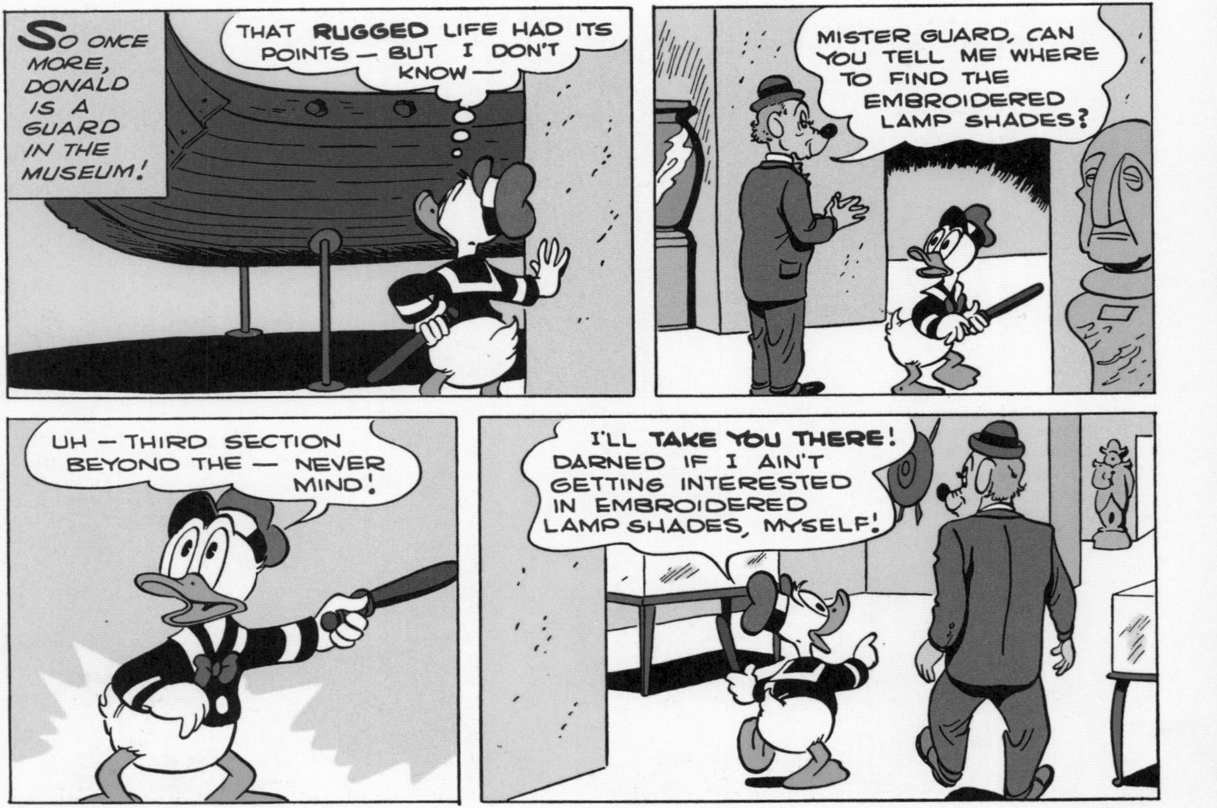
SO ONCE MORE, DONALD IS A GUARD IN THE MUSEUM!
THAT **RUGGED** LIFE HAD ITS POINTS — BUT I DON'T KNOW —
MISTER GUARD, CAN YOU TELL ME WHERE TO FIND THE EMBROIDERED LAMP SHADES?
UH — THIRD SECTION BEYOND THE — NEVER MIND!
I'LL **TAKE YOU THERE!** DARNED IF I AIN'T GETTING INTERESTED IN EMBROIDERED LAMP SHADES, MYSELF!

THE END

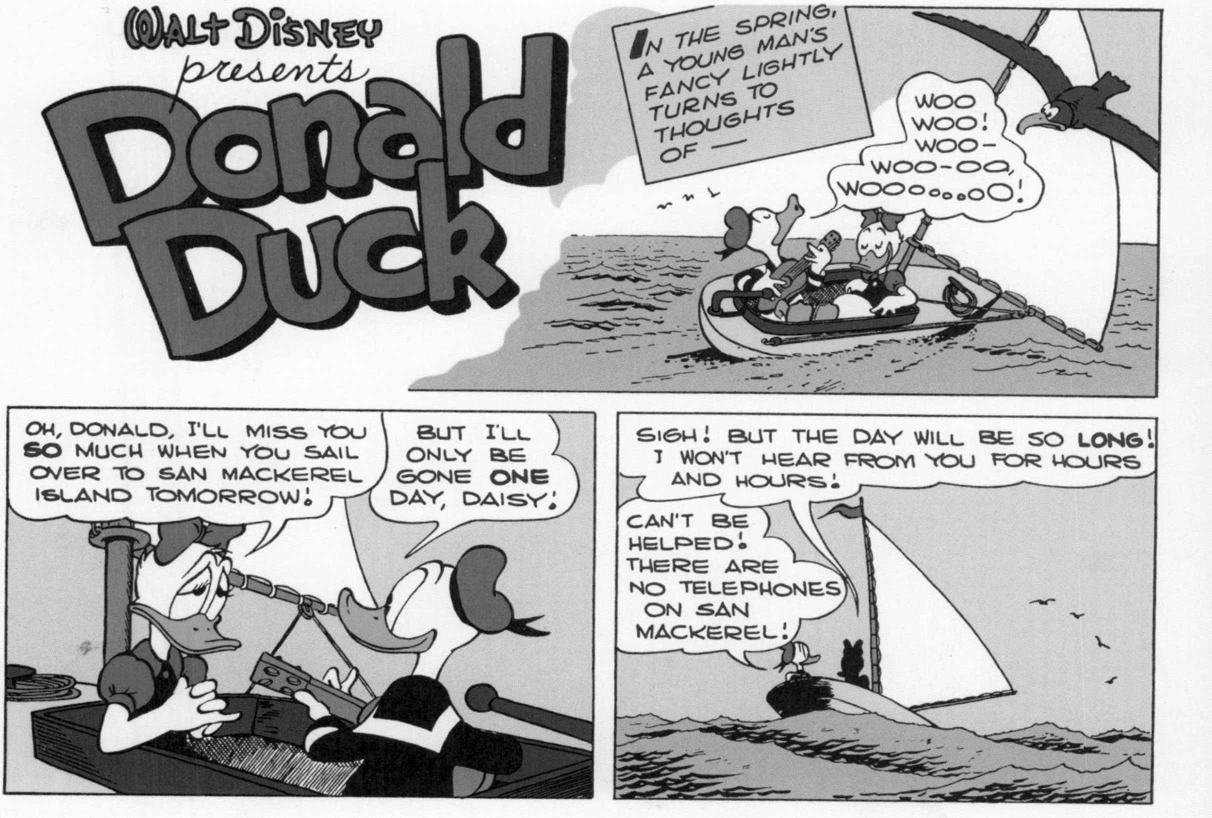
WALT DISNEY
presents
Donald Duck
IN THE SPRING, A YOUNG MAN'S FANCY LIGHTLY TURNS TO THOUGHTS OF —
WOO WOO! WOO- WOO-OO, WOOooooO!
OH, DONALD, I'LL MISS YOU SO MUCH WHEN YOU SAIL OVER TO SAN MACKEREL ISLAND TOMORROW!
BUT I'LL ONLY BE GONE ONE DAY, DAISY!
SIGH! BUT THE DAY WILL BE SO LONG! I WON'T HEAR FROM YOU FOR HOURS AND HOURS!
CAN'T BE HELPED! THERE ARE NO TELEPHONES ON SAN MACKEREL!

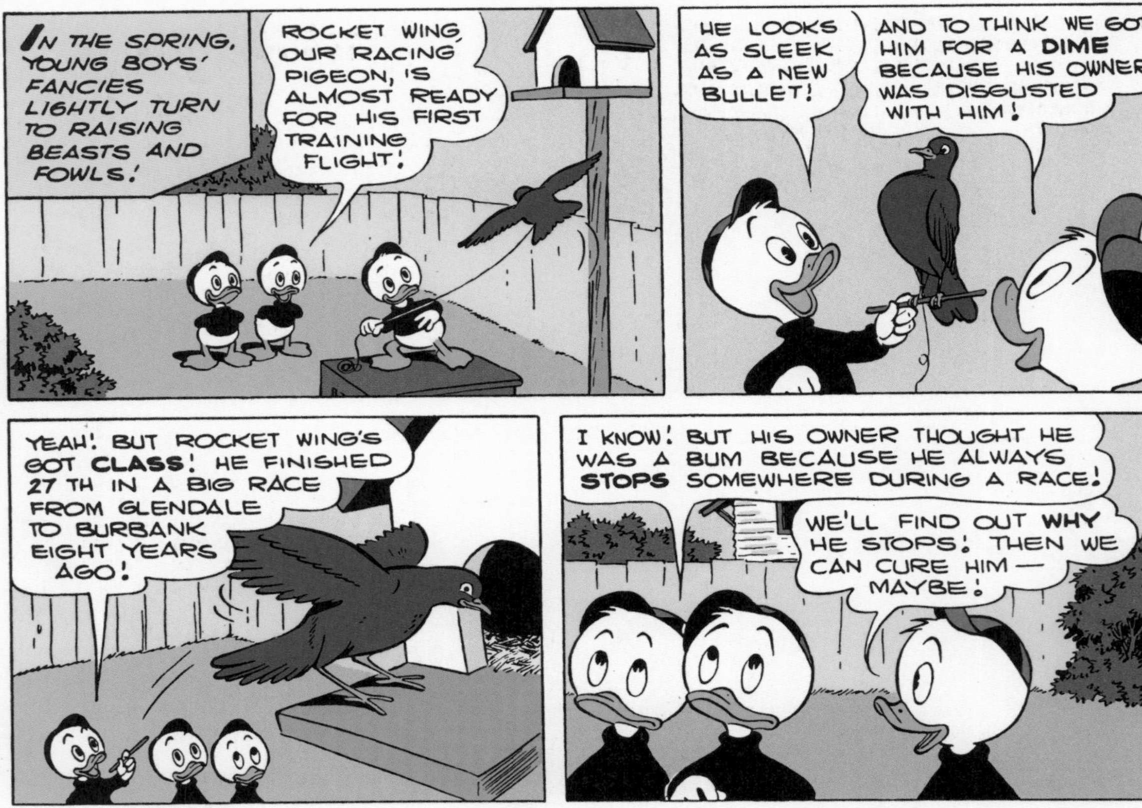
IN THE SPRING, YOUNG BOYS' FANCIES LIGHTLY TURN TO RAISING BEASTS AND FOWLS!
ROCKET WING, OUR RACING PIGEON, IS ALMOST READY FOR HIS FIRST TRAINING FLIGHT!
HE LOOKS AS SLEEK AS A NEW BULLET!
AND TO THINK WE GOT HIM FOR A **DIME** BECAUSE HIS OWNER WAS DISGUSTED WITH HIM!
YEAH! BUT ROCKET WING'S GOT **CLASS**! HE FINISHED 27 TH IN A BIG RACE FROM GLENDALE TO BURBANK EIGHT YEARS AGO!
I KNOW! BUT HIS OWNER THOUGHT HE WAS A BUM BECAUSE HE ALWAYS **STOPS** SOMEWHERE DURING A RACE!
WE'LL FIND OUT **WHY** HE STOPS! THEN WE CAN CURE HIM—MAYBE!

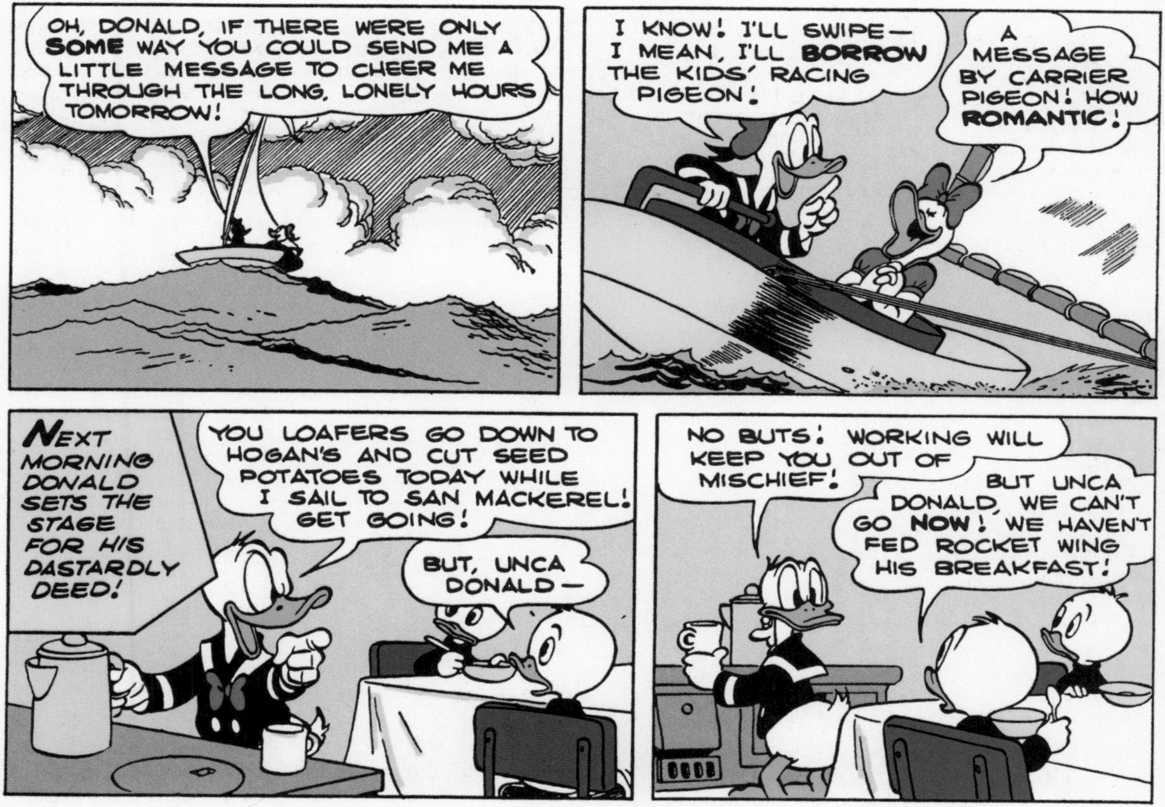
OH, DONALD, IF THERE WERE ONLY **SOME** WAY YOU COULD SEND ME A LITTLE MESSAGE TO CHEER ME THROUGH THE LONG, LONELY HOURS TOMORROW!
I KNOW! I'LL SWIPE— I MEAN, I'LL **BORROW** THE KIDS' RACING PIGEON!
A MESSAGE BY CARRIER PIGEON! HOW **ROMANTIC**!
NEXT MORNING DONALD SETS THE STAGE FOR HIS DASTARDLY DEED!
YOU LOAFERS GO DOWN TO HOGAN'S AND CUT SEED POTATOES TODAY WHILE I SAIL TO SAN MACKEREL! GET GOING!
BUT, UNCA DONALD—
NO BUTS! WORKING WILL KEEP YOU OUT OF MISCHIEF!
BUT UNCA DONALD, WE CAN'T GO **NOW**! WE HAVEN'T FED ROCKET WING HIS BREAKFAST!

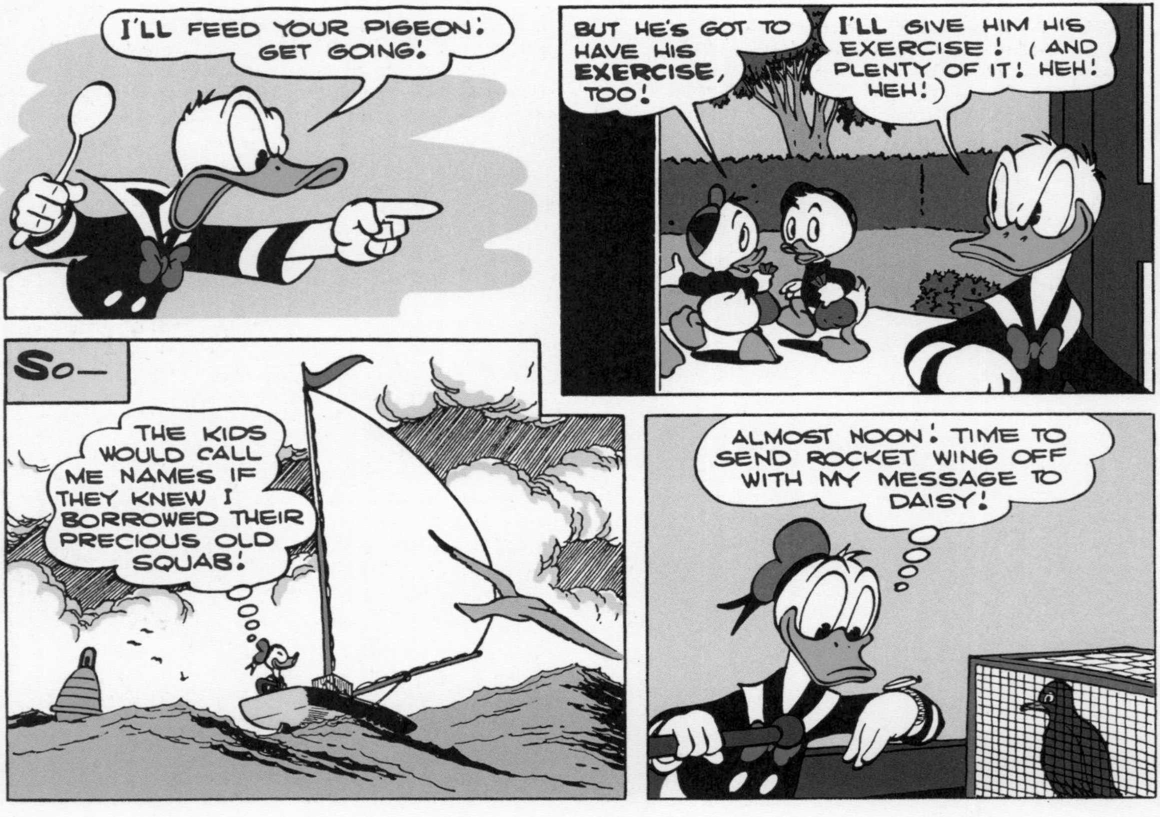
I'LL FEED YOUR PIGEON! GET GOING!
BUT HE'S GOT TO HAVE HIS EXERCISE, TOO!
I'LL GIVE HIM HIS EXERCISE! (AND PLENTY OF IT! HEH! HEH!)
SO—
THE KIDS WOULD CALL ME NAMES IF THEY KNEW I BORROWED THEIR PRECIOUS OLD SQUAB!
ALMOST NOON! TIME TO SEND ROCKET WING OFF WITH MY MESSAGE TO DAISY!

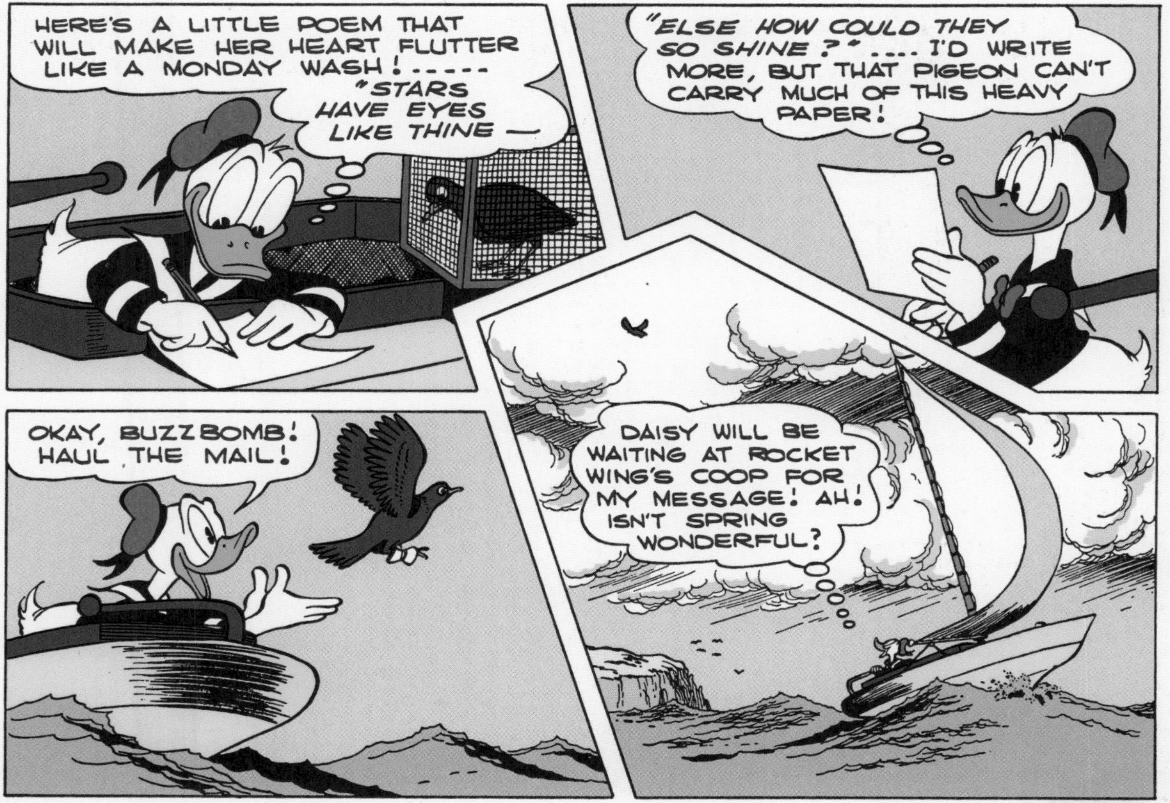
HERE'S A LITTLE POEM THAT WILL MAKE HER HEART FLUTTER LIKE A MONDAY WASH! ..... "STARS HAVE EYES LIKE THINE —
"ELSE HOW COULD THEY SO SHINE?" .... I'D WRITE MORE, BUT THAT PIGEON CAN'T CARRY MUCH OF THIS HEAVY PAPER!
OKAY, BUZZBOMB! HAUL THE MAIL!
DAISY WILL BE WAITING AT ROCKET WING'S COOP FOR MY MESSAGE! AH! ISN'T SPRING WONDERFUL?

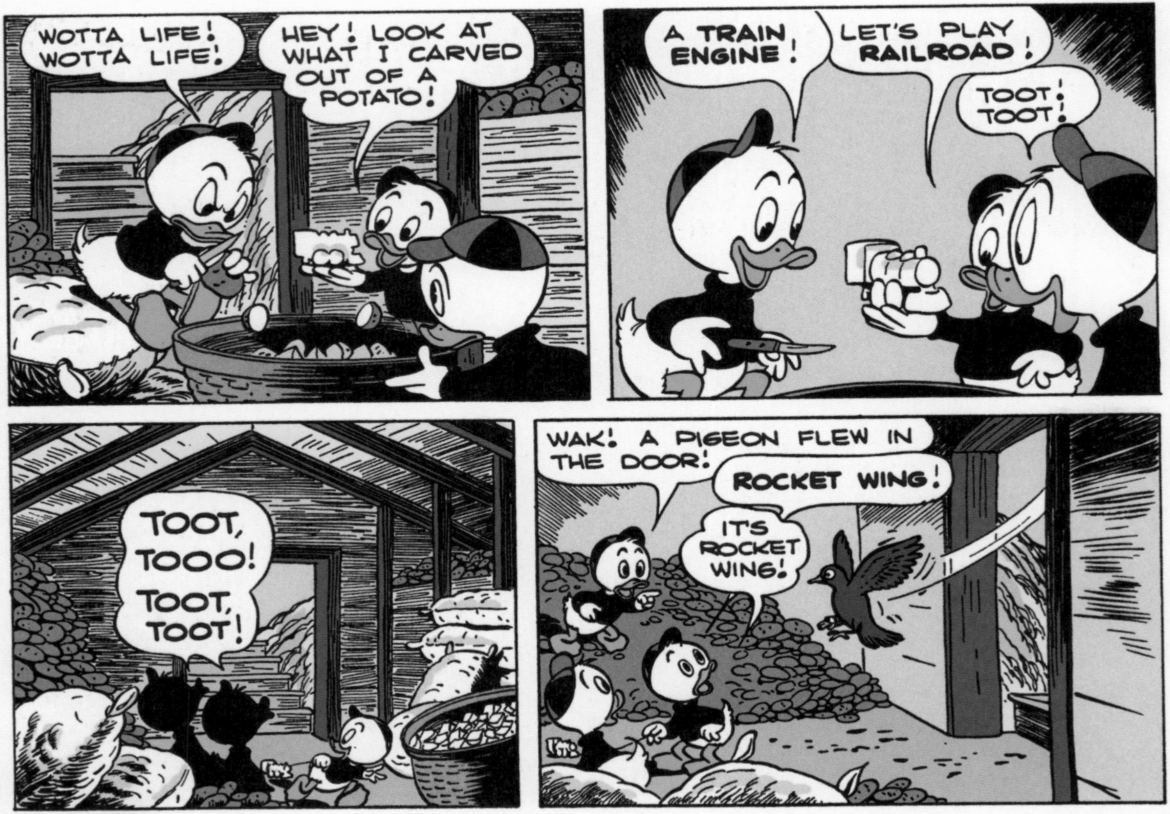

WOTTA LIFE! WOTTA LIFE!
HEY! LOOK AT WHAT I CARVED OUT OF A POTATO!
A TRAIN ENGINE!
LET'S PLAY RAILROAD!
TOOT! TOOT!
TOOT, TOOO! TOOT, TOOT!
WAK! A PIGEON FLEW IN THE DOOR!
ROCKET WING!
IT'S ROCKET WING!

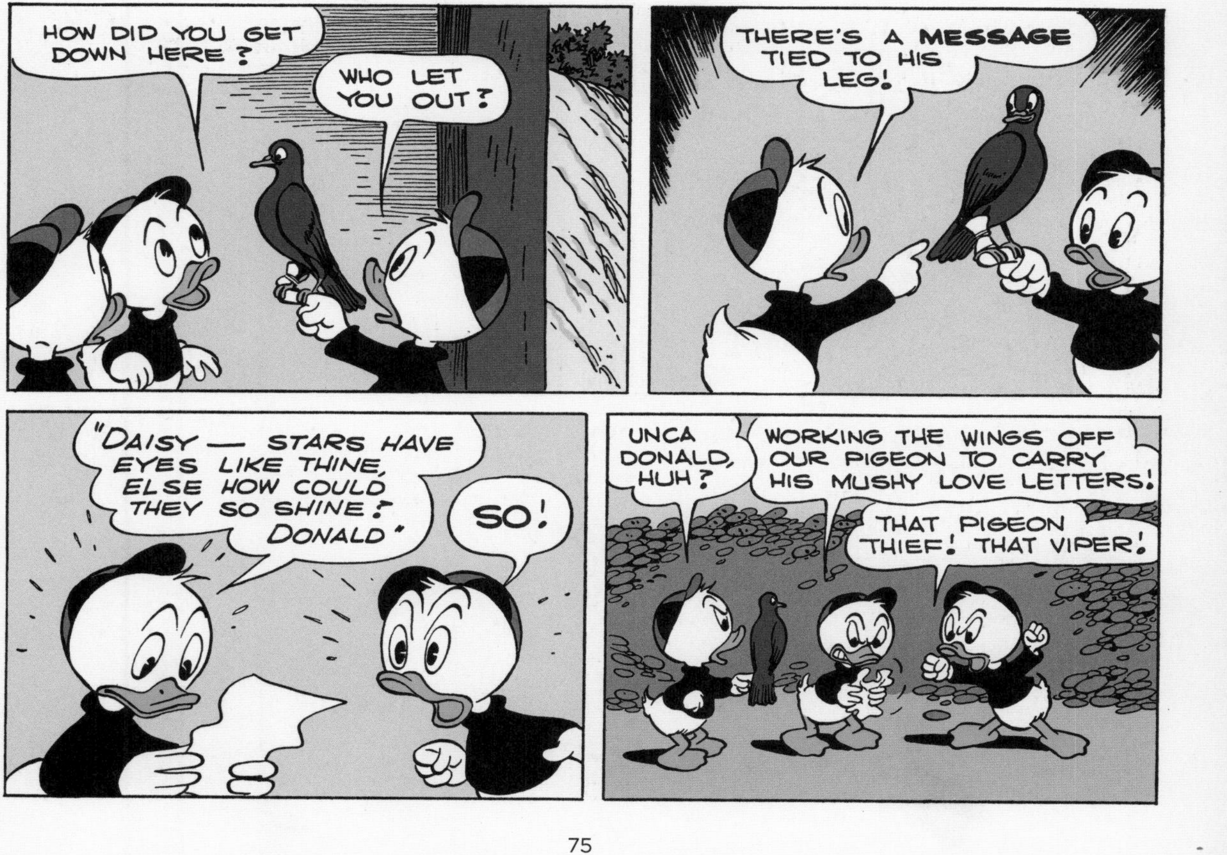
HOW DID YOU GET DOWN HERE?
WHO LET YOU OUT?
THERE'S A **MESSAGE** TIED TO HIS LEG!
"DAISY — STARS HAVE EYES LIKE THINE, ELSE HOW COULD THEY SO SHINE? DONALD"
SO!
UNCA DONALD, HUH?
WORKING THE WINGS OFF OUR PIGEON TO CARRY HIS MUSHY LOVE LETTERS!
THAT PIGEON THIEF! THAT VIPER!

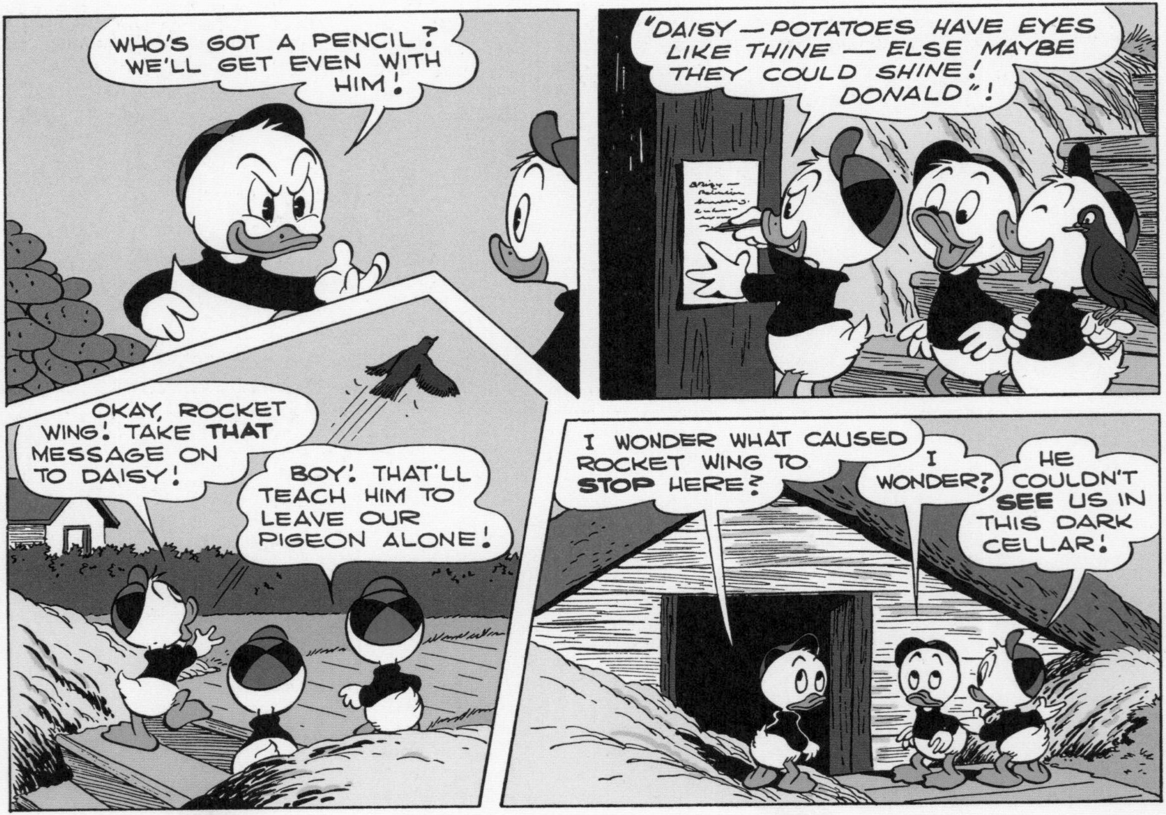
WHO'S GOT A PENCIL? WE'LL GET EVEN WITH HIM!
"DAISY — POTATOES HAVE EYES LIKE THINE — ELSE MAYBE THEY COULD SHINE! DONALD"!
OKAY, ROCKET WING! TAKE THAT MESSAGE ON TO DAISY!
BOY! THAT'LL TEACH HIM TO LEAVE OUR PIGEON ALONE!
I WONDER WHAT CAUSED ROCKET WING TO STOP HERE?
I WONDER?
HE COULDN'T SEE US IN THIS DARK CELLAR!

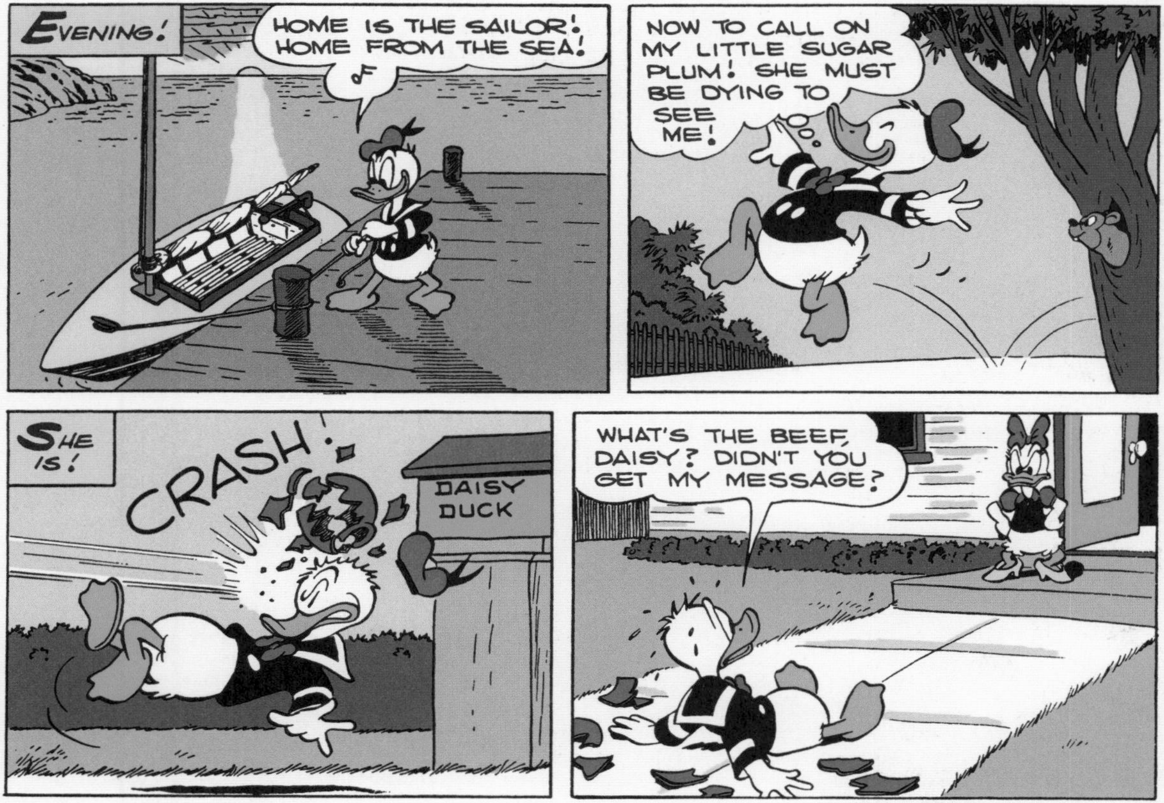
EVENING!
HOME IS THE SAILOR! HOME FROM THE SEA!
NOW TO CALL ON MY LITTLE SUGAR PLUM! SHE MUST BE DYING TO SEE ME!
SHE IS!
CRASH!
DAISY DUCK
WHAT'S THE BEEF, DAISY? DIDN'T YOU GET MY MESSAGE?

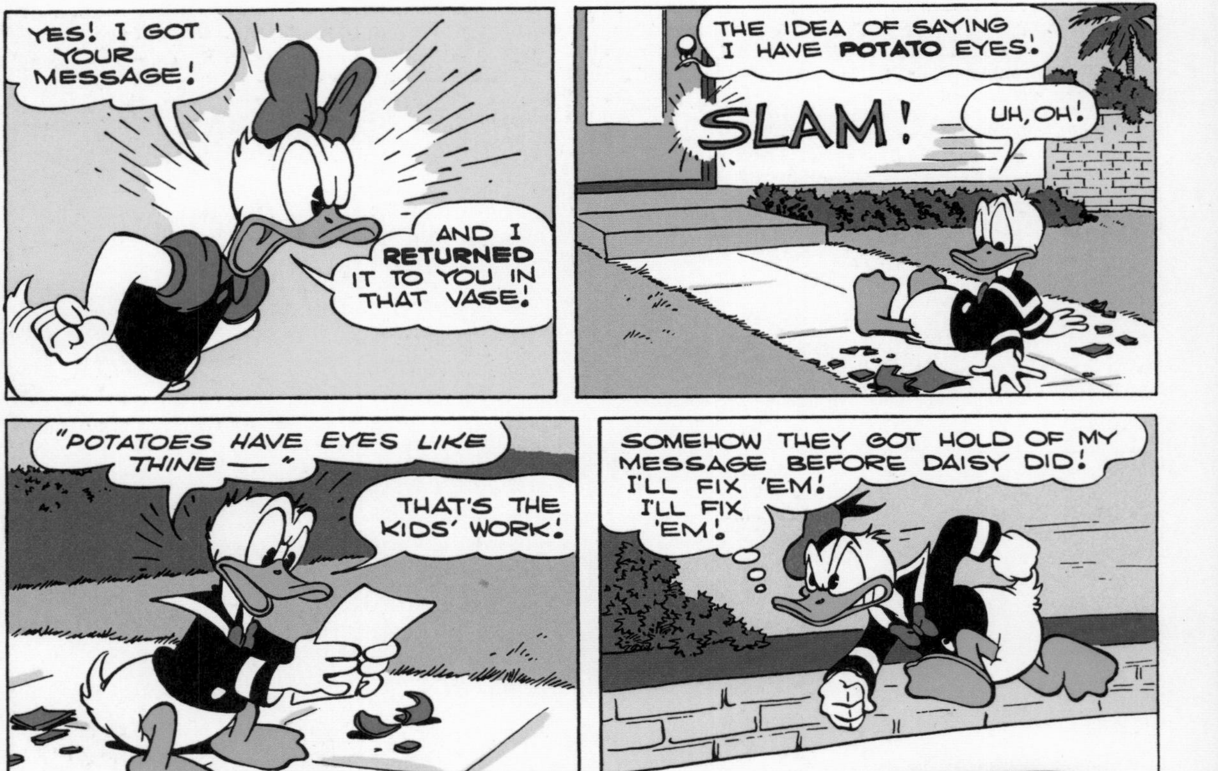
YES! I GOT YOUR MESSAGE!
AND I **RETURNED** IT TO YOU IN THAT VASE!
THE IDEA OF SAYING I HAVE **POTATO** EYES!
SLAM!
UH, OH!
"POTATOES HAVE EYES LIKE THINE — "
THAT'S THE KIDS' WORK!
SOMEHOW THEY GOT HOLD OF MY MESSAGE BEFORE DAISY DID! I'LL FIX 'EM!
I'LL FIX 'EM!

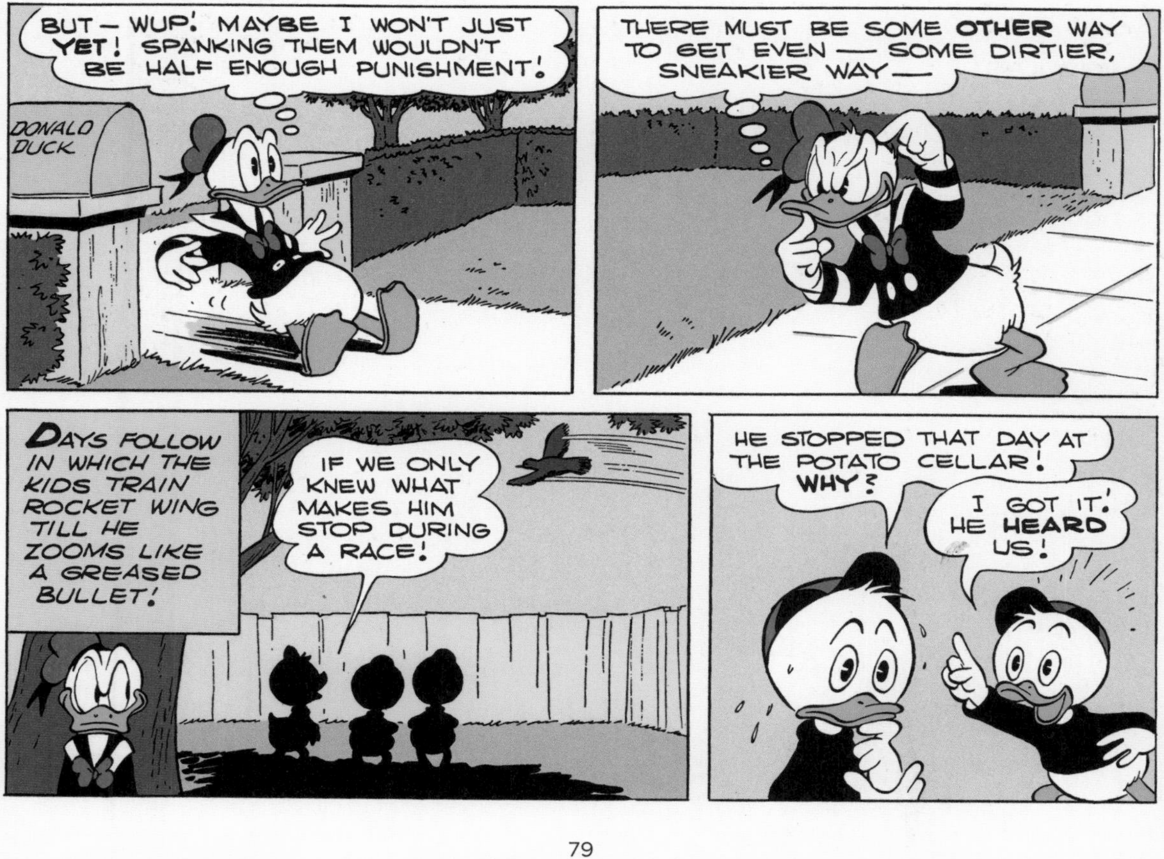
BUT — WUP! MAYBE I WON'T JUST YET! SPANKING THEM WOULDN'T BE HALF ENOUGH PUNISHMENT!
DONALD DUCK
THERE MUST BE SOME OTHER WAY TO GET EVEN — SOME DIRTIER, SNEAKIER WAY —
DAYS FOLLOW IN WHICH THE KIDS TRAIN ROCKET WING TILL HE ZOOMS LIKE A GREASED BULLET!
IF WE ONLY KNEW WHAT MAKES HIM STOP DURING A RACE!
HE STOPPED THAT DAY AT THE POTATO CELLAR! WHY?
I GOT IT! HE HEARD US!

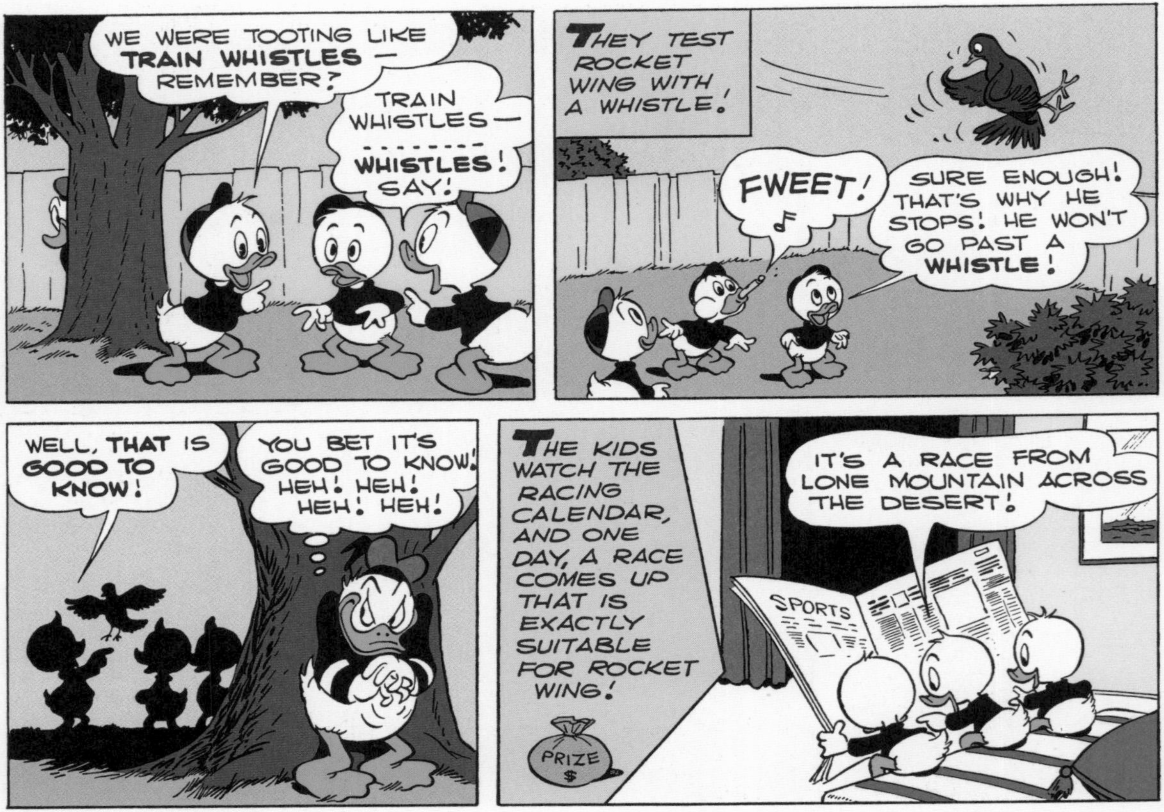
WE WERE TOOTING LIKE TRAIN WHISTLES — REMEMBER?
TRAIN WHISTLES — -------- WHISTLES! SAY!
THEY TEST ROCKET WING WITH A WHISTLE!
FWEET!
SURE ENOUGH! THAT'S WHY HE STOPS! HE WON'T GO PAST A WHISTLE!
WELL, THAT IS GOOD TO KNOW!
YOU BET IT'S GOOD TO KNOW! HEH! HEH! HEH! HEH!
THE KIDS WATCH THE RACING CALENDAR, AND ONE DAY, A RACE COMES UP THAT IS EXACTLY SUITABLE FOR ROCKET WING!
PRIZE $
IT'S A RACE FROM LONE MOUNTAIN ACROSS THE DESERT!
SPORTS

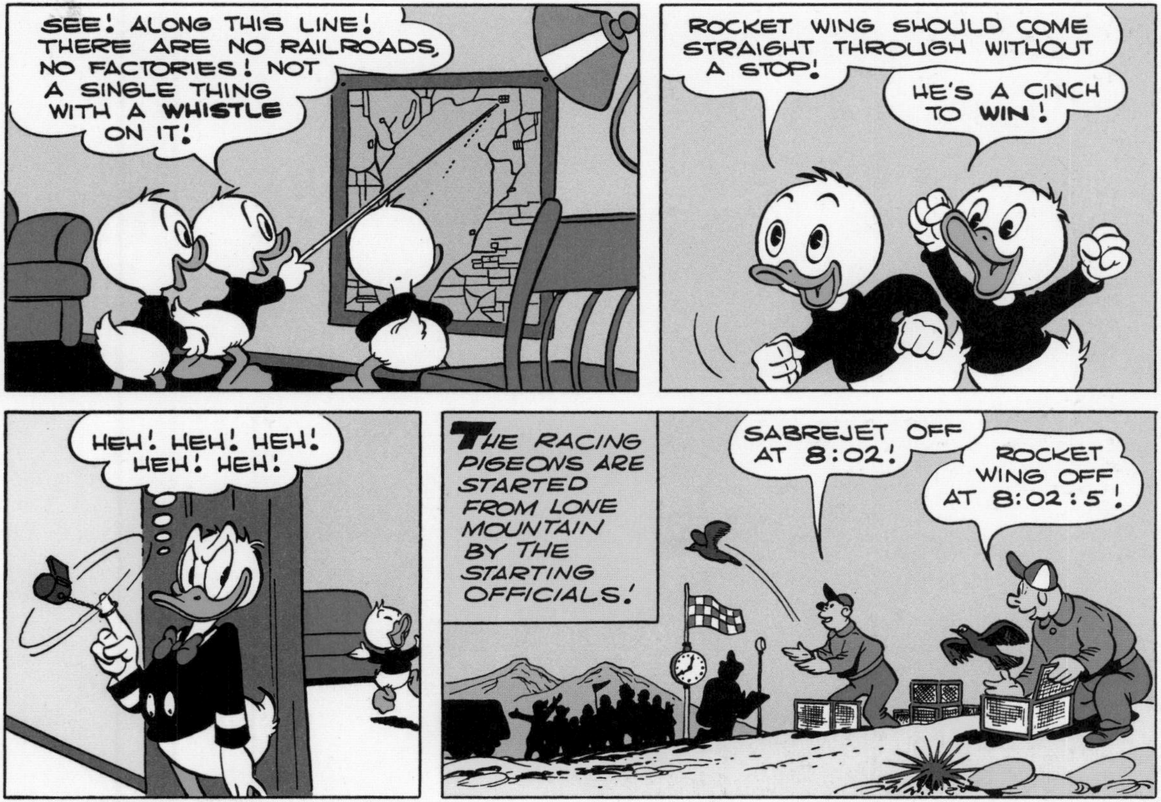
SEE! ALONG THIS LINE! THERE ARE NO RAILROADS, NO FACTORIES! NOT A SINGLE THING WITH A **WHISTLE** ON IT!
ROCKET WING SHOULD COME STRAIGHT THROUGH WITHOUT A STOP!
HE'S A CINCH TO **WIN**!
HEH! HEH! HEH! HEH! HEH!
THE RACING PIGEONS ARE STARTED FROM LONE MOUNTAIN BY THE STARTING OFFICIALS!
SABREJET OFF AT 8:02!
ROCKET WING OFF AT 8:02:5!

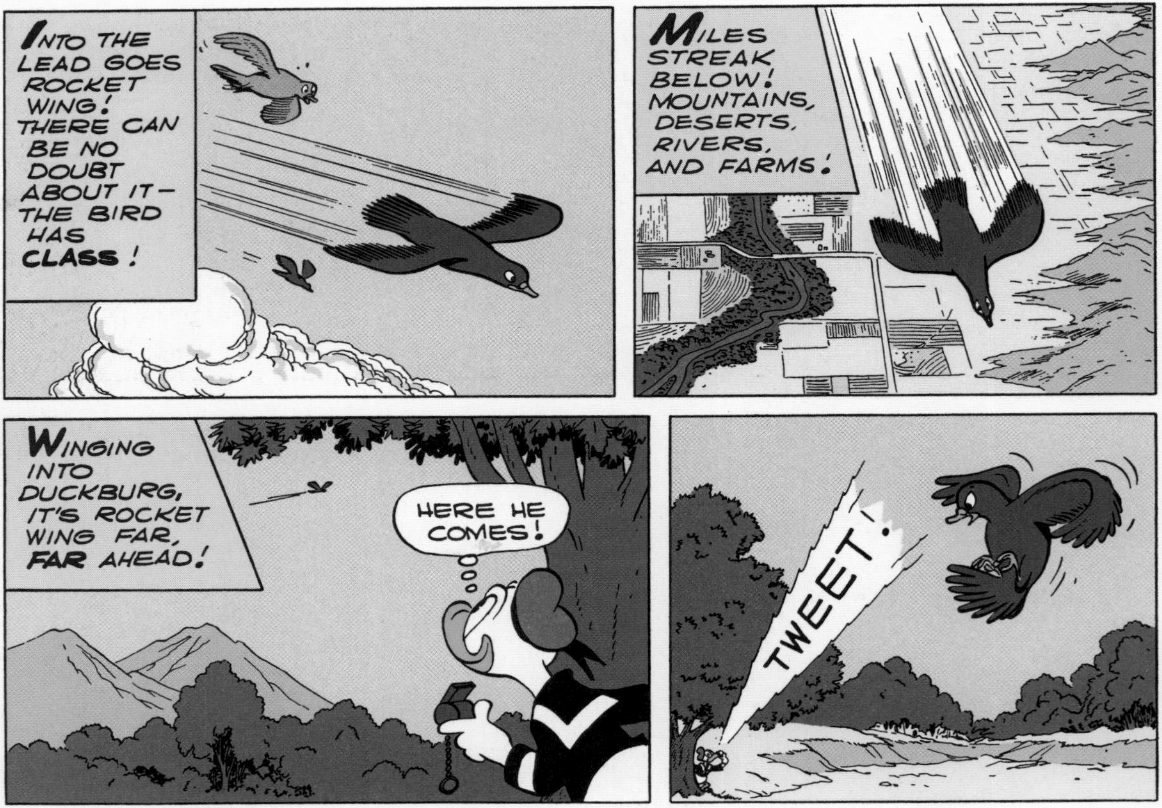
INTO THE LEAD GOES ROCKET WING! THERE CAN BE NO DOUBT ABOUT IT— THE BIRD HAS CLASS!
MILES STREAK BELOW! MOUNTAINS, DESERTS, RIVERS, AND FARMS!
WINGING INTO DUCKBURG, IT'S ROCKET WING FAR, FAR AHEAD!
HERE HE COMES!
TWEET!

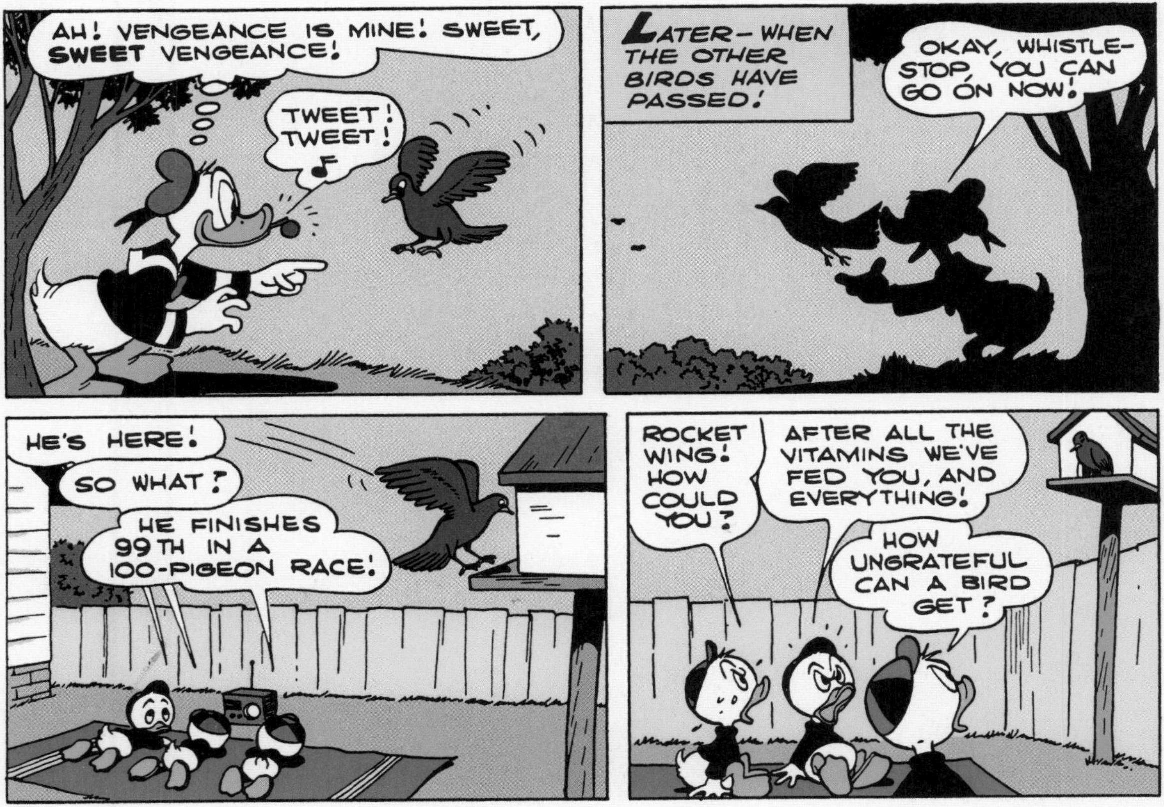
AH! VENGEANCE IS MINE! SWEET, **SWEET** VENGEANCE!
TWEET! TWEET!
LATER—WHEN THE OTHER BIRDS HAVE PASSED!
OKAY, WHISTLE-STOP, YOU CAN GO ON NOW!
HE'S HERE!
SO WHAT?
HE FINISHES 99TH IN A 100-PIGEON RACE!
ROCKET WING! HOW COULD YOU?
AFTER ALL THE VITAMINS WE'VE FED YOU, AND EVERYTHING!
HOW UNGRATEFUL CAN A BIRD GET?

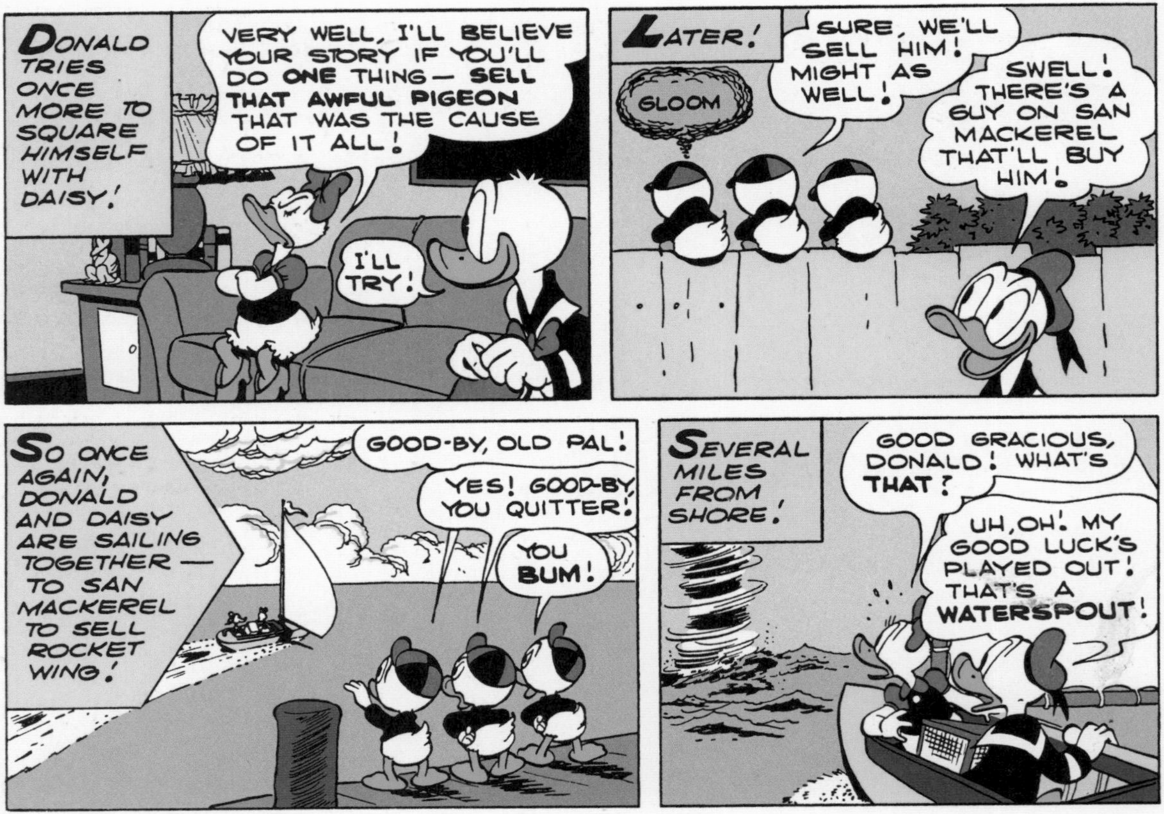
DONALD TRIES ONCE MORE TO SQUARE HIMSELF WITH DAISY!
VERY WELL, I'LL BELIEVE YOUR STORY IF YOU'LL DO ONE THING— SELL THAT AWFUL PIGEON THAT WAS THE CAUSE OF IT ALL!
I'LL TRY!
LATER!
GLOOM
SURE, WE'LL SELL HIM! MIGHT AS WELL!
SWELL! THERE'S A GUY ON SAN MACKEREL THAT'LL BUY HIM!
SO ONCE AGAIN, DONALD AND DAISY ARE SAILING TOGETHER — TO SAN MACKEREL TO SELL ROCKET WING!
GOOD-BY, OLD PAL!
YES! GOOD-BY, YOU QUITTER!
YOU BUM!
SEVERAL MILES FROM SHORE!
GOOD GRACIOUS, DONALD! WHAT'S THAT?
UH, OH! MY GOOD LUCK'S PLAYED OUT! THAT'S A WATERSPOUT!

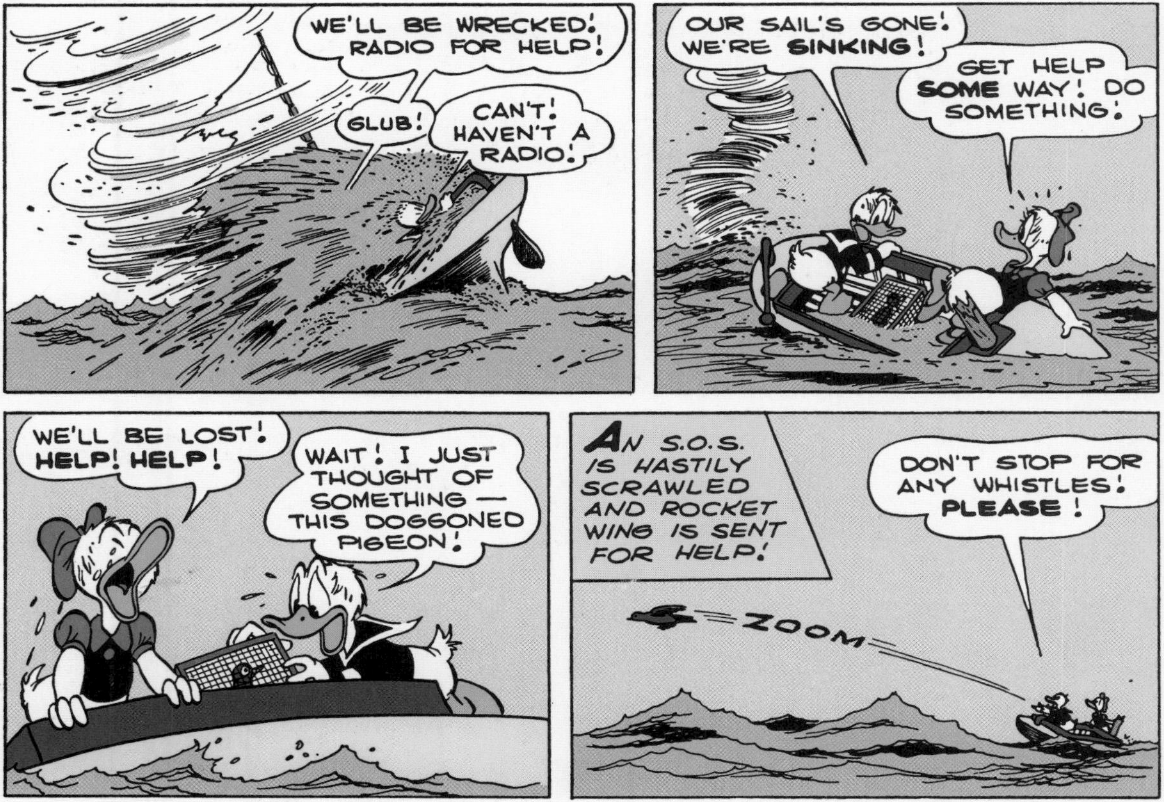
WE'LL BE WRECKED! RADIO FOR HELP!
GLUB!
CAN'T! HAVEN'T A RADIO!
OUR SAIL'S GONE! WE'RE **SINKING**!
GET HELP **SOME** WAY! DO SOMETHING!
WE'LL BE LOST! **HELP! HELP**!
WAIT! I JUST THOUGHT OF SOMETHING — THIS DOGGONED PIGEON!
AN S.O.S. IS HASTILY SCRAWLED AND ROCKET WING IS SENT FOR HELP!
DON'T STOP FOR ANY WHISTLES! **PLEASE**!
ZOOM

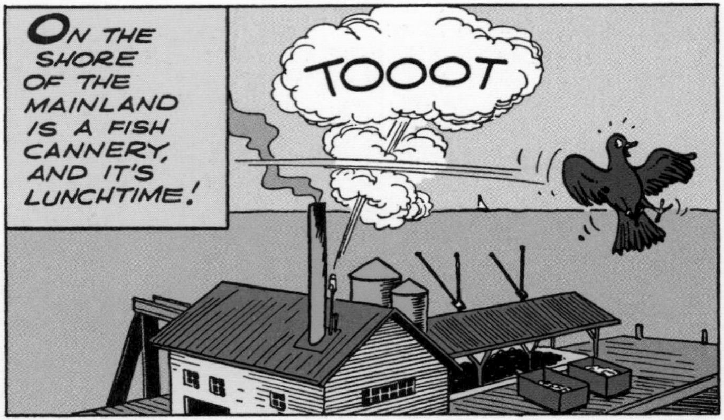
ON THE SHORE OF THE MAINLAND IS A FISH CANNERY, AND IT'S LUNCHTIME!
TOOOT

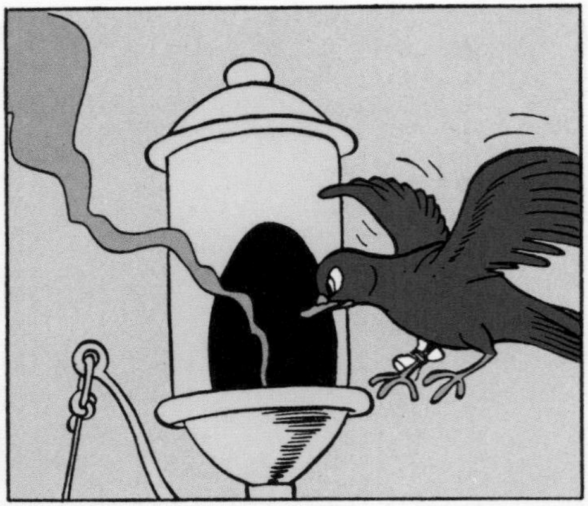

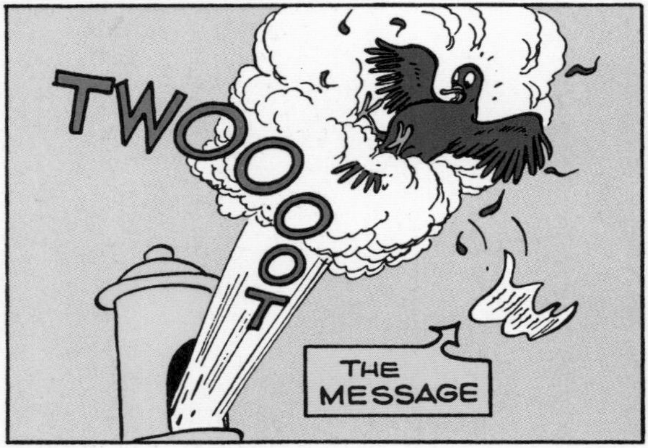
TWOOOOOOT
THE MESSAGE

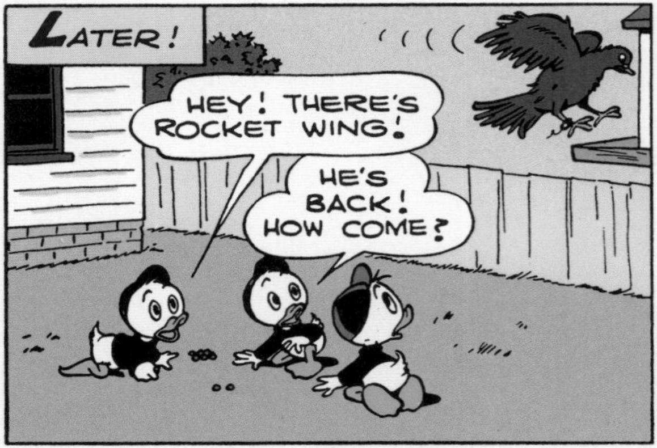
LATER!
HEY! THERE'S ROCKET WING!
HE'S BACK! HOW COME?

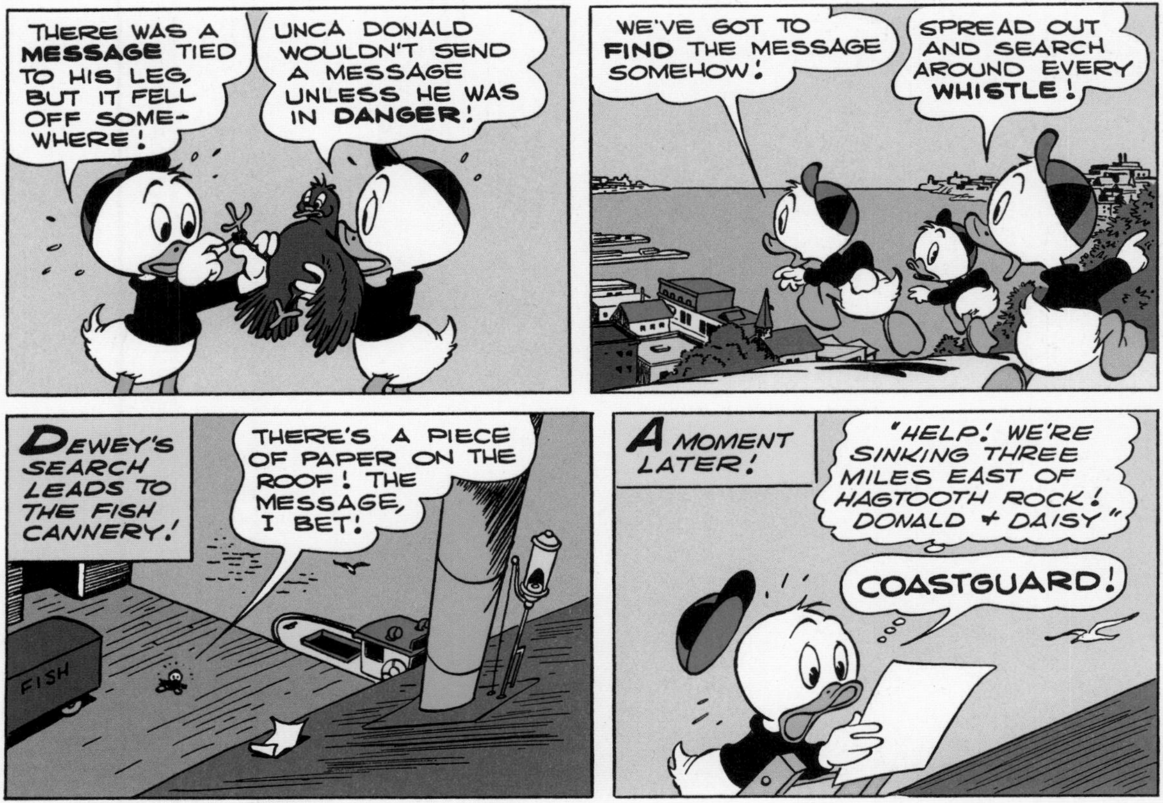
THERE WAS A MESSAGE TIED TO HIS LEG, BUT IT FELL OFF SOMEWHERE!
UNCA DONALD WOULDN'T SEND A MESSAGE UNLESS HE WAS IN DANGER!
WE'VE GOT TO FIND THE MESSAGE SOMEHOW!
SPREAD OUT AND SEARCH AROUND EVERY WHISTLE!
DEWEY'S SEARCH LEADS TO THE FISH CANNERY!
THERE'S A PIECE OF PAPER ON THE ROOF! THE MESSAGE, I BET!
FISH
A MOMENT LATER!
"HELP! WE'RE SINKING THREE MILES EAST OF HAGTOOTH ROCK! DONALD + DAISY"
COASTGUARD!

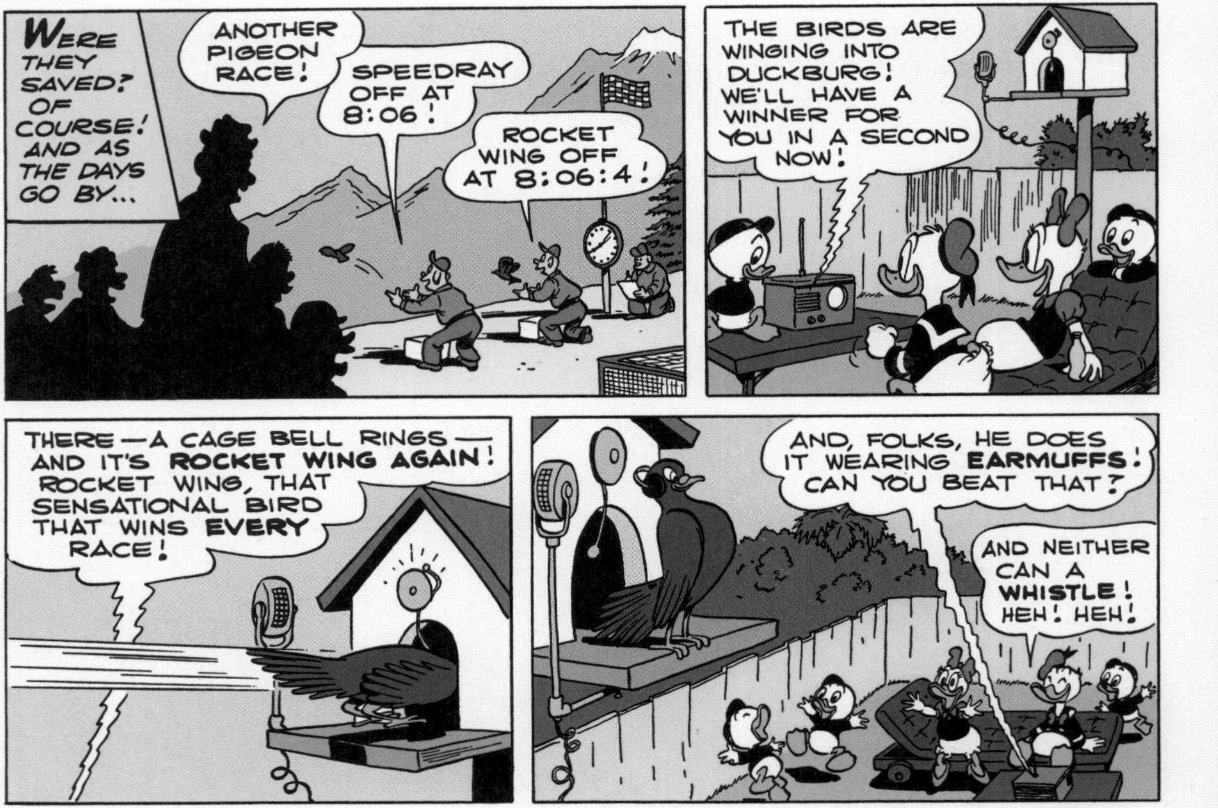
WERE THEY SAVED? OF COURSE! AND AS THE DAYS GO BY...
ANOTHER PIGEON RACE!
SPEEDRAY OFF AT 8:06!
ROCKET WING OFF AT 8:06:4!
THE BIRDS ARE WINGING INTO DUCKBURG! WE'LL HAVE A WINNER FOR YOU IN A SECOND NOW!
THERE—A CAGE BELL RINGS—AND IT'S **ROCKET WING AGAIN**! ROCKET WING, THAT SENSATIONAL BIRD THAT WINS **EVERY** RACE!
AND, FOLKS, HE DOES IT WEARING **EARMUFFS**! CAN YOU BEAT THAT?
AND NEITHER CAN A **WHISTLE**! HEH! HEH!

THE END

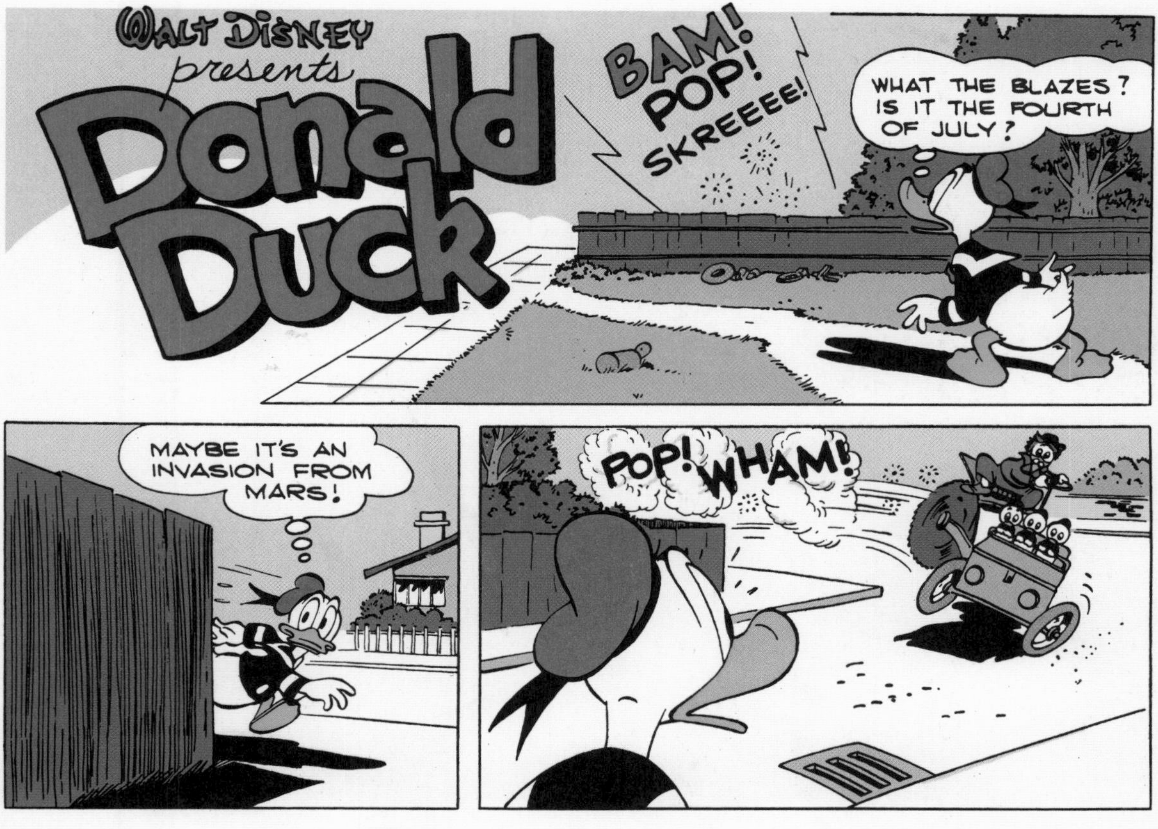
WALT DISNEY
presents
Donald Duck
BAM! POP! SKREEEEE!
WHAT THE BLAZES? IS IT THE FOURTH OF JULY?
MAYBE IT'S AN INVASION FROM MARS!
POP! WHAM!

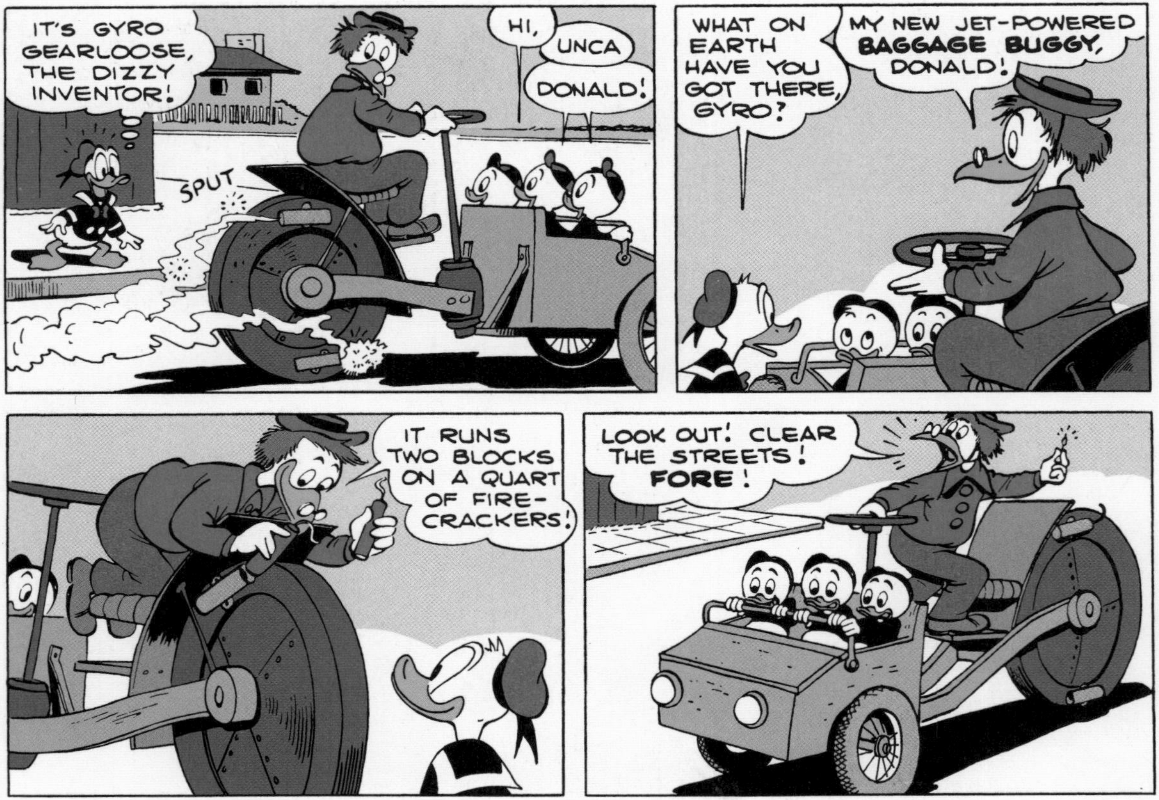
IT'S GYRO GEARLOOSE, THE DIZZY INVENTOR!
HI,
UNCA
DONALD!
SPUT
WHAT ON EARTH HAVE YOU GOT THERE, GYRO?
MY NEW JET-POWERED **BAGGAGE BUGGY**, DONALD!
IT RUNS TWO BLOCKS ON A QUART OF FIRE-CRACKERS!
LOOK OUT! CLEAR THE STREETS! **FORE**!

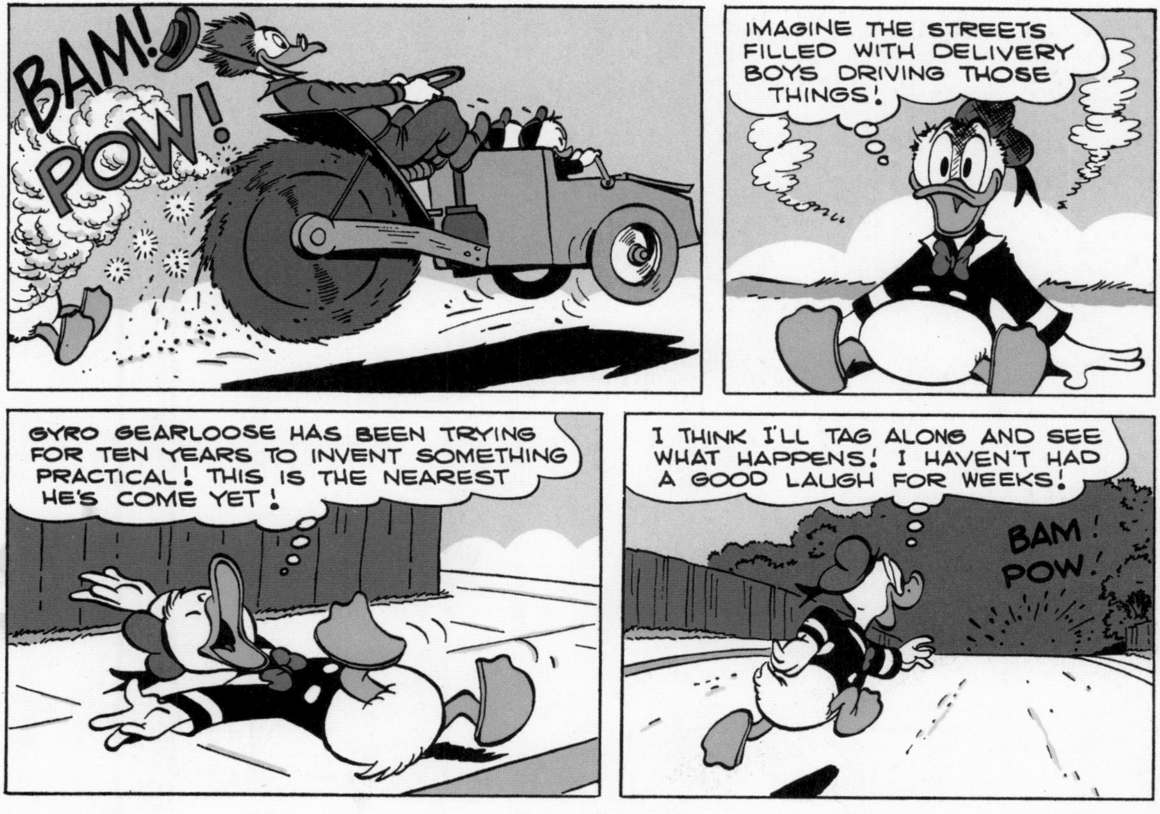
BAM!
POW!
IMAGINE THE STREETS FILLED WITH DELIVERY BOYS DRIVING THOSE THINGS!
GYRO GEARLOOSE HAS BEEN TRYING FOR TEN YEARS TO INVENT SOMETHING PRACTICAL! THIS IS THE NEAREST HE'S COME YET!
I THINK I'LL TAG ALONG AND SEE WHAT HAPPENS! I HAVEN'T HAD A GOOD LAUGH FOR WEEKS!
BAM!
POW!

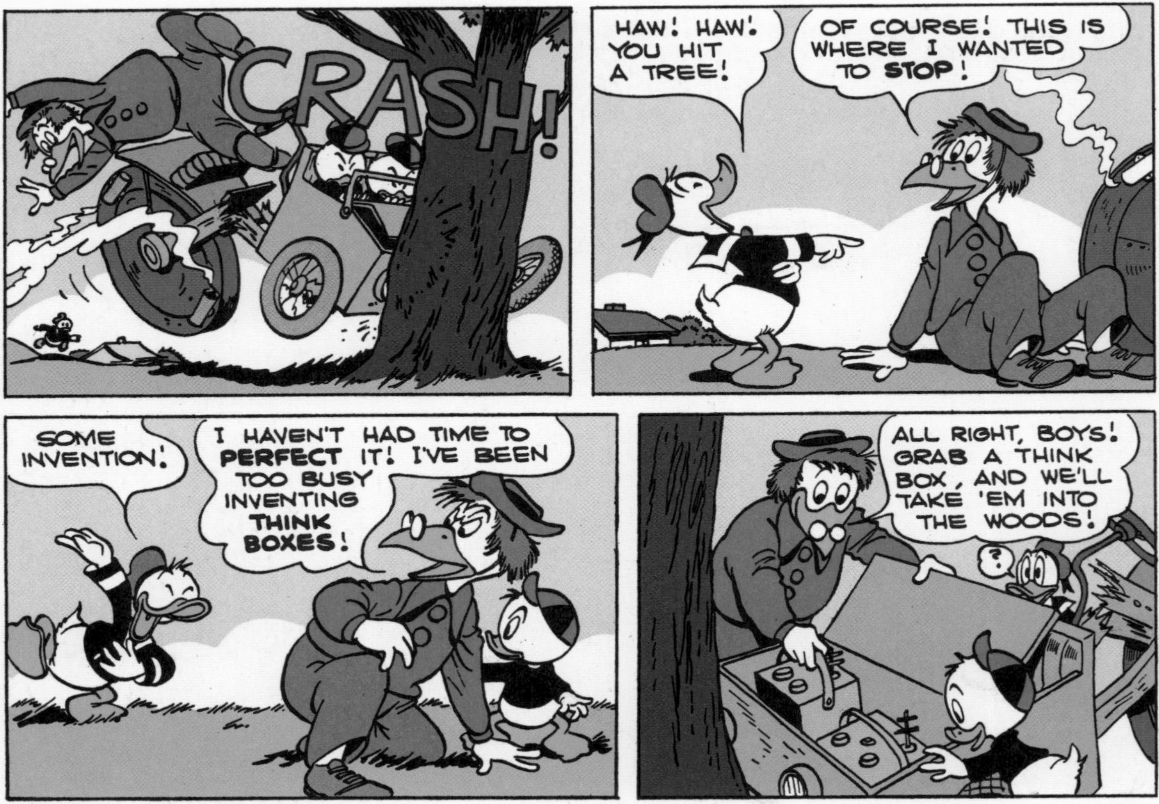
CRASH!
HAW! HAW! YOU HIT A TREE!
OF COURSE! THIS IS WHERE I WANTED TO **STOP**!
SOME INVENTION!
I HAVEN'T HAD TIME TO **PERFECT** IT! I'VE BEEN TOO BUSY INVENTING **THINK BOXES**!
ALL RIGHT, BOYS! GRAB A THINK BOX, AND WE'LL TAKE 'EM INTO THE WOODS!
?

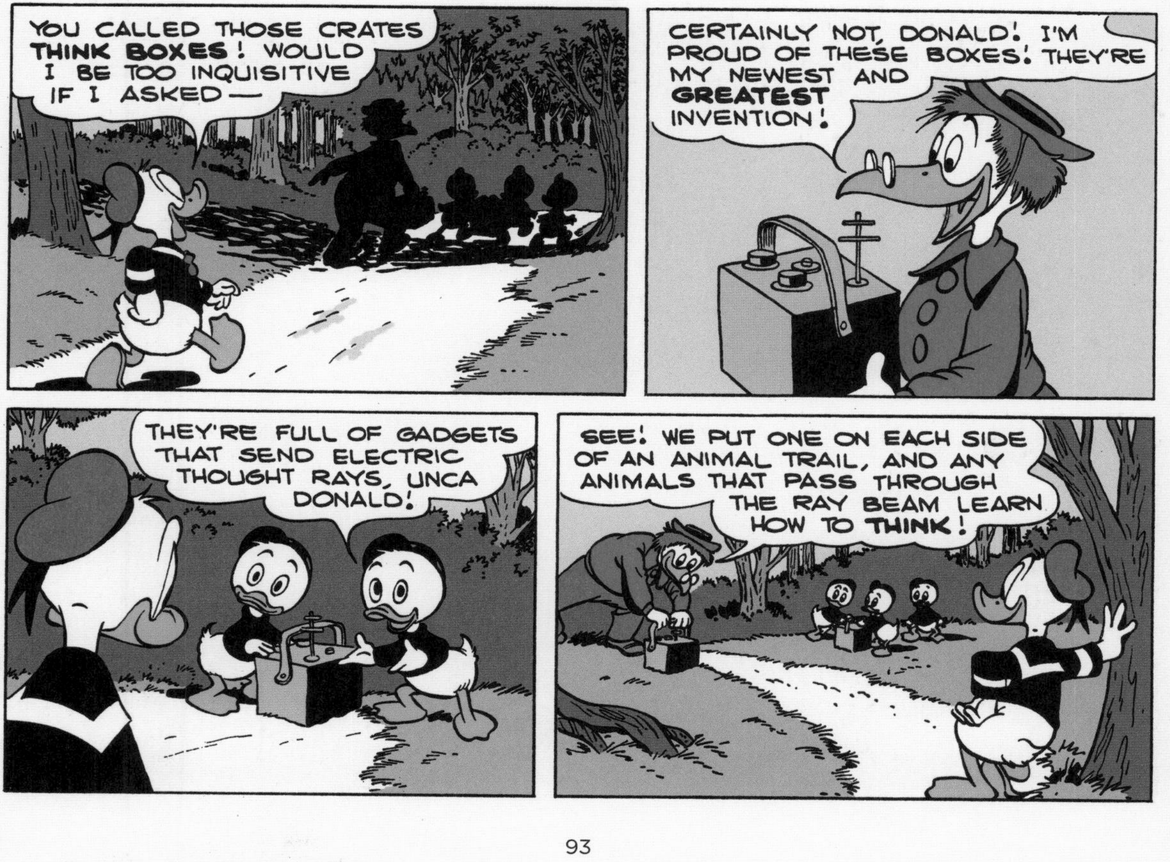
YOU CALLED THOSE CRATES **THINK BOXES**! WOULD I BE TOO INQUISITIVE IF I ASKED—
CERTAINLY NOT, DONALD! I'M PROUD OF THESE BOXES! THEY'RE MY NEWEST AND **GREATEST** INVENTION!
THEY'RE FULL OF GADGETS THAT SEND ELECTRIC THOUGHT RAYS, UNCA DONALD!
SEE! WE PUT ONE ON EACH SIDE OF AN ANIMAL TRAIL, AND ANY ANIMALS THAT PASS THROUGH THE RAY BEAM LEARN HOW TO **THINK**!

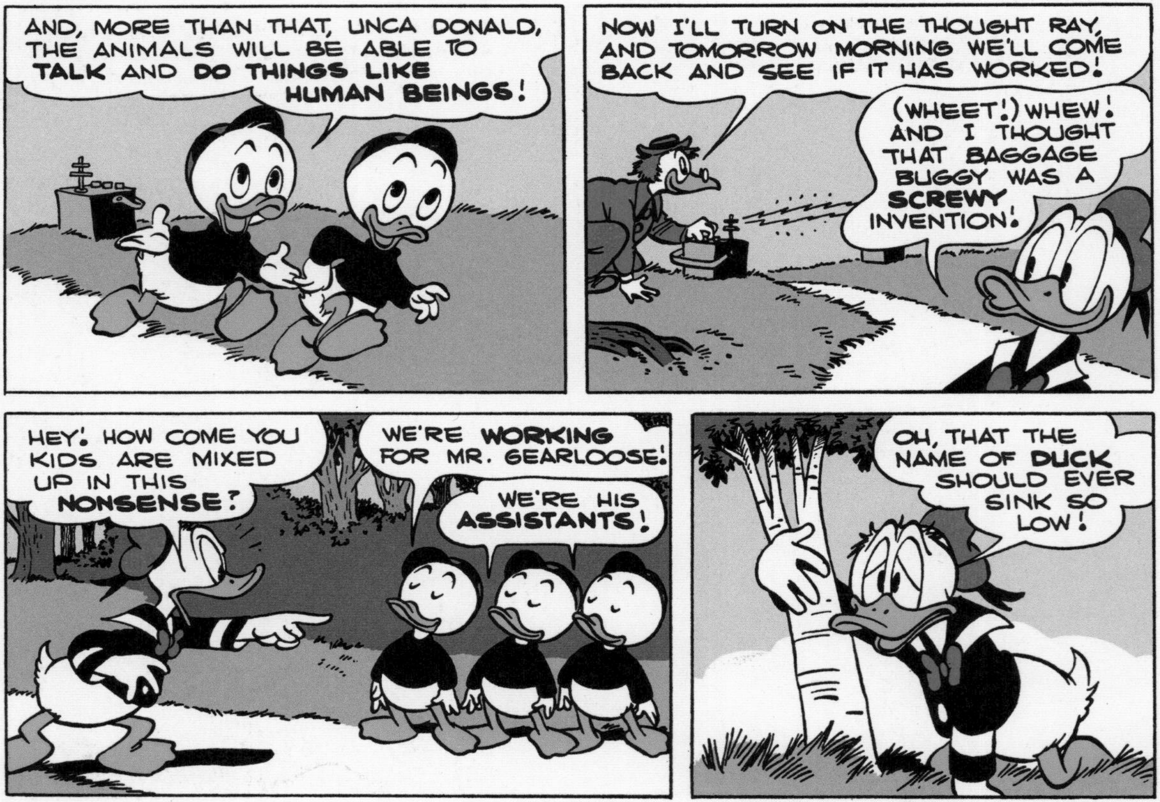
AND, MORE THAN THAT, UNCA DONALD, THE ANIMALS WILL BE ABLE TO **TALK** AND **DO THINGS LIKE HUMAN BEINGS**!
NOW I'LL TURN ON THE THOUGHT RAY, AND TOMORROW **MORNING** WE'LL COME BACK AND SEE IF IT HAS WORKED!
(WHEET!) WHEW! AND I THOUGHT THAT BAGGAGE BUGGY WAS A **SCREWY** INVENTION!
HEY! HOW COME YOU KIDS ARE MIXED UP IN THIS **NONSENSE**?
WE'RE **WORKING** FOR MR. GEARLOOSE!
WE'RE HIS **ASSISTANTS**!
OH, THAT THE NAME OF **DUCK** SHOULD EVER SINK SO LOW!

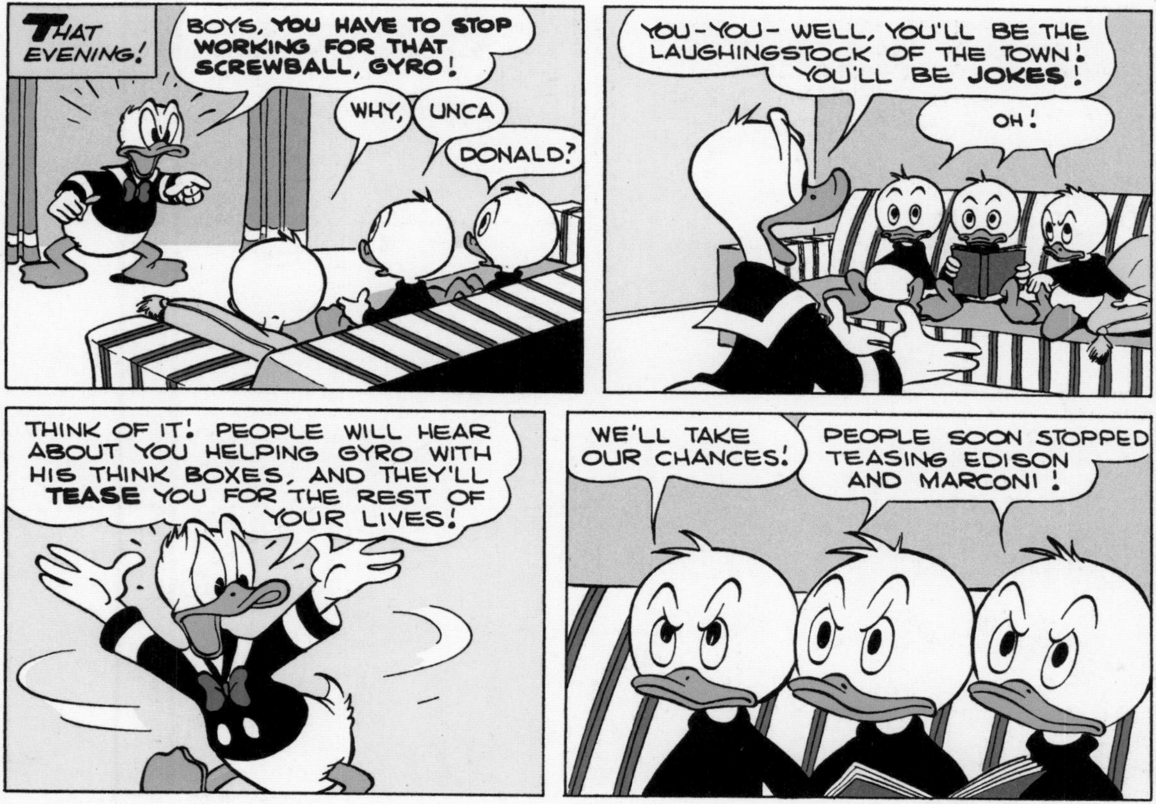
THAT EVENING!
BOYS, **YOU HAVE TO STOP WORKING FOR THAT SCREWBALL, GYRO!**
WHY,
UNCA
DONALD?
YOU-YOU- WELL, YOU'LL BE THE LAUGHINGSTOCK OF THE TOWN! YOU'LL BE **JOKES**!
OH!
THINK OF IT! PEOPLE WILL HEAR ABOUT YOU HELPING GYRO WITH HIS THINK BOXES, AND THEY'LL **TEASE** YOU FOR THE REST OF YOUR LIVES!
WE'LL TAKE OUR CHANCES!
PEOPLE SOON STOPPED TEASING EDISON AND MARCONI!

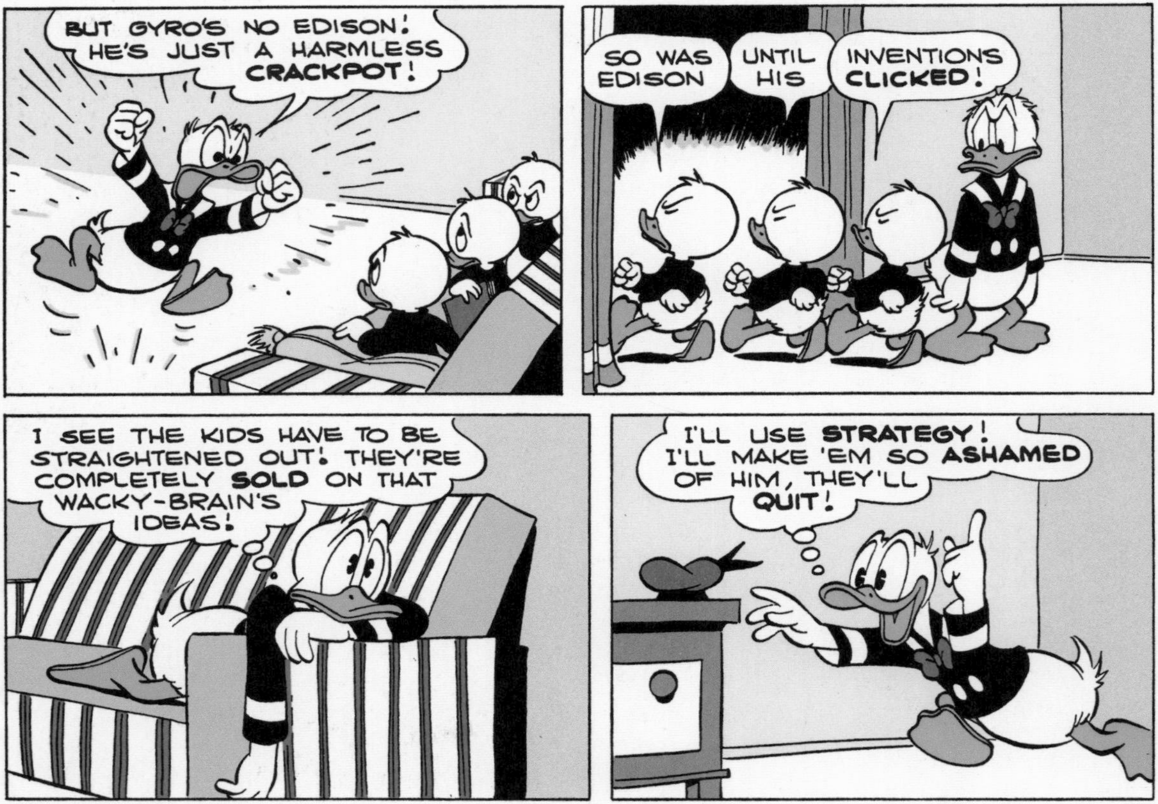
BUT GYRO'S NO EDISON! HE'S JUST A HARMLESS CRACKPOT!
SO WAS EDISON
UNTIL HIS
INVENTIONS CLICKED!
I SEE THE KIDS HAVE TO BE STRAIGHTENED OUT! THEY'RE COMPLETELY SOLD ON THAT WACKY-BRAIN'S IDEAS!
I'LL USE STRATEGY! I'LL MAKE 'EM SO ASHAMED OF HIM, THEY'LL QUIT!

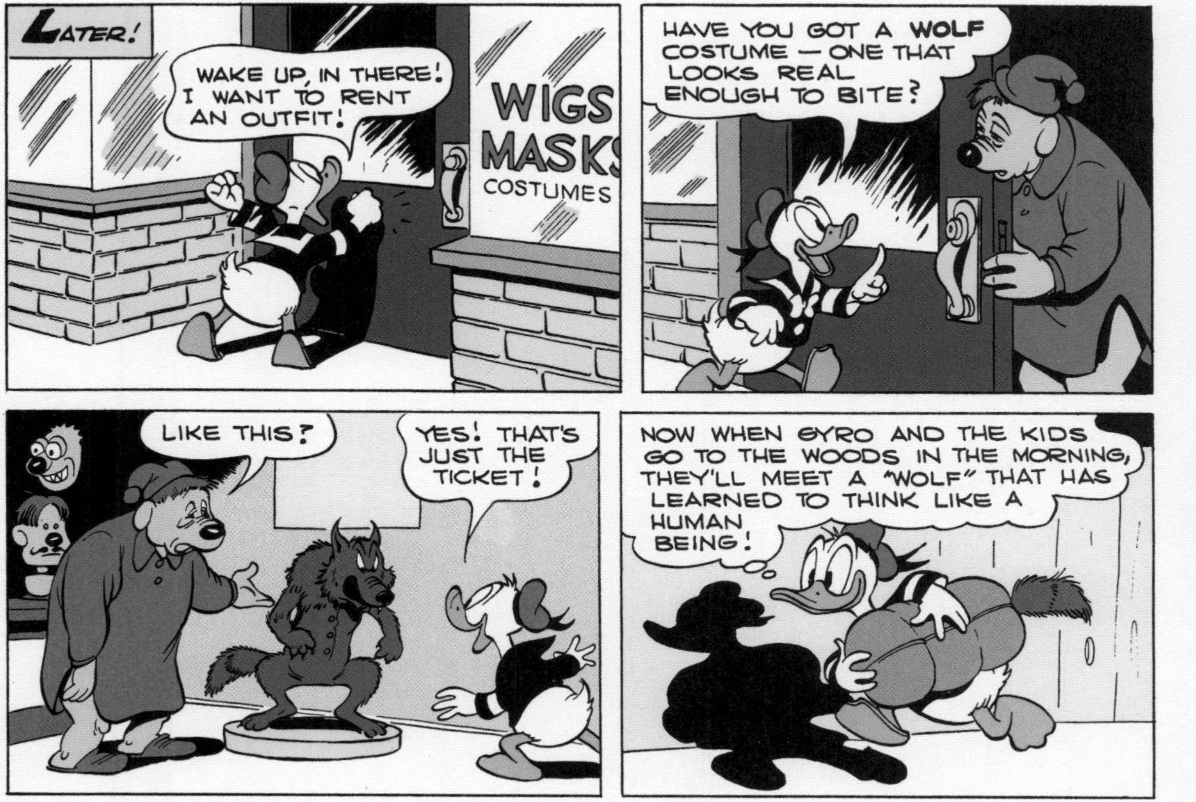
LATER!
WAKE UP, IN THERE! I WANT TO RENT AN OUTFIT!
WIGS MASKS COSTUMES
HAVE YOU GOT A WOLF COSTUME — ONE THAT LOOKS REAL ENOUGH TO BITE?
LIKE THIS?
YES! THAT'S JUST THE TICKET!
NOW WHEN GYRO AND THE KIDS GO TO THE WOODS IN THE MORNING, THEY'LL MEET A "WOLF" THAT HAS LEARNED TO THINK LIKE A HUMAN BEING!

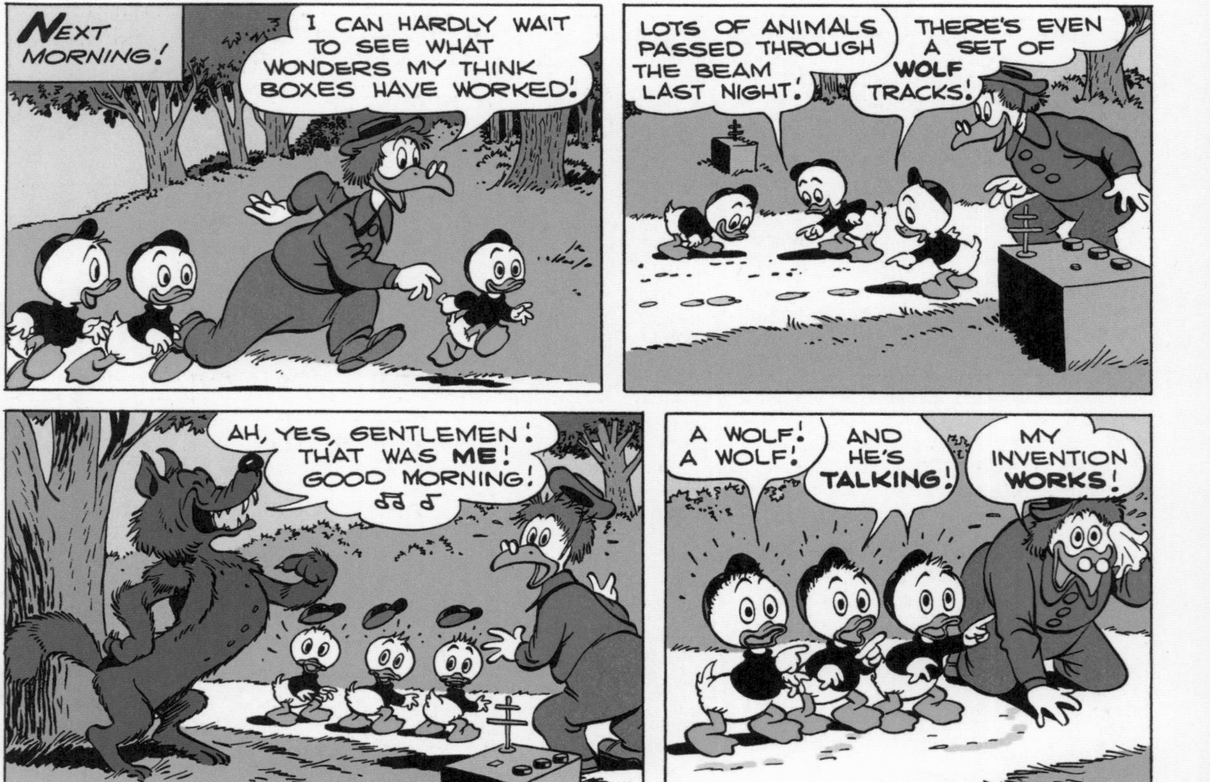
NEXT MORNING!
I CAN HARDLY WAIT TO SEE WHAT WONDERS MY THINK BOXES HAVE WORKED!
LOTS OF ANIMALS PASSED THROUGH THE BEAM LAST NIGHT!
THERE'S EVEN A SET OF **WOLF** TRACKS!
AH, YES, GENTLEMEN! THAT WAS **ME**! GOOD MORNING!
A WOLF! A WOLF!
AND HE'S **TALKING**!
MY INVENTION **WORKS**!

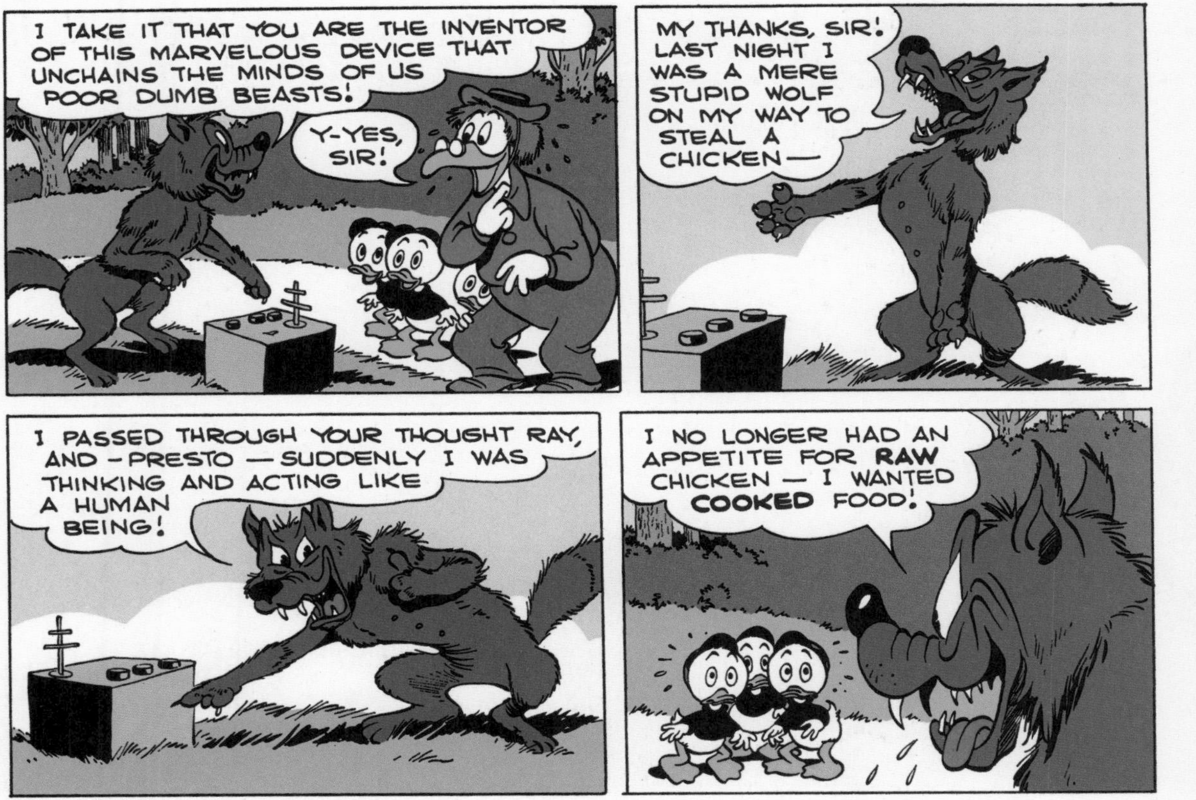
I TAKE IT THAT YOU ARE THE INVENTOR OF THIS MARVELOUS DEVICE THAT UNCHAINS THE MINDS OF US POOR DUMB BEASTS!
Y-YES, SIR!
MY THANKS, SIR! LAST NIGHT I WAS A MERE STUPID WOLF ON MY WAY TO STEAL A CHICKEN—
I PASSED THROUGH YOUR THOUGHT RAY, AND - PRESTO — SUDDENLY I WAS THINKING AND ACTING LIKE A HUMAN BEING!
I NO LONGER HAD AN APPETITE FOR **RAW** CHICKEN — I WANTED **COOKED** FOOD!

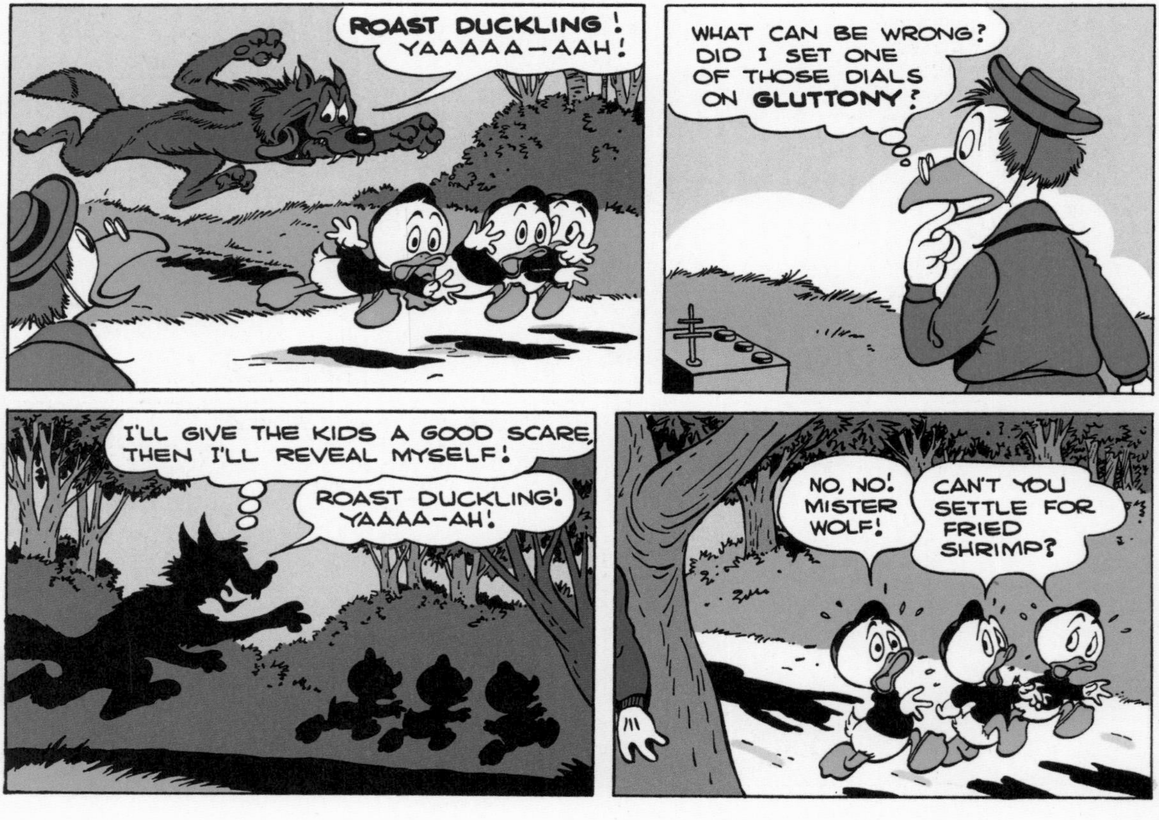
ROAST DUCKLING! YAAAAA-AAH!
WHAT CAN BE WRONG? DID I SET ONE OF THOSE DIALS ON GLUTTONY?
I'LL GIVE THE KIDS A GOOD SCARE, THEN I'LL REVEAL MYSELF!
ROAST DUCKLING! YAAAA-AH!
NO, NO! MISTER WOLF!
CAN'T YOU SETTLE FOR FRIED SHRIMP?

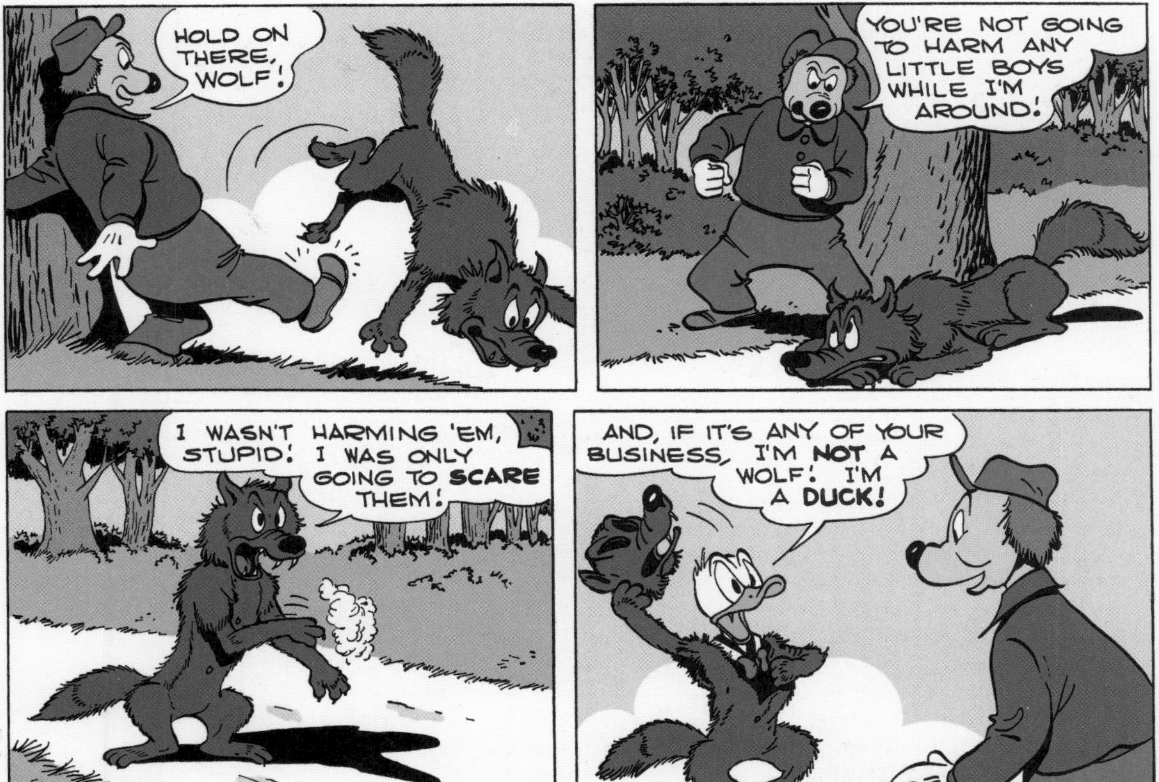
HOLD ON THERE, WOLF!
YOU'RE NOT GOING TO HARM ANY LITTLE BOYS WHILE I'M AROUND!
I WASN'T HARMING 'EM, STUPID! I WAS ONLY GOING TO **SCARE** THEM!
AND, IF IT'S ANY OF YOUR BUSINESS, I'M **NOT** A WOLF! I'M A **DUCK**!

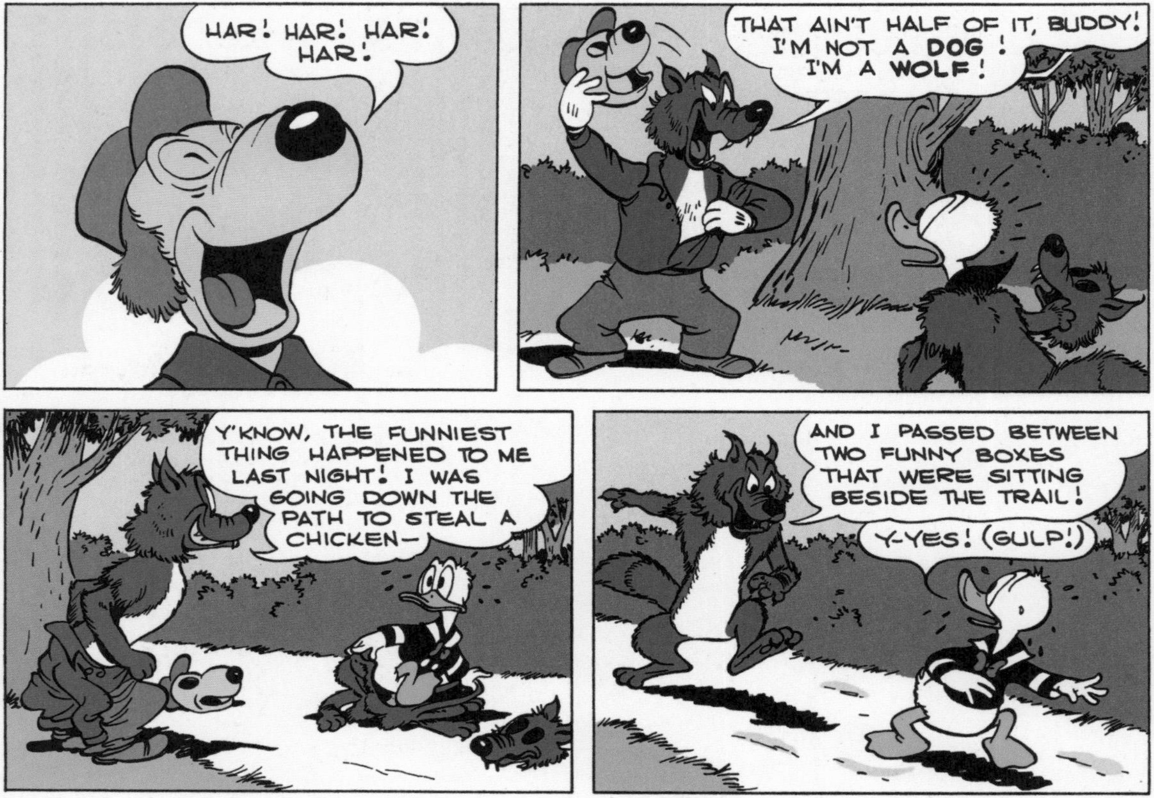
HAR! HAR! HAR! HAR!
THAT AIN'T HALF OF IT, BUDDY! I'M NOT A DOG! I'M A WOLF!
Y'KNOW, THE FUNNIEST THING HAPPENED TO ME LAST NIGHT! I WAS GOING DOWN THE PATH TO STEAL A CHICKEN—
AND I PASSED BETWEEN TWO FUNNY BOXES THAT WERE SITTING BESIDE THE TRAIL!
Y-YES! (GULP!)

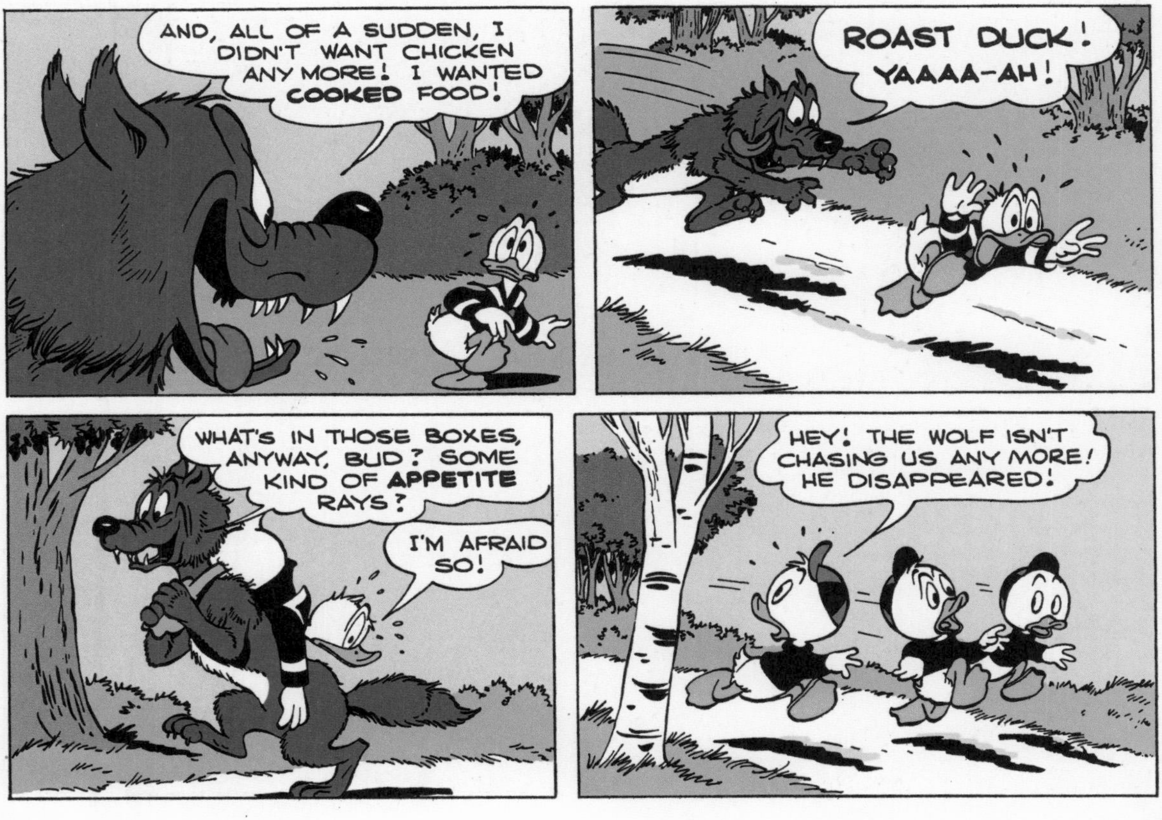
AND, ALL OF A SUDDEN, I DIDN'T WANT CHICKEN ANY MORE! I WANTED **COOKED** FOOD!
ROAST DUCK! YAAAA-AH!
WHAT'S IN THOSE BOXES, ANYWAY, BUD? SOME KIND OF **APPETITE** RAYS?
I'M AFRAID SO!
HEY! THE WOLF ISN'T CHASING US ANY MORE! HE DISAPPEARED!

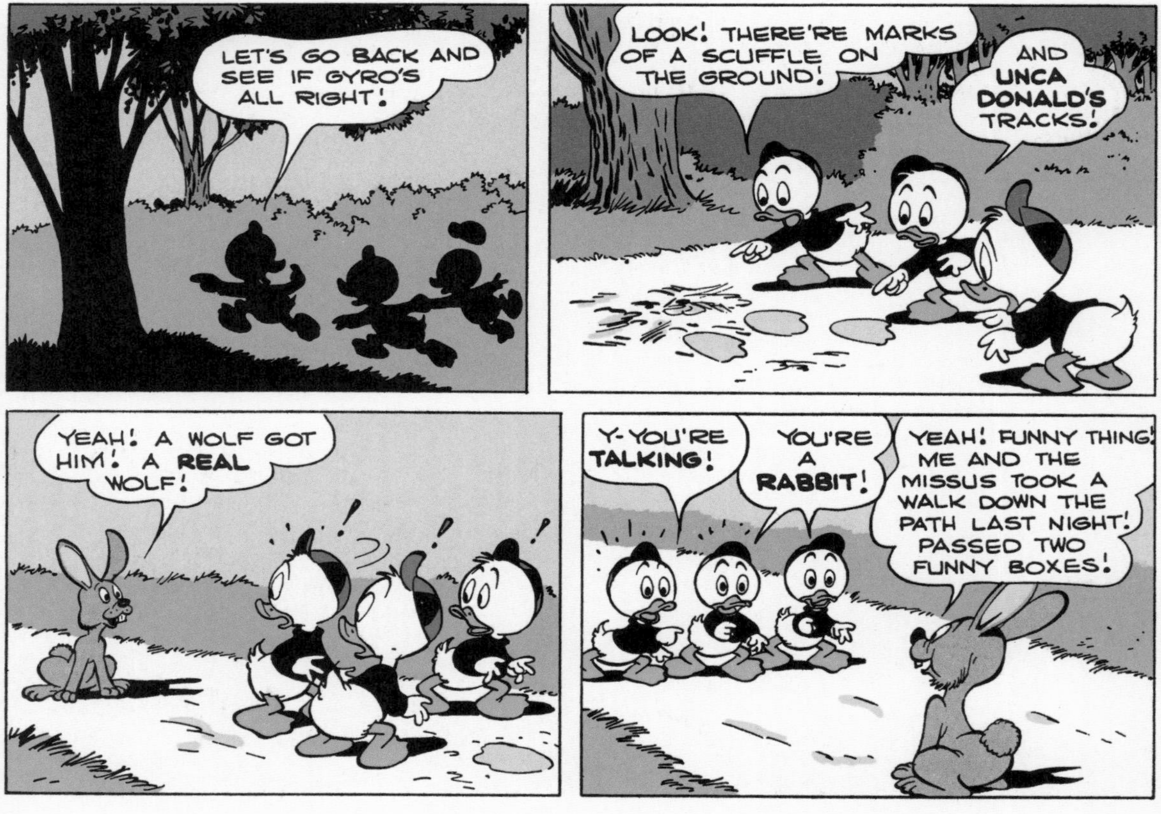
LET'S GO BACK AND SEE IF GYRO'S ALL RIGHT!
LOOK! THERE'RE MARKS OF A SCUFFLE ON THE GROUND!
AND UNCA DONALD'S TRACKS!
YEAH! A WOLF GOT HIM! A REAL WOLF!
Y-YOU'RE TALKING!
YOU'RE A RABBIT!
YEAH! FUNNY THING! ME AND THE MISSUS TOOK A WALK DOWN THE PATH LAST NIGHT! PASSED TWO FUNNY BOXES!

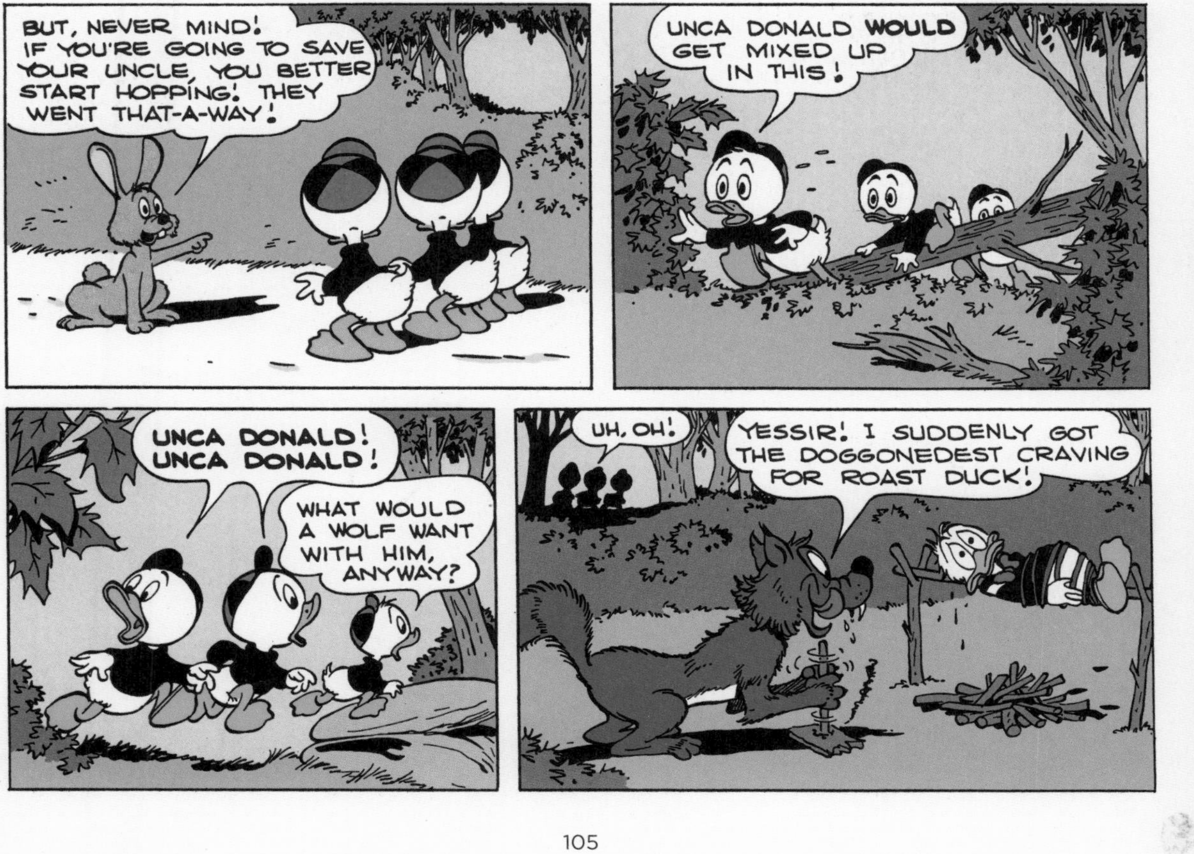
BUT, NEVER MIND! IF YOU'RE GOING TO SAVE YOUR UNCLE, YOU BETTER START HOPPING! THEY WENT THAT-A-WAY!
UNCA DONALD **WOULD** GET MIXED UP IN THIS!
UNCA DONALD! UNCA DONALD!
WHAT WOULD A WOLF WANT WITH HIM, ANYWAY?
UH, OH!
YESSIR! I SUDDENLY GOT THE DOGGONEDEST CRAVING FOR ROAST DUCK!

WE CAN'T TACKLE THAT WOLF WITH OUR BARE HANDS! WE'VE GOT TO GET GYRO TO HELP US!

GYRO! GYRO! MR. GEARLOOSE! CAN YOU **REVERSE** THOSE THINK BOXES —

MAKE 'EM UNSMART A WOLF?

WHY, YES! I CAN DOUBLE THE BEAM BACK FROM 'B' BOX TO 'A' BOX, CAUSING THE POLAR NEGATIVE TO BREAK UP THE COSMIC POSITIVE —

NEVER MIND THE DETAILS! WE'VE GOT TO BREAK UP A DINNER DATE!

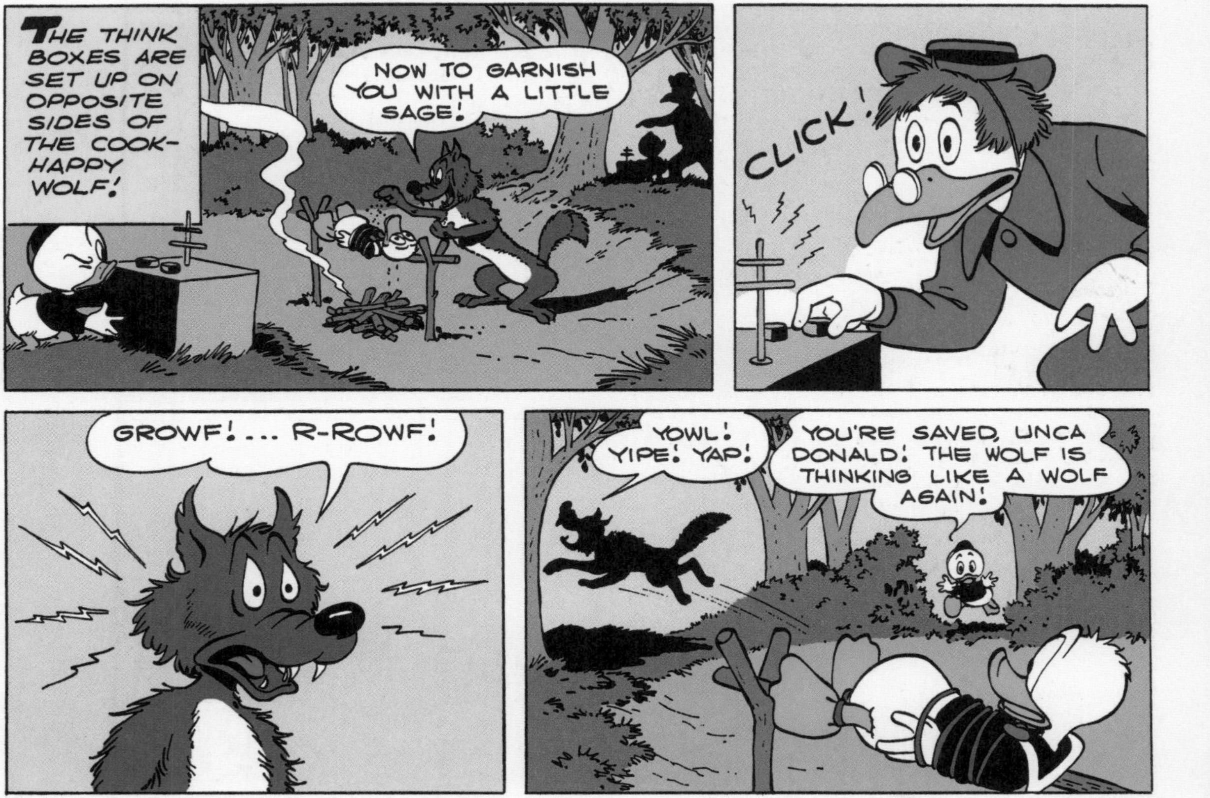
THE THINK BOXES ARE SET UP ON OPPOSITE SIDES OF THE COOK-HAPPY WOLF!
NOW TO GARNISH YOU WITH A LITTLE SAGE!
CLICK!
GROWF! ... R-ROWF!
YOWL! YIPE! YAP!
YOU'RE SAVED, UNCA DONALD! THE WOLF IS THINKING LIKE A WOLF AGAIN!

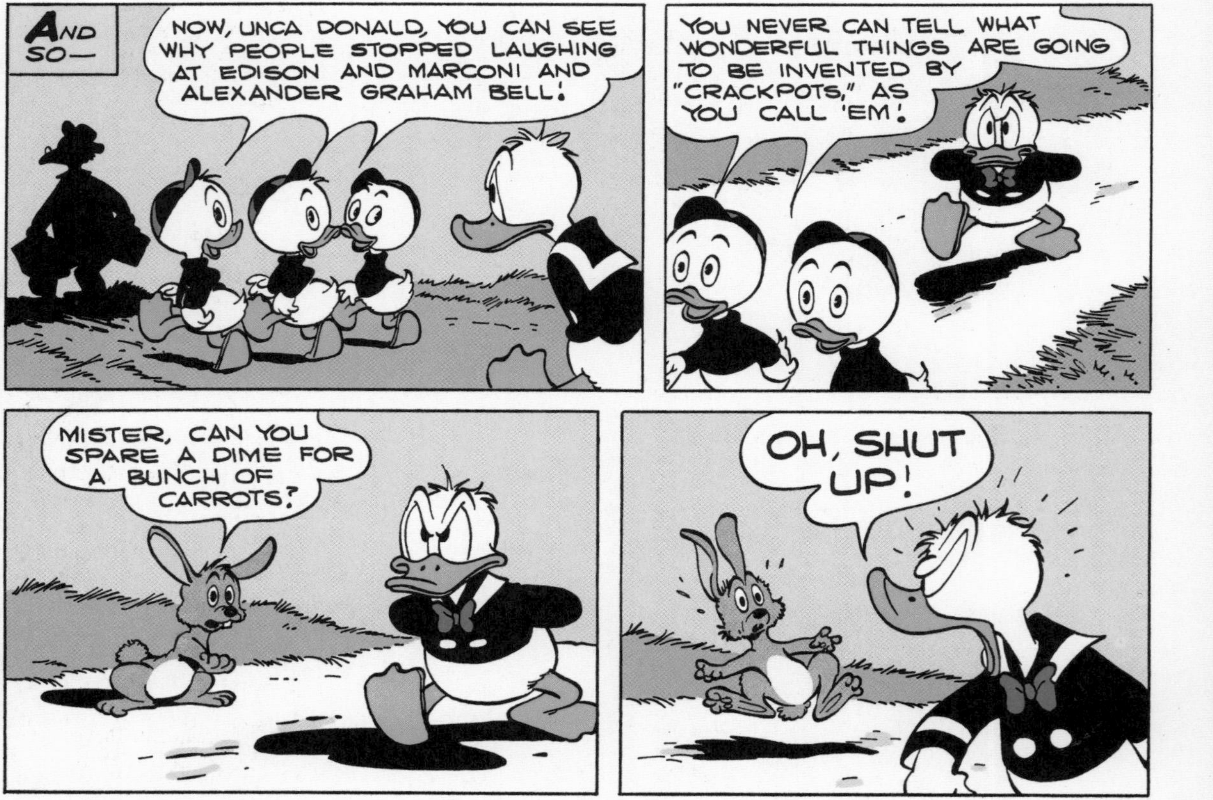
AND SO—
NOW, UNCA DONALD, YOU CAN SEE WHY PEOPLE STOPPED LAUGHING AT EDISON AND MARCONI AND ALEXANDER GRAHAM BELL!
YOU NEVER CAN TELL WHAT WONDERFUL THINGS ARE GOING TO BE INVENTED BY "CRACKPOTS," AS YOU CALL 'EM!
MISTER, CAN YOU SPARE A DIME FOR A BUNCH OF CARROTS?
OH, SHUT UP!

THE END

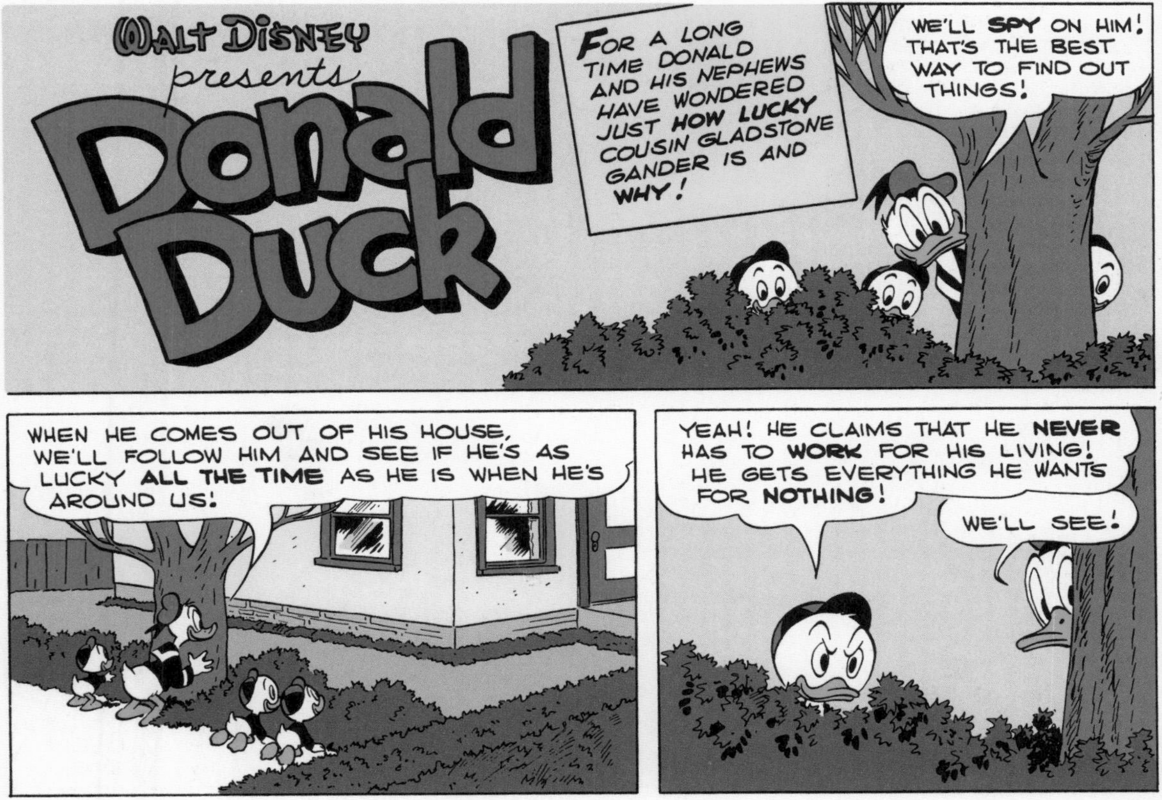
WALT DISNEY presents
Donald Duck
FOR A LONG TIME DONALD AND HIS NEPHEWS HAVE WONDERED JUST HOW LUCKY COUSIN GLADSTONE GANDER IS AND WHY!
WE'LL SPY ON HIM! THAT'S THE BEST WAY TO FIND OUT THINGS!
WHEN HE COMES OUT OF HIS HOUSE, WE'LL FOLLOW HIM AND SEE IF HE'S AS LUCKY ALL THE TIME AS HE IS WHEN HE'S AROUND US!
YEAH! HE CLAIMS THAT HE NEVER HAS TO WORK FOR HIS LIVING! HE GETS EVERYTHING HE WANTS FOR NOTHING!
WE'LL SEE!

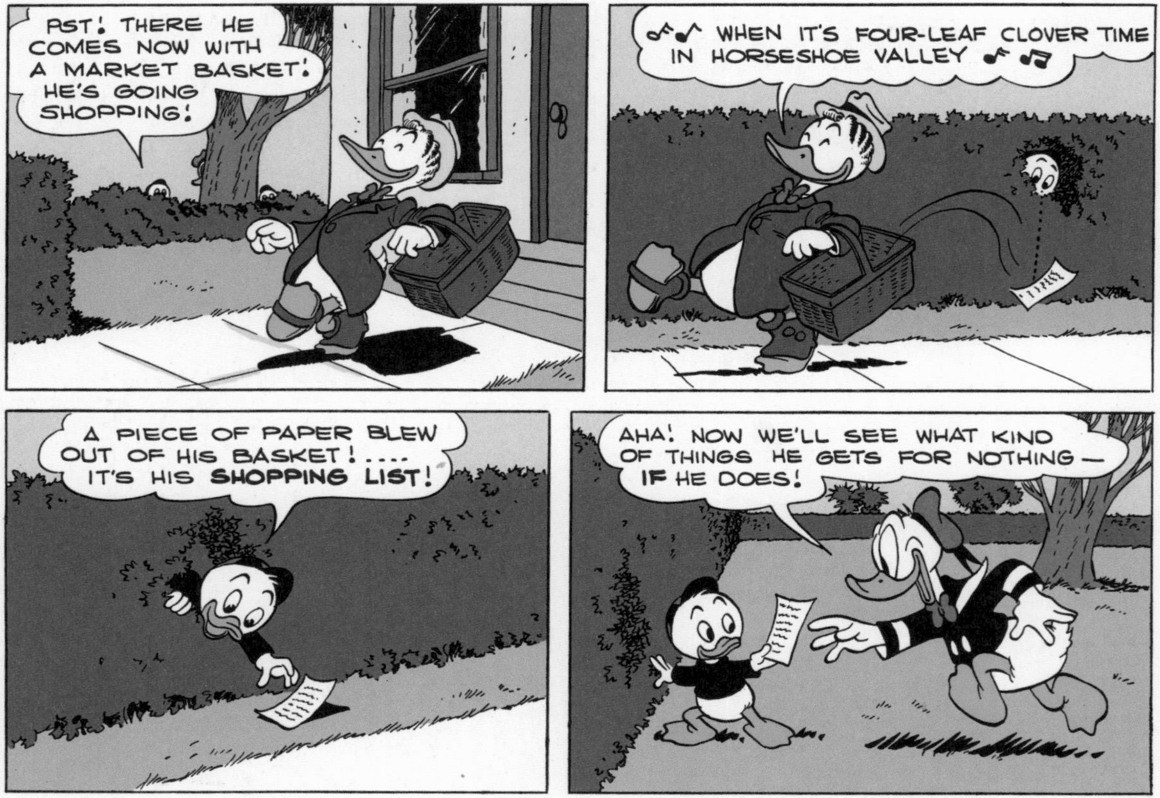
PST! THERE HE COMES NOW WITH A MARKET BASKET! HE'S GOING SHOPPING!
WHEN IT'S FOUR-LEAF CLOVER TIME IN HORSESHOE VALLEY
A PIECE OF PAPER BLEW OUT OF HIS BASKET! .... IT'S HIS **SHOPPING LIST**!
AHA! NOW WE'LL SEE WHAT KIND OF THINGS HE GETS FOR NOTHING— **IF** HE DOES!

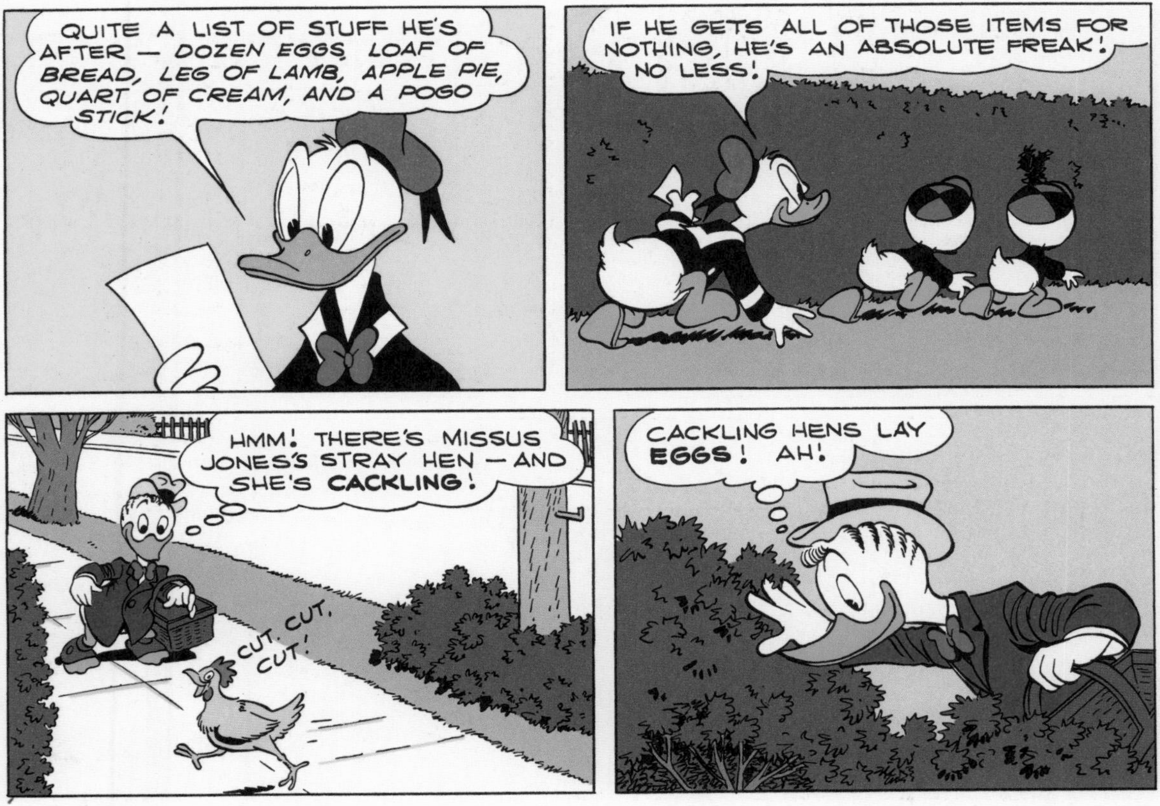
QUITE A LIST OF STUFF HE'S AFTER — DOZEN EGGS, LOAF OF BREAD, LEG OF LAMB, APPLE PIE, QUART OF CREAM, AND A POGO STICK!
IF HE GETS ALL OF THOSE ITEMS FOR NOTHING, HE'S AN ABSOLUTE FREAK! NO LESS!
HMM! THERE'S MISSUS JONES'S STRAY HEN — AND SHE'S CACKLING!
CUT. CUT. CUT!
CACKLING HENS LAY EGGS! AH!

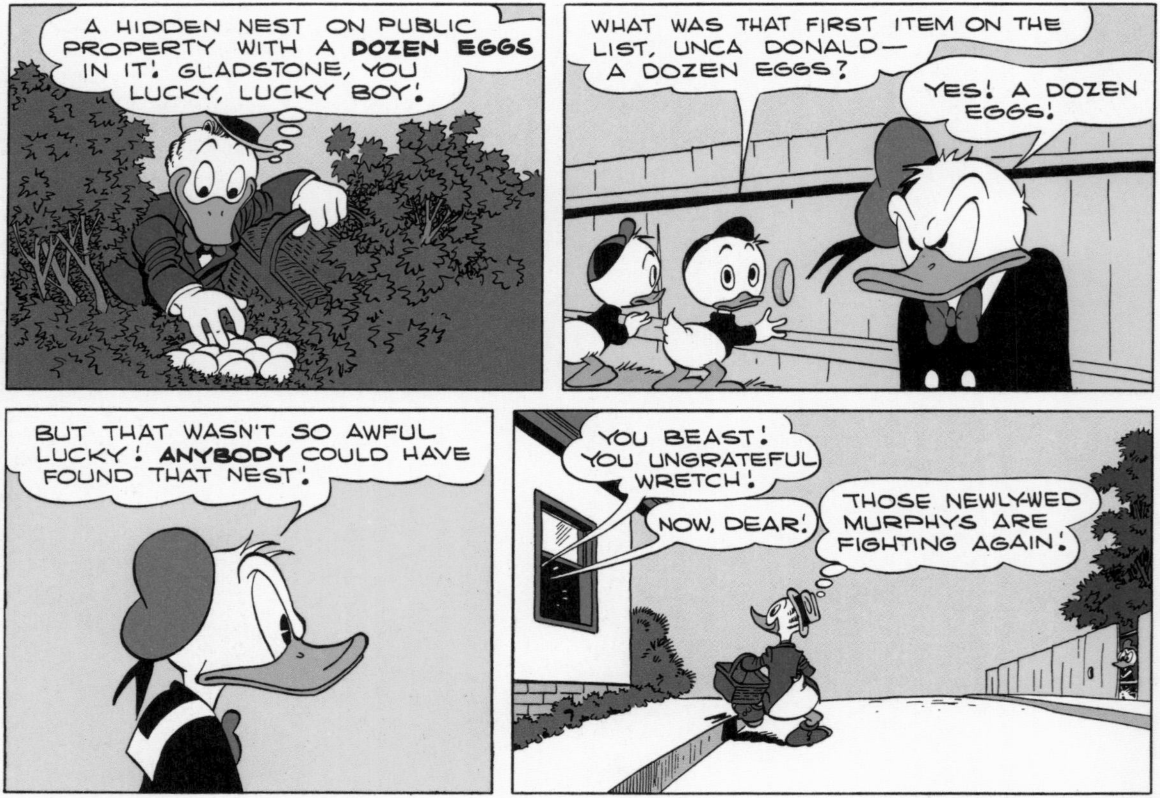
A HIDDEN NEST ON PUBLIC PROPERTY WITH A **DOZEN EGGS** IN IT! GLADSTONE, YOU LUCKY, LUCKY BOY!
WHAT WAS THAT FIRST ITEM ON THE LIST, UNCA DONALD— A DOZEN EGGS?
YES! A DOZEN EGGS!
BUT THAT WASN'T SO AWFUL LUCKY! **ANYBODY** COULD HAVE FOUND THAT NEST!
YOU BEAST! YOU UNGRATEFUL WRETCH!
NOW, DEAR!
THOSE NEWLY-WED MURPHYS ARE FIGHTING AGAIN!

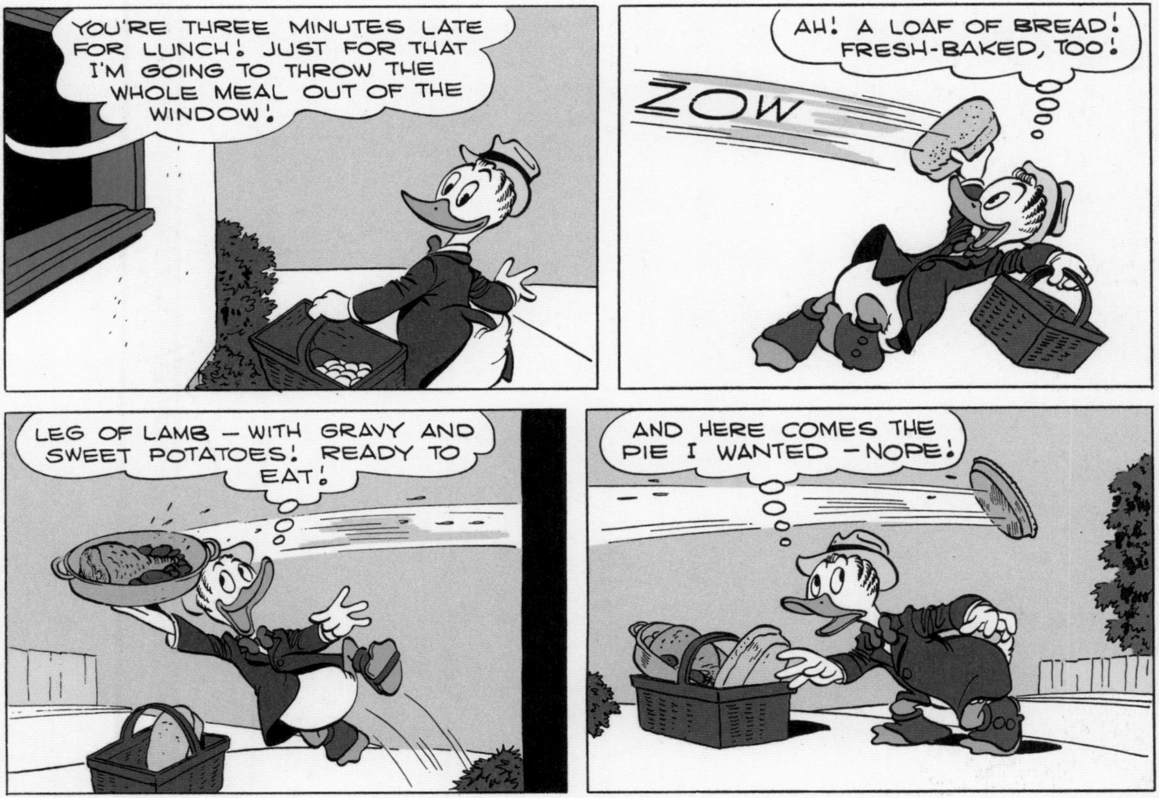
YOU'RE THREE MINUTES LATE FOR LUNCH! JUST FOR THAT I'M GOING TO THROW THE WHOLE MEAL OUT OF THE WINDOW!
AH! A LOAF OF BREAD! FRESH-BAKED, TOO!
ZOW
LEG OF LAMB — WITH GRAVY AND SWEET POTATOES! READY TO EAT!
AND HERE COMES THE PIE I WANTED — NOPE!

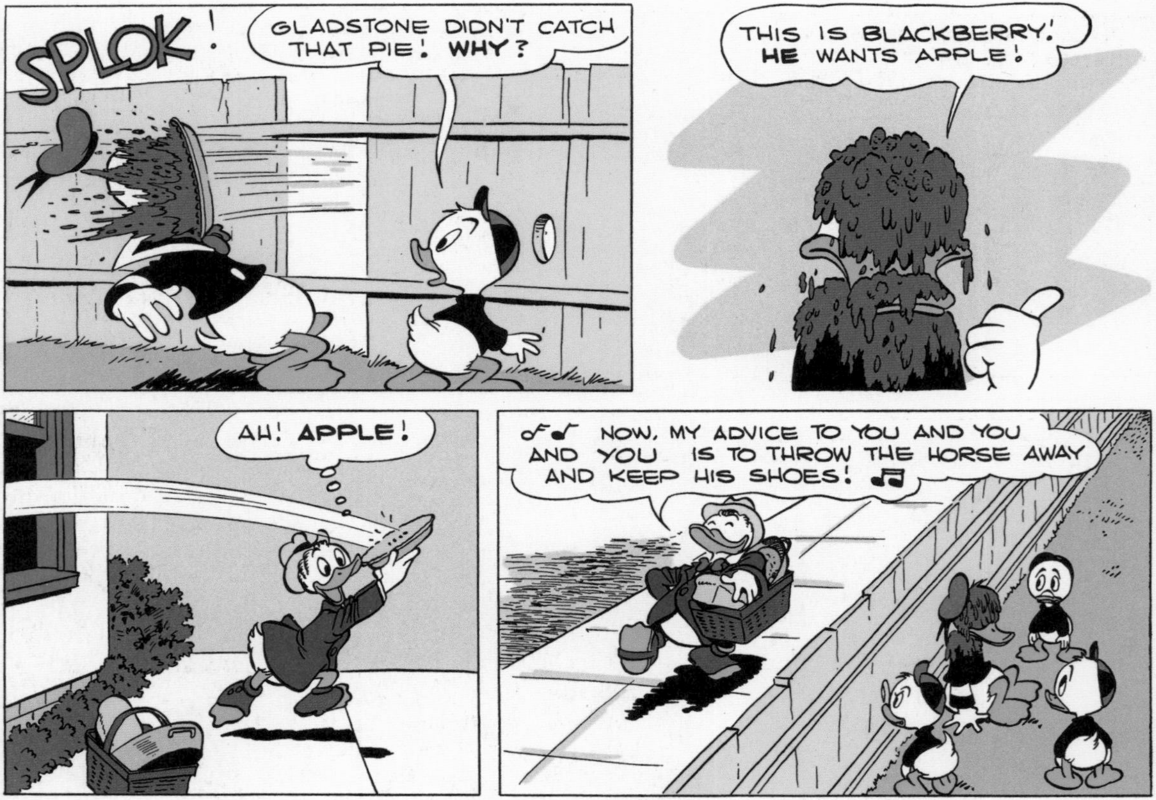
SPLOK!
GLADSTONE DIDN'T CATCH THAT PIE! **WHY**?
THIS IS BLACKBERRY! **HE** WANTS APPLE!
AH! **APPLE**!
NOW, MY ADVICE TO YOU AND YOU AND YOU IS TO THROW THE HORSE AWAY AND KEEP HIS SHOES!

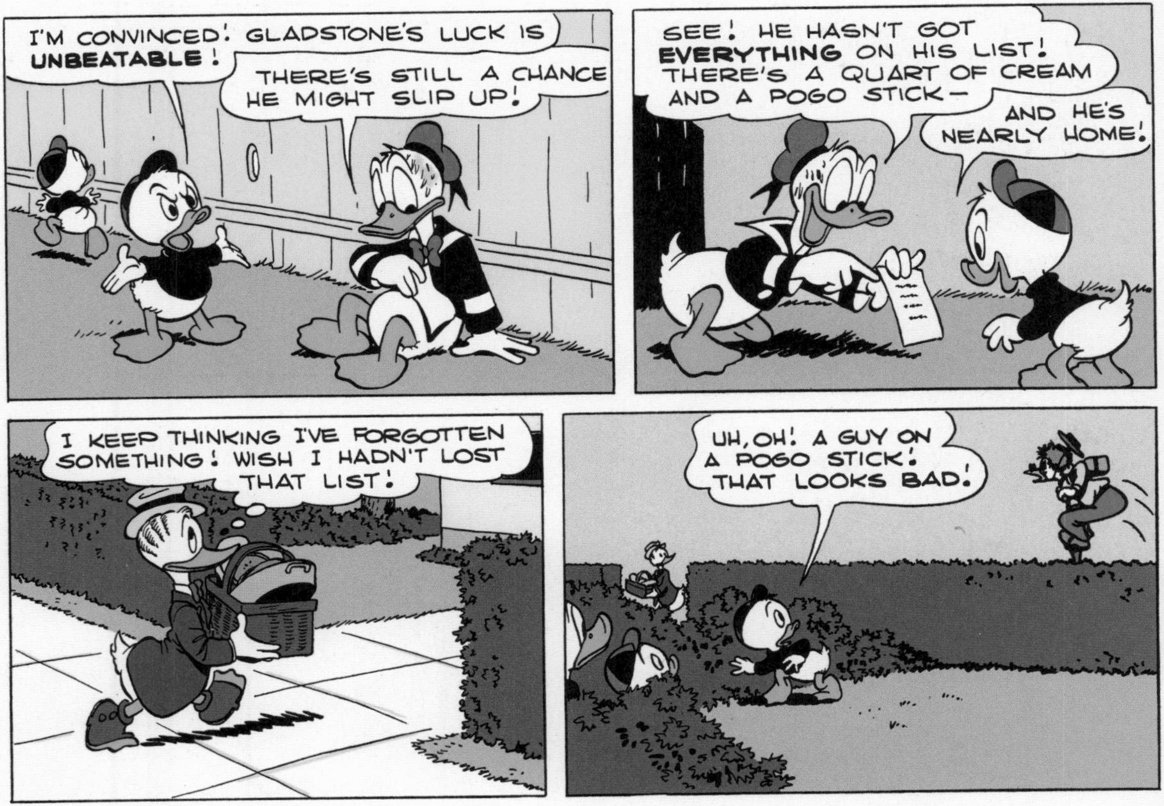

I'M CONVINCED! GLADSTONE'S LUCK IS UNBEATABLE!
THERE'S STILL A CHANCE HE MIGHT SLIP UP!
SEE! HE HASN'T GOT EVERYTHING ON HIS LIST! THERE'S A QUART OF CREAM AND A POGO STICK—
AND HE'S NEARLY HOME!
I KEEP THINKING I'VE FORGOTTEN SOMETHING! WISH I HADN'T LOST THAT LIST!
UH, OH! A GUY ON A POGO STICK! THAT LOOKS BAD!

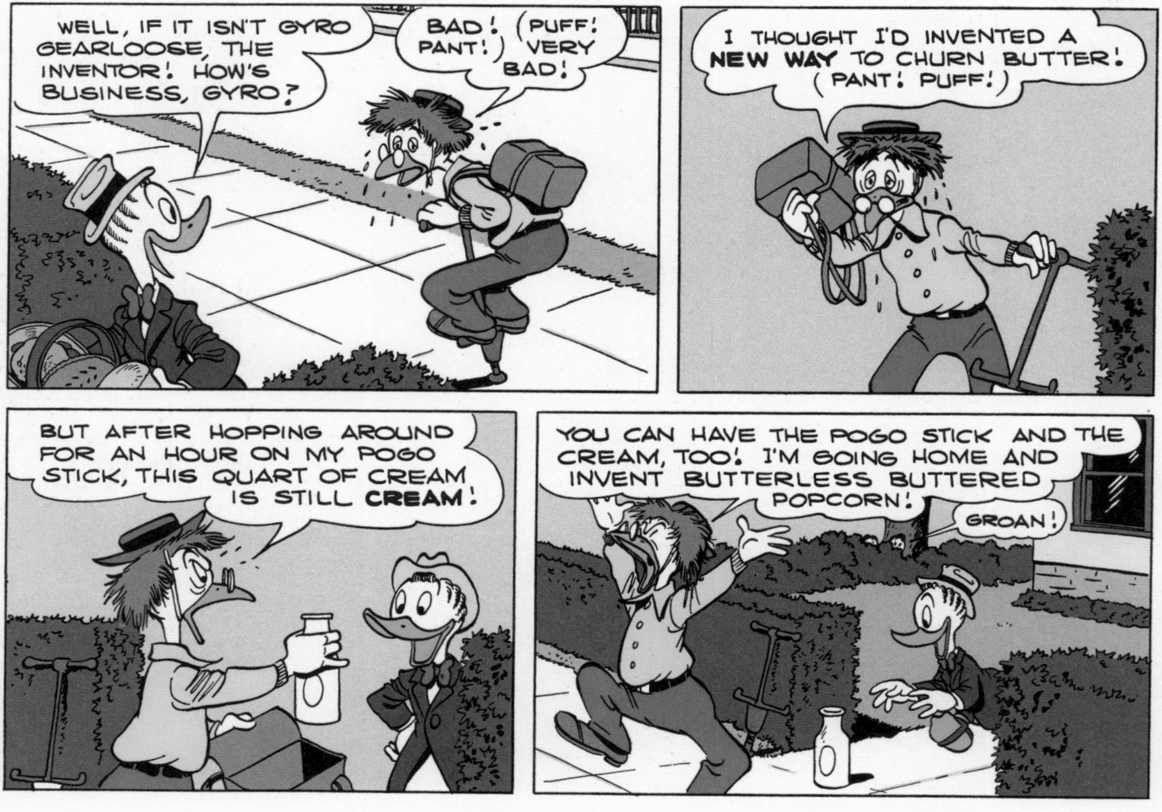
WELL, IF IT ISN'T GYRO GEARLOOSE, THE INVENTOR! HOW'S BUSINESS, GYRO?
BAD! PANT!
(PUFF! VERY BAD!
I THOUGHT I'D INVENTED A NEW WAY TO CHURN BUTTER! (PANT! PUFF!)
BUT AFTER HOPPING AROUND FOR AN HOUR ON MY POGO STICK, THIS QUART OF CREAM IS STILL CREAM!
YOU CAN HAVE THE POGO STICK AND THE CREAM, TOO! I'M GOING HOME AND INVENT BUTTERLESS BUTTERED POPCORN!
GROAN!

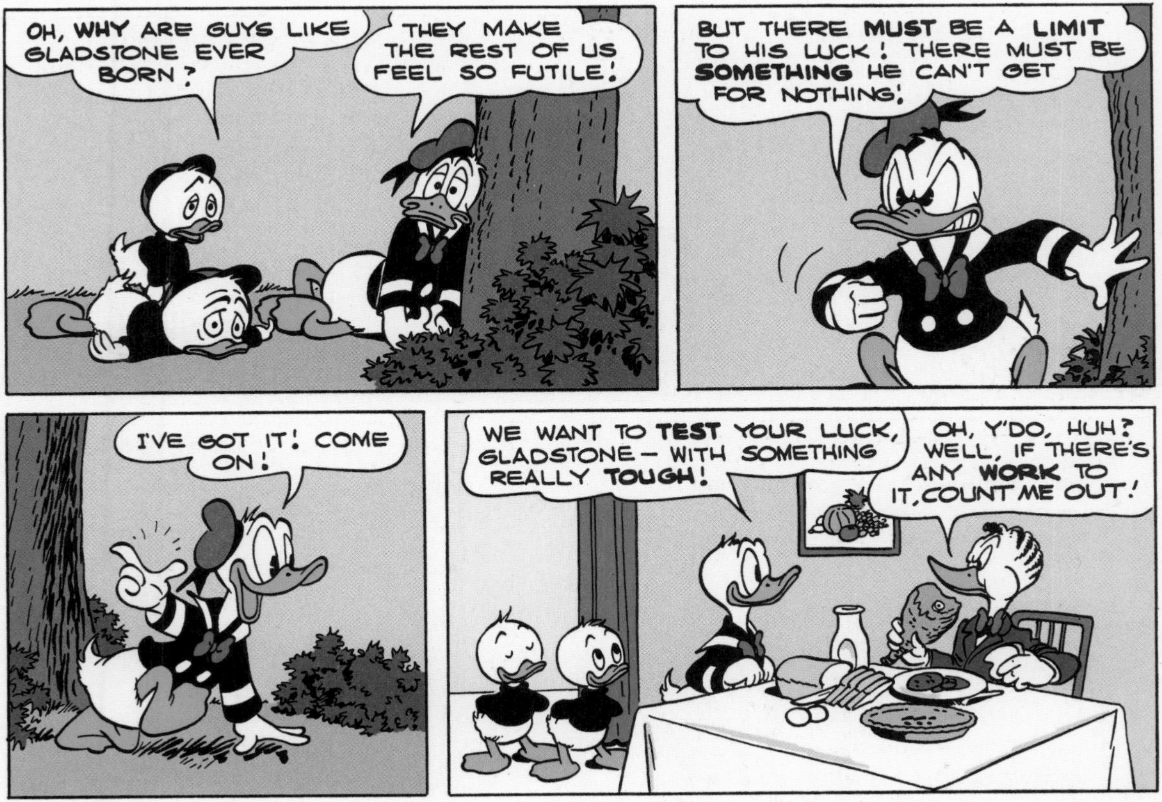
OH, WHY ARE GUYS LIKE GLADSTONE EVER BORN?
THEY MAKE THE REST OF US FEEL SO FUTILE!
BUT THERE MUST BE A LIMIT TO HIS LUCK! THERE MUST BE SOMETHING HE CAN'T GET FOR NOTHING!
I'VE GOT IT! COME ON!
WE WANT TO TEST YOUR LUCK, GLADSTONE — WITH SOMETHING REALLY TOUGH!
OH, Y'DO, HUH? WELL, IF THERE'S ANY WORK TO IT, COUNT ME OUT!

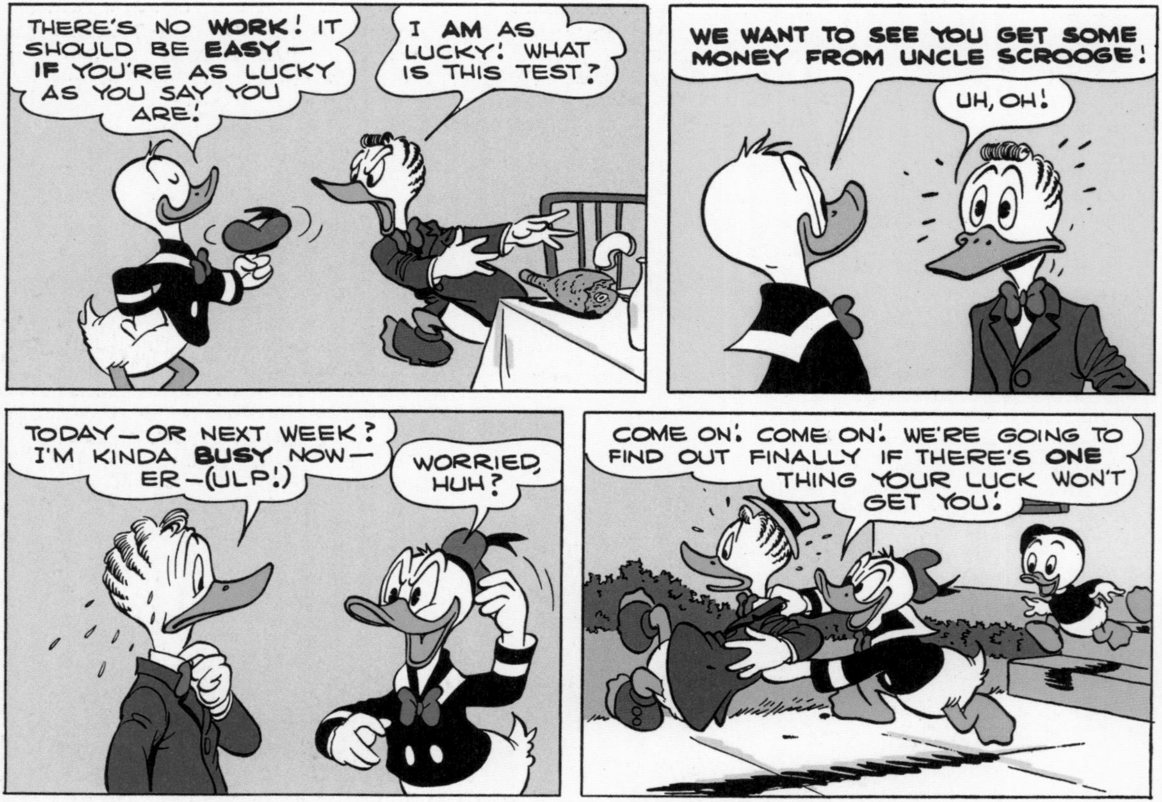
THERE'S NO WORK! IT SHOULD BE EASY— IF YOU'RE AS LUCKY AS YOU SAY YOU ARE!
I AM AS LUCKY! WHAT IS THIS TEST?
WE WANT TO SEE YOU GET SOME MONEY FROM UNCLE SCROOGE!
UH, OH!
TODAY—OR NEXT WEEK? I'M KINDA BUSY NOW— ER—(ULP!)
WORRIED, HUH?
COME ON! COME ON! WE'RE GOING TO FIND OUT FINALLY IF THERE'S ONE THING YOUR LUCK WON'T GET YOU!

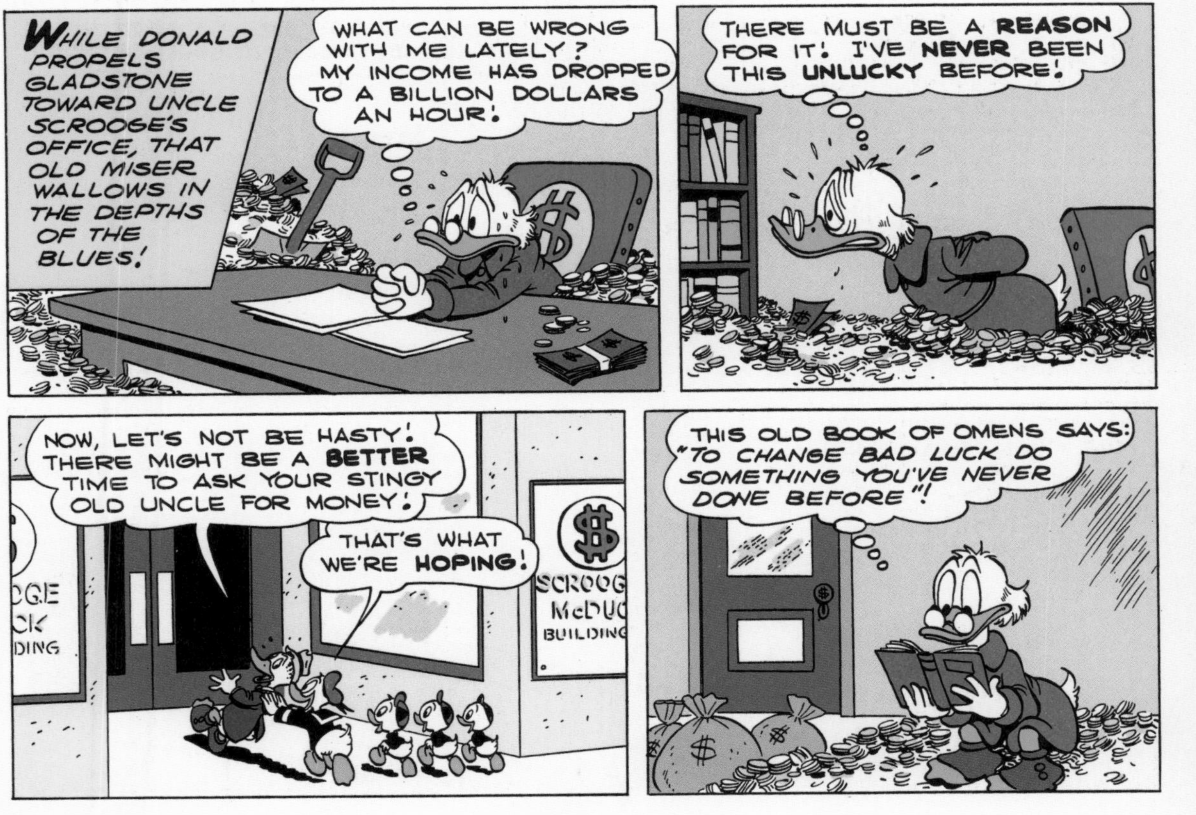
WHILE DONALD PROPELS GLADSTONE TOWARD UNCLE SCROOGE'S OFFICE, THAT OLD MISER WALLOWS IN THE DEPTHS OF THE BLUES!
WHAT CAN BE WRONG WITH ME LATELY? MY INCOME HAS DROPPED TO A BILLION DOLLARS AN HOUR!
THERE MUST BE A **REASON** FOR IT! I'VE **NEVER** BEEN THIS **UNLUCKY** BEFORE!
NOW, LET'S NOT BE HASTY! THERE MIGHT BE A **BETTER** TIME TO ASK YOUR STINGY OLD UNCLE FOR MONEY!
THAT'S WHAT WE'RE **HOPING**!
SCROOGE McDUCK BUILDING
THIS OLD BOOK OF OMENS SAYS: "TO CHANGE BAD LUCK DO SOMETHING YOU'VE NEVER DONE BEFORE"!

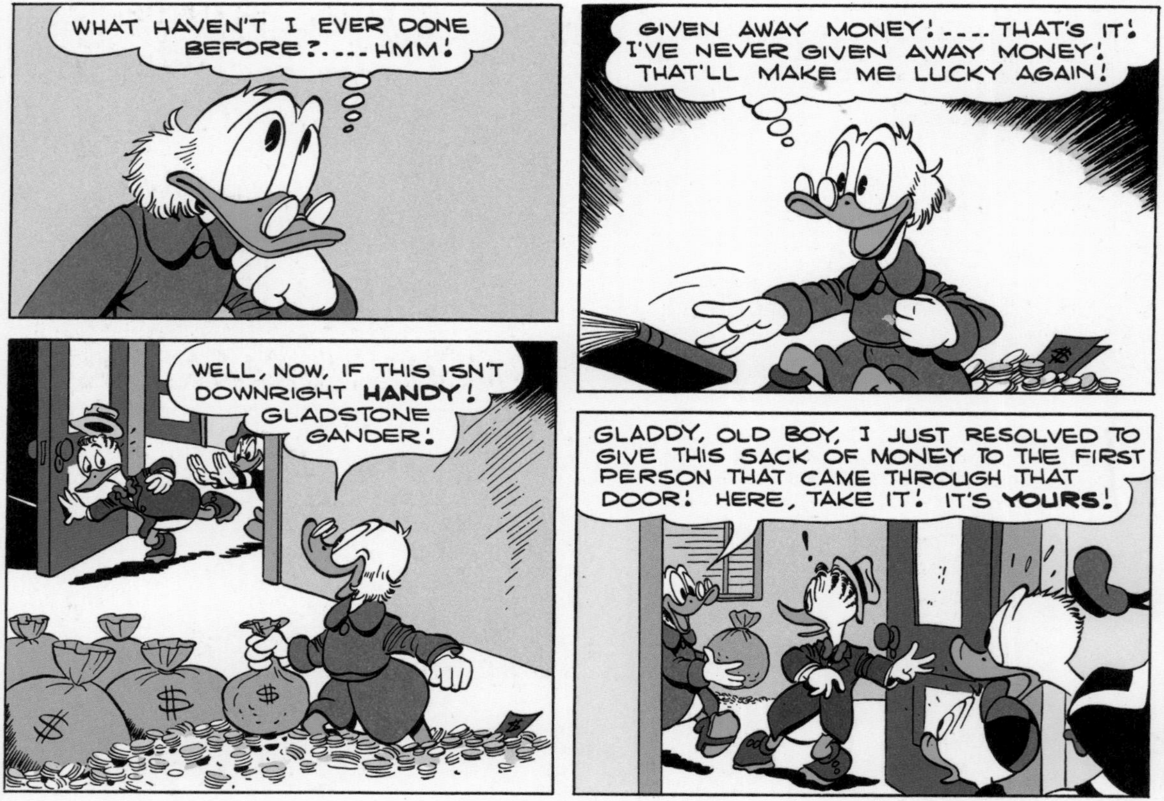
WHAT HAVEN'T I EVER DONE BEFORE?....HMM!
GIVEN AWAY MONEY!....THAT'S IT! I'VE NEVER GIVEN AWAY MONEY! THAT'LL MAKE ME LUCKY AGAIN!
WELL, NOW, IF THIS ISN'T DOWNRIGHT **HANDY**! GLADSTONE GANDER!
GLADDY, OLD BOY, I JUST RESOLVED TO GIVE THIS SACK OF MONEY TO THE FIRST PERSON THAT CAME THROUGH THAT DOOR! HERE, TAKE IT! IT'S **YOURS**!
!

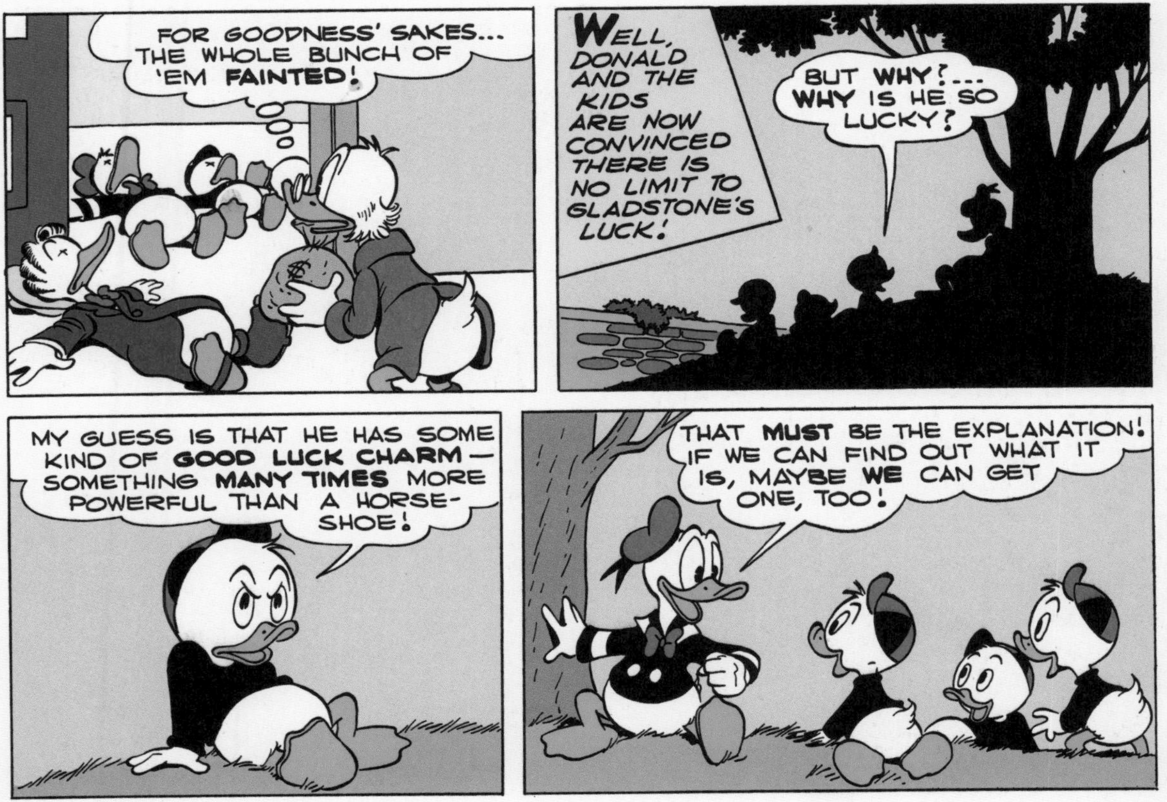
FOR GOODNESS' SAKES... THE WHOLE BUNCH OF 'EM **FAINTED**!
WELL, DONALD AND THE KIDS ARE NOW CONVINCED THERE IS NO LIMIT TO GLADSTONE'S LUCK!
BUT **WHY**?... **WHY** IS HE SO LUCKY?
MY GUESS IS THAT HE HAS SOME KIND OF **GOOD LUCK CHARM** — SOMETHING **MANY TIMES** MORE POWERFUL THAN A HORSE-SHOE!
THAT **MUST** BE THE EXPLANATION! IF WE CAN FIND OUT WHAT IT IS, MAYBE **WE** CAN GET ONE, TOO!

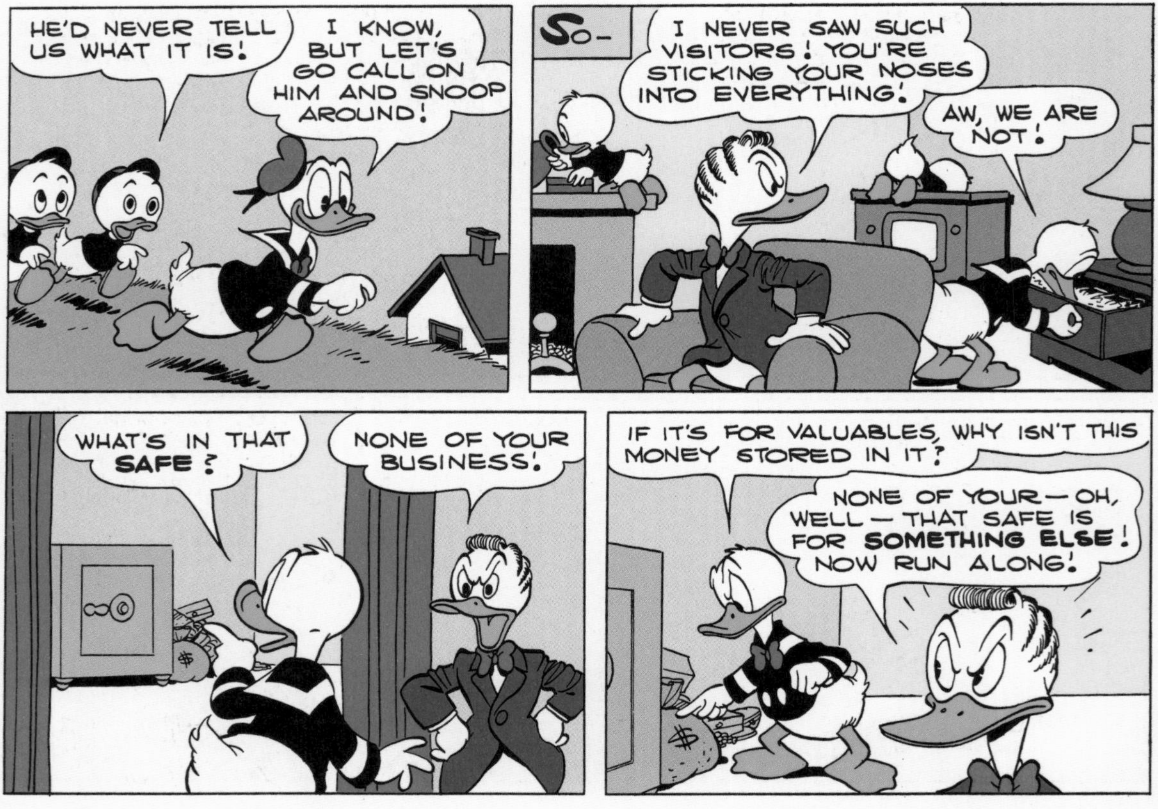
HE'D NEVER TELL US WHAT IT IS!
I KNOW, BUT LET'S GO CALL ON HIM AND SNOOP AROUND!
SO-
I NEVER SAW SUCH VISITORS! YOU'RE STICKING YOUR NOSES INTO EVERYTHING!
AW, WE ARE NOT!
WHAT'S IN THAT SAFE?
NONE OF YOUR BUSINESS!
IF IT'S FOR VALUABLES, WHY ISN'T THIS MONEY STORED IN IT?
NONE OF YOUR—OH, WELL—THAT SAFE IS FOR SOMETHING ELSE! NOW RUN ALONG!

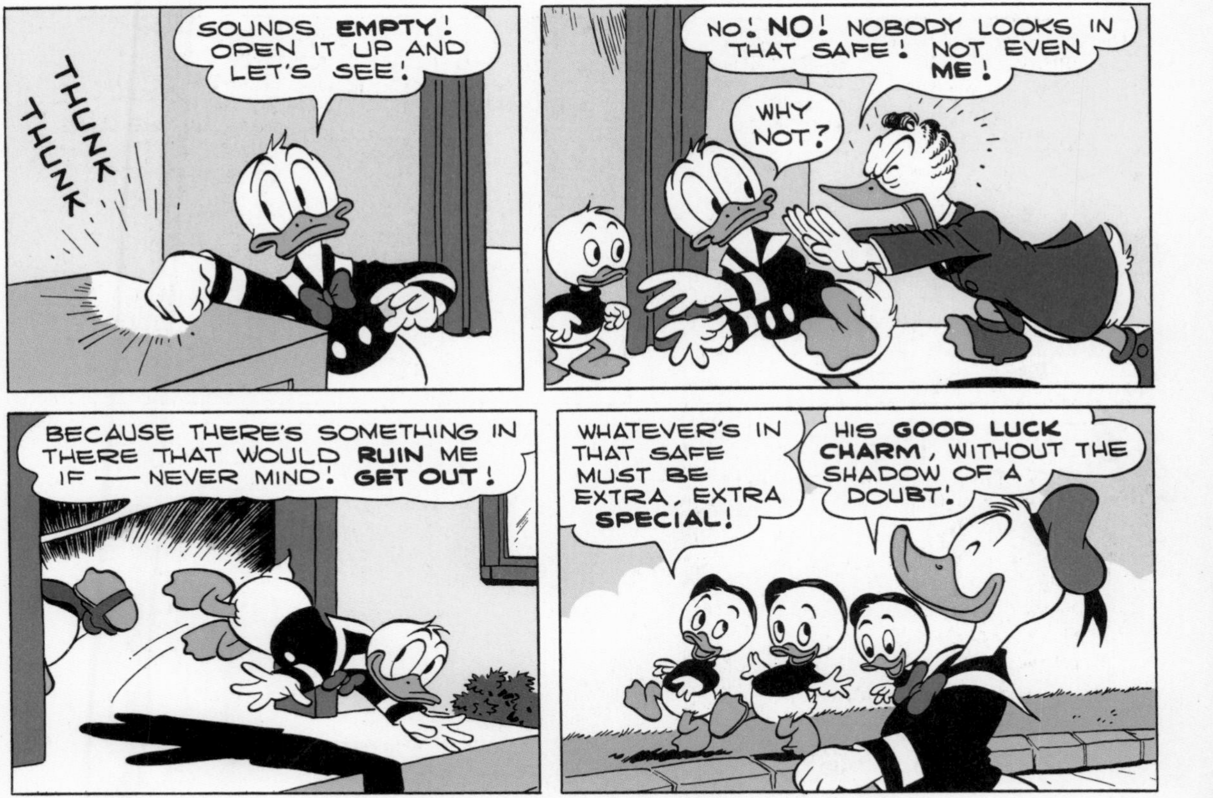
SOUNDS **EMPTY**! OPEN IT UP AND LET'S SEE!
THUNK THUNK
NO! **NO!** NOBODY LOOKS IN THAT SAFE! NOT EVEN **ME**!
WHY NOT?
BECAUSE THERE'S SOMETHING IN THERE THAT WOULD **RUIN** ME IF — NEVER MIND! **GET OUT**!
WHATEVER'S IN THAT SAFE MUST BE EXTRA, EXTRA **SPECIAL**!
HIS **GOOD LUCK CHARM**, WITHOUT THE SHADOW OF A DOUBT!

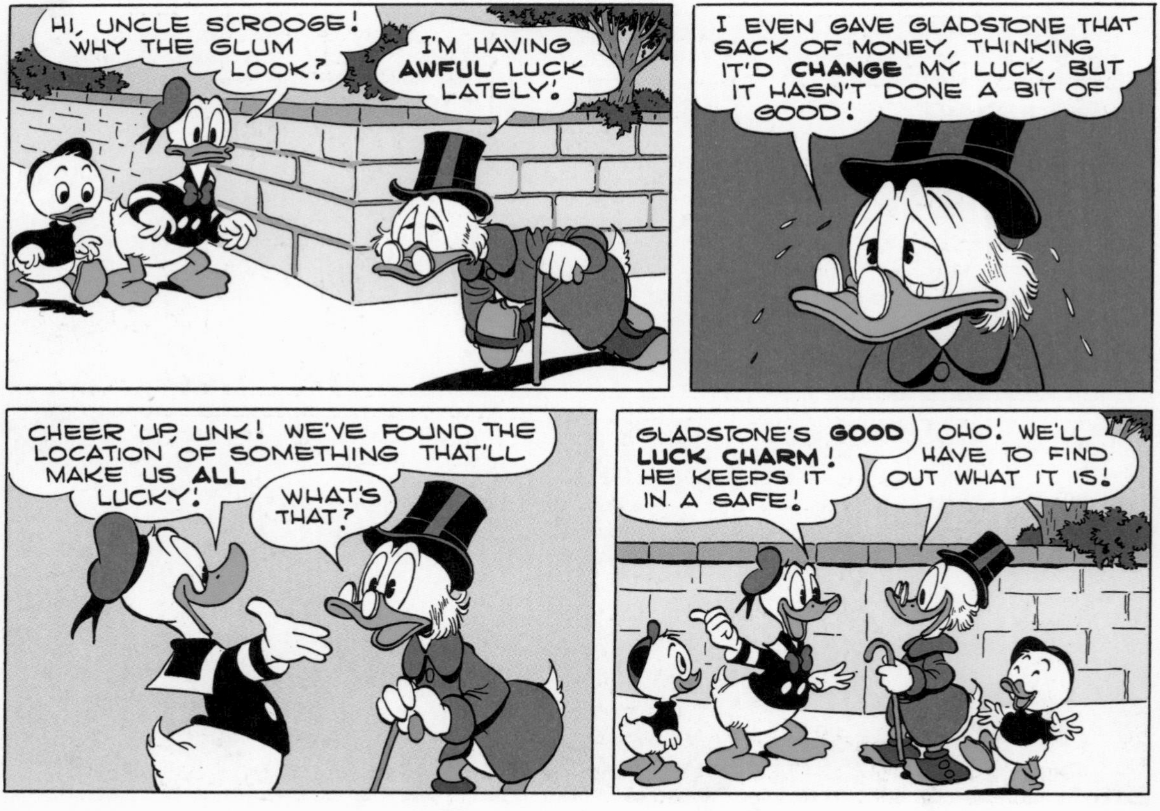
HI, UNCLE SCROOGE! WHY THE GLUM LOOK?
I'M HAVING **AWFUL** LUCK LATELY!
I EVEN GAVE GLADSTONE THAT SACK OF MONEY, THINKING IT'D **CHANGE** MY LUCK, BUT IT HASN'T DONE A BIT OF GOOD!
CHEER UP, UNK! WE'VE FOUND THE LOCATION OF SOMETHING THAT'LL MAKE US **ALL** LUCKY!
WHAT'S THAT?
GLADSTONE'S **GOOD LUCK CHARM**! HE KEEPS IT IN A SAFE!
OHO! WE'LL HAVE TO FIND OUT WHAT IT IS!

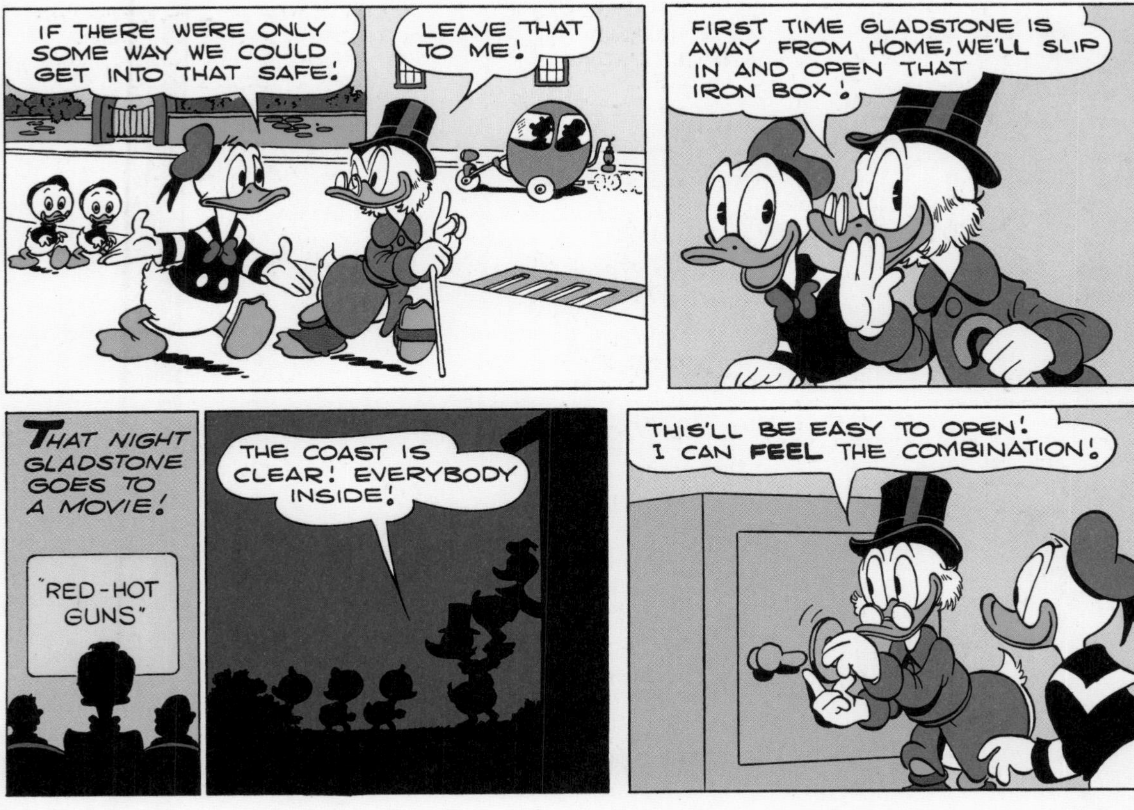
IF THERE WERE ONLY SOME WAY WE COULD GET INTO THAT SAFE!
LEAVE THAT TO ME!
FIRST TIME GLADSTONE IS AWAY FROM HOME, WE'LL SLIP IN AND OPEN THAT IRON BOX!
THAT NIGHT GLADSTONE GOES TO A MOVIE!
"RED-HOT GUNS"
THE COAST IS CLEAR! EVERYBODY INSIDE!
THIS'LL BE EASY TO OPEN! I CAN FEEL THE COMBINATION!

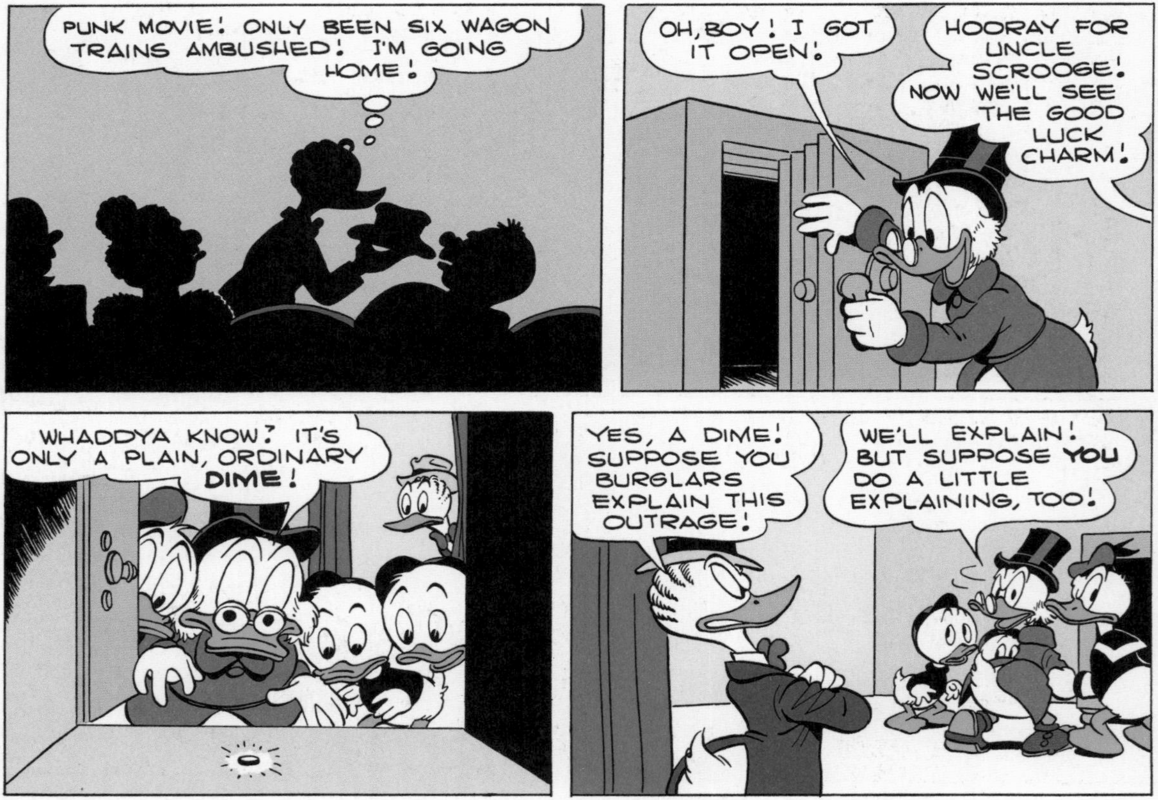
PUNK MOVIE! ONLY BEEN SIX WAGON TRAINS AMBUSHED! I'M GOING HOME!
OH, BOY! I GOT IT OPEN!
HOORAY FOR UNCLE SCROOGE! NOW WE'LL SEE THE GOOD LUCK CHARM!
WHADDYA KNOW? IT'S ONLY A PLAIN, ORDINARY DIME!
YES, A DIME! SUPPOSE YOU BURGLARS EXPLAIN THIS OUTRAGE!
WE'LL EXPLAIN! BUT SUPPOSE YOU DO A LITTLE EXPLAINING, TOO!

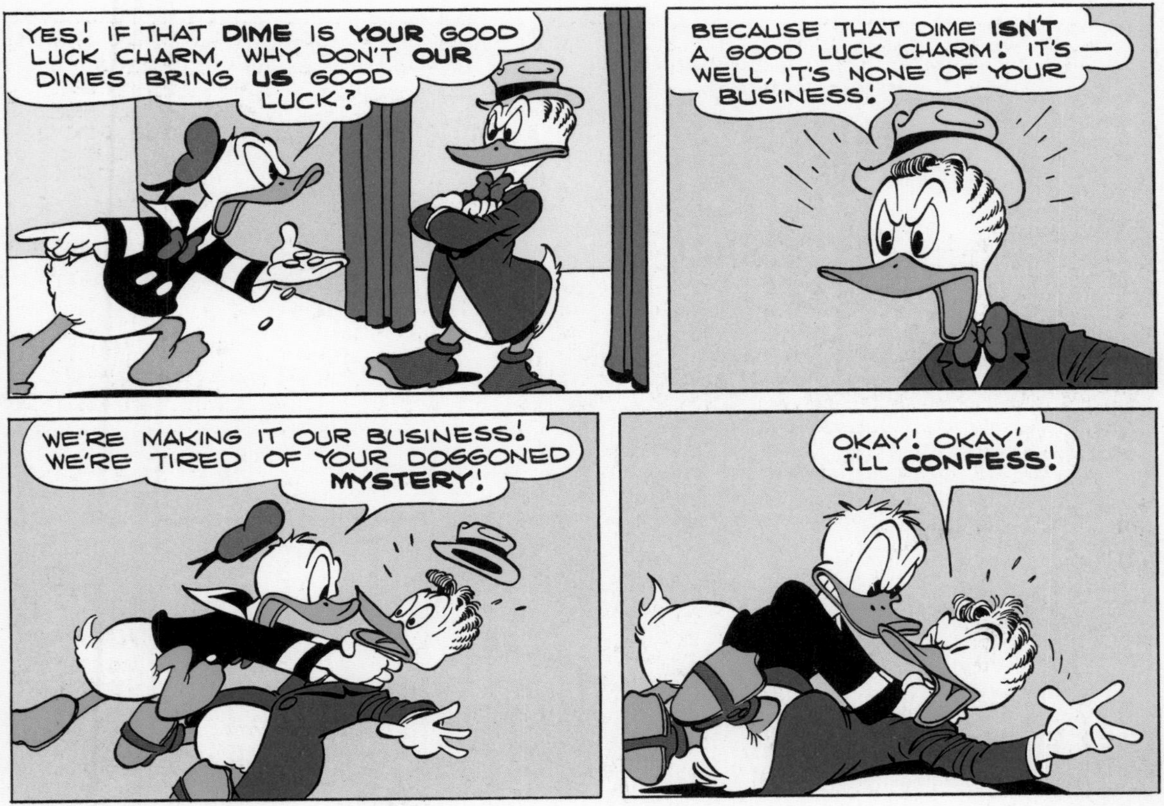
YES! IF THAT DIME IS YOUR GOOD LUCK CHARM, WHY DON'T OUR DIMES BRING US GOOD LUCK?
BECAUSE THAT DIME ISN'T A GOOD LUCK CHARM! IT'S — WELL, IT'S NONE OF YOUR BUSINESS!
WE'RE MAKING IT OUR BUSINESS! WE'RE TIRED OF YOUR DOGGONED MYSTERY!
OKAY! OKAY! I'LL CONFESS!

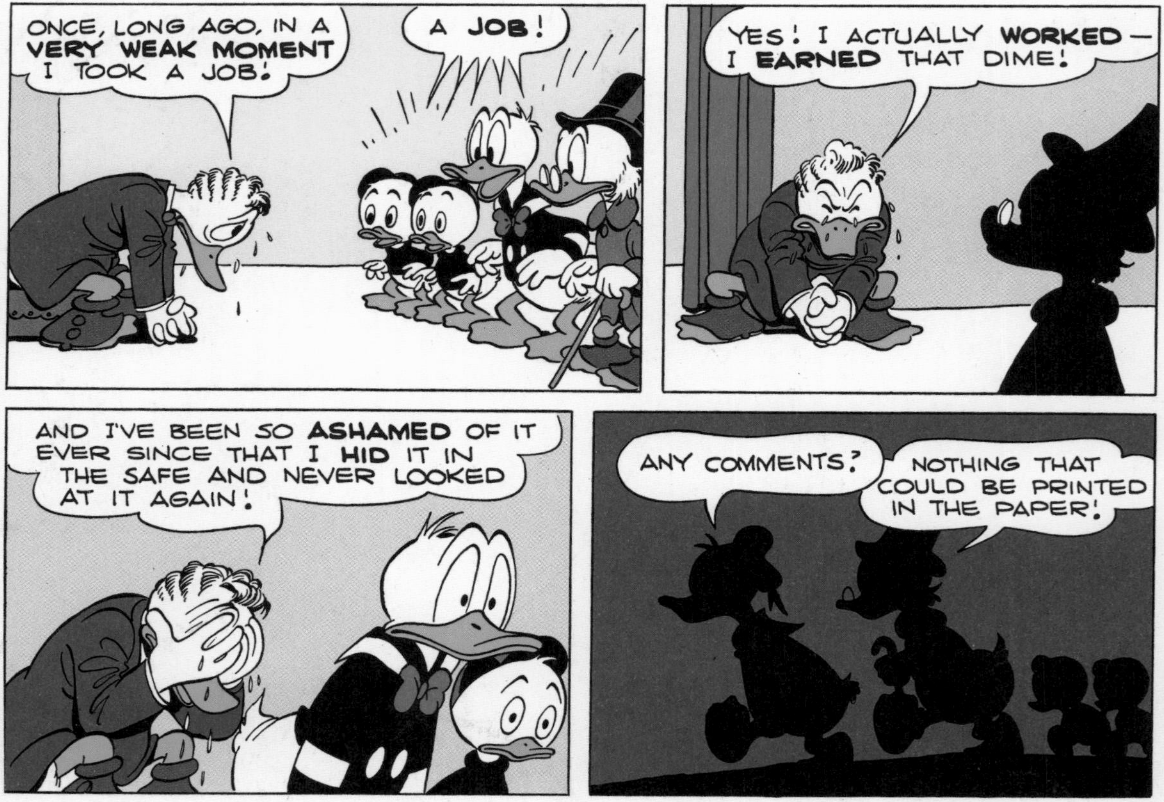
ONCE, LONG AGO, IN A VERY WEAK MOMENT I TOOK A JOB!
A JOB!
YES! I ACTUALLY WORKED— I EARNED THAT DIME!
AND I'VE BEEN SO ASHAMED OF IT EVER SINCE THAT I HID IT IN THE SAFE AND NEVER LOOKED AT IT AGAIN!
ANY COMMENTS?
NOTHING THAT COULD BE PRINTED IN THE PAPER!

THE END